# The
# Jungle's
# Edge

# The Jungle's Edge

## A Southeast Asian Mystery

## Jerry Craven

ANGELINA RIVER PRESS

ISBN: 978-0-9883844-7-7
Library of Congress Control Number:  2015921473
cover painting: Peter Kim
back cover wood carving: "Dragon Snake" by Sabak Embring

Angelina River Press, LLC
Fort Worth, Texas

# Acknowledgments

I am grateful for the advice, inspiration, encouragement, and support of many people in the writing of this novel. Among those who had a hand, directly or indirectly, in the making of *The Jungle's Edge* are Lionel K. H. Low, A. Ramez Kutrieh, Schelle Miller, Linda Cook, Phillip Gensler, A. William Hinson, David Rindlisbacher, Terry Dalrymple, Andrew Geyer, Pam Sybert, Clay Reynolds, Jim Sybert, Richard Moseley, Shari Wood, Jerry Bradley, and Barry Wood.

Fiction by Jerry Craven

*Women of Thunder*
*The Wild Part*
*Tiger, Tiger*
*Searching for Rama's Spear*
*The Big Thicket*

For more information see www.jerrycraven.com

for Schelle
who shares my love of Malaysia

Other books from Angelina River Press

*Adventures from the Last Century*
*Field Guide, Essays and Stories*
*Memoirs of a Biologist, a Coyote Ate my Cat and Other Tales*
*Nature Nurture Neither*
*Oklahoma and Else*
*The Wild Part*

For information on these and other books, go to
www.angelinariverpress.com

# 1

Art and nature, nature and art
Tell what dwells in the human heart.
                    —Coleman Farquart, *Asean Doublets*


Kent saw the customs official at the Kuala Lumpur-Subang International Airport pull something from Noland's suitcase, but he paid little attention until the inspector snapped upright and said something to the guard beside him. The guard jerked his M-14 rifle up and thrust the muzzle at Noland's stomach.

"Dadah?" the guard asked.

"I think yes," the customs official said. He looked at the baggy of white power he had taken from Noland's suitcase.

"*Dadah*?" Kent asked. "You think you found drugs?" Kent knew it had to be a mistake.

"Point that cannon somewhere else, partner," Noland said.

"Please to raise hands," the guard said. Two other uniformed guards appeared behind Noland. They took his arms and twisted them behind his back.

"Easy there, little fellows," Noland said. "There's no reason to break my arms."

Kent half expected Noland to turn around and slug the man who kept twisting one of his wrists, but he looked at the M-14 and apparently decided to accept the pain. It took some minutes for the men behind him to fumble around with handcuffs, open them, and clamp them on Noland's wrists.

"Baking soda," Noland said to the customs inspector. "That there is nothing but soda for cleaning my contact lenses. Back in Texas, it didn't occur to me that you folk would be so all-fired touchy about how I packed my baking soda, or I sure as hell would have put it in a can. Taste the stuff. It ain't nothing but baking soda."

"Taste dadah?" The inspector seemed astounded at the thought. He picked up the baggy and looked at it as if he were inspecting a scorpion. "It look same as I found ago five months. Six. In suitcase of Australian. Big man, look like you. Government hang him." He shook his head. "You bring dadah into Malaysia? You hang. It not smart business, not in Malaysia. We catch. You die."

"That's the dumbest bunch of cow flop I ever heard. Look at the stuff. Smell it. It's baking soda, for chrissake. Tell them, Kent. Tell them it's only baking soda." When Noland turned to Kent, so did the customs man and two more men with rifles.

"You and him friends?" the customs official demanded.

"Yes. Why not do a test on the soda? It isn't drugs." Kent heard the certainty in his voice, but he had begun to doubt. Until just hours ago, he and Noland were strangers. The customs man seemed not to hear Kent's suggestion.

"Put suitcase there." He pointed, then gave his attention to Noland's luggage again, this time pulling out all items, examining each with elaborate show. Two rifle barrels pointed at Kent's stomach, less than a meter away. Curious faces in the other lines turned their way.

Kent noticed the European-looking man he had seen earlier with the medals and ribbons penned to his vest hurry through the green line where there were no inspectors and pause in the exit doorway for a brief glance at Noland and Kent.

The inspector set the empty suitcase aside and opened Noland's guitar case. Inside he found only a battered guitar, some picks, and an extra set of strings. He then attacked Kent's luggage.

Guards took Noland's arms, pulling him toward a staircase. "Kent, get me a lawyer," he called over his shoulder. "For the luvva god, make them analyze the soda, Kent. Do they really hang folks they think push drugs in this country? A lawyer, Kent I'll pay . . ." his voice trailed off as the partition beside the stairs came between him and Kent.

The customs official gave Kent's clothing the same scrutiny he had given each item in Noland's suitcase. Kent told himself to relax, that nothing could go wrong. But it did little good: Noland no doubt thought nothing would go wrong with a routine customs check, either. That is, if the baggy did contain genuine baking soda. Kent shook his head, annoyed with himself. Of course it was baking soda, he told himself. Everything about Noland suggested him to be as innocent and naive as he appeared. And the big cowboy was such a romantic, Kent thought, a man on a quest to find the perfect soulmate—much like my own quest here in the orient, though mine has to do with art, not with romance.

Will my search put my life in danger, as Noland's has? Kent shook his head, trying to deny any validity to the question, for surely his new friend couldn't be in mortal danger over a simple misunderstanding. Or was he?

Kent Day first noticed Noland Fritch in the Dallas International airport while boarding a flight to Denver. And in Denver, he saw Noland get on the same plane he did for Seattle. It wasn't hard to notice Noland because of his height, exaggerated by a white Stetson, and what Kent regarded as his almost comical western dress. He wore light blue, brushed cotton jeans; lizard cowboy boots; a hand-tooled belt that said NOLAND FRITCH across the back and had a four-inch buckle in front; a tight red and blue shirt with pearl-covered snaps instead of buttons, and flaps over the pockets; and a string tie clasp with a scorpion enclosed in clear plastic.

On the flight to Denver, Kent took out his sketch pad and a box of pastel chalk. He drew Noland in caricature, making the figure stoop to keep from bumping his head on the ceiling of the plane. Beside him, Kent put a stewardess looking up at him in awe, her chin brushing Noland's gigantic belt buckle. He drew Noland's legs toothpick thin, his hips almost non-existent, and his shoulders impossibly broad. On Noland's handsome, square-jawed face, Kent drew a confused, stupid look. Why am I doing this, Kent wondered, even as he began shading the absurd cowboy clothing in the very colors Noland was wearing. Why caricature someone who is already a caricature?

After they had sat together for the long flight across the Pacific, after he had learned of Noland's quest in the Orient, Kent chided himself even more for lampooning Noland with commercial art.

And now? Kent looked at the rifle barrels pointed at him. Now I'm in trouble with the local law over a silly misunderstanding. But Kent knew enough about the quirky nature of people to realize he was in real danger.

When the woman sitting next to Kent had said, "That is terrific," Kent began to regret doing the drawing. "You are a real artist," the woman said. "Would you do one of me? I would buy it from you, of course."

Kent flushed crimson and closed his sketch pad. Being a commercial artist was, he wanted to believe, a thing of his past. He had worked as artist-in-residence for two years at the Hotel Galvez in Galveston, drawing caricatures of the tourists and charging a fat enough fee to be able to bank the money he needed to go to art school to learn to be a real artist. Even while studying at The University of Houston, he returned to Galveston during the summers to do his time as a hack so that, one day, he could put what he regarded as crass commercial art behind him. When the day arrived—when he managed to be among the first in an artists' exchange program between Selangor in Malaysia and the state of Texas, what do I do? he asked himself. I go back to mucking around in caricature work, that's what. He shook his head.

There were other heads from the past shaking, looking with disapproval at him. The one Kent was most aware of wore the garb of a Roman Catholic nun. Sister Corazon. Kent felt certain that she would have scorned his work at the Hotel Galvez.

He had been in East Texas, at Jefferson City shopping Center in Port Arthur, doing several days in a starving artist show, making not much at all, when, out of frustration over nobody noticing him, he began singing "Your Cheating Heart" as loud as he could. People up and down the sidewalk stopped to stare. "Who's the nut?" they wanted to know, and grinning faces crowded around. Before long, he was doing a booming business in caricatures, and he jacked his prices up a few bucks. When the crowd around him thinned, he broke into song again, singing whatever came to mind: "Does Your Chewing Gum Lose its Flavor on the Bedpost Over Night?" and other odd-ball classics of the Texas hit parade from years ago. He knew he couldn't sing worth a damn, but he was loud, not at all self conscious, and outrageous enough to draw plenty of attention. The crowd loved him. A man from the *Port Arthur News* took his photograph, and an article appeared in the paper the next morning about the singing artist. That day, the manager of the Hotel Galvez became one of his customers, and by the next day, Kent was packing up to move to Galveston to become artist in residence at the hotel, though not without feeling guilty about it.

The guilt aside, it was a good life, Kent reflected, living at the hotel and making big bucks, by a young artist's standards. But it wasn't what he wanted, and he knew one day he would abandon such commercialism forever. And yet here he was, twenty thousand feet over the high plains of Texas, blasting that poor cowboy in coarse, commercial form just to amuse himself, and there was the woman next to him, the epitome of all the wealthy tourists who wandered through Hotel Galvez, offering money for his services as commercial artist. He looked again at the woman beside him. Fortyish, he decided, beautiful, aware of her appeal to men and used to it. He glanced at her tight pants, her stylish blouse that revealed a slight bit of cleavage. Oil money, maybe, or cattle dollars bought that outfit, he thought. She looked as if she just stepped out of Neiman Marcus.

"I'll do a drawing of you," he said, "but only under the condition that you pay no more than you think it's worth and that you not pay anything at all if you don't like it."

She protested, flashing charm, sexuality, and a smile that revealed the expensive, subtle wiring Kent had seen before in mid-life orthodontics. He insisted on his terms. "Don't look until it's finished."

Kent put away the pastels and got out a black pen. He would do her in ink, he decided, with care and with real artistry. And just maybe a little meanness for her catching him at the piece of fluff he zapped Noland with. He had her sit on the aisle seat, leaving an empty one between them so he could turn and look at her with more ease. Then he drew her as if she were sitting in the plane with not one scrap of clothes on.

Doing the piece reminded Kent of all those nights he studied Brenda Watson through the window of the house next door. Almost every night she undressed and paraded around her room, lights on and curtains open, and he sat just feet away in the darkness of his room, feeling the juices flow with vigor through his thirteen-year-old body, telling himself that he was making a study of anatomy for drawing later that night. As soon as she turned out her lights, Kent turned his on and got out the special sketch pad he kept under his chest of drawers. "Fantasy Girl" he had labeled the pad, just in case anyone ever found it and wondered who the model was. Not that anyone would wonder. He was always careful to put Marilyn Monroe's face on the body.

He wasn't that good at drawing the body, though certain parts he did an outstanding job with. One day, on impulse, he showed the pad to

Esmund Drakes, a new kid in school he wanted to be friends with, a kid who could draw comic strip characters with amazing speed and accuracy. Kent didn't tell about the nighttime modeling sessions, though. He would just as soon Esmund think the girl was supposed to be Marilyn Monroe. Esmund was so impressed that, when he left Kent's home, he sneaked out with Kent's sketch pad tucked inside his own.

The next day, Esmund took Kent's drawings of Brenda to school and handed them out to various guys in the cafeteria. Marilyn-Brenda, the fantasy girl Kent had kept such a secret for so long, created a sensation, and before he knew what was going on, boys were coming up to Kent, asking for more such drawings. At one table, a scuffle broke out between Haines Cunningham and Jim Hudson, a couple of the school's track stars, over ownership of a drawing. "Lookit them tits," Haines said. Jim tried to look, but Haines held the drawing away, repeating, "Wouldja just lookit them tits." Jim made a snatch for the drawing, and Haines punched his arm. Other guys gathered around the table, gawking and pushing each other to get a look. The activity caught the attention of Sister Charlotte—Sherman Tank Charlotte, the kids called her. Guys scattered at her approach, all but Jim Hudson and Haines Cunningham, who had their backs to her and were too involved in their contest over the drawing to notice much of anything.

Kent watched in agony as Sherman Tank Charlotte's eyes went round and her puffy lips formed a huge O, making her face, encircled by the nun's habit, look like a gigantic circle with three smaller circles drawn inside, the three connected by a banana that was her nose. Kent sketched the face on his napkin even as Sister Charlotte grabbed up Jim Hudson and Haines Cunningham by their collars. She lifted them from their chairs and banged their bodies together before dropping them in a confused heap in front of her. "Hand me that trash," she said in the high, fluting voice that she used in moments of great distress, "and you two come with me."

The rest of the afternoon proved to be one of the longest of Kent's life. He expected to be called to the main office to talk with the new principal, Sister Corazon, who had come to Bishop Green Intermediate School with the reputation of being a tough lady to deal with. But the summons did not come.

That night, he watched Brenda with less than his usual

6

enthusiasm, and afterward he found he could not draw a thing. During second period the following day the summons came.

Sherman Tank Charlotte herself delivered the message to Kent, and as he left math class to follow her down the hall, he heard uneasy laughter from some of the guys in the class.

The hallway felt longer, narrower, and darker than Kent remembered it. He noticed some cobwebs near the ceiling, and in a couple of places the dark, excremental flecks of chewing tobacco that some of the guys dropped on the floor while scooping out a jaw full of Bull Durham. This is it, he thought. Endsville. He got a vision of Sister Charlotte tying a blindfold over his eyes while Sister Corazon lined up a firing squad, headed by Esmund Drakes and Brenda Watson. "Do you want a final chew of tobacco before the execution?" Sherman Tank Charlotte asked.

"I don't chew," Kent said.

"What was that?" Sister Charlotte held the door to the principal's office open.

Kent looked at her with alarmed confusion. "Uh, after you." Kent felt dizzy.

"Stuff the charm." She scowled. "Nothing can save you now."

He knew that was true, but to hear it from Sister Charlotte made his knees turn to jelly. As he walked in, Esmund hurried out, his eyes down-cast. Kent thought Esmund looked much like his dog did when it got caught piddling on the floor. Sister Charlotte gestured into the private office of the principal and gave Kent a shove in that direction.

He looked around the room in a panic. No windows. And the only door was behind him, blocked by a Sherman tank. He took a deep breath and let himself into the principal's office.

Sister Corazon stood by a window, the backlight ringing her so it was impossible for Kent to make out her facial features. Except for being smaller, she might have been Sister Charlotte standing there. "Please sit down, Kent Day." She indicated a chair in front of her desk, then walked to her chair and sat, looking at Kent in a most disconcerting and steady way.

Kent met her gaze, something he had taught himself to do with people when he decided he wanted to learn to draw faces. But holding eye contact with Sister Corazon was tough.

"You realize, of course, that you have committed a number of offenses?" She picked up a stack of his drawings and dropped them a little closer to him on her desk. "Do you?"

"Do I what?" Kent asked, then realized what she meant and stammered, "Yes, uh, yes I did. Do."

"The human body," she held eye contact as if she were challenging him to be the first to look away, "is the temple of the soul. You realize that, of course?"

He said nothing. It seemed to him as if she had penned him down with her steady gaze.

"You have tried to draw that divine temple in a rather poor way. Marilyn Monroe once was a real, live, breathing human being, but no more. Now she is a myth, an unreal entity, a chimera, a kind of dream that people try to give substance to in their dreams. You tried that, and you failed. Miserably. Do you understand what I have said?"

"No."

"That, at least, is honest. This," she broke eye contact for the first time, and Kent felt as if someone had just taken a knife from his throat. "This," she picked up the drawings of Marilyn-Brenda, "is bad on a number of counts. It isn't a good rendering of the myth. It concentrates on making a woman's body something it is not, on making it into a thing, an object. And remember that a body is holy. Always remember that." She walked to the trash can and dropped the drawings into it, then stood for a few seconds, looking at the contents of the can.

She turned to Kent. "The first offense was drawing without working out what the body looks like. You brought talent to the task, along with ignorance." She went to a bookcase, removed a book, and opened it on her desk. "Come look at this."

Kent stood with uncertainty and looked at the book. It was some sort of anatomy text, and the picture she had opened to showed a human body with no skin in order to illustrate the shapes of the body's muscles.

"That is part of the foundation." Sister Corazon pointed. "This one is female. On the next page is the male."

Kent turned a page, caught by the lines of muscles wrapping the body. He picked the book up and turned another page, then looked up, embarrassed.

"Would you like to borrow the book?"

At that point he understood what Sister Corazon was up to.

Kent looked at various parts of the woman's anatomy as she sat in the airplane seat, fidgeting, unsure of how to respond to the intensity and frankness of the way he looked at her. He thought of the shape of her body, only partly hidden by her clothing, of the smooth flow of muscles under her skin, and moved his pen with precision. She was beautiful, and his pen celebrated her beauty. Sister Corazon, could she see the drawing, would approve, for he was drawing the beauty of this woman, and was catching something of her tentative, nervous and yet self confident personality. A human being, Kent knew. Alive, beautiful, perhaps aging a bit, but not an object.

His next attempt to draw Brenda, which came just days after the interview with Sister Corazon, showed her in profile, standing beside a bed, with no clothes on—in fact, with no skin on. "She is beautiful," Sister Corazon said when she looked at the drawing. Even the facial muscles were there, wrapping the jaw and encasing the eyeball. Some of the perspectives were not quite right. Her head was too small, and her pectorals too large.

At the principal's suggestion, he drew skeletons, working on getting the dimensions of the various bones the proper size in relationship to each other. At night he studied Brenda, then drew her bones in the various positions he saw her take in her room: sitting before the mirror, combing non-existent hair with skeletal fingers grasping a comb; lying on the bed, reading through empty sockets; standing with one bony finger poised over the light switch. Watching her and seeing bones and muscles and light and shading became exercises in self control and objectivity. He never told Sister Corazon about his model, even when he showed her drawings of Brenda wrapped in flesh and wearing the self-satisfied, flirtatious and naughty grin she often had when glancing in the direction of his darkened window. Sister Corazon always approved, for he was learning, and he was being honest.

"You have great talent," she told him once. "Use it for creating truth and beauty. Never be dishonest as an artist." Was drawing caricatures being dishonest? He wasn't sure, but suspected it was at least doing less than he should be doing, less than he was capable of. But there was the persistent need for money, and caricatures brought plenty of that.

Kent completed the drawing of the nude lady. It would be easy to drape her in clothes, but to alter the drawing at this point would do bad things to it. He knew the piece was as good as anything he had done lately, yet he wasn't pleased with it. He handed her the drawing with much the same feeling he used to have when showing Sister Corazon a new drawing of Brenda. Then he remembered his original motives for striping his subject of clothing. A mean-spirited motive. Kent blushed, ashamed to have allowed himself to act on such a base feeling.

The woman looked at the drawing, then at Kent. "This is wonderful," she said. "Don't be embarrassed over it."

Kent made no attempt to correct her analysis of his blush. He watched her study the drawing.

"You captured some things about me that not many people know." She moved into the seat next to him again. "I've posed nude for other artists, but you did a better job than any of them, and I was fully dressed." There was awe in her voice. "Would you please sign the drawing?"

As the two parted in the Denver airport, the woman handed him a folded hundred dollar bill, blushing as she did so. Her awkwardness made Kent feel awkward, though he was quite used to people handing him money for his work. The woman hurried off, and Kent looked at the bill she had given him, realizing that there was another hundred wrapped inside it.

He wadded up the bills and jammed them into a pocket, glad to have the money and at the same time disappointed and more than a bit angry at himself. So what has happened, he had wondered, to my affirmation that I have given up commercial art, that if my life is to mean anything, I must seek something else in my art?

These men, Kent thought as he looked at the soldiers pointing rifles at him, know nothing of art. But they would understand a chain of com-mand in their government. He reached into a pocket for the letter that might help him with the zealous customs agent.

A guard threw an arm around his neck. The rifles advanced to his chin, and someone said, "Please to keep hands in sight. Better to hold them up."

"I was," Kent struggled to get a breath, "just reaching for a letter in my pocket. From the Sultan of Selangor." His statement had a surprising effect. The arm around his neck dropped away, and the M-14 rifles lowered.

"I'll get," a voice behind him said. Kent turned so the man could reach into his pocket. The letter was an official welcome from the Sultan and an invitation to his home in Shah Alam. Kent was the first of a series of Texas artists to be sent to Malaysia in a cultural exchange program between Texas and Selangor, one of the more populated states in Malaysia.

The customs official and two of the guards puzzled over the letter for a while, becoming increasingly impressed. "I sorry for inconvenience," the customs man said. As he talked, he began gathering Kent's clothing and folding them.

As soon as he checked into a hotel, Kent decided, leaving the customs desk and heading for the taxi stand outside, he would try to contact Ms Suppriah Krishna for advice on helping Noland out of his scrape. Getting the matter straight would be no problem—unless something else went wrong. He considered the possibilities: the police could store the baggy with others like it that had real drugs in them, then get the wrong baggy for chemical analysis. Or, unknown to Noland, some drug smuggler had switched out his soda for something a little stronger. There was, after all, that odd-looking man with the medals and ribbons on his chest who seemed to take some interest in Noland in the airport. That odd man could be a genuine drug smuggler.

But all that speculation is ridiculous, he told himself, and based on seeing too many American movies set in California. Next I'll be expecting to run into a mysterious, beautiful blond woman and get involved in a shoot-out chase scene through an old warehouse. We would end up at her apartment, showering together and madly in love, soulmates like Noland wishes for. Kent laughed out loud, and several bearded men with white turbans turned to stare at him.

The serious problem at hand now, Kent told himself, is to figure out how to help Noland—innocent, romantic Noland who, Kent had to admit, could present people with an inaccurate first impression.

Kent had watched Noland wander around the airport, wait in the same section he did, and board the same plane to Seattle. As Kent watched, he revised his estimation of Noland. The man was neither silly nor stupid. Kent took out the caricature he had done and altered some lines and shading, making Noland's face amiable and friendly.

Later, when it became clear that both of them were waiting in Seattle for the same flight to Japan, Kent introduced himself to the man he still regarded as a movie-set cowboy. They sat together on the long flight to Tokyo. Noland talked most of the way.

He was no fake cowboy but "the honest-to-gawd real thing," he explained. Or he was the real thing some few years before. Noland came from Shamrock, a tiny Texas Panhandle town 90 miles east of Amarillo, just off Interstate 40. "I was Born and raised there," he told Kent, "and even went to Shamrock high school."

Kent, a city Texan, had never heard such a thick accent. He tried spelling some of the words as Noland spoke them: "Ah wuz barn n razed thar, n eben wenta Shum Rock ha school." But Kent found Noland's account of himself so colorful that he soon paid little attention to the way he flattened vowels, squashed diphthongs, and jammed words together.

Noland was going to Malaysia as a geologist for EXXON, but the true reason for his venture into Malaysia was to find a perfect wife. He had read somewhere that Malaysian women were both beautiful and dedicated to giving their lives to making their husbands happy. "Girls back in the states, shoot, they go for making life miserable, seems to me, for everbody around them," he told Kent. "Even Virginia." Noland sighed. "Time was when I knew she and me was soulmates. Virginia was about the best thing ever to come out of Shamrock, Texas, and she up and married a diesel mechanic."

Kent saw his lower lip tremble a bit. He's fighting for control, Kent realized with surprise. But then it makes sense, Kent knew, for Noland to hide his feelings. Weren't most men that way—especially Texas men? Especially the macho type, Kent thought. He gave Noland a few seconds to get himself in hand, then steered the subject away from Virginia.

"So what did you do after graduating from Sham Rock High School?" Kent asked.

Noland explained that he worked on his father's ranch, doing what most cowboys do and had done for over a hundred years in Texas: ride horses and move cows around and drink themselves into a stupor on

Saturday night. Kent was amazed to learn that there were still cowboys. "There sure is for a fact," Noland said. "And the old hands on the ranch, some of them taught me a passel of songs. I change them up some, though. And old Hank Simon, he taught me how to stay alive in the Avalon."

"The Avalon?" Kent asked.

"It's a big dance hall and bar on Amarillo Boulevard." Noland went on to explain how it was a Saturday-night hangout for cowboys who drove from out-lying ranches for a good time in Amarillo, an evening of Lone Star beer and dancing on a hardwood floor sprinkled with coarse-ground corn meal. And maybe a good fight or two. "Old Hank told me you don't go into the Avalon without cavalry support."

"You can get yourself kilt in there," Hank had warned, "unless you know a thing or two about banging heads and busting asses." Hank let it be known that he regarded himself as calvary support enough for Noland.

When a cowboy in the Avalon punched Noland in the eye, knocking him and his chair over, Hank stepped up to the fellow and said, "Just whatja go and do that for?"

The cowboy looked down at Hank, a bent, skinny old guy with graying hair. "Pops," the cowboy said, "you tell your grandson there about not talking to another man's girl." Hank raised one hand to scratch his head. His other hand flew out, hitting the cowboy in the stomach. Hank belted the man several more times. The bouncer at the Avalon had to pick the cowboy up and drag him out the back door.

The next day, Hank Simon took Noland to the barn and began instructing him in ways to survive in Texas bars. "That there is one helluva shiner," Hank said. "Your mistake was letting him get close enough to you to tag your eye like that. If a guy gets close, you step back quick or else hammer him into the floor before he expects anything." Then Hank instructed Noland in the art of hammering a man into the floor.

Kent disliked Noland's account of learning how to brawl. "So what did you do after you got over losing Virginia?" Kent felt a bit mean about mentioning her name again.

"Nobody ever gets over loving someone like I loved that girl. I did, for a fact, mourn too much—but finally had to get over mourning."

After a couple of years of lamenting the loss of Virginia and wishing for a suitable replacement, Noland decided he would do better if he got some education. So he enrolled in Amarillo College and picked up a two-year certificate. Then he moved to Canyon, a little farther down the road, and took a few geology courses from West Texas A&M.

In Amarillo and Canyon, he kept an eye out for the perfect life mate, but knew it was hopeless. "College girls are a pushy lot," he told Kent. "You hold a door open for one, treating her like she was a lady, and like as not she will bloody your lip or bite you on the leg. I used to treat college girls like ladies, but I learned to treat them like prickly pears or pole cats. They can be mighty pretty, but only at a distance."

Without having finished a degree from West Texas A&M, Noland managed to talk his way into a job as a geologist with a small oil company. And after a couple of successful years, he got on with EXXON, which sent him to Malaysia.

"This here," he showed Kent a photograph of a beautiful woman who looked as if she came from India, "is Suppriah Krishna. This girl put an ad in *The Dallas Morning News*. Here," he took out a newspaper clipping and read, "'Loving, lonely Malaysian Indian girl looking for soul-mate with view to marriage.' Sounds good, huh? Did to me, anyway. Of course, any dumb old ugly sow can put an ad in a paper, and there are lots of them, to be sure. But I wrote to this Suppriah and sent a photograph, and she wrote back with this here photo and the sweetest letter you ever saw. Maybe nothing will come of it, but then what do I have to lose? Besides, I got a couple more leads, one in Thailand, just up from Malaysia. Found them in the same paper."

Later, after Kent and Noland had caught the plane from Japan to Kuala Lumpur, Noland wrote Suppriah's phone number and address on a slip of paper and handed it to Kent. "Don't know exactly where I might be staying right off, so I want you to have this so you can contact me. She will know where to find me."

"What if you and she don't hit it off?" Kent asked.

"We already have. Shoot, we're going to be friends, even if soul-mates turns out to be out of the question."

As he stepped outside the airport beside a line to taxi cabs, each with the word *Teksi* written somewhere on the car Kent looked at the slip of paper with Ms Suppriah Krishna's phone number on it. At least, Kent thought, I can call someone for advice about how to help Noland. The man was innocent—innocent to the point of being foolish, carrying the soda in a baggy like that into Malaysia.

## 2

> UGLY AMERICAN: How can anyone stand to watch something
> so silly as a shadow play for more than five minutes?
> YAP AH LOY: The shadow play is the oldest art form in Malaysia.
> But any art, however new or old, can be put to serious use.
> —Butch Gaston, *Playwright's Notebook*

Dressed as Yap Ah Loy, Butch Gaston parked his car by Central Market and walked to the Mandarin Hotel. He waited close to the entrance so he could follow the drug dealer through his first full day in Kuala Lumpur.

When the cocaine dealer emerged, Butch stepped to the sidewalk and pretended to examine the rings a vendor had displayed on the strip of carpet in front of him. Butch noted that the gangster still carried his art pad. A clever disguise, Butch thought—but not clever enough to fool me.

Kent blinked, startled by the brilliance of the morning sun. He steadied himself on the door before allowing it to shut behind him. Jetlag, he told himself, but he knew it was more than that. It was the exotic strangeness of Kuala Lumpur that threw him off balance. He had experienced some of that the previous afternoon and evening, in spite of being dead tired from travel, and in spite of the hassle at the P.J. Hilton, where his reservation had been lost. After almost an hour of frustration, he decided to go to Kuala Lumpur for a hotel. A cheaper one, he told the cab driver.

It wasn't the uncertainty of finding lodging, though, that contributed to the odd feeling of dislocation: it was the orchids growing with such abundance among the shrubs in front of the P.J. Hilton; the fan-shaped travelers palms along the Federal Highway; the arch over the highway announcing entry to the federal capitol, an exotic arch with antique cannons along the bottom and minarets on top; the Klang River lined with hovels made from uneven gray boards and rusted-out corrugated zinc and framed by the magnificence of the Kuala Lumpur skyline; the railway station that looked like the grandest mosque Kent could imagine. And, more than anything, the faces of the people. So many faces, and all so interesting, alive, beautiful.

Sensory overload always made Kent dizzy, for he wanted to see it all, memorize all the details of new and strange images so he could capture them on paper or on canvas. The morning street scene in front of the Mandarin made him stumble and catch his breath. Walls of buildings across the street, cracked and stained from age, had cliff bushes growing on them here and there, some the size of small trees, their roots snaking into the cracks and running down the smooth walls. A man, blacker than Kent thought possible, walked past wearing a white toga and a turban, his back straight, his chin up, his face announcing him to be pleased with himself, perhaps, Kent thought, because he had managed live to such antiquity. A bag woman sat on the steps of the Mandarin, her hair uncombed and her face still showing the mark of the sidewalk where she had slept. She hummed snatches of a song and threw crumbs from the pastry she was eating to the sparrows in the gutter. Taxis and delivery trucks already crowded the narrow street, driven by men whose faces Kent wanted to see better. But then he wanted to see everything better, and it was the attempt to take it all in that gave him that feeling of disorientation.

From his vantage point beside the ring seller, Butch watched Kent stumble, grasp the door, and seem uncertain if he could even walk. Butch allowed himself a mean, tight smile. Gathering the damning evidence would be easier than he thought. The cocaine dealer was himself a drugger, having hooked himself on the very poison he peddled, dulling his senses, causing him difficulty with something so simple as walking. Butch looked at Kent with scorn and contempt, wondering how such a man could enjoy life if he were so drugged he couldn't even see the things around him.

The previous evening, when Butch had picked up Colman at the airport, Cole took Butch's arm, leaned into his face, and declared that he had just seen some high drama at the customs desk. "Two American drug gangsters tried to get into the country," he said. "One of them actually made it—the one who carries a Grumbacher art pad got past the police. You should have seen the silly way the other dealer dressed. He looked like Roy Rogers from an old movie, only much taller."

Butch stepped back from Cole and extricated his arm. He looked at the medals and ribbons Cole kept pinned to his shirt and smiled. You're in no position to make fun of how anyone dresses, he thought.

"I went out the main door and watched the arrest through the glass wall," Cole said. "The guards packed off the rhinestone cowboy, but for some reason they let the other one go. I guess it was because the cowboy had the drugs in his suitcase."

Butch told Cole that he figured the cowboy came from Chicago or New York, maybe Miami, so the western outfit had to be a ruse to throw the locals off track.

A brilliant ploy, Butch thought, using a costume to throw the police off. And such a smart choice. Malaysians had seen plenty of western movies, and the Marlboro man was posted in billboards all over the country. Who would suspect the Marlboro man of trafficking in drugs? Brilliant or not, the pseudo cowboy got caught. The accomplice had escaped.

And Butch was determined to see him nailed. Not through any sort of direct interference, of course. Police work was the business of gumshoes. A playwright had other ways of seeing that justice was done. Subtle ways, Butch reflected, watching the American drug dealer stumble in the doorway of the Mandarin Hotel. He checked his costume again, admiring the flawless way he had made himself look like Yap Ah Loy, the 19th century Chinese kingpin of the city of Kuala Lumpur.

Butch had found Cole's account a bit long-winded, especially when Cole recited some of his poetry, something about a dibbledy Mugs who took drugs. Butch waved the poetry aside and demanded some useful information. He had no time for poetry.

"They only got one of them," Cole repeated, "Just one. The other is headed for his hotel."

"Which hotel?"

"Seems to me," Cole said, frowning and rubbing his chin, "one of them mentioned going to the P.J. Hilton. They talked a great deal on the plane, and I was close enough to hear. But I didn't pay much attention because I didn't know they were gangsters, then."

That was clue enough. Butch took Cole to his house and got away as soon as he could. Cole kept insisting he join the Batu Blue group that night, but Butch resisted. He had research to do, he explained.

Research for his next play. Besides, Cole's odd-ball group had enough writers in it to warn Butch that he needed to keep his distance from them. He wanted to keep his art pure from foreign influences.

Butch drove straight to the P.J. Hilton after dropping off Cole. He wanted to slap on some make-up, but there wasn't time, so he parked his van in front of Thrifty and walked across the street to the Hilton.

Cole's description of the pusher was so good that, when Butch saw him at the registration desk, there was no doubt he had found his man. Butch stood nearby and listened.

The drug pusher kept insisting he had a reservation, but the clerk could find no record of it. As Butch walked up, the two seemed to be settling the matter: the clerk could find no cancellations, and the pusher agreed, with reluctance, to go to another hotel.

It had been an easy matter to follow the taxi that took the drug dealer into Kuala Lumpur. Butch parked in the alley beside the Mandarin and entered the hotel through a side door, then took the stairs to the mezzanine so he could stand on the balcony above the registration desk and watch.

The drug pusher set his suitcase down and put his sketch pad on the counter. Butch strained to see what room the man got, but it was not possible. Without a costume or even rudimentary make-up on, Butch knew he would have to be discrete in his observations lest the pusher notice him and maybe remember what he looked like.

He felt naked and vulnerable without a costume on while doing field research, but no matter. Butch Gaston was not a man to let an opportunity such as this go by. He could, if he were careful how he went about it, gather plenty of material for a play, perhaps a wildly successful one. Successful in getting rid of a dealer in cocaine—that was the main thing. And maybe successful enough with audiences to get Butch what he knew was some well-deserved fame and fortune. Butch had felt that he could go home, get a good night's sleep, and return—dressed in a proper costume—the next morning in time to check on the activities of the pusher.

Kent looked at the ring seller sitting in a lotus position under the arched covering of the sidewalk, his back to the wall. In a guide book, Kent learned that the English had encouraged Malaysians to build their buildings so that the second floor covered the sidewalks in order to allow shoppers to continue their business in spite of the rain. And in Malaysia, it rained plenty. He looked at the covered walkway, wanting to study it longer, but finding his attention drawn to the ring seller.

The vendor was a racial mix, with Chinese predominating. His hair had been bleached, which made it an odd carroty color, called red by people who were careless about naming colors. His face was huge but gentle, and Kent wanted to draw it. Then he looked at the man examining the vendor's wares.

He seemed vaguely Chinese to Kent because of the outrageous oriental gown and elaborate coolie-style pointed hat. But that face. Not oriental at all, Kent observed. And something else about it didn't seem right. What that was, though, Kent couldn't pinpoint. There was some obscure quality there that needed to be drawn in order to be understood. Kent opened his sketch pad, only to discover the man was aware of him, and he didn't seem too pleased with Kent's attention. He stepped behind the sidewalk pillar, which Kent took as a clear sign that his artistic interest had been interpreted as invasive.

Kent decided he would ask permission to draw those who might be offended by his seeming to stare. No caricatures, though—at least not unkind ones like the one he had done of Noland.

The thought of Noland gave him a bad moment. The poor fellow was no doubt in some Malaysian jail worrying about being hanged for a crime he had not committed, so far as Kent could tell. But what could he do? He had tried to call the number of Suppriah Krishna that Noland had given him but got no answer. Kent would try again that day, and if he still had not reached her by early afternoon, he would go looking for a lawyer on his own.

Kent took a deep breath, enjoying the varied odors: curries, frying onions, fresh fish and other vague and unidentifiable pleasant smells jumbled with some not-so-nice things like the hydrocarbons from the taxis and trucks and a faint odor of stagnant water, perhaps sewage. He turned left and headed for Petaling Street, one block over, which the bell hop had assured him was Chinatown at its best. Beside the ring seller, he paused long enough to see that most of the rings were brass set with cheap-looking gemstones.

Along the covered walkway, Kent found he had to move around a variety of street merchants. One woman read fortunes using some kind of cards laid on a board with Chinese writing all over it. Another sold lottery tickets. A European man leaned against the wall, smoking. He stood in stockings while a wrinkled little Chinaman cobbled new soles onto the man's shoes. Kent paused and did a fast sketch of the woman with the fortune cards, catching her only in broad lines, then looked at her, hoping he would later be able to remember the details to sketch in. Most of the time he could, but then he was not often bombarded with so many new images to try to remember.

He passed an alley lined with food stalls. Customers sat beside tiny tables eating soupy looking food full of noodles. Most ate with chopsticks, wielding them with an expertise Kent envied. Some of the stalls had dried, cardboard-like pork hanging on racks; others had smoked duck suspended from hooks, their bodies still intact from bill to clawed toes. Kent drew one of the ducks, then, pretending still to be examining the duck, he drew the face of the Chinese man serving food at the stall.

Kent walked around a food stall attached as a side-car of a motor-cycle. The cyclist specialized in freshly-boiled corn-on-cob. A bird vendor beside a wall with no overhanging sidewalk cover tried to get Kent interested in looking at an assortment of tiny birds with brilliant orange beaks. "Sing good," the vendor assured him. "Feed red peppers to clear throat, and they best singing bird in Malaysia."

By the time Kent reached Petaling Street, only half a block from the entrance to the Mandarin, he had made half a dozen quick sketches, as well as the one carefully-drawn piece of the roasted duck and the food stall operator. When he looked to the left down Petaling Street, Kent realized he would never make it a single block, not in one day, anyway. There was too much to look at, too much to try to capture on paper.

Vendors crowded the edges of the street, pushing the stream of cars, delivery trucks and taxis into a single lane in the middle. The bell hop had mentioned that at night the street was closed to traffic in order to make room for those selling merchandise.

Buildings hung over the sidewalks along both sides of the streets, making the shops that opened to the walks look as if they were entrances to caves. The sidewalks themselves were lined with an odd assortment of merchandise, some from the shops, some from street hawkers choosing a spot to display their goods: watches, brassieres, tee shirts, jewelry, kitchen utensils, batik. Above the covered walkways, carved into the side of the building, hung balconies and windows. On most of the buildings, along the cracks, grew jungle plants, and cliff swallows darted in and out of the arches over the walks.

In one window a short way down the street, Kent saw an interesting face, an old woman who appeared to be watching with great interest the activity of the merchants below her. Kent opened his pad to a new page and walked down the street, trying not to be distracted by all the interesting people, trying to keep his attention focused on the old woman. When he was across from her, he stopped and began drawing.

Kent wasn't sure he could read the expressions of an oriental face, but the more he looked at that woman, the more he was convinced that she had a streak of spitefulness in her. Maybe it wasn't a permanent thing with her, but it sure seemed to be there right then. He moved his hand fast over the paper, capturing the spite in the lines around her eyes, in the set of her jaw, in the thin arrogant line that was her lips.

The old woman leaned forward, produced a large glob of spittle, aiming it at someone below her. As soon as she had dropped her bomb, she vanished from the window.

Kent watched the object fall and land in the hair of a watch vendor. He swatted at his head as if shooing away a fly, then got back to the business of arranging watches on the table in front of him. Kent drew the vendor, his arm reaching over the table to a watch, his hair holding a spot of gooey liquid that caught the morning sun like a jewel. Kent considered telling the man about the loogie in his hair, but decided it would be wiser not to become involved in the politics of the neighborhood.

Across from him, Kent saw a coffee house that seemed quite active. *The Sun Wah*, the sign above the place said. He got out his pocket Malay-English dictionary and looked up *wah*. "An expression of surprise," the book said. That made perfect sense to Kent, who had read in his guidebook about how much it rained in that part of the world. Malaysia, the book said, had the oldest rain forest jungles in the world, dating back some 134 million years. All that rain explained the cliff plants growing into the cracks of the buildings. Kent figured it was the jungle trying to reclaim the city, which in geological time had been lost to people for only the blink of an eye. The sun would crack the buildings and the plants would break them apart with their roots, and, with the aid of a few hundreds of millions of inches of rainfall, the city would collapse and green over into primordial rain forest again.

Meanwhile, Kent figured, vendors would set up shops in the street and spiteful old women would lay a few loogies on their heads. On days when the sun came out to steam away the rain, people might well emerge from the crumbling, time-doomed and dripping buildings, look up and exclaim in delight and surprise, "The Sun. Wah!"

Butch Gaston watched Kent go into the Sun Wah, a place that in his mind was at best of doubtful reputation. A week before, when Butch had been in there, examining some of the gemstones sold by hucksters at the tables near the entrance, a tall young Chinaman had encouraged him to "come with me to see best gems in Kuala Lumpur." And he had gone, only to find himself led to a sidewalk vendor with an assortment of polished iron pyrite and tiger eye. So Butch went back to the Sun Wah. When he arrived, the proprietor maneuvered him aside.

"Beware of the con men," the proprietor said. Butch looked puzzled. "This place is full of many types of con men," the proprietor explained. "Most would just sell you bad merchandise for big prices. Others might get you to go with them, take you into an alley, and rob you. Maybe beat you up." Butch had looked around the café, noting that there was indeed an assortment of thugy-looking people there.

So when he saw Kent go into the place, Butch was sure it was to make some drug sales. He decided he would find a table in the back, get a cup of coffee and watch.

Kent paused by the table at the entrance to look at the assortment of gemstones, rings, and coins. One of the coins was a 1799 Liberty Head silver dollar. He picked it up and looked at the face on the coin. It wasn't quite right: the nose stood a little too pointy and the hair looked etched by an amateur. "American silver coin," the hawker sitting at the table said. "Genuine. Only three hundred ringgit."

"The coin is a clever fake," Kent said.

"For man like you," the salesman said, "I sell for five ringgit." Kent walked past him to the next table, also covered with gemstones and assorted pieces of jewelry. The man at the first table picked up the coin and held it toward Kent. "Two ringgit. How much? You say how much?"

Kent ignored the offer and looked at the polished gemstones. The table held an astounding variety, and most of them looked like the real thing to Kent. He saw lapis, carnelian, bloodstone, lace agate, amethyst, rose quartz, jadeite, and some low-quality emeralds with inclusions throughout. But he didn't pick anything up lest he involve himself in bargaining. What he wanted to do was sit down, have a cup of coffee, and look around the café, to inspect the furnishings and the people. He took a chair at an empty table beside the second display of gemstones and ordered coffee.

Two walls had white strips of paper about a foot wide hanging on them; the paper was covered with Chinese writing. Nice decoration, Kent thought. One wall had a cigarette ad with the Marlboro man on it, a ruddy little cowboy hovering near a campfire, smoking, with snow-covered mountains in the background. Kent hated the ad. It didn't belong in Kuala Lumpur, not in a Chinatown café named The Sun Wah. And it reminded him of his failure to do anything for Noland, but he thrust aside that thought and the stab of guilt it brought. After all, there was nothing he could do about Noland right then.

Kent's coffee came in a clear cup that held what looked more like dark cane syrup than coffee. It sat in the cup on top of a puddle of some kind of white goop that Kent decided had to be condensed milk sweetened beyond all reason. He sipped the drink, trying not to shake it lest the sugary mess in the bottom dissolve into the coffee.

The peculiar-looking man in the Chinese robe and funny hat whom Kent had seen in front of the Mandarin came in and sat at a table nearby. Again Kent noticed that the man's face didn't seem right, and he decided that if he drew it, perhaps he could figure out what was wrong. But the fellow had seemed so touchy when he caught Kent looking at him earlier that it seemed wise to ask permission before doing any drawing.

"Kopi," the man told the waiter, "tidak susu. Tidak gular."

"You want coffee without cream or sugar?" the waiter asked. The man nodded and squinted in what Kent thought an unnatural way.

"Excuse me, sir," Kent said, "but I find you to be a most interesting person. Can I draw you?"

The drug pusher was, Butch decided, playing the artist role to the hilt. Butch had watched the man observing the neighborhood, taking notes in what others who were not in the know would assume to be a sketch pad. But Butch knew the man wasn't drawing anything; he was learning his new market, taking notes that would be of some use to him when he began pushing his deadly ware. And just maybe he sees me as his first customer, Butch thought. He will flatter me with some attention, then no doubt try to get me involved in a conversation that will turn to the subject of cocaine. Pretending to be an artist is a pretty damn good ploy, an ice-breaker that would allow him to get to know something about his potential customers before making the sales pitch. Clever, Butch thought. A pusher had to be damn careful in Malaysia, where the authorities hang you for selling drugs.

Butch squinted his eyes to emphasize the oriental look he had put into his make-up, seemed to consider Kent's question, then nodded. "Can," he said. If there had been a way to avoid talking with the drug dealer, Butch would have taken it. But how was he to respond to the silly request from the fake artist? Butch shivered. He disliked direct involvement with those he studied when doing field research, but sometimes there seemed no getting around it.

Kent nodded his thanks, took another careful sip of the coffee, and got to work. His subject looked oriental in a vague way, at least if Kent didn't look close. Trouble was, since he began drawing in earnest—since those days back in junior high when he sat in the dark and, with the encouragement of the school principal, sought to see the reality of Brenda, to see beyond the jiggle of her breasts and dark fascinating triangle of body hair in order to catch with his pencil the actuality of her physical being as well as the essence of those coquettish glances she made toward his window —Kent had not been able to look casually at any face that interested him. In practical terms, that meant that he tried to look deep into at every face he saw.

The drawing began to take shape, though Kent was hesitant to put in the lined details of the face until he understood them better. As he examined the light and shadow on the man's face and began to sketch in some shading, it became clear to him that the thing wrong was the artificial shadows. Around the eyes, especially. Kent looked in astonishment at his subject. The man had allowed some master make-up artist work on him, shading in shadows with such clever artistry that it took Kent's expert eye for light some time to see the hoax. But when he caught on, it became obvious. There was no way some of the shadows could be made by facial contour. Kent rubbed away the shading he had been tricked by and read the face for what lay under the makeup.

The drawing that emerged was of an American face, one that Kent found sensitive in an odd kind of way. There was both bitterness and cynicism in the man's eyes and the set of his lips. Kent captured as best he could both qualities. There were others he got glimpses of from time to time as the man drank his coffee and glanced at him. Anger. Or at least some little flashes of it. And contempt. And rigidity—that was there, Kent thought, hoping to catch some of it in the man's stubborn insistence in holding his facial muscles taut: the raised brows, the half-shut lids, the steady grip of his cheek muscles in holding the corners of the mouth turned downward. Kent found his subject interesting, but it was a bit distressing to draw him, to see all the uncomfortable emotions the man seemed to keep right under the surface.

And it was a little defeating for Kent to realize, as he often did, that his art couldn't hope to capture all of what he saw. Others who didn't understand the difficulties he faced—the impossibilities he yearned to make realities—people like that lady on the flight from Denver, whom he drew nude in an attempt to capture more of her personality, might praise Kent's work for how much of a person he managed to get into his art. But when he compared how much more he saw to what he drew or painted, Kent knew the true inadequacy of his art. That sense of failure, or of partial failure, along with the sure knowledge of some faint success drove

Kent to push himself to be better, to make his hands get more of reality into his work.

Just as he was giving up on his drawing—*finishing it*, others might call it, though Kent almost always regarded his stopping as giving up on capturing everything he wanted to be there—just as he was about to turn to a blank sheet, an American woman came into the Sun Wah. Kent glanced at her as he was trying to figure out a graceful way not to show the drawing to the pseudo Chinaman. How might the man react if he knew he had been found out? Kent didn't want any unpleasant scenes, so he covered the drawing with a clean sheet and took a final sip of his coffee, now cold and dangerously close to the sugar paste in the bottom.

The American woman, whom Kent found more interesting than attractive—though she was attractive enough—stood by one of the tables of gemstones, closed her eyes and let her hand float over the collection of stones.

It was that relaxed, almost beatific look that Kent wanted to capture, a look he felt he had to get down. In his excitement, he forgot the false Chinaman and turned his full attention to the woman. When she opened her eyes, they were looking straight into Kent's, though it took a fraction of a second for her to seem to see him. She gave him a slight embarrassed smile and looked at the gemstones.

Kent rushed to block out the general configuration of the woman standing by the table, her hand over the stones. But he knew he would never be able to get even a fraction of who the woman was without studying her for some time. And that meant, for the sake of avoiding an embarrassing scene, he must ask permission to draw her. Doing so surreptitiously was out of the question, for she kept glancing at him, aware of his interest in her.

Kent left two ringgits on the table to cover both coffee and tip, and stepped over to the woman. He waited until she and the gem seller paused in conversing about a star sapphire. "Excuse me," he said. "I am an artist, and I couldn't help noticing you." He held the sketch pad so she could see the beginning of the drawing of her by the table. "Would you mind if I did a more thorough job of drawing you?"

"Just stand there a minute." She stepped back. "No, don't move." She looked at him in a way that made Kent wonder if she, too, were an

27

artist. Then she began looking around him, as if she were studying the outermost lines of his figure. "Murky," she said. "But interesting. Could I see an example of your signature?"

"I beg your pardon?"

"Your signature. Could I see a sample of it?"

Kent had heard right the first time, but doubted he had since he could make no sense of her request. Perhaps it was a way she had of making introductions, Kent thought, doubting the assessment even as he scrawled his name across the bottom of his sketch pad. He held it out to her.

"Firm," she said, running her finger across it, then lifting the sheet and feeling the underside. "Artistic, tentative in a good way, striving." She took the pad from his hands and looked at the signature. "Genuine talent. Not egotistical, and honest. Yes, Mr. Kent Day, I will."

"Genuine star sapphire," the gem seller said. "From Burma. Watch." He produced a penlight and held it over the stone. "Star, you see?"

"Not from Burma," the woman said. "A printed stone, but a beautiful one."

Impressed with her knowledge of gemstones, Kent said, "Yes, the Lende Star is a man-made stone, but it is nice."

"This real stone," the huckster said. "How much you pay?"

"Not today," the woman said. "Next time." She dug into her purse and produced a card.

"'Libby LeMaster,'" Kent read, "'Gemologist.' No wonder you know so much about these stones."

"How much? You say how much?" The man at the table held up the fake sapphire.

"You seem to know much about gems yourself. And an artist, too. Where would you like me to pose for you? I did a bit of that kind of thing back in college days, standing before an art class in the buff. But my body was ten years younger then. It is, I must admit, a little flattering that an artist would still be interested in my posing."

Kent swallowed hard, searching for the proper response. All he had wanted to do was to sit down and draw her while she stood over the table of semi-precious stones. But how could he say that without it coming out as an insult, without her hearing something like "Well, no, you see madam, I haven't the slightest interest in looking at your body for my art, seeing as how it's ten years out of college-girl prime. I just want to draw you in your current frumpy condition, hovering over a man-made gemstone." Not that she was at all frumpy, Kent thought, glancing down at her figure. When he looked up, their eyes met and he saw that she had watched his eyes as he made a quick assessment of her body. He blushed.

"Innocent, too." Libby looked at her watch. "I suppose we could go for the modeling session at my place this afternoon. Unless you had something else in mind."

"Twenty dollar," the huckster said. "Best price for Burmese star sapphire."

"Uh, yeah," Kent hedged. He wanted to get out of the Sun Wah, away from the persistent gem seller, away from the false Chinaman, who seemed to be taking great interest in their conversation. It was all rather embarrassing, especially with the American under the makeup, watching. Without doubt he understood the absurdity of the situation Kent got himself into, Kent believed, since he had asked to draw him, too, and there had been no question of nude posing, or posing of any kind. "Let's go," Kent said.

As he and Libby stepped into the street beside the watch vendor, Kent remembered the old woman in the upper window, and he looked up. A large block of ice teetered on the edge of the window and dropped toward him and Libby.

Kent grabbed Libby and pushed her, leaning into the push and jumping so the two of them fell onto the display of watches. The ice crashed into the street, shattering into a number of chunks and sending ice splinters all over the street.

Libby, who had made no sound except for a slight grunt when the table collapsed under her and Kent, sat up and looked at the shards of ice. "Thanks, Kent," she whispered.

Kent glanced up but saw no one in the window. He looked at Libby, checking for damage. She had an imitation Rolex with a day and date readout and a silver band on one of her shoulders and a number of imitation Dunhills and Piagets were in a heap in her lap. One knee had a scraped, bloody spot on it.

A crowd began to gather. Many people talked in loud, excited voices and pointed to the window the ice had fallen from. Kent helped Libby to her feet, then the two helped the watch vendor gather his ware from the street. Kent noticed that the man still had a spot where his hair was plastered together from the woman spitting on him.

"Your knee," Kent said.

"Not bad. But it's dirty, which can pose a problem in the tropics where germs grow so fast."

"Let's get to a drug store," Kent suggested, "for some antiseptic ointment of some kind. My hotel is just around the corner. We can go there and you can get cleaned up."

"It's a deal," Libby said. "Only, around here, they call the drug store 'The Chemist.' The Chinese use an herbalist, and the traditional herb drug stores are reliable. There's one right down Sultan street, across from the Mandarin Hotel."

After they had walked for a way, Libby said, "Someone did that deliberately."

Kent considered the opinion. It was possible, though there was no sense to it. But then he saw no sense to the woman spitting on the watch vendor's head. That didn't mean she had no motivation, just that Kent was ignorant of it.

"Someone was trying to kill me," Libby added.

Butch Gaston, watching Libby walk away with the cocaine man, felt tempted to go after them, to take Libby away from that scum, to tell her that if she hung around him, all kinds of bad things could happen to her. Like almost getting killed by that block of ice someone aimed at the drug dealer.

Butch figured the local gangsters had added up the facts just as he and Coleman had, and they came to the conclusion that this Kent Day, as he called himself to Libby, was out to take over their territory for drug dealing. So they decided to get rid of him. That could spell real danger for Libby, not to mention the fact that Kent had tagged her as a customer for his poison.

Butch had been sure the dealer was about to make a pitch to him. Kent was sizing up the customer—Butch—by pretending to draw him.

Then in came Libby, and the drug dealer perceived her to be an easier mark, so he dropped the approach to Butch, alias Yap Ah Loy, and made his pitch for her.

And it was such an obvious one, one a man could see right through. Libby should have, being a psychologist and all, Butch reflected. But then she was a woman and hence vulnerable to the flattery of the fake artist. What a smooth operator that Kent was. Asking her to pose nude for him so he could steer her into bed, so he could get some sexual power over her, weaken her, use her to satisfy his perverse lust, and then get her dependent on him as a supplier of dope.

Butch clinched his fists in anger. No, he couldn't run after Libby, not when doing so might screw up his chance to get some evidence of that Kent fellow's corruption. Libby wouldn't believe him, anyway, and she would be angry.

Butch would just as soon not have Libby angry at him.

3

Hey and a dibble-de dabble-de mugs
Panhandle Noland got busted for drugs.
—Coleman Farquart, *Asean Doublets*


Miles Osborn moved about the living room, agitated. He looked at Coleman's book of poetry and rolled his eyes. Cole and his stupid poetry, he thought, and his even stupider party last night. Images from the party kept popping into his head, increasing his agitation. That beautiful Malay woman watching him. The wild man from Borneo. Libby slapping that lawyer, and the cold fury in his eyes. The Malay woman there in the dark laundry room, right beside me without my knowing it—watching Libby slap the lawyer. Then she made it clear she wants something from me. Damn. Miles took a deep, ragged breath and looked again at Cole's book.

Poetry, for chrissake. Nobody in his right mind reads poetry. Miles scowled at the manuscript. There was something outrageous about being assigned a roommate who was a poet, especially one who insisted you read his garbage. Miles walked around the coffee table, glancing at the bound manuscript sitting there, waiting. Today's title, written in carved calligraphic letters on a gummed label and stuck on the cover read *Asean Doublets*. Under that, in larger carved letters was *by Coleman Farquart*.

The only thing Miles liked about the cover appeared at the bottom, in red and black print: *Clearly the Best*, a label Coleman had snipped off the dust jacket of a dictionary. Miles liked the absurdity of that label. In his mind, it was an ironic statement, something he himself might have written and stuck there as an indictment of the crappy verses that Coleman was so proud of.

Miles stood by the sliding glass door, open because of the late afternoon heat, and looked at the triangular patterns made by the wrought iron door. "Like a goddam insect," he said. He thrust a fist through one of the triangles and shook it, aiming the gesture at Coleman, who was out there in Petaling Jaya somewhere, at the chicken-shit university in the city that brought him to Malaysia, under paid him, and stuck him with a poet to room with, at the whole effing world for the way it crowded him and cramped him and bottled him up.

For Miles, the diamond pattern made by the iron door caused the world to look like he imagined it did to a grasshopper or fly, all cris-crossed and regimented. If he wanted, he could take the key from its peg above the curtains and unlock the grating and thus be able to see out without having to look through the patterned iron. He was aware of that. But he also knew that the annoyance of the grating helped keep him aware of the way the world was out to confine him, to make him be certain ways, behave certain ways. As long as he remained aware of what the bastards were up to, he could stay free enough to say what he pleased.

And the iron door was there to keep out thieves. "Indonesians sneak over here and steal," a Malaysian cab driver had assured him. When Miles was in Bali, the porter at the hotel explained the barred windows of the beach cottage Miles rented: "They keep out the Javanese, who come to Bali at night to steal." Everyone seemed to believe it was never a neighbor who did anything nasty to you. But Miles knew better. Those bars were there to keep his neighbors out. He knew it had to be neighbors and colleagues— even roommates—who were the nastiest people in the world.

He looked beyond the grate at the bougainvilleas, the frangipani blossoms, and the oleanders growing in his yard. "Poisonous," he said, meaning the oleanders. He glanced back at Coleman's manuscript. "That, too," he said. "Pure poison."

Miles sighed and picked up the volume. Coleman would be in shortly, and he would ask if Miles had read the latest entries. Sure, he would pretend not to be all that interested, waiting for Miles to bring the matter up. Cole would go to the fridge and get them a couple of Anchor beers and would sit in the living room and make small talk about the latest rumors concerning the wild success of Ringling University. "It's slowly edging out the Texas program," he would say. "Even The Big Ten people are starting to sweat about us." But all the while he would be glancing at his poetry there on the coffee table, expecting Miles to interrupt with wild praise for the latest entries.

Miles opened the book from the back, flipped beyond the blank pages, the ones destined to have some of the great poetry of the ages scrawled upon them, and stopped at the last verse. As was often the case, it was a two-liner. Under the title, the words *by Coleman Farquart* appeared, in calligraphy. After the two lines there was a dash and *Coleman Farquart* written again. An abominable habit, Miles thought, this insistence of putting his name on every page, twice.

The verse itself was worse than usual, Miles decided. *Panhandle Noland*? That sounded familiar. Oh yeah. That Texan who got jailed for bringing drugs into the country. Cole had come home from the airport yesterday evening, babbling about some guy who sat in front of him on the trip from Japan, something about the security guards catching the fellow with dope in his luggage. Miles hadn't listened because Cole introduced the subject by saying he had just written a poem about it. The drugger wore a cowboy outfit, Miles remembered—Cole had gone on a while about how tall he was and about his name being tooled on a belt about three inches wide.

What kind of perverted mental gymnastics, Miles wondered, would cause a drugger to fly into Malaysia? The idiot. Malaysians would string the sucker up—after a publicized trial, of course. The same as they had done with that tall Aussie pusher several months back, and there wasn't a damn thing anyone could do about it. As far as Miles was concerned, whoever Panhandle Noland was had it coming, too. Not for pushing drugs—that wasn't an issue Miles had ever given much thought to. For being stupid. It was written on his airplane tickets, for chrissake, in plain English: death is the penalty for bringing drugs into Malaysia. And it was on posters all over the effing airport, even in the toilets. People needed to by god take serious what they read in public toilets.

"Hey and a dibble-de dabble-de mugs," Miles read, doing a little tap dance to the rhythms of the verse. That part wasn't so bad, what with the heavy anapests and the wonderful potential of the word *mugs*. Miles could see it written on the wall above a urinal in a public whizzer somewhere in Ohio. Bowling Green, maybe—in that grungy little bar on main street where all the jerks from the university hang out. But it had to have a stronger second line, something that made use of *mugs* to slap the pomposity out of some square-jawed jock who shaved three times a day and rubbed Aqua Velva all over his body and knew all the girls were dreaming up ways to trip him so he would fall forward, right on top of them. The guys who used the urinal would read the message and know right off who the jock was, and they would go out laughing and repeat the graffiti to other guys who would tell the girls and some of them might write it in the booths of their whizzers to spread the word better, and like as not the Big Man with the super-slick mug and the Aqua Velva body would get the squashing he deserved.

That's if the second line were done right. Miles frowned at the page. Put the way Cole did it and patched into a book, even if it was just an unpublished manuscript, made it a poem rather than something more useful, like graffiti. Poetry was bullshit stuff in literature books full of names like William Shakespeare and John Maysfield. Miles winced at the memory of Maysfield.

"I should have done it like this." Miles set aside Coleman's book. "My heart's in the highlands," he put one hand over his crotch, "My heart is not here. My heart's in the highlands a-chasing a deer."

He thought of a high school English teacher, Miss whatzername—Gertrude Bagby Duckfat or Briggot Bilgewater, Maggoty Meg, or perhaps Rita Rottencrotch. He had given her an abundance of names on the restroom walls of Thomas Jefferson High School, all richly deserved. She had made him memorize the deer-chasing poem and recite it while standing before the class, hand over his heart for emphasizing the "delicate feelings and poignant nostalgia the poem offers the reader."

Delicate feelings, my ass. Miles still remembered the sniggering from the guys in the class and the sweet put-down smiles from the girls. From Dee-Dee Jolsen, who sat beside him in class with her faint perfume and thick, auburn hair and breasts. Of course, all those jerk-heads had to recite something similar—but that was different. Standing up there, with everybody watching, smirking, some of them outright laughing was the hardest thing he ever did in his life.

And that was poetry. Reciting dog doo with his hand over his heart. That and reading impossible stuff by men with three names. Henry Wadsworth Longfellow. James Whitcomb Riley. Alfred Lord Tennyson. Or else they had names like *Dryden*. "Dry-den" Miles had written on the gym locker room wall at Thomas Jefferson High School. What was the rest of it? He couldn't remember, but it was a fine piece of graffiti, and it stayed up there for weeks. Even Coach Mac had laughed about it. Trouble was, Miles had to write serious bullshit on exams about lines he thought might as well be written in Swahili.

Dee-Dee Jolsen said she just adored poetry. She carried around little books of it in her purse—*Sonnets from the Portuguese* and volumes by Rod somebody or other with titles like *Listen to the Warm*. Miles adored Dee-Dee, and he spent weeks trying to figure out how to get her to notice him. She was all agog over Keith Furgeson, a big stupid jock who hung out with all the popular kids. Furg hated poetry—perhaps his only redeeming characteristic, to Miles' way of thinking.

Furg was the competition, and he looked unbeatable with his Hollywood good looks and weight lifter's body. But he was dumber than hammered shit (a phrase Miles had applied to him, with satisfactory results, in some restroom graffiti). How an intelligent, sensitive girl like Dee-Dee Jolsen could fall for such a moron was beyond comprehension. But he had that straight jaw and even teeth and unpimpled skin and muscles—none of which Miles had.

His ace-in-the-hole was his intelligence and his ability to write. Poetry, if necessary. He spent an afternoon in a Hallmark card store, borrowing lines from cards, and put together a poem sure to win the heart of any girl who liked poetry.

In his first period class—algebra with old lady Mercer—he proof-read the poem one last time and folded it. During Miss Mower's health class, second period, he folded it a couple more times. Third period, while Mr. Landry explained something about the American civil war, Miles gave the poem several more folds. By the time sixth period came, it wasn't possible to fold the paper again. He tried, sitting next to Dee-Dee, working up the nerve to give it to her, but all he had to work with was a fat little rectangle that looked less like a poem than the spit wads he used to make for firing from rubber bands.

While the English teacher, Slobber-faced Sal, was writing some crap on the blackboard, Miles tossed the poem to Dee-Dee. It landed on her knuckles and bounced across the sheet she was taking notes on. "For you," Miles whispered, holding his hand over his heart. Dee-Dee put her fist over the wad of paper and glanced up at the teacher. Then she looked at Miles and gave him a tiny, puzzled smile.

It took her what seemed hours to get the poem unfolded. She performed the job like a ritual, inside the book slot of her desk, out of sight of old Twat-Brain, who spent a long time reading to the class what she had written on the board.

"Twat-Brain reads the board," Miles once wrote on the cork board in Mercer's algebra class, "because she thinks she is the only one in the room who knows how to read."

When Dee-Dee got the sheet flat enough to read, she took what felt to Miles like another hour to read the poem. He pretended to take notes, spending most of the time rubbing the sweat off of his palms on his jeans and glancing at Dee-Dee. It annoyed him a little that she moved her lips while reading, the same way Furg always had to do in order to understand anything. When she finished, she smiled with her lips, though her brow was knit up all wrong for a smile, and she mouthed the words "How sweet," to Miles.

The response both pleased him and angered him. *Sweet*? A bullshit word if he ever heard one. Fuzzy-eared rabbits were sweet. Teddy bears were sweet. Little things, unimportant things that in no way were to be taken seriously were *sweet*. Still, Dee-Dee could have responded in a worse way. She could have laughed.

Between classes, Dee-Dee showed the poem to Furgeson, and he didn't laugh, either. What he did do was to catch Miles just outside the library, stiff-arm him up against the wall, and nail him in the stomach with five or six punches. Miles doubled over and fought for breath. He wanted to tell Furg what a mistake he had made in punching someone with power over words. Never offend an artist, he wanted to shout, and he might have, too, but for the fact that he couldn't get enough air to breathe, much less to form the words. Later, he was glad he had not been able to speak. After all, no one knew he was a graffiti artist, and his power lay in such anonymity. Furg didn't say anything, but his muteness was born of ignorance and stupidity; Miles was certain of that. He would make it his business to let everyone know just how ignorant and stupid Furg was.

But he would do the most damage to that bitch, Dee-Dee Jolsen. Anyone who would take a love poem that pure and beautiful and let someone like Furg read it had to be the lowest form of human scum. Even as he watched Furg huff away, leaving him crumpled against the wall, Miles was forming the basis of a graffiti campaign aimed at Dee-Dee:

Dumb dumb Dee-Dee de dumb

masturbates with her thumb.

Nobody would mistake that for a poem, Miles knew, considering where they would find it.

Kids passing in the hall stared as he struggled to stand up straight. One guy laughed, and Miles took note that Charles Brownell would get a few vicious strokes from the pen. The braying jackass.

The next day, Mr. Stocker, the assistant principal, had Furg and Miles into his office. He lectured them on the uselessness of violence in solving personal problems. While he droned on, Miles amused himself by making up phrases like "Stocker is the Ass. Princ. of the hole school." By god that was a good one, he thought, grinning at the genius of it. Stocker and Furg took the grin to mean that there were no hard feelings about the matter, and that was just fine with Miles. He rather liked the idea of their being so fooled. He shook hands with Furgie the Frog Frigger when the Ass. Princ. asked him to, and he smiled, thinking of all the places he could write brilliant phrases about Furgie as a buggerer of frogs.

Miles had never before attempted to mass produce any of his graffiti, but then never had anyone offended him as had Dee-Dee Jolsen. While he and his parents were visiting his uncle Silas Osborn in Beaumont, Miles walked over to Shelby Office Supplies a couple of blocks away and ordered a rubber stamp and an ink pad of permanent ink.

The next week, Miles hung around the library after school until nearly everyone had gone, then ducked under a little-used office desk in the back of the library. He waited what seemed two hours before coming out. When he got on with his job, it took less time than he had anticipated.

With indelible ink, on every toilet seat in the entire school, he stamped "Dee-Dee Jolsen sits here." Then he let himself out a back door and threw the stamp and pad into a garbage Dumpster.

Two days later, he selected three toilet booths in different places around the school for his jingle about Dee-Dee whacking off with her thumb. Then he waited a week, checking out the graffiti around school to see if anything he had done would inspire some of the lesser graffiti wits. One piece appeared in a booth of the boy's room on the second floor:

38

I sits upon dear Dee-Dee's throne
a-wishing she was with me
to offer her a naked bone
and hope that she would kith me.

"Goddam amateur," Miles said. But he was pleased: it was a beginning. In the booth of another boy's room, someone wrote, "Dee-Dee sucks her thumb," and below that, someone else wrote "I'd suck Dee-Dee's thumb while she's using it." In most boy's rooms appeared drawings of huge thumbs with assorted poorly-written graffiti beside them, all naming Dee-Dee in some way.

Miles decided it was time for stage three, for his final piece on Dee-Dee. After that, he would consider scores evened. Anything other would-be wits put up would be bonus blasts at her, and Miles had no doubt that she deserved them.

Confident of his power, he wrote the last piece of the vendetta on only two walls, though he did pick the busiest restrooms in the school. He hung around school until nearly everyone had gone, then slipped into the boy's room near the front entrance and wrote in large block letters beside the mirror: "Dee-Dee the Thumb does it on toilet seats." Then he went across the hall and did the same in the girl's room. Just as he was capping the pen, the door opened and one of the women janitors came in. "Scuse me honey," she said, and headed to the booths with her cleaning equipment. She never looked up, or she would have responded to a boy being in the wrong room. Miles left, his heart racing from the close call.

By the next day, someone had marked out his graffiti in the boy's room so it was unreadable—probably the cover-up was the work of old Fart Faced Furg. After the close call with the cleaning woman, Miles dared not check out the wall across the hall. In any case, he decided, the damage was done. The jerks who felt the need to write on walls but lacked imagination scribbled everywhere Miles' note about Dee-Dee doing it on toilet seats. And even some of the popular kids—the ones who sat on the Student Council and took turns raising the flag every morning—sniggered about the Dee-Dee jokes.

Miles had watched her every day in English class. He hadn't spoken to her since Furg belted him in front of the library, and she had seemed too embarrassed to say anything to him. As the graffiti campaign picked up its pace, Dee-Dee seemed to wilt. She sat in a listless fog, drawing triangles and cubes in her English notebook instead of taking notes. She seemed so depressed that Miles had to resist feeling sorry for her.

She sat a table away from him in the cafeteria the day one of the popular kids shouted across the room, "Hey, Dee-Dee. Show us your thumb." Miles saw her wince a bit, as if someone had struck her but she seemed determined not to respond. Miles smiled a nervous smile and told himself that he had hit her just then, and he tried to feel good about it. The bitch, he affirmed. She deserves all she gets. And he managed a tiny bit of elation until he saw a single tear run down Dee-Dee's cheek. Miles felt his stomach tighten and a sour taste come into the back of his mouth.

The slap at Dee-Dee Jolsen was the most successful graffiti campaign Miles had ever conducted, even if he felt guilty about how far he had taken it.

The close call in the girl's room made him decide that he had to change the way he operated. It was too risky to spend so much time scribbling on walls when just anyone could walk in. He experimented with writing notes on paper and taping it to walls, but that proved unsatis-factory since someone took it down before it got a large enough audience.

He tried making his notes durable with various glues. People ripped at the paper, which left an ugly splotch of gluey pulp on the wall but was effective in removing his artwork. Just before he graduated from high school, Miles hit upon the combination that served him for years to come: he wrote or typed out his note, laminated the paper in clear plastic, and stick it to a wall with quick-set epoxy. Miles was so pleased with the relative permanence of his glue-on graffiti that he purchased his own lamination machine for plastic-coating paper, and he bought epoxy by the carton.

The stick-on graffiti did something for him he had not anticipated: it lifted the limitations on length of his writing, enabling him to write entire essays running to several pages—though he regarded the short, pithy remark the best, one that a person could read in under 45 seconds, the amount of time Miles calculated the average person took to urinate. If I had thought of epoxy and plastic lamination earlier, Miles had told himself, I could have honed in on Dee-Dee with more precision, given her what she deserved without hitting her quite so hard.

The keys to success as a graffiti artist, Miles knew, were the ability to turn a memorable phrase and the fact that he had the good sense to do so with proper anonymity.

But that stupid Coleman Farquart lacked the good sense to keep a low profile. Miles picked up the book of poetry again and flipped through it. Some of the verse was almost good enough to go on the wall above a urinal just as it was, but most of it limped along, inferior, unfocused, and flawed by Coleman's name over and under it.

Miles regarded it as his bad luck when Coleman walked up to the iron grating and found him examining the poetry. A sneaky habit, coming to the living room to look in before going to the front door, Miles thought. Coleman carried some plastic grocery bags, heavy ones, making the handles into tight little strands that turned his fingers purple. Miles chuckled to himself. You would think Cole had bought junk food enough to last him weeks for the party he had insisted on last night. If you could call it a party, Miles added to himself, scowling at the memory of the Batu Blue gang that he regarded as escapees from the booby hatch. Coleman looked with approval at Miles standing there with his poetry, then tried pushing aside the grating. "This locked?"

Miles nodded. He was tempted to tell Cole that it was kept locked to prevent poets and other perverts from wandering into the house. Miles found himself tempted to tell people such things, but he never did—except in his graffiti, which was safe and anonymous.

Cole went to the front and let himself in with his house key. When he got to the living room, he said, "Why not keep the grate open while you are home?"

"Cats come in and annoy me."

"Not while anyone is at home, they don't." Cole went to the kitchen. Miles listened for the opening of the fridge, the rattle of utensils, the popping of two beer bottles. The jerk never asks me if I want a beer, Miles grumbled to himself. And do I want a beer? Only an idiot would drink a beer on an empty stomach. Gives you a headache.

"Good reading?" Cole asked, nodding toward his poetry book on the coffee table. He handed Miles a beer.

"Thanks." Miles took a sip and looked with contempt at the medals

41

on Cole's shirt. Likely he walked all over Tokyo with those or other similar medals on, then paraded about the airport wearing them so people could see what a hot-shot he was. Anyone unlucky enough to be seated next to him on the flight would have to listen to explanations of the stupid decorations.

He had three new ones on, new to Miles, anyway. No doubt Cole would explain them, and no doubt he would have, in Miles' view, some stupid reason for wearing them. Coleman wore a long sleeved batik shirt and five—no, six medals that Miles could see. Likely, Miles knew, Cole had a couple more somewhere. In his pocket, maybe, or penned under his collar. The Gajah Brown hung over his left shirt pocket. If Miles had a favorite of what he regarded as the stupid medals, it was the Gajah Brown. It was a brass casting with an excremental brown ribbon hanging under it. The casting was of a book being splattered by elephant turds. It was supposed to represent the clever way one of Coleman's mock epics blasted the Malay literary critic, Kamal Mahir, who had published what Cole considered an unfair and scurrilous attack on Malaysian poets who chose to write in English.

Miles had suffered through the ceremony in which Cole received the medal the evening before at the stupid party, one of the monthly meetings of The Order of the Batu Blue, a group Cole had put together. Miles never had figured out the purpose of the group, except as an agency to award medals to Cole. But what brought the other members to the meetings, and what did they perceive as the goals of the group? Some of them got medals, but all had the good sense not to wear them in public. Miles had asked what the group was for at the party, but did I get an answer? He scowled at Cole. Not on your life.

The Batu Blue often met in the home Miles and Cole shared, though, Miles noted, no one ever asked him if he minded that 15 or 20 lunatics would be invited over for an evening. Even worse, Cole had the unmitigated gall to put Miles in charge of final preparations for the party. "I know you won't mind giving me a hand with the preparations," Cole had said, "Seeing as how I will have to be in Japan for the JALT conference until late in the afternoon of the meeting." Cole went on to explain the "vital importance" of the timing of the meeting: ceremonial awards had to be made before the group went on its first annual retreat to Genting

Highlands on the weekend. Cole's reasoning about timing eluded Miles, and he had grumbled and written bits of graffiti about the Batu Blue even while he put the house in order for the meeting.

"What do you think of the latest ones in the work?" Coleman asked, nodding toward his manuscript.

"Interesting. The best line is the one that goes something like 'dibble-de dabble-de mugs.' It reminds me of some of the Victorian poets." Miles had in mind writers of nonsense verse—what were their names? He strained to remember and came up with Lewis Carroll and somebody-or-other Lear. "Lewis Carroll and those guys," he added. Miles regarded it a first- class put-down to compare anyone's writing to Lewis Carroll's.

"Thanks," Cole said. He frowned in a furious sort of way that always irked Miles. It seemed to him that Cole's knit brow was an attempt to look as artsy-fartsy and intellectual as possible. The frown always was accompanied with a lowering of his voice as if he had something of earth-shaking importance to say. Miles took a long drink of his beer and waited for Cole to tell him the solemn, honest-to-god truth about something of no significance at all.

"You know, I've been thinking about the title of the work. *Asean Doublets* does have the right ring about it, don't you think? I mean, it says it all: the mysterious east coupled with poetry, which everyone knows is the art of the irrational, the mystical." Cole squinted his eyes and wrinkled his brow into an intense frown.

Miles grunted, knowing Cole would interpret the sound as a sign of understanding and agreement. It was something of a minor surprise that Cole left the title of the manuscript alone. In fact, Miles thought Cole had just set a record by not changing the title for six days running. "I thought you would have an opinion on the matter," Coleman said. "Maybe I'll ask some of the Batu Blue folk about the title in the meeting this weekend at the Highlands."

Miles laughed to himself. Fat chance Cole would get any kind of straight answer from any of those Bedlams who showed up for the party. Miles thought about the Malay woman with her startling beauty. About Libby slapping the lawyer. The party had been full of experiences to ponder and puzzle out. Miles took another sip of the Anchor beer. Maybe, he admitted, just maybe, I enjoyed the party more than I realized at the time.

When people had began arriving the previous evening, Cole met them at the door, where they removed their shoes before entering. Normally, Cole and Miles wore shoes in their house, but knowing the Malaysian visitors would remove theirs, the two were stocking-footed for the evening. A stupid habit, Miles thought, walking around on marble floors barefooted. It was enough to give a guy fallen arches.

Miles had to put his set of Anchor beer glasses out of sight and use only plastic cups. Some of the guests would be Moslem, and they for sure would not drink out of glasses in which alcohol had been served—unless they had some assurance that the containers had been scrubbed out with dirt several times. As far as Miles was concerned, a glass scrubbed out with dirt wasn't fit to drink from—unless perhaps it had been rinsed with alcohol. Miles imagined having an Islamic roommate with whom he traded off washing the glasses: Mondays, Wednesdays, and Fridays they got soap and water for use as beer mugs; Tuesdays, Thursdays, and Saturdays they got the dirt treatment out in the yard. An Islamic roommate, Miles concluded, just might be worse than Coleman, especially if he was a poet.

Cole had outlined the other rules: no beef served on account of the Hindus; no pork on account of the Moslems; and no restrictions at all for the Chinese. "There would be one *Orang Asli*," Cole warned. "That dark little aborigine. But I haven't the slightest idea what dietary taboos he might have."

It was too much for Miles to worry about. He got Syed's Restaurant across from the P.J. Hilton to cater the refreshments. The man from Syed's brought sugar cane juice and an assortment of fried puffy things that Miles eyed with distrust. He broke open several and found them to be stuffed with either green goo and potatoes or brown goo that smelled like fermented coconut. Miles took care to eat some real food before the meeting. The guests, especially the *Orang Asli*, loved the food.

Miles could smell him even before opening the door. The Wild Man from Borneo, Miles thought. He was not quite five feet tall, had a broad, flat face and nose, and wore a fuzzy salt-and-pepper beard. The other times Miles had seen the man, he was panhandling on Petaling Street in Kuala Lumpur. Then, he had worn a shirt that Miles was sure ought to go into *The Guinness Book of World Records* for having been worn longer than any other garment in the world without being washed. He also wore tattered black pants held up with a rope belt and a pair of the dirtiest feet in Malaysia.

At the party, everyone called the Wild Man "Berak" or "Mr. Berak." He still had those dirty feet and the black pants, but had exchanged the shirt for a long sleeved batik, a rather fancy one that Miles recognized as belonging to Cole. The shirt had been gathered and penned in several places to make it smaller, and still it billowed around the tiny man as if he were a young boy wearing his father's shirt.

Most of the guests gathered around the table, eating with a frenzy that quite astonished Miles. Berak seemed to consume at least half of the fried bread with the green goo inside. From time to time, he issued a loud, resonate belch like the ones Miles used to practice back when he was in junior high school. Some of the other guests grinned at Berak when he belched, and several let loose small burps to show that they, too, enjoyed the food. Others glanced around unsmiling.

Miles stayed away from the table because of Syed's gooey bread puffs and because he feared that Berak, who smelled like a goat even before he began belching, would fill the air with odors of gastric juices. When the food was gone, they broke into little groups. Miles went from group to group, trying to discover what brought such an assortment of people together.

He met a man of Chinese ancestry who had been brought up on Crab Island, a fishing village off the west coast that was an island only at low tide. The man had become a fish broker, choosing to sell fish instead of catching them, and before long he had become wealthy. The fish monger was of the opinion that the group met to address some of the societal injustices in Malaysia. Which ones, Miles wanted to know. "Racism," the fish monger said, and launched into a barely-coherent condemnation of everyone who sought special favors by virtue of belonging to a particular race.

In another group, Miles met a man wearing a Sikh turban who owned controlling interest in a factory that made batteries. The Sikh was of the opinion that Cole's group met to encourage freedom of all sorts—especially free enterprise. "Da danjur ist da communists," he

45

explained. Miles worked to pay attention to what the Sikh had to say but felt defeated by the man's accent. He found himself looking at the fellow's turban. Miles thought of the Malaysian law that people who rode motorcycles had to wear helmets, except for those wearing the head-wrap that Islamic men wore to the Mosque, or else a Sikh turban. Not much protection, Miles concluded, unless some special Krishna power lived in the cloth. Miles looked at the way the turban was wrapped and doubted anything divine would want to occupy that particular wrap on account of the line of body oil and dandruff ringing the lower part of the turban.

Libby LeMaster approached Miles from one side and took his hand. "Miles Osborn," she said. "So very good to see you. Have you ever had your palm read, Miles?" She turned his hand over.

"I don't go in for that kind of thing." Miles withdrew his hand and thrust it into a pocket.

"Too bad. It looked most interesting. The abundance of lines and the elongated palm indicate an artistic personality—the same thing your aura tells me."

"My aura?" Miles asked. It made him uneasy that someone might look at the electrical field generated by his body and find out things about him. And if anybody could do it, he knew it would be Libby. She taught psychology at Ringling University and did experiments in parapsychology. Miles had once found one of her books, published by a Singapore press, in a bookstore. The book explained various psi phenomena and reported on the abilities of some Malaysian bomohs, or spiritual healers. Libby's book had impressed Miles with its many pages of statistics, charts, and graphs.

He looked uneasily at the air around him.

"You can't see your own aura," Libby said. "But if you have the gift, maybe you can see someone else's. That Chinese-looking man over there by the curtain talking with Cole, for example."

"You mean Che? He isn't Chinese. He's Malay. His full name is Haji Che Mothar bin Dr. Hazri. One of Cole's screwballs. Cole says he makes paintings out of scraps of butterfly wings, but that must be just a hobby. He told me he is a lawyer. A Malay lawyer."

"He looks Chinese, anyway. Try fuzzing your vision a slight bit and looking at the space around him."

46

"Fuzzing my vision?" Miles tried seeing as Libby directed, to no avail. He tried crossing his eyes some.

"He has a large, turbulent aura. Many dark colors, and a lot of movement. Whoever that man is, Miles, he has a lot of personal power. Look at the way the colors explode and swirl."

"I guess I just don't have the knack of it," Miles said. He did, though, notice nosy Rosey watching him and Libby. Now there is a woman to distrust, he thought. Not that he trusted Libby, or any other female, for that matter. Libby was a little scary and, at the same time, attractive in an odd way. At 5 foot nine inches, she stood a bit too tall for Miles' comfort. Her blond hair got her more attention in Malaysia than Miles thought she deserved. More than anything else, Miles was awed by her because she was always nice to him.

But that Roseta. She always seemed to be prying into everything. She might be the most beautiful Malaysian woman Miles had ever seen—maybe the most beautiful woman, period. But he didn't like the way she seemed to ask questions even when not asking anything.

Berak watched, too, but he looked frightened. Miles had seen that look before when Berak observed Libby, a kind of round-mouthed terror that made Berak something of a comical figure.

"It takes practice." Libby kept her attention on Che.

"Libby, what is the purpose of the Batu Blue? What brings everybody together like this?"

"Different needs, I suppose. Some need to be noticed. Others are looking for some sort of sense of power that might be lacking in their own lives. This can be a nurturing group, you know. Coleman sees to that partly with the medals he keeps coming up with."

"For himself," Miles snorted.

"Yes. For himself. But that's innocent enough. Miles, he does do much for the other people. Did you know he has cooked up an award for that pitiful Mr. Berak? And that he even gave the man one of his better batik shirts for the occasion."

Miles remained silent. He could find little kind to say about Cole. Libby gave her attention to Che.

"That man is an enigma," She said.

"Coleman Farquart? An enigma?" Miles sputtered.

"No. The one you called Che. Look at his body language. One minute his bearing is almost regal, then he thrusts that left shoulder up like a cheap hood and looks around like man with homicide on his mind. I would like to have him as a volunteer for some of my tests, but a man like that would never allow it."

Coleman caught Libby's eye from across the room and gestured to her. Miles watched Cole nodding and patting people's shoulders, extricating himself from the conversation so he could join Libby. Before Cole made it over, Miles muttered through his teeth, "Libby, there comes Shakespeare, and here goes Miles." He turned his back and edged away, but stayed close enough to hear.

"Libby the magnificent." Cole bowed. "I salute that in you which is divine."

Libby templed her fingers and muttered something nonsensical that sounded to Miles like a chant with a lot of *um* and *ohm* sounds in it.

"You will come to the First Annual Batu Blue retreat this weekend, of course?" Cole asked.

"I'll come on one condition. You must tell me why you include me with this group."

"You have a deal, my uh, friend."

"Cole, you almost called me 'my dear.' But you caught it almost in time. Good, good."

Cole frowned and leaned toward Libby. "You teach me better ways, though I learn slow. You are an artist of people, Libby, an artist of people." He drew the corners of his mouth down and nodded with approval. "Friday. Remember Friday. I'll call." Cole turned away. Miles watched him frown and nod and pat shoulders as he worked his way across the room. Libby tugged at Miles' sleeve.

"You heard all of that," she said. "Don't you admit that Cole is a charmer?" She held up her palms to halt Miles' sputtering response. "I know, I know. You see him quite differently."

"He didn't tell you what you wanted to know. That's just like him. You never get a direct answer out of a poet."

"You mean about why he includes me in the Batu Blue group? But he will, Miles. Cole just wasn't ready for that yet. He will want you to go, too. Has he asked?"

"Yes."

"And you said?"

"I said, 'yes, to be sure Genting is an interesting place, for those who like to gamble,' or some such nonsense."

"That kind of hedging, Miles, says that you have some interest in going."

"I do not. I'm just curious about what he is up to—the same as you."

"But, Miles, I think I know what he is up to." She smiled with an air of mystery, raised her brows and turned away.

Miles wanted to ask Libby what she meant, but he knew better. She would just laugh and tease and tell nothing. Probably she knew nothing about the matter, anyway, he thought.

Miles wandered to a group of people where he met a Malay who said he owned "a small rubber holding north of P.J." When Miles asked, the man said he thought the Batu Blue met to serve as a link between businessmen and the fine arts. Coleman had earlier mentioned to Miles a new member who was a rubber baron. "He owns one of the largest plantations of rubber trees in the state. He already contributes more ringgit than anyone else to the group's treasury. I think he is a bit odd, though."

Anyone Cole regarded as odd, to Miles' way of thinking, had to be one of the world's genuine weirdos. When Miles met the rubber baron, he was talking to a group that included Roseta.

Cole and Che joined the group. Cole turned to Miles, putting his face within inches of Miles' nose, and made introductions. Miles stepped back and Cole moved forward, bent upon invading Miles' space, as Miles viewed the matter. He always does that, Miles thought. That and squinting his eyes, thinning his lips, and speaking in low tones as if delivering some bit of secret information. "Miles, this," Cole said, turning his invasion of space to the rubber baron, "is Othar, the fine fellow I mentioned to you earlier who understands the need for a bridge between the arts and the sciences of money-making. Othar, Miles is the one who cooked all that fine food in there. And you know Che."

Othar, who seemed not at all bothered by Cole's habit of standing too close, nodded then held his hand out. Miles reached for it, but the man allowed a mere brush of finger tips, then withdrew his hand, touching his fingers to his heart.

Miles noticed that Roseta seemed to watch Che with great attention, which relieved Miles a bit since that meant she was not prying into his private affairs. "Mr. Coleman," she said, "I presume you will be reading some of your wonderful poetry tonight."

Miles winced. Wonderful? Was the woman as simple as she was beautiful? He remembered a line he had stolen from Robert Heinlein that he had laminated in plastic on index cards and epoxied over several urinals in Kuala Lumpur restaurants: "A poet who reads his poetry in public probably has other nasty habits." That was a by god good line, pithy and ringing with truth.

Miles looked at Roseta. She wore a long silk dress printed with frangipani blossoms and bougainvilleas. Her hair fell in shoulder length waves and shined blue-black under the artificial lights. So beautiful, Miles thought, and so dumb. He excused himself from the group before Cole got going about his poetry.

Che joined Miles, taking his arm and pulling him to the side of the room. "That European woman," Che demanded, "What is her name?" He gestured toward Libby.

"Not European. American."

"Yes, yes. Americans are children of Europeans, are they not? Except for the black Africans. Who is she?"

"Her name is Libby LeMaster. She teaches at the university with me and Cole."

"Libby, you say? This Libby has been watching me all evening. I think she must like Malay men. You will tell her that I am interested."

Miles grunted his neutral, non-committal sound that most people took to mean what they wanted it to. He was astonished that this man had the temerity to ask him to act as a go-between, and he began framing a bit of graffiti to put up later: "Che would make a pimp of any man who knows a blond woman." Miles decided he might just by god epoxy that to the elevator wall in the building where Che had his law offices.

"I knew I could rely on you." Che clapped Miles' arm.

When medal-awarding time came, Coleman stood in the center of the living room and announced, "The first award tonight is the Batu Samuel, named after the great literary critic, Samuel Johnson. Tonight it goes to Mr. Miles Osborn, who teaches English and technical writing at Ringling University."

Miles, who was only half listening, stared in amazement. Cole continued talking, but Miles caught only snatches of it—something about his sensitivity to poetry and his love of clear communication making him an artist in his own right. He struggled to keep his astonishment from turning into anger. People began applauding, and hands started pushing Miles into the center of the room.

It was being put on that kind of public display that he dreaded most and most angered him. He stood before Coleman and forced a smile while Che stepped forward and pinned a medal on his shirt.

Berak got the next medal. It was a brass casting of a frog that looked as if it had been flattened by generations of truck traffic. While he pinned the medal on the grinning Berak, Cole announced, "This award is the Batu Royal, given for environmental concern. Mr. Berak has taken several nights of his own precious time to make sure the frogs in front of Batu Caves Temple survive when they cross the parking lot from the pond to the grassy area." What Berak had done, Cole explained, was to tear up the speed bump in the parking lot and replace it with one that looked identical but had a pipe in the center for the frogs to travel through. He had permission from the keepers of the temple, but only if he worked at night, and if he did not disrupt the flow of tourists by having the project interfere with traffic.

Miles, who had retreated to the far side of the room to nurse his anger at Cole into some smashingly brutal graffiti, found the award to Berak so silly that he almost forgot the way he had just been embarrassed. *A toad tunnel?* he said to himself. Did frogs wiggle into fifty feet of pipe laid under asphalt where the tropic sun would heat the tunnel like an oven? Wherein was the environmental improvement, Miles wondered, if Berak merely switched the method of frog execution from squashing them to baking them?

The next medal went to Che, who, according to Cole, had just won a court case in favor of a Malaysian writer that the state government was trying to censor. Miles saw Roseta smirk and seem to laugh in a way that said she didn't believe a word of the praise of Che, but no one else seemed to notice her.

When the party began breaking up and most people were in the area of the front door, searching for their shoes, Miles saw a quick exchange between Libby and Che. Miles had gone into the kitchen to get away from everyone, and when he heard someone coming, he stepped into the dark laundry room where he could not be seen. He did not want anyone asking to see his silly medal or commenting in any way about his being a critic and lover of poetry.

Libby came into the kitchen, perhaps to get a drink. Che followed her in and said something to her. Miles saw him reach toward her, but did not see what he did. But he did see the quick flash of Libby's hand and heard the slap as it connected with Che's cheek.

"In my country," Libby said, "A gentleman would never touch a woman he just met in such an insulting way."

Che stepped back, rubbing his cheek. "In my country," he said, his voice a growl, "a woman might not survive striking a man like that." As he left the kitchen, Miles could see the murderous intensity flashing in his dark eyes.

When Libby left the kitchen, Miles shifted his position somewhat and brushed against someone. Startled, he jumped to the doorway and hit the light switch. "Roseta," he said. "What the hell?"

"We are both observers of the human comedy," Roseta said. "So we both found a good spot to watch others. That little drama with Che and Libby was chilling, no?"

Miles found himself at a complete loss for words. Ordinarily, someone catching him hiding away like that would have angered him. But Roseta was doing something worse—spying on people—and she didn't seem a bit bothered.

"I thought you might be also a secret observer of others. Perhaps we can get together sometime and share some of the things we know?"

"Perhaps." Miles found the idea of getting together with Roseta both scary and attractive.

"That Che is a bad one. I suspect he just might try to carry out his threat to harm Libby. Maybe in the worst sort of way."

Roseta had stepped up to Miles and given him a quick hug, then hurried out of the laundry room.

Miles took another sip of the Anchor beer and thought about that hug. At the time, the gesture made his heart pound, and even as he remembered it, sitting there beside the wrought-iron grillwork in his living room, he felt his pulse quicken and his cheeks flush. Cole looked up from his book of poetry.

"Miles." Cole frowned. "You're red as a beet. I think you ought not drink beer during the day." He looked back at his collection of poetry, and Miles rolled his eyes, suppressing a sigh.

# 4

For the little people of the Malayan jungles, Nature is the supreme artist, and people are just another part of the web She weaves into a cosmic tapestry.

—Dr. L. LeMaster, "The Psychology of Primitive Art"

When he calmed down enough to make a cool assessment of his situation, Noland Fritch decided that protesting his innocence to police was a waste of energy. Nothing he could say would change the murderous intensity in the eyes of the airport guard who kept a rifle barrel pointed at Noland's stomach. Kent would get him out of the mess. Besides, Noland would use his one phone call to get in touch with the Malaysian EXXON office, and the rich oil firm would get him the best legal help in the country.

So he submitted to the handcuffs behind his back and the rough shoves he got when his guards put him into a police van for the trip to the Kuala Lumpur city jail.

He would have found the drive interesting if he had been less tired from travel and if he could find a way to get his arms comfortable. By the time the police decided to get him out of the airport security room, darkness was coming, and Noland was aware that, by body time, it was the early hours of the morning. Back in Amarillo, the sun would not be rising for another hour or so.

From inside the police van, Noland could see well enough to be aware of the modern freeway into the city. He hoped the jail would be as modern as the highway into Kuala Lumpur.

It turned out not to be so different from the Amarillo City Jail, which Noland had seen when he visited one of his friends, arrested for smoking marijuana in Thompson Park. In the outer office of the Kuala Lumpur jail, Noland waited while his suitcase, guitar, and Stetson were inventoried by a clerk who, Noland guessed, typed about four words per hour. The man examined every piece in the suitcase, taking what seemed to Noland hours to list each article. "Now please give watch and all things from pockets," the clerk said.

"I guess I could make a stab at digging in my pocket with my elbow," Noland said. "But if you want my watch, you better take off my boots, so I can try to get at it with my toes. No guarantees, though."

The clerk stared blankly. "Please, the watch and pocket items?" He held out his hand.

Noland made an exaggerated attempt to reach into a pocket, turning so the man could get a good look at the handcuffs behind him. "This could take four or five hours, but I suppose you couldn't mind too much, seeing as how you enjoy a job that is stretched out some."

The clerk said something in Malay, and Noland's guards removed his watch and took out everything from his jeans pockets. The clerk examined various items, typed something, and dropped them into a large envelope. When he finished, he rolled the paper from his typewriter and placed it on the desk before Noland. "Read list, please, and sign if it is okay." He held out a pen.

Noland stared in disbelief. "I'll tell you what, Jack, you read it and sign for me."

"You read," the clerk said with annoyance. "Sign. And I not Jack. I Wan."

"It all looks fine to me, One. Just show me where to sign, put the pen in my mouth, and I'll make my mark."

Wan looked blank, then raised his brows in surprise and leaned around to look at Noland's cuffed hands. He went to another desk across the room and held an animated discussion with another clerk, then returned. "We wait for permission to take off cuffs so you can sign."

"Wait? Here? How long?"

Wan shrugged. "Chief gone for tea. Twenty minutes, maybe. Hour."

"Look, One, these cuffs are cutting off the circulation. You wait an hour, and gangrene will set in. The prison doctor will have to amputate my hands, and I'll still have to sign with the pen in my mouth."

"No sign with mouth. Use hand. We wait." Wan sat down.

"Put the papers over there, on that chair, put the pen in my hand, and give me a little help, and I'll sign the papers. Can you try that?"

Wan looked at the chair, considering the proposal. "Can," he said.

Noland thought the process would break one of his arms, but he did manage to scrawl something of a signature on the paper. Wan picked it up and examined it. "For why you write only *N. Fritch*? Passport say you *Noland Fritch*."

Noland puffed out his cheeks in exasperation. "The guys back on the ranch, they all the time call me N. My mama even called me N. Sometimes NF. 'N,' my mama used to say, 'you get in here this minute.' I always used to know when mama was mad, because that's when she used to call me by my full name, NF."

"You sign passport name." Wan put the papers back on the chair. Noland sighed and tried for another signature. Wan looked at it and nodded.

"When can I make my phone call?"

"Make phone call?" The clerk seemed genuine in his bewilderment.

"Yes, phone call. When can I talk on the phone? Haven't I been a good boy about long enough around here?"

"You watch too many American television shows. Not make call here."

"No calls at all?" Noland raised his voice in disbelief.

"Yes, yes, you get to use phone. Tomorrow. Next day. Maybe. Now you go to jail room." Wan took the paper Noland had signed to a filing cabinet, muttering something to the guards as he did so.

After being jerked by his cuffs through a dimly-lighted room occupied by several secretaries, Noland stood before a locked door while his guards spoke gibberish into a box on the wall. A buzzer sounded somewhere inside the door, and the guards opened it, then pushed Noland across the threshold.

He tripped, not realizing that the doorway opened to a flight of stairs going up. The guards made fussing noises in Malay and pulled him to his feet. The stairs were uneven in height, some only a few inches above the last, others far too high. Noland kept stumbling, but managed not to fall again. The stairwell narrowed, and the ceiling dipped so low Noland had to duck to keep from bumping his head. The floor gritted beneath his boots, and Noland noticed the edges of the stairs were covered with rat droppings.

When he got to the top of the stairs, he and his guards had to wait on a landing while a jailer on the other side of a door made from iron bars inspected them, then tripped a switch behind his desk that caused the barred door to slide to one side. Once inside, the guards motioned to Noland that he had to take off his boots.

He tried, but it was no use. Taking off his cowboy boots with his hands locked behind his back was impossible. One of the guards who escorted him from the airport struck him. Not hard, and not in anger; he hit Noland in frustration for Noland's inability to follow orders.

"Let be, let be," the jailer said, then spilled a torrent of Malay. The escorts grumbled, but they retreated beyond the sliding bars and the jailer locked them out. He produced a key and unlocked Noland's cuffs. "So sorry for treatment. You sit there." He got a three-legged wooden stool from behind his desk and set it by Noland. "Take off shoes. We give slippers, there," he pointed with his thumb toward a hallway that contained a series of cells.

Noland rubbed his wrists. His hands tingled and his arms ached. But he did sit and pull off the boots. The jailer took them to a door by his desk and threw them inside. He turned and smiled. "Actually, my jail not so bad. Not good. Jail never good. But here," he gestured around him, "not so bad. Indonesian jail bad. Jakarta. Ah. That bad. Bangkok. No, no, no. They beat you with cane. Very bad. Here, locks best guard. I do nothing. I wait. Not have gun. Not use cane. Him," he pointed to a man sleeping on a bench in the dark end of the room, near the door to the cells, a man Noland had not noticed until that moment, "have gun. But no use, just have. Why you here?"

Noland cleared his throat, unsure of what to say. Before he could formulate an answer, the jailer continued speaking. "Call me Hashim. You act good, we be friends. That good. Maybe you get to stay in Hashim's good jail, maybe you get lucky and go to federal prison. It good place. Actually, it not bad way to get to know Kuala Lumpur. Federal prison in Guinness book of records, you know that? Now you stand up, follow Hashim."

Noland followed Hashim past the sleeping man, who stirred, opened one eye and fixed it on Noland for a few seconds before it glazed over in sleep again. The man wore a pistol holster strapped to his hip. Noland worried some about the federal prison being in *The Guinness Book of World Records*. For what? Having the most fatalities among foreign inmates?

"In Hashim's jail, you get food. Bath. Same as in federal prison, but better." He led Noland by a series of empty cells on the left side of the hall, one of which was enormous and had a floor tiled like the bathrooms Noland had seen in some motels back in Texas. On the right was an iron wall with tiny windows covered by sliding sheets of metal. Hashim stopped by a door on the iron wall and banged on it. He yelled something in Malay, then spoke English: "Get back from door. Get back. We have new friend." He got a key from his belt and opened the door. "You go in. It totally not bad place, actually."

When Noland stepped inside, the door behind him slammed. Then the window in the door opened and Hashim spoke through it. "You need anything, you call Hashim, yes? But you not need much, you understand?" The window slid shut, and Noland turned to survey his cell.

It was far bigger and gloomier than he had expected. Once his eyes adjusted to the dimness, he could see metal bunks suspended from the walls, some of them covered with what might have once been thin mattresses but were now lumps of flattened, stained cotton. The floor was gray cement; the ceiling a low, black presence. Some twenty or so men sat on various bunks or on the floor. Some of them smoked; a few looked with dull curiosity at Noland, but most ignored him.

For Noland, the worst part about the place was the smell. Body odor. Urine. Noland thought the place smelled like a cross between the pig farms around Happy, Texas, and the goats some degenerate Texas farmers kept around. He walked around the cell, aware of his socks catching on the floor. Other prisoners were barefooted, except for those who came out of what had to be the toilet room at one end of the cell. They wore slippers, which they took off just outside the door.

Noland decided he better make use of the facilities, then see if there was any way he could get some sleep. Near the toilet door, he felt his socks get wet. He stepped back and looked at the floor. The entire floor around the toilet entrance glistened with what Noland hoped was water. He put on a pair of slippers, scrunching his socks up between his toes in the process, and forced himself into the room. The smell was worse than the outdoor privy Noland had used as a kid on his grandparents' farm in Shamrock. "A six-holer," Noland muttered to himself, "but they got no seats."

The commodes were urinal-looking devices set into the cement floor, their tops level with the gray, wet cement. Behind each hung a hose attached to a faucet protruding from the wall. No wonder the floor is wet, Noland thought. Those things would be hard to hit standing up. Then he remembered that all of the Malaysian men he had seen were a foot or more shorter then he. They don't have as far to shoot, he concluded. And maybe they aim better. Much of the water came from the hoses, all of which dribbled water onto the floor.

Noland got out of there as soon as he could. He decided the place was crawling alive with microbes that could do you in, unless the AIDS virus had killed off everything less toxic.

Outside the door, he stepped out of the slippers and walked as far as he could away from the toilet, his damp socks sticking to the floor, making a soft ripping sound each time he lifted a foot. It didn't seem to matter where he went in the cell; the smell from the toilet permeated the entire room. Locating an unoccupied bunk, he sat down and inspected what used to be its mattress. It was a mass of yellow and black cotton held together in places by a few shreds of striped cloth. Noland got up and turned it over, but the other side was worse. His disturbing the mattress released a powerful smell of body odor and urine.

He went to another bunk, and finding it just as bad, he tossed the mattress on the floor and reclined on the bare metal, the chains suspending it from the wall creaking and objecting. Hell, Noland told himself, sleeping on a slab of pressed steel was no big deal. He had bedded down on worse surfaces when he worked as a cowboy—like the hard scrabble in west Texas, for example. At least in the Kuala Lumpur jail, he didn't have to contend with prickly pear or worry about tarantulas and rattlesnakes.

As soon as he stretched out and closed his eyes, he remembered his contact lenses. "Damn," he muttered. Sleeping with them in was out of the question. He sat up, took out the lenses, and put them into the watch pocket of his jeans. He had done that a couple of times before when he got caught out on a field trip for EXXON and had forgotten his lens case.

He laid back down and fell asleep. During the night, Hashim awoke him three times with his banging on the door to announce the arrival of a new friend. Each time, Noland shifted his position somewhat, looked at the new arrival, and went back to sleep.

To his surprise, Noland slept until morning, an event announced by all the lights in the jail switching on. They blinked in neon fury, then lighted the room with bone white light. Noland sat up and dug his contact lenses out of his pocket. He put them into his mouth to get them moist, then put them on his eyes, blinking from the sting. The lenses were in the wrong eyes, he concluded, and reversed them. Then he looked around. The man on the next bunk motioned to him.

"*Orang putih*, you come sit here. We talk, yes?" Noland looked at the dark-faced man beckoning to him. Noland had seen a few men of African descent in Texas who were plenty black, but never had he seen anyone whose skin was as black as a burnt-out campfire. Nor had he ever seen a black man with such a fine, thin nose and thin lips. White wash that fellow, Noland thought, and he would pass for one of the O'Riley clan in Shamrock, Texas. Noland stood up, stretched, walked to the other bunk and sat where the Black O'Riley indicated.

"Mehinder Deyavanthi," the man said, offering his hand.

"Do what?" Noland said, taking the offered hand.

"Mehinder. Mehinder. My name."

"Noland. Glad ta meetcha."

"Nolan Gla Ditmitja? You American? That a strange American name."

"By jiggers, that's a good one. Nope. My name is Noland Fritch."

"What you in this place for, Mr. Noland?"

"Fritch. Mr. Fritch—either that or just plain old Noland." Noland looked with greater care at Mehinder. Wasn't he one of the new guests the jailer had brought in during the night? And why, Noland wondered, did he want to know what Noland was charged with doing?

Another man approached the bunk and squatted just a few feet from Noland and Mehinder. Noland looked him over, startled by how tiny and how fierce the man looked, like a pit terrier. "Morning to you," Noland said.

The man nodded. "*Selamat pagi.*"

"Ibrahim say 'good morning,'" Mehinder translated. "Because why you here, Mr. Fritch Noland?"

A third man wandered close to Noland's bunk. Noland thought the man looked Chinese and considerably cleaner than the other inmates.

"It's all a big mistake, boys." Noland was aware that another man had wandered over and that others were glancing his way. "I'll tell you about it, Mehinder Dave-a-whatever, if you will tell me how come you called me an orange poot."

"Oren put?" Mehinder looked confused.

"*Orang putih*," the scrubbed-looking Chinaman said. "*Orang* is man; *putih* is white. The, ah, gentleman called you a white man."

"And morning to you, too. Folks call me Noland Fritch."

"Chung Lee. Good morning." Chung smiled and raised his brows.

"And the word for black, Chung?" Noland asked.

"*Hitam.* That's the Malay word."

"In that case, Mr. Mehinder Dave, you sure enough are *hitam orang*, by a long shot more than anybody I ever saw in Amarillo. Black as the bottom of a boot. I got put in this wonderful jail on account of getting punched in the stomach." Noland surveyed his audience. Chung's grin grew wider; Mehinder looked more confused than ever, and Ibrahim curled his lips into a snarl.

"No reason to get all bent out of shape, Abraham. I'm not accusing you of throwing the punch. Last night, I was wandering through the park here in Kuala Lumpur, when this big guy jumped out of the shadows and caught me right in the gut with a round house. Stuck his fist nearly through my stomach to my backbone, and I commenced to barfing." Noland saw Mehinder and Ibrahim were puzzled. "Texas English, gents. Sorry. The way it was is this: I just came out of a restaurant, full as a tick. That is, I had just eaten much food. The walk through the park seemed a good idea, until that man hit me right here, hard. I bent over with the wind knocked out of me, and he went to feeling around for my wallet, but he didn't get it, because all that food got knocked loose and I started throwing it up, a goodly portion of it on him. He backed off and bunched up his fist for another poke at me, when something scared him off. I didn't pay him much mind, you see, on account of being busy getting rid of the dinner. What scared the guy off was a cop—a policeman—but I didn't see him, not right off. All I knew was that there was somebody yelling at me in words that didn't make sense. Seems I was throwing up on a statue of some big

61

shot, and the policeman got hopping mad about it. Thought I was drunk and disrespectful. So he busted me, dragged me to the station, and booked be for being drunk and disorderly, which was not the case at all. So you see, Mehinder Dave, I got put in jail, like I said, because somebody hit me in the stomach."

"You not here because man hit stomach," Mehinder affirmed. Ibrahim shook his head and furrowed his brow, and Chung laughed.

"Mehinder, old buddy, as long as we've been friends, do you think I would pull your leg?"

Mehinder glanced uneasily at his leg. Chung laughed again.

"Tell you what. Just to set the record straight, I'll tell you the honest- to-goodness truth. I made up that story about getting hit in the stomach."

"Yes," Mehinder said.

"The truth is, I got thrown into the poky for dancing with the wrong woman. In a little joint over by the park, it was. A woman at the next table got all lathered up and asked me to dance, so I did it. Turned out she was married to the owner of half the rubber plantations in Malaysia. Just a little squirt of a man, her husband, but he took exception to my dancing with his woman and invited me to step outside. You would have laughed right out loud, Mehinder Dave, if you had been there to see how it was. I could have picked up the husband and hung him on a peg on the wall, and he was standing there like a bandy rooster, telling me to step outside with him. So I did it, and he had his men there with rifles and grenades and machine guns. Then he called his bought-and-paid-for cops, and they brought me here. All that for one little dance. What got the husband real mad was when I told him his wife wasn't pretty enough to get all that riled up about."

"An excellent story, Mr. Fritch," Chung said, "But I'm afraid your colorful language is beyond your old friend here. For my part, I enjoyed it more than the story about throwing up on the statue."

"You here for drugs," Mehinder said. "Not for woman who dance. Drugs."

"He must have understood some of it." Noland turned to Chung.

"Drugs." Mehinder leaned close to Noland and lowered his voice. "You tell where you put drugs and I pay. Much money. Get you out of prison, give you Mercedes."

Ibrahim, remaining in a squatting position, duck-walked closer to Noland, nodding and frowning. "You tell, you tell. You get rich."

"Abraham, you're one of the new guests who arrived in the night. And you, Mehinder, came after I did. I suppose the police downstairs pumped you full of cow flop about me and my package of baking soda. If you want stories, I got plenty of them. But for drugs you got to go somewhere else. I don't even smoke."

Mehinder stood up. "You be good man and tell Mehinder about drugs and get rich. Not be nice," Mehinder slit his eyes, "and maybe get hurt. Hurt bad."

Noland looked at the man in astonishment. He looked big, bigger than most men he had seen so far in Malaysia. But not that big. Not that size always meant so much, Noland cautioned himself. Hank Simon taught him that. "Some of them runts in the Avalon are tough as a bull's pizzle," Hank had said, "and can take you right out of a fight while you're still thinking they're harmless as a lap dog." Noland didn't question Hank's judgment on the matter seeing as how Hank was a runty little guy who often beat up big guys in the Avalon.

Noland stood, bunched his fists in front of him, and looked down at Mehinder, who stood six inches shorter. When Mehinder blinked and stepped back, Noland knew he had him. "One more threat like that, Mehinder, and you and me have to stop being buddies. I'd hate to do it to a nice fellow like you, but I would break at least four of your ribs and hammer your nose down right flat."

Mehinder retreated across the room, much to Noland's relief. "You might get by with a threat," Hank had told him one evening during a training session in the barn, "because you're a big fellow. But never count on it." Noland didn't want to get into a fight in the jail.

Ibrahim stood up. "You big," he said. "Strong. But Ibrahim not like Mehinder. Ibrahim mean. You remember what I say. Mean beat strong, ever time. I know right time to get mean, then you tell. You tell ever thing. Mean all the time beat strong." He joined Mehinder.

Noland sat on his bunk.

"May I sit next to you, Mr. Fritch?" Chung asked.

"Suit yourself."

"You tell a good story, Mr. Fritch. I always appreciate a clever wit and a good sense of humor."

Noland nodded. "Thanks. I always figured a guy had to keep a sense of humor about him, or he would be lost in a right mean world."

"Some parts are meaner than others. When you get out of this place, stay in well-lighted places at night, and watch out for Ibrahim. He is a mean little fellow with a knife. But Mehinder is a different story. He isn't a totally bad man. Just almost totally. His one redeeming characteristic is that he is a coward. In my business, I have to deal with such people, unfortunately."

"Is that a fact? What is your business?"

"Four digits. The government likes to hold a monopoly on four digits, but there are so many punters out there with money to give away that I get my share."

"You talk like somebody from England. What I mean is, you talk nearly regular English—close enough so I get what you say, most of the time. But all that stuff about digits and punters is just so much noise."

"Sorry. *Four digits* is our term for a popular form of lottery, which is legal when the government sells the numbers but illegal when I do. A *punter* is a person willing to make bets. I suppose you Americans would say that I run a numbers game."

"And you got caught and put in jail?"

"Not at all. I was foolish enough to ignore some traffic tickets. A rather large number of them, as a matter of fact. The idiot traffic control people in Kuala Lumpur put up a no parking sign right in front of my place of business."

Chung went on to explain that he ran a legal business selling herbal medicines just off Petaling Street, a profitable enough way to make a living, but not so lucrative as dealing in numbers. He did not explain that the herbs in his shop were mainly sold as aphrodisiacs. Americans he had met found the idea of aphrodisiacs too foreign, and were prone to ridicule him for dealing in them.

Chung's uncle was the real owner of the shop for herbal medicines, but he was in semi-retirement and had turned over most of the running of the business to Chung, whom he had raised.

64

After graduating from a Chinese school in Kuala Lumpur, Chung, at his uncle's prompting and with his uncle's money, went to the United States to study. He got a degree in biology from the University of Houston, then returned to Kuala Lumpur, where he found many jobs unavailable to him because he was Chinese and not Malay.

He explained his bitterness to Noland. "I applied for a driver's license and had to deal with the Malay bureaucracy. They sit in their offices, playing crossword puzzles, and refuse to wait on you. Then, when one finally looked up and I said I had come about a license, they wouldn't speak to me in English. They all know English well enough, but they pretend not to understand it. 'Speak Malay,' they kept telling me. But I don't like Malay, so I made my request in English. One of them said, 'Learn Malay, if you want to be a Malaysian. If you want to speak English, go live in London.' Is that a way to treat me? I was born in Malaysia. My father and his father were born in Malaysia. I am Malaysian. I speak four languages—English, Cantonese, Tamil, and Malay—all learned in Malaysia. They sit in their tenured sinecures, stupid and ignorant, protected by their special status because they breed like bacteria and have more votes than the Chinese Malaysians and the Indian Malaysians combined, and tell me in their arrogance and ignorance to learn their primitive language, if I want to be Malaysian. The government of this country is run by stupid bullies and mean little men like Ibrahim. Ah, but the business and industry of the country are run by the Chinese. Forgive me, Mr. Fritch, for carrying on so. You have your own problems to worry about."

"They don't look so bad to me this morning, with me all rested up. Everybody and his dog in Malaysia think I came here with some kind of drugs, when all that was in my suitcase was a little baggie of baking soda. But the boys at the airport will discover their mistake—or the cops here will, soon as they take a close look at the soda. Then I'll get out."

"You must come see me and my uncle. Our shop is near the corner of Petaling street, just down from the Mandarin Hotel."

"Mandarin? Like a Mandarin orange?"

"Yes. An area of China, from which the orange gets its name."

Hashim opened the window in the door and announced, "Some of our guests go downstairs now. Everyone I call please to come to door." He read a list of names that included Noland, Chung, Mehinder, and Ibrahim.

Noland watched as the men rushed to the door, elbowing and shoving each other in an attempt to be first in line. Only he and Chung held back. "What's all this about?" Noland asked Chung.

"I'm not sure. Perhaps we will be let out of jail? It would make sense— that way they would not have to feed breakfast to so many. Not that you would want to eat the swill they call food around here."

When Noland made it through the door, he found Hashim's sleepy friend, now awake, standing at the end of the hall, his pistol in hand. The sight gave Noland some alarm, though the other prisoners seemed not to notice the man at all.

In the area of Hashim's desk, a bored looking man beckoned them to the door through which Hashim had thrown Noland's boots. "Find shoes, find shoes," Hashim announced, "then queue by the stairs."

Noland thought his boots looked rather sad and mashed up from the other men trampling on them. About the same shape I'm in, he thought, rubbing a shoulder gone numb from bedding down on a slab of iron.

Guards escorted the men down in threes, then had them sit on what Noland thought looked like pews back in the Eleventh Street Baptist Church in Shamrock. Four armed guards surrounded the group, and they made it clear that a part of their job description was to enforce silence.

The prisoners waited three hours before a policeman came in to announce the processing had begun. Another hour passed before he returned to name a man to step through the door at the front of the room. When Noland's name was called, Chung whispered, "Across from the Mandarin Hotel," and offered Noland his hand.

"You bet." Noland shook Chung's hand.

A guard escorted Noland to the same room where the clerk had inventoried his personal possessions the night before. "Mr. Noland?" Wan said, holding out a large envelope. "Please to check and sign here."

"What's all this about? Are you saying I go free, or what?"

"Sign. Then go. Suit case there. Guitar, hat, over there. You sign now?"

Noland looked through his billfold, finding no money, though his traveler's checks were there. "My money is missing."

"Money?" Wan took the list and examined it. "No money listed."

He shrugged.

"And my pocket knife is gone. And my watch. Look, One, keep the money. It wasn't much. And the knife wasn't worth much. But I want that watch. How about giving it back?"

"No watch on list. Look. You signed here to say list good."

"You remember the watch, One. You tried to get me to take it off with my toes, on account of my hands being cuffed. I want that watch."

"Toes?"

"One of the guards had to take it off my wrist because of the handcuffs. You remember."

"Not on list. You want to file objection? Here." Wan dug around among the papers on his desk, picked up several sheets, and handed them to Noland. "You fill these out. Three copies."

"But these forms are not in English."

"You not in England. You in Malaysia. Forms in Malay."

"I don't read Malay. Do you have any other suggestions for my getting that watch back?"

Wan shrugged. "You want to look for watch, you fill out forms. Not want, not fill out forms."

"Keep your papers. And I hope you find it hard to enjoy a stolen watch." Noland jammed his billfold into his pocket, put on his hat, and picked up his suitcase and guitar. He turned to the door, but a policeman blocked his way.

"You not sign papers, you not take anything out of room," Wan said.

Noland sighed, set the guitar down, and returned to the desk. "Where do I sign?"

"You not want to look in suitcase, in guitar case?"

"Why? if they're empty, I would have to fill out three million forms, none of which are in a language I can read, and even then I would have to wait lord knows how long to get anything back, if I ever did. Isn't that right?"

Wan shrugged; Noland signed.

When he got outside, Noland was startled at the brightness of the sun and the lack of shadows. Nearly noon, he told himself. He walked to the curb and a cab pulled out of the traffic. Noland got into the cab.

"Where you want to go?" the driver asked.

"I need a bath, a shave, a meal, a watch, a pocket knife, and a room to put my stuff in. Can you suggest something close?"

"Can. You want good new hotel? Cheap old hotel?"

Noland thought for a moment. "The Mandarin, is that a good one?"

"Cheap old hotel. Yes, a good one."

Noland had to go to the money changer in the hotel in order to get the cash to pay the cab driver. When he went back outside, the driver said, "Two men follow us." He pointed across the street. Mehinder smiled and waved; Ibrahim scowled, pulled a knife from his belt and began cleaning his fingernails. "Them bad men. You take care of wallet when they around."

"Thanks."

"You want knife, watch? Go there, to Petaling Street. Many cheap watches, knives, anything you want. But you must bargain or get cheated."

While Noland registered for a room, Kent and Libby turned the corner from Petaling Street, heading for the Chinese drug store across from the Mandarin. "I thought you said a drug store was called 'chemist' here in Malaysia," Kent said. "I don't see any sign to that effect."

"The place we're going isn't exactly a chemist either. We're going to a traditional herbalist. Right here." Libby and Kent entered a shop that had bins of dried leaves, twigs, flattened out turtles dehydrated into gray wrinkles, seeds, nuts, and dried fish that looked to Kent as if they had been squashed by road machinery until they were wafer-thin, then dried into a form that resembled a soda cracker with a head and tail. Bottles of various kinds lined shelves behind a long counter.

"You're going to buy something for your knee here?"

"Me Sing Ng," Libby said to a Chinese man sitting on a stool, one leg propped up on a chair, "my honored master. It's good to see you."

"You come at bad time." Ng scowled. "Chung Lee not here. You want to learn more about curing in modern ways, no can. All knowledge I have is ancient."

"Mr. Ng, that is the only kind of knowledge I want."

Kent fingered his drawing pad, leafing forward to a clean sheet. The old man's face was such a study in dichotomies that Kent wanted to draw it.

"But today, all I really want is something to put on a scratch." Libby lifted her skirt above the knee to show the abrasion. "Do you have *manggis hutan*?"

Ng leaned forward and squinted at her knee. "Yes. But that not so good. Even chopped and boiled with sulfur and peppercorn, *manggis hutan* too complicated. You would have to stay away from water for three days." He stood up, reached for a cane leaning against the counter, and hobbled to a shelf lined with jars. "Have you learned of *akar kait-kait merah*?"

"Is that the same as *kekait*?"

Ng turned to her, his face showing that he was impressed. "Same family, yes. Some master senseh has been teaching you well."

"You refer to yourself, for you are my guru of herbs."

"Of course. Only one other in all of Malaysia knows as much as I about uses of plants, and she is old lady of the *orang asli*, living in jungles. If she still lives." Ng turned back to the jars.

"*Orang asli*," Libby said to Kent, "are the original people, the forest people who were here before even the Malays. And a *senseh* is a Chinese-Malaysian master, in this case an herbal doctor."

Kent nodded. He was too busy drawing Me Sing Ng to respond with words. Kent's hand moved with a speed that astonished Libby. She watched the pencil move over the paper, leaving behind it an emerging portrait of Ng. What amazed her the most was that it didn't seem to matter to Kent how much Ng moved around. Kent's portrait showed Ng sitting on the stool, one leg propped up, his head tilted to one side in a gesture Libby realized was characteristic of Ng, though she had never noticed it before.

Ng took a handful of dried leaves from a jar, put them in a pan on the counter, then set up a gas burner attached to a hose that ran somewhere behind the counter. He poured water from a bottle into the pan and lighted the fire under it. Kent shifted around, glancing from his pad to Ng.

"Take that spoon and stir the *kait-kait* until it boils," Ng told Libby. He returned to his stool. "And tell me who this man is and why he keeps looking at me as kingfisher looks at goldfish."

"I'm sorry. I meant to introduce you. Mr. Ng, this is Kent Day.

69

Kent, this is Me Sing Ng, the most knowledgeable *senseh* in Kuala Lumpur. Kent is an artist."

"Please accept my apologies. I should ask permission before drawing anyone. But your face is so lined with much wisdom that I simply began drawing. May I continue?"

Ng tilted his head and waved his hand, indicating that he was indifferent about the matter. "See to it that your medicine does not boil over."

Kent got back to his drawing. He had spoken the truth: he did see wisdom in some of the lines of Ng's face. But he also saw a crafty shrewdness that wasn't so flattering, and something else. What? Kent asked himself, straining for understanding even as his hand put down some of the traits he was trying to name. Arrogance? There was some of that, showing in flashes as Ng talked to Libby. Kent paused and looked at what he had done. Dishonesty? That wasn't it. It was more a sort of egotism born of insecurity, Kent decided. He altered some shading, taking off the more obvious arrogance he had put around the eyes and mouth. At a glance, Kent realized, Ng's face looked impenetrable, perhaps inscrutable. Bad word, inscrutable, one to avoid, a cliché. I must not deal in clichés in my art, Kent admonished himself. Beyond the first glance, for those who cared or were able to look deeper, there were the other things, some of them in Kent's drawing. He made a few more alterations to the shading of the face that emphasized Ng's wisdom, then gave attention to the details of his posture on the stool. When he got to the hands, Kent drew them clasping one another, though he had not seen Ng hold them that way.

"This is boiling," Libby said.

"Stir and count to fifty, slow, then turn off fire." Ng watched her, his lips twitching. "Fifty," he said, even as Libby reached for the valve at the base of the burner. "Let cool. Then strain with that wire strainer into a clean jar. There, below the counter."

Kent hurried, knowing he had just a few more minutes to complete the drawing. He put in the details of Ng's body, the leg on the stool, the sandal hanging from one toe.

Libby set down the pan and looked at the liquid in the jar. "It's red," she said.

Kent looked at the jar. *Red* was stretching it somewhat. He would call it *rust,* but then, he acknowledged, he was pickier than most when it came to naming colors.

"Wash wound with that," Ng directed. "Three, four times every day for three days. Use only clean cloth. If you run out or spill, come back. Or buy alcohol and use it. But alcohol burns like dragon."

Libby thanked Ng so profusely that Kent decided she understood Ng's insecurities quite well. She picked up the bottle of medicine. "Would you like to see Kent's drawing of you, Mr. Ng?"

"I knew an artist once who read nature of soul. He was n old man, much older than this gecko-eyed youth, and possessed wisdom of generations. But he is dead now. You come back when Chung is here, and he will show you medicines useful for men such as your Kent Day, ones you might benefit from, if you find him interesting." Ng clasped his hands and looked down, dismissing them.

Outside, Kent asked, "What was that all about?"

"I think it was something of a joke. But it is hard to tell with old Me Sing Ng."

As they crossed the street, Kent saw Mehinder and Ibrahim leaning against a building, smoking. "Those men," Kent said, looking back at them, "have a predatory look about them." Libby stopped and looked for a moment.

"Mushy little black auras. They're harmless."

Kent didn't contradict her, but he knew her to be wrong.

When they got to his room in the Mandarin, Libby got a wash cloth, wet it with Ng's concoction, and dabbed it to her knee. She put her foot on the arm of a stuffed chair, lifted her skirt nearly to the thigh, bent forward and applied the medicine. Kent sat on the bed, opened his pad to a new sheet, and began blocking out a drawing of Libby in that posture, for it said much to him about who she was. Trusting—both of him and of Ng. Sexy in an unselfconscious way. Very sexy. A little naive, perhaps, but self assured.

"This stuff doesn't burn at all."

"Don't you think a little antibiotic ointment from a regular drug store might be safer?"

"Maybe. But I doubt it. Ng knows a great deal. His mentioning alcohol did much for raising my estimation of his concoction of red thistle leaves." She looked up. "What? Are you already at it? Hang on just a second and I'll get into the proper model's pose."

In a conservation of motion that quite startled Kent, she stepped out of her skirt and pulled her blouse off, going from dressed to nude in a matter of seconds. "Should I stand or sit?"

"Do what's comfortable." Kent hid his disappointment that she felt compelled to undress. Not that she was unattractive—far from it. He looked with genuine appreciation at her smooth, young body. A swimmer, he decided. Or a runner. At one time she worked out with weights, but not in the way a man would; whatever exercises she did emphasized and complemented her natural form.

What disappointed him was the loss of something offered by the lifting of her skirt to doctor her knee. Mystery, maybe. That wasn't it. Trusting innocence, perhaps.

And yet her new pose added a confidence and surety to her face that Kent found attractive. He kept his previous blocking of Libby with one foot on the arm of the chair and gave his attention to drawing her face, to trying to capture the emotions he had seen earlier as well as the confidence in the way she lifted her chin and held her eyelids since removing her clothes.

Then he added details, capturing the smooth, athletic nature of her body, but keeping it clothed as he had seen her when she dabbed her knee with a cloth.

When he decided he had done all he could, Kent looked at the drawing, noting with satisfaction that the innocent sexuality and trust were both there. Yet he felt he hadn't captured something else, a kind of naive and dedicated sincerity. Maybe some of that was there, more in her posture than anything else.

But he dreaded showing the drawing to her. After all, she had posed nude, responding to a request she only imagined he had made. And he drew her with clothes on. Might she be angry? When the woman on the plane to Denver had posed dressed, he had drawn her nude—and she had been pleased. But this was different, somehow. In that moment, Kent knew Libby would be insulted, and he blushed, not wanting to displease her.

"That blush tells me you have stopped looking at me as an artist does and are seeing me as would a charming, interested, and innocent male." She put her clothes back on. "May I?" she held out her hand.

Kent sighed. "Please don't . . . I mean, I . . ."

"You quit that. It isn't fair to try to structure how I see your art." She took the sketch pad and looked at the drawing. "But, Kent," she began, then sat on the easy chair and examined the drawing.

When she looked up, her lips were parted and her brow knit. Kent sighed in relief.

After Libby had gone, Kent drew her again, a quick sketch in broad strokes of ink, using tiny lines and spacing to simulate shading. What he wanted was to get that puzzled, pleased look she had on her face when she looked up from his art pad. There was more than a touch of awe in that look, and—what Kent most wanted to ponder—affection.

Maybe I should be doing a self portrait, he thought, if I want to examine affection. In a single morning, Libby had gone from a bizarre image of a woman poised with her hand above gemstones, feeling for some sort of vibrations, to far more than a stranger, more than a model. How much more? he asked himself, then set the question aside. The block of ice teetering on the ledge above them did it, or at least started it—that and working to find a way to doctor the scratched knee she got when I shoved her and we dived into that display of watches, he thought. And the cantankerous old Chinaman. An altogether strange morning to base any sort of romance on.

Even as he completed the drawing, he thought of Noland. He hurried his hand, something that always resulted in concentration on technique rather than the art of capturing feelings. Noland is in jail while I'm . . . . Kent threw the sketch pad on the bed in frustration. What good was it to work only with technique, to draw a perfect drawing, if it was lifeless? He looked at the drawing feeling both satisfaction and anger. Sister Corazon would approve. A younger Kent would admire many of the lines. The surprise was there in the lines of Libby's face, in the stress of her upper body, and perhaps some of the awe. Perhaps. But Kent saw nothing more, other than a perfectly-executed ink drawing that in its very perfection lacked the living vitality, the completion that he so wanted to be there.

Kent called Suppriah's number again, this time getting an answer from a pleasant, British-sounding female voice. He established that he was speaking with Suppriah, then fumbled through an introduction, getting out an explanation of Noland's current situation in as few words as possible.

"Noland who?" Suppriah asked.

"Fritch. The one who answered your ad in the Dallas paper."

"I am so sorry, Mr. Kent, but I have never been in Dallas, nor has anyone named Noland written to me. Surely he passed along to you the wrong telephone number?" Befuddled by the odd situation, Kent fell silent for a moment. "Hello? Hello?" the woman said.

"Yes?" Kent groped for words. "Well, uh, I'm sorry to disturb you."

"But do wait, Mr. Kent. Since your friend is in trouble and you are new to Malaysia, perhaps I could be of help somehow?"

"More than anything else, I need the name of a good lawyer."

"Unfortunately, I know none. But—yes. Do wait a moment, yes?"

Kent heard her set the phone down, then heard the rattle of paper.

"There is a man whose name is in the newspaper much of late, a lawyer with court victories of several kinds. Here it is." Kent heard the snap and fold of the paper. "Mr. Che Mothar bin Dr. Hazri. He has offices right here in K.L."

"K.L.?"

"It's what we call Kuala Lumpur. Can I be of further help?"

As he set the phone down, Kent thought of something he wished he had explored with Suppriah. Perhaps Noland had given him the wrong number, but could he have given both the wrong number as well as the name *Suppriah*? That matter, he decided, was Noland's worry. Kent had a lawyer's name, which was all he wanted from the phone call, anyway.

When Kent called the lawyer's office, Che's secretary said for him to come to the office right away. Such promptness gave Kent a good feeling about Che. Lawyers, Kent knew, don't operate thus in Texas.

When he arrived, the secretary sent him through a door bearing a brass plate with the name Che on it. Another surprise, Kent thought—no waiting in an outer office. He had brought his sketch pad with him so he could draw while waiting to see the lawyer.

The office he went into reminded Kent of the principal's office in

Bishop Green's Intermediate School: an enormous desk, rows of book shelves—even a window beside the desk with a shadowy figure standing before the window. Only when the figure stepped forward, away from the back lighting, could Kent make out facial features.

"I am Che," he said, stepping up to Kent, his hand extended.

"Kent. Kent Day." Kent gripped the proffered hand, gave it a couple of formal pumps, and released it. Che drew his finger tips to his breast, impressing Kent with the eloquence of the gesture.

Kent got the mandatory small talk over as fast as possible and began relating the incident at the airport. Che held up his hand. "One moment, Mr. Kent," he said, "I must have some assistance at this point." He pressed a button on his desk, and Kent heard a buzz in an adjoining room.

"Both of my names sound like last names," Kent said. "That is often confusing. *Kent* is the first name, though. You are not the first to call me 'Mr. Kent.'"

"Ah, yes, the quaint European custom of using the last name. Here, Mr. Day, we do not use our last name in that way. My last name is my father's name, not mine. So we put *Mr.* and *Mrs.* in front of the first name."

The door opened and a figure clad in black came in. "Mr. Day, may I present you to Miss Ros." Kent stood, unsure if he should offer his hand, bowing instead. Ros stared at the carpet in front of her feet and mumbled something, then took a chair at the side of the room, beside a wall of book cases. "Please be seated, Mr. Day," Che said.

A bit startled to find himself still standing and looking at the peculiar figure of Ros, Kent sat down. Ros looked to Kent like pictures he had seen of Saudi Arabian women, except she did not have a veil over her face. The black garment she wore looked at first glance like a single piece of cloth that covered everything about her except her face. But it was several pieces of cloth, Kent decided upon closer examination: a hood of some sort that flowed past her shoulders, then a large, shapeless gown, like the robes scholars wore at graduation, only longer. Black shoes. Black gloves. Kent turned so he could look at both Che and Ros.

"Miss Ros is a competent lawyer, a junior member of my firm. She will take notes on what you say, and her evaluation of the situation will be of help to me later."

As Kent related the events at the airport, he glanced from Che to Ros, finding Ros the more interesting. She would be a real challenge to draw. Only occasionally did she dare a look in Kent's direction, and that for less than a second each time. But it was enough for Kent to see glimpses of a personality far firmer than the domesticated and slavish person her lowered chin and rounded shoulders seemed to suggest. Ros wrote as Kent talked, and he got the feeling that she was taking down every word he said.

Che listened in silence, and when Kent concluded the account, he had no questions. "Can you help Noland?" Kent asked. "Get him out of jail?"

"If he brought no drugs into the country, the police will release him, though it might take them weeks. Yes, I can help. I will have him out of jail in a matter of days, perhaps, if he is innocent."

"Is there anything else I need to tell you?"

"Nothing just now. There remains only the small matter of a professional fee. The custom is to make a modest deposit."

"How much?" Kent reached for his wallet.

Che waved his hand. "Pay the secretary, please. It will be only two hundred ringgit."

Kent saw a slight change in Ros's face when Che named the sum. So I am being had, Kent realized. But no matter. Noland will return the money, and it's worth the cost to get him out of jail.

When Kent left, Che stood, stretched, and looked out the window. "Ros," he said, not looking at her, "Take care of this matter as best you can and have a report on my desk tomorrow afternoon about your progress. I will be out of town until shortly after noon. That will be all."

Ros returned to her office without a word. She consulted her log, confirming that Che was due to have an out-station taxi pick him up within ten minutes. She knew the taxi would take him to Genting Highlands where he would meet some gangsters from Manila. She wondered if Che would be shocked to discover Ros had that information. Probably not. He wouldn't care. To him, she was little more than a useful item around the office. A legal machine who could get things done. But

76

certainly not a human being.

Ros didn't care, though. She preferred him to think of her an a utilitarian piece of machinery, to be confident that while he headed for the resort at Genting, she would be doing the drudgery required to run a law office.

When she heard Che leave, Ros waited a few minutes, flipped her rotary file to the card with "Miles Osborn" on it, and reached for the phone.

# 5

Artists in the Batu Blue
With art will forge a country new.
　　　　　—Coleman Farquart, *Asean Doublets*


　　Miles Osborn set the phone in its cradle, asking himself why he had agreed to meet Roseta.

　　Probably she wants to talk about that gross fellow who slapped Libby, he thought. Or something similar—hadn't she mentioned getting together for exchanging information? Miles concluded that Roseta had some insight into people; how else would she have known him to be an astute observer of humanity? The fact that Roseta was the most beautiful woman he had ever met was something Miles did not let himself dwell on for long. He thought about it, then dismissed the thought with a look at the clock. Nobody would set up a date with romance in mind in the early part of a hot afternoon. Roseta, he told himself, finds me interesting only as a source of information.

　　Miles looked out a window, scowling at the force of the sun. *Mata Hari*, Miles thought, *the eye of the day*. He fumbled with his pocket, pulling his graffiti pad out. *Mata* meant *eye* in Malay, but it meant *kill* in Spanish, and Miles felt there was some worth-while graffiti to be had from the pun, since he was certain the sun in Malaysia could do him in. They oughta announce *tiempo de mata*, Miles thought: *killing time*. The length of time a person could survive in the sun without proper protective clothing, something like the way radios in Marquette way up on the upper peninsula of Michigan announced freezing time in the winter—the length of time it would take a person in normal clothing to freeze to death.

　　But who would catch the pun? Nobody in Malaysia knew Spanish, and his graffiti would be a waste. He put the pad back into his pocket and again wondered why he had agreed to meet Roseta.

It meant cleaning up, putting on some uncomfortable, hot clothes, and going to the center of K.L., which in Miles' estimation was the hottest city on the face of the earth. It meant having to make conversation with a person he knew only slightly. Worse, that person was a girl.

*Girl?* He thought about the word. It had a number of rhyme words: curl, pearl, swirl. Graffiti would could be built around such a word with little effort.

In the midst of Central Market swirl,

I met a magnificent girl.

God, Miles thought, now I'm sounding like Cole. He took off his tee shirt, went into the bathroom, and lathered up his shaving brush.

Besides, he told himself, squinting at the mirror, Roseta is a woman, not a girl. A forward, aggressive woman. Scary. He applied the lather to his face and picked up a safety razor. A petite, sensual woman who wore tight, shimmery dresses and spoke in soft ways when she addressed him. A magnificent woman.

Even more scary. Miles nicked his chin, sending a trickle of red through the lather on his neck.

Roseta stepped out of the shower with a sigh. It's such a luxury, a shower, she told herself, one she hoped never to have to do without again. Her flat was too small; she had only a black-and-white TV; her stereo droned a cheap electronic hum—but she had a good shower. A matter or priorities.

She toweled herself dry and went to the wooden hutch that served as a closet, frowning at the black dresses on the left side. Potato sacks, she thought. Useful, perhaps, but so terrible to wear. She had once overheard some American women discussing the black Islamic dresses and hoods. "These women walk around," one of them said, "in this tropical heat— often in the direct sun—covered with black except for their faces. Can you imagine the build-up of heat? Can you imagine what it does to their bodies?"

Apparently, Roseta had decided, the two American women could imagine what the black sacks did to a woman's body. But they had no idea the damage it did to her soul.

To my soul, at least, Roseta corrected. Some women didn't seem to mind being bound up in a way that obscured the fact that they possessed sexuality. The potato sacks, Roseta thought, made people into lumpy, shapeless blobs, marking women as inferior creatures in a society where males had the freedom and power to live as they wished. It was enough to drive a woman to hysteria or even *latah*.

Roseta feared being *latah,* for that meant a lack of control, perhaps being directed by some sadistic male to mimic the behavior of an animal. Maybe a dog or a chicken. Or it meant screaming in public about her vulva, then not remembering the attack.

Hysteria was something else, though. Roseta knew about hysteria; she once made use of it.

Everyone in her village had, at one time or another, witnessed an outbreak of hysteria. Roseta had seen her own grandmother in the grips of such behavior. After complaining that Roseta's grandfather was late for dinner again, the old woman moved around the kitchen with increasing agitation, then began screaming phrases about cold food. She picked up the two pots containing her husband's dinner, ran out the door, and threw them into a sewer ditch. After only a few minutes, she returned to the house, a dazed look on her face, and was aghast to find the food she had prepared gone.

To Roseta's surprise, no one chastised her grandmother for her odd behavior. Instead, they brought in the village bomoh to cast out the demons that made her hysterical.

The attack of hysteria that Roseta participated in gave her a certain amount of freedom. It occurred after a history teacher disciplined a class for not learning enough. Abdul, the teacher, singled out only the girls to chastise, though the girls in the class knew the material better than the boys. Nor'in, a pretty girl, as usual caught the brunt of his wrath.

The next day, while the class was busy writing, Nor'in leaped to her feet, swept the papers from her desk, and threw her book at Abdul. He tried to duck, but was too slow; the book hit the side of his face, sending his glasses flying through the air. Roseta watched as the glasses bounced off the blackboard and landed, unbroken, behind the trash can.

As soon as she threw the book, Nor'in began screaming incoherent phrases, some of them obscene. Abdul dropped to his knees and began groping around on the floor in search of his glasses. The two girls on either side of Nor'in began screaming also. One of them ripped up her history papers, the other jumped up and began snatching history books from other desks and throwing them out the window.

Roseta looked at the glasses, lying some distance from where Abdul was searching. A pity they did not break, Roseta thought. She glanced at the screaming girls, and inspiration came to her.

Roseta stood up with such determined vigor that she overturned her desk. She had not intended to do that, but the gesture pleased her. She began screaming, dotting her incoherent phrases with an occasional obscenity, as the three other girls were doing, as her grandmother had done; and she headed for the trash can. Setting her shoe on Abdul's glasses and giving her foot a slight twist, she picked up the trash can then ran to the window.

Abdul heard the crunch of his glasses shattering and let out a little moan as he crawled in the direction of the sound. Roseta dumped the trash out the window, then turned and threw the can at Abdul.

The can bounced in front of him just as he put his hand on what was left of his glasses. Startled by the noise and the sudden motion in front of him, Abdul jerked his hand back, slicing a long gash in his palm as he did so.

Roseta looked at the other girls for a clue about what to do next. They were still yelling and scattering books and papers. Roseta looked at Abdul, who sat on the floor holding his broken glasses in a hand that dripped blood. She decided she had accomplished enough. Rolling her eyes back, as she had heard women often did when coming out of hysteria, she let herself drop to the floor, and she twitched her feet and hands a few times before sitting up, her face composed into a puzzled frown.

Abdul had to miss two days of school while awaiting new glasses to be ground. When he returned, he was subdued and curbed his berating of the girls. For the rest of the year, he avoided criticizing Nor'in.

Did Nor'in feign her hysteria? Roseta wondered. Did the other two girls? Roseta suspected that they did not. None of the school officials suspected the bout of hysteria to be anything but what it appeared to be: another instance of that mysterious behavior Malay women seemed to be so prone to. The headmaster called in a bomoh, who mumbled prayers in the room, scattered some magic water, and pronounced the girls freed from evil influences.

When Abdul's new and kinder behavior became apparent, Roseta believed the bomoh; the evil influence had indeed been exorcized. But the bomoh, who took credit, had not accomplished the exorcism. Nor'in had done so by bashing Abdul's face with the book, and Roseta had done so by crunching the glasses and causing Abdul to suffer a nasty cut on his hand.

Roseta felt she was the only one in the community who understood what had happened, though she remained uncertain about the exact nature of the hysteria suffered by the other girls.

Miles would like this one, Roseta thought, taking a red dress from the closet. It fit around her hips and was cut so that it emphasized her tiny waist. Only a dour member of the Islamic ecclesiastical police could object, for the dress design was what Roseta called a "Bumi suit," and except for the tightness at the hips and waist, it resembled what many somewhat conservative Malay Bumiputra women wore. Roseta would rather wear the mini skirt and the tight, knit blouse hanging in her closet. Miles would go for such a costume. But those items she reserved for particular occasions. Besides, her variation on the Bumi suit had always caught his attention.

In the street by her apartment building, Roseta was aware that when compared to the Chinese Malaysian women in their short skirts and tight blouses, and compared with the Indian Malaysian women in waist-revealing saris, her own dress looked conservative. But go a few kilometers out of Kuala Lumpur, to Shah Alam—or even to Petaling Jaya where Miles lived—and she would appear to many as a radical feminist. To those in black potato sacks, Roseta would be sinful, perhaps even a harlot. She thought of the way Che had looked her over at Coleman's party, and she laughed out loud. When she dressed as Roseta, Che almost drooled when he looked; but when dressed as Ros, the frumpy, black-sacked lawyer, Che didn't see her at all. Not as a woman, anyway. She laughed at the thought that Che had no idea conservative Ros and sexy Roseta were one and the same.

She caught a taxi and directed the driver to take her to Central Market.

Miles entered Central Market, relieved to get out of the sun. He arrived early so he could cool down some before Roseta saw him. None of the Malaysians ever seemed to sweat or even be bothered by the heat. For sure his students appeared impervious to high temperatures. If he turned on the classroom fans in his early morning classes, the students would shiver and glare at him, even while Miles found the temperature in the room too hot in spite of the fans.

They call this air conditioning, Miles grumbled, pausing inside the main doors of Central Market. The building was an enclosed mall, and the temperature inside was considerably cooler than the oven air beyond the doors. But Miles wanted the air to be as it was in malls in the United States during the summers: cold enough that sales clerks wore sweaters. He took out his handkerchief and mopped his brow then looked at the damp spots on his shirt.

The display of fake primitive art would do as well an any, he decided, moving to a nearby stall. He reached for an ugly little carving at the back of the display, hesitated, and pretended to have noticed something else closer to him. His arm still extended, he lowered his head as for a closer look at something, turned his head and took a quick, surreptitious sniff of his armpit.

"Yes, sir?" the stall owner said.

"Not bad," Miles said, picking up the ugly carving, which was an attempt to portray a Malaysian aboriginal woman nursing a child. "Not bad at all, considering the heat." He put the carving back and moved on before the sales clerk could engage him in bargaining.

Taking out his note pad, Miles wrote in square, clear print, "K.L. is Hell." He said the phrase to himself several times, altering his imagined intonation each time. Not bad, he thought and looked around for a place to put the graffiti. But Central Market was too crowded; someone would see him if he taped the paper to a wall or a sales display. The public toilet would be crowded, also. Besides, it wasn't a place he wanted to go unless he had to. It smelled too terrible. He put the note pad back into his pocket, and in doing so remembered the poem, also in that pocket, that Cole had pressed upon him as he left the house.

Just as he headed out the door, Cole came rushing out of his office, waving a sheet of paper. "Miles." He came far too close, frowning in a furious sort of way. Miles stepped back. "Miles, I just did something you need to read."

It struck Miles as unlikely that anything Cole ever wrote was something anyone needed to read. He took another step back. "Something new?"

"Yes, yes. And different." Cole spoke in low, secretive tones. "Remember that man I told you about who sat next to me on the flight from Japan?" Miles nodded. He did not remember, but neither did he want Cole to launch into an explanation. "That story he told me about the general's wife who drowned when the passenger plane crashed in the Hong Kong bay? I got it down. No kidding. In a poem." He offered Miles a sheet of paper.

Miles looked at the paper as if he were being handed the business end of a black cobra. "That's great, Cole. Only, I gotta run to K.L. right now."

"I didn't mean you had to read it right now. Here." Cole folded the sheet several times, stepped closer and stuffed it into Miles' shirt pocket.

Miles moved back again, crossing the threshold and almost falling from the unexpected step down. "Thanks." He tried to make his stumble seem something he had done on purpose. "I'll read it later. In the taxi to town." He turned and walked toward the gate.

"One more thing," Cole said. Miles stopped in the sun, winced, and stepped into the partial shade of a hibiscus bush. "The retreat at Genting Highlands, Miles. It's important that you go. Batu Blue needs you. Malaysia needs you." Miles nodded a non-committal response and left. As far as he was concerned, Cole was getting crazier.

He had not thought again about the poem Cole pressed upon him until it got in the way of returning his graffiti note pad to his pocket. "Motivated forgetting," Miles mumbled. He looked around for Roseta, almost hoping not to find her.

Libby LeMaster left the Mandarin feeling better than she had in weeks. She stopped just beyond the doors to look at the men Kent thought were predatory. The small one playing with a knife didn't look up; the tall black one grinned when he saw her looking his way. He pursed his lips, and Libby knew that if it were not for the traffic noise, she would be able to hear him making kissy noises at her. The jerk. Libby hated the way so many lower class Malaysian men insisted on making those obscene smacky sounds if she made eye contact with them. She raised her brows, lowered her eyelids, and turned away, icing the fellow as best she could.

She walked the two blocks to the Klang Bus Station, crossed the street to where the taxis waited, and caught a cab to Tunku Abdul Rahman street so she could browse around in The Globe Silk Store and the little import shops that lined the street.

Noland looked down from his hotel window at Mehinder and Ibrahim, waiting across the street. Mehinder's attention was on some girl in front of the hotel. Noland couldn't see the person, but he knew it was a girl by the look on Mehinder's face—the pursed lips followed by the almost drooling grin.

Noland opened the window and leaned out. He could see a blond woman walking off to his right with Mehinder staring after her. All men in the area, he noted, turned to watch the blond—all except the mean-looking little fellow, Mehinder's friend.

After a quick shower, Noland went to the hotel coffee shop for a lunch that included warm vegetables. They weren't cooked, as he understood the term. Mixed among them were shrimp, pieces of liver, and some sort of horrible-looking things with rubbery tentacles. He also had a bowl of rice, but couldn't figure out what the waiter had in mind in setting it there.

When Noland had looked at the menu, he saw nothing he recognized, so he asked the waiter to bring him "something good—like the specialty of the house, maybe." Such instructions always got him a fine meal in Dallas or Fort Worth when he went into fancy restaurants and didn't know what to order. But here, he ended up with that plate of uncooked and unidentifiable vegetables mixed with a few shrimp, the rubber things that Noland thought might pass for plastic bass lures, and liver. Guts, he thought, that's what liver is, and I don't eat guts.

He ate the shrimp and took a few bites of the raw vegetables. Noland noticed an odd-looking white man with a beard and mustache at a nearby table who seemed to be paying a good deal of attention to him. I'll bet that guy has eaten here before, Noland thought, and is sitting over there laughing his ass off at me trying to find anything edible in this joint.

Noland ordered a glass of milk. "Cow's milk?" the waiter asked.

"For sure I don't want goat's milk or frog's milk."

"Goat's milk, don't have. Maybe cow's milk. I check."

When the waiter brought a glass of milk, he set it on the table and retreated to the bar, where he, the cashier, and another waiter stared round-eyed at Noland, who poured the milk over his rice, spooned some sugar into the bowl, and ate the concoction with a ceramic soup spoon.

When he got outside, he adjusted his Stetson to shade his eyes and looked across the street at Mehinder and Ibrahim. "Howdy, boys," he said, then went off to the left toward the street where the cab driver had told him he could buy a watch.

On Petaling Street, Noland found a vendor with a display of watches on a rickety-looking table. He selected a fake Rolex, argued some about the price because the cab driver had told him he should, and ended up paying what he considered a low price for a watch of any kind, fake or real. Mehinder and Ibrahim, he noted, watched the exchange from down the street.

Noland went to another hawker whose display consisted of household goods. Among the items, Noland found a large lock-back, stainless steel pocket knife. He haggled half-heartedly and paid for it. Turning toward Mehinder and Ibrahim, Noland opened the knife, tossed it into the air so that it turned several times, and caught it by the handle. With an exaggerated wink at his former jail-mates, Noland folded the knife and dropped it into the pocket of his jeans.

After touring her favorite shops along Tunku Abdul Rahman street, Libby caught a cab to Central Market. She had heard about a new vendor there who sold gemstones, and she thought she might as well check it out while she was downtown. It seemed unlikely that a stall in Central Market could sell stones as cheap as those hawked along Petaling Street, but then it was possible the stones would be of higher quality.

Inside Central Market, Libby wished she had carried a light jacket with her. The Globe Silk Store had been colder than a meat locker, as had several of the import shops. Public buildings in Malaysia were too cold to suit her, though she was grateful that such buildings were not kept as cool as were their counterparts back in the States. Still, the abrupt change from a comfortable, humid, day to the refrigerated air in the mall caused her skin to ripple in protest.

In the crowd ahead, she saw Miles Osborn mopping his brow with a handkerchief. Miles sweated more than anyone Libby had ever known. How he managed to continue emitting water like that in the frigid air of Central Market was beyond her. She began making her way through the crowd toward him when she saw Roseta appear by his side.

Miles and Roseta talked with exaggerated histrionics. Roseta waved her arms about and pointed several directions with her thumb. Libby smiled at the gesture. Malays regarded pointing with their index finger as an obscene sign, the same as Americans did holding up the middle finger. So what is the Malay solution? Libby thought. They point with their thumbs, that's what—or at least the higher class ones did. That way they do several things at once, Libby figured; they indicated a direction; they pro-claimed themselves to better than the rabble who made that ugly sign with their index fingers, and they reminded anyone watching of the obscene gesture by the studied omission of it. Libby laughed. By being so coy about the matter, they insured that they and everyone around them thought about sexual matters. All in the name of being polite.

Roseta took Miles' arm, and the two headed toward the Malay restaurant in the center of the mall.

Miles and Roseta? Libby wondered in amazement. That he would allow any woman to take his arm was mind-boggling. Libby thought of how he had jerked his hand away at Cole's party when she offered to read his palm. He seemed fearful of being touched by a woman. And yet there he was, allowing Roseta to lead him about.

Libby had on several occasions watched Miles look at Roseta like he was the pimply junior high school nerd and she the popular cheerleader. He made disparaging remarks about her, but he often had a kind of hang-dog look about him when she was near.

Libby wanted to follow and listen to what they had to say, but felt such behavior to be inappropriate. She knew she would resent it if Miles followed her and Kent around.

Libby turned and looked at her reflection in the plate glass front of the Selangor Pewter store. "Me and Kent?" She mouthed the words, startled by how easy it had been to think of him in such a possessive way.

Roseta had suspected Miles would be a little difficult, but she had not expected him to balk at going somewhere private. Even when he agreed to go to the Malay Restaurant in the mall, the one without walls, she had to drag him there.

So Miles had no real experience with women, Roseta thought. The insight gave her courage to carry through with her plans since it meant it would be difficult for him to know she had no experience with men, either. Moreover, he would not be comparing her to women he had known.

Roseta picked a table away from other diners, one large enough for only two people. "I must admit to being a little intimidated by this situation, Mr. Osborn." She leaned on the table so their faces were closer.

Miles sat back in his chair. "Please," he said, "call me Miles. And why should you be intimidated?"

"I'm just a nobody from a small *kampung* in a place no one has ever heard of, while you, Miles, are a sophisticated university lecturer and a world traveler. I'm sure you must find me a bit ordinary and dull."

"You? Ordinary or dull?"

She could tell that Miles was astonished at the notion, a response that pleased her. "What about me could be otherwise than ordinary?"

What, indeed, Miles thought. He could name quite a few things. Her startling beauty. Her intelligence. Her self-confidence. But he lacked the courage to name them out loud. He leaned forward, delighted with the situation. Then he remembered Roseta had some other traits, ones he liked less well. She is one helluva nosy woman, he thought. And sneaky—like when she hid in the laundry room so she could spy on anyone who happened along. And pushy as hell. He sat back in his chair again.

Watching Miles and Roseta from a safe distance, Libby moved around the hawker stalls near the restaurant. She could read little of what was going on, but then, she told herself, it was better that way. Maybe she could get Miles to tell her about his rendezvous.

To amuse herself while she waited, Libby bargained for and bought several pieces of jewelry that she liked and a key chain she did not like. It would have to be a gift to someone who deserved such an object, she thought, looking at the scorpion encased in plastic hanging from the chain.

The long, copper-enameled earrings matched her batik skirt. And a necklace she picked out would go with her orange floral dress. The orange in the necklace, the hawker assured her, came from Malaysian butterfly wings embedded in clear glass beads.

When she saw Miles and Roseta stand up, Libby moved closer, peering at them from behind a display of tee shirts. Miles wore a goofy-looking grin, and Roseta looked pleased with herself. Just before parting, she offered her hand, and Miles took it without hesitation. Roseta clasped Miles' hand with both of hers, then drew her hands back, touching them to her heart.

What the hell is that all about, Libby wondered. Miles watched Roseta leave the mall through the side door; Libby watched Miles. He appeared to Libby like an adolescent stricken with romantic agony. Then he turned with startling abruptness and energy and walked out of the area of the restaurant, toward the main entrance of Central Market.

That sudden, explosive movement, so unexpected after the apparent serenity of watching Roseta, reminded Libby of Al Lutz. That's an unfair and unflattering comparison, Libby thought. Still, Miles often had a blank compulsiveness, devoid of any sense of how comical he might appear to others—a trait Al had in the extreme.

When Al had come into the San Francisco clinic where Libby was serving her internship, the director of the clinic assigned Al to Libby for counseling. Dr. Salaman made the assignment with a certain amount of smirking and knowing smiles at the other members of the staff, all of whom had worked there much longer than Libby.

She began to understand the non-verbal fooleries during Al's first session. He came to her, he explained, because he had discovered the cause of all psychosis in the world, and he had worked out a cure. "My device will stop all mental illness, everywhere." He jumped to his feet and walked around the room.

Libby let him pace for a while, then suggested that he sit in the easy chair and tell her some things about himself. To her surprise, Al sat in the chair she indicated, going from an arm-waving, pacing intensity to the posture of a man who adored relaxation above all else. He lolled his head, opened one eye with what looked like the effort of the newly awakened and looked at her. "Go for it, lady." His voice came out soft and thick. "Ask me what you want to know."

Al answered a few questions with quiet frankness. He came from Cut-and-Shoot, Texas, he said, a tiny town he hated. Libby didn't believe that such a town existed, except in Al's mind, but later when she looked the name up in a Texas road atlas, she found it. "I'm a left-over hippie," he told Libby, "A flower child who found out how to Peter Pan. Dad, back in Cut-and-Shoot, tells everybody in the town barber shop and at the general store that I went off to college in California and fried my brain on LSD, but then Dad has to see everything in black-and-white terms and blame something tangible for the way I dress and the cut of my hair and the fact that I refuse to come home and take over his junkyard business."

Without warning, Al leaped to his feet, exploding from almost trance-like serenity into the pacing, gesticulating person he had been when he first entered Libby's office. "It will work. It will." He turned with passion to Libby. "And you can help by explaining to the other doctors here about it."

"What will work, Al?"

"My prosthetic foreskin." He began digging in the back pocket of his jeans. "Like I was telling you, I found out the cause of mental illness. Circumcision. I got to noticing it over in Haight Ashbury, then at some of the nude beaches down the coast. I'll bet you didn't realize it, but every person who suffers from mental disturbance of any kind has been circumcised. Every single one. When the realization first came to me, I couldn't believe how simple the explanation was, so I watched more carefully. I've had some bouts myself with mental aberrations, so I know the signs to watch for. And every person I have ever looked at on those beaches and elsewhere who seemed a little out of it, you know, crazy—every single one of them had been circumcised. What do you think of that?"

"I find that very interesting."

"Oh ho. It's much more than interesting. It's revolutionary. At least with this, it will be." He pulled a tiny piece of plastic from his pocket and held it out for Libby to inspect.

"And just what is that?"

"Can't you tell?"

"It looks like a piece of Saran Wrap."

"Maybe it was that, once. But I cut it carefully and treated the ends with heat. Now it's a prosthetic foreskin, the most revolutionary thing in psychiatry since Freud. Who knows what the consequences of my discovery will be? Certainly the medical world will cease the brutal practice of sniping away such a vital part of an infant's body, but that won't help the millions who are already maimed, no siree bobtail, it won't. The world will go on having wars and mass murders and building clinics like this one, not to mention all the loony bins they put up all over the place to warehouse the victims of circumcision, and all for what? Just to tear them down in a single generation when circumcision is stopped after my discovery becomes known and all mental illness is wiped out, banished from the face of the earth, from the solar system, from the entire universe."

"Do, uh, you wear one of those?"

Al looked at her in a wild way. "Just think about that question for a minute. Think about it. A waste of breath. Of course I wear a prosthetic foreskin. How else could I possibly know the device works? Not that one case proves anything, you understand. I have distributed some around the beach and over in Haight Ashbury. Every single person I gave one to is better. Every one. That's one hundred percent. One hundred. Proof positive that my device works, and I might add, proof that my theory is right."

"What about women?"

"What about them?"

"Do you know any women with mental disturbances?"

As soon as she said it, she regretted it. Al's face fell and his shoulders slumped. "Yeah." He turned to the door. "Yeah, what about women?" At the door, he turned back to Libby. "Do they ever circumcise women?"

"In some places, I'm sad to say, female circumcision is practiced."

"How do they do it? I mean, the machinery is completely different." He walked back toward Libby, a hopeful look on his face.

"With a knife, I think—or a sharp stone, maybe. I don't know. What they do is remove the clitoris."

"Then that's it, by god." Al snapped his fingers. "This," he held up the piece of Saran Wrap, "would cure only half of the people in the world. Why didn't I think of that before? Of course. I'm a man, so I thought only about men. But women. They need a device to help them out, too. A prosthetic clitoris. Thanks, Dr. LeMaster. It will take some careful measuring to develop one that would work. I'd better get right on this."

Maybe it isn't a fair comparison, Libby acknowledged, watching Miles push his way through the crowd. But there did seem to be something of Al Lutz in Miles, in the way he lurched about, hurrying to the door. It took real effort for her to catch up with him.

"Miles Osborn." She touched his arm. "What good luck to run into you here. Is there a chance you're heading home, and if so, how about sharing a cab?"

"Hello, Libby. I was just going toward the bus station, but with you to share the cost, it would be better to ride in an air conditioned cab."

When they got into a taxi, Libby said, "Miles, I thought I saw you and that beautiful lady what's her name, Roseta, in Central Market."

"Is that right?" Miles asked. Libby's statement seemed to make him nervous. He reached for his pocket as though for a cigarette, though Libby knew he didn't smoke. When he touched the pocket, he seemed to remember something. "Right before I left the house today," he said, "Cole pressed a copy of his latest poem on me. I haven't had a chance to read it yet."

Libby felt a twinge of disappointment that her fishing around for information about Miles and Roseta failed so completely. But she also felt a little guilty for bringing the matter up when she saw how flustered it made Miles. Libby saw the relief in his eyes when he realized he had a ready and easy way to guide the conversation to something other than Roseta.

Miles took a folded sheet of paper from his pocket. "Is that the poem?" Libby asked.

"Yeah. And I'll bet a dollar to a silk hat that it's as bad a piece of verse as you could find in Malaysia."

"Miles." Libby knew his opinion of Coleman's poetry, even if Coleman did not—though how Cole remained so ignorant about his own roommate was a mystery to her.

"You have to admit that he writes real garbage."

"Privately, and only to you, Miles, I will admit I do know that. But every poet in the world writes garbage. Some of them also write really good things, from time to time."

"Not Cole. Do you want to hear this one?"

"Is it short?"

"Yes. Most of his poems are short, and that, I might add, is their only virtue."

"Miles. Read it and then decide."

"He calls this one '1970: the flight of the Vietnamese general's wife.' Cole said it was inspired by a story he heard from a passenger on his last flight from Japan, something about a woman drowning when her plane overshot the runway. Cole wrote 'by Coleman Farquart' right under the title. He always does that.

When the airplane went beyond its track

92

into the Hong Kong Bay,
the general's wife dropped bubbling slack
down into the China Sea,
dragged by gold that weighed two stone
stitched into the leather band
that wrapped her slender waist;
dragged by gold into the night
and anchored to the rocky sand,
the general's wife lies seaweed laced
and flashes green and gold and white
when the dead and crab-picked bone
catches rays of surface light.

Right after the poem, he put a dash and his name again. He always does that, too."

"Miles, read that again. That is really good."

"Good? Good?" Miles stared.

"Yes. Let me look at it." She took the sheet from his hands and read it. "It's a tragedy, Miles. The poor woman has been exploited by men."

"What? What was that?" Miles leaned over and looked at the paper as if to make sure she had the same poem he had just read.

"He captures it beautifully: she isn't even a person in her own right. She's just 'the general's wife,' and not a human being at all. Don't you see, Miles? The values of a warped male world where war and theft are a way of life place a premium on gold even more than on women. The general made her into an object, a thing. She is little more than a pack mule. And her death is nothing much—just an event that turns her from one object into another. When the wife is not being a living wheel barrow for the general's gold, she is merely a sex object to him. That's suggested by the reference to 'her slender waist,' which in itself is a pun on *waste*."

"A pun? I like puns, though never have I found one in any of Cole's poems."

"Definitely a pun. It's Cole's subtle way of letting the reader know that he is just reporting on the male chauvinist piggery of the world rather than endorsing it. He is suggesting that it is a tragic *waste* to subject a woman to such treatment, to weight her down and throw her into the sea to drown like an unwanted cat."

Miles put his fingers on his temples. "I feel as if I'm back in an

93

English class in high school and you're the teacher, the wizard who could noodle out meaning from words that, to me, look like so much gibberish. Maybe all that hidden meaning is there, but I find the poem gross. That line about 'the dead and crab-picked bone' is revolting."

"It is, isn't it? But that's the beauty of the line, Miles. You're supposed to be repulsed by what happens to the poor woman."

"Miss Duckfat said the same sort of things, back in high school."

"Who?"

"Never mind. I guess I don't understand poetry."

Noland watched Ibrahim jerking his finger in his direction and saying a few words to Mehinder. They both know how to frown in a right ugly way, Noland thought. He turned his back to them to show his contempt and gave his attention to the wares of the hawkers who were still setting up displays along the edge of the street. When he stopped to examine a display of odd-looking fruit, Ibrahim poked a finger into the small of his back.

Turning around, Noland found Ibrahim looking up at him, a knife in one hand, and Mehinder standing a little farther back. "Don't crowd me like that, little fellow." Noland stepped back.

"I little," Ibrahim said. "You big. But I mean. You remember what I say. Mean beat strong. You come with Ibrahim and Mehinder, yes?" He moved closer to Noland.

Remembering Hank's advice about not letting anyone get too close to you in a dangerous place like the Avalon, Noland jerked a quick left punch into Ibrahim's stomach. The blow nearly lifted Ibrahim off of his feet. He fell back, cracking his head on the pavement.

Mehinder watched Ibrahim, an amazed look on his face. It seemed to occur to him, too late, that Noland might hit him next. As he lifted his hands, Noland's fist caught him over his left eye. He staggered back to keep from falling, and Noland stepped into him, delivering two blows to his ribs, another to his left eye, and a solid punch to his nose.

Mehinder scrambled back, away from the American. The cartilage in his nose popped from the last blow, and blood gushed over his mouth.

Noland pulled a red bandanna from a hip pocket and wiped his knuckles, watching Mehinder stagger to the building across the street and grasp at the wall for support. Ibrahim was on his hands and knees in the middle of the street, vomiting. Noland walked over to him, picked up his knife and looked at it with elaborate interest.

It was a slender, poorly-constructed hunting knife with a sharp point and no edge to brag about. Noland set the handle of the knife in the gutter and leaned the point against the curb. He stomped the knife with the heal of his boot, snapping the blade from the handle.

Noland picked up the blade and the handle, walked over to Ibrahim, who was beginning to crawl across the street, and dropped the pieces of knife in front of him. "Sometimes, Abraham, old buddy, big beats mean."

And that, Noland told himself, was a damn good line. A punch line, he added, pleased with the pun. He looked around. All the hawkers up and down Petaling street stared at him, and shopkeepers stood in their doorways, watching.

Crappo, Noland thought, this could land me back in Hashim's jail. He started back toward the hotel. When he got to the stall where he had bought the fake Rolex, the vendor said, "Where you from?"

"Texas. But I can't stay to chat."

"No worry." The vendor pointed down the street. "Look."

Noland looked back. All the merchants had gone back to their businesses. Except for Mehinder and Ibrahim leaning against the wall of a building, the street looked much as it had when Noland first turned the corner. "If police come, no one here know nothing. But police come here almost never." The vendor lowered his voice and nodded toward Mehinder and Ibrahim. "Them bad. Nobody like. You ever need favor from me? From others," he waved his hand, indicating the merchants along the street, "You get favor. You hero here for knocking bad men in stomach. In face. You want another watch? I sell for my cost."

"Thanks."

The vendor looked around and lowered his voice to a whisper. "One thing I give. Burning Tiger. There Badder men than Ibrahim in Burning Tiger. Badder than Mehinder. Smarter men. It good you have knife. Better for to have gun, when Burning Tiger come."

"This Burning Tiger is a gang of some kind?"

"Not say name so loud. Better not say at all," the hawker whispered, then resumed his normal voice. "You want another Rolex?"

"Not just now. Thanks, especially for the information." Noland wandered back toward the hotel, taking his time so he could calm himself from the adrenaline surge that came with hammering on the two men in the street. He wondered if he needed to worry any about the gang the watch vendor mentioned. Probably not, he decided, at least for a while. *Burning Tiger* struck him as a silly-sounding name, one made up by little boys playing at being tough men. He had other things to concern him, like calling EXXON to report that he was in the country. Not that he was expected to report to work soon. And there was Suppriah.

On his walk toward Sultan Street, toward the Mandarin Hotel, Noland forced a smile for the shopkeepers and vendors, who grinned and nodded to him. But he didn't feel much like smiling. Having to fight like he was some sort of animal always upset Noland.

# 6

The play's the thing
Wherein I'll catch the King of Cocaine

Butch Gaston, *Playwright's Notebook*


Butch followed Libby and Kent down Petaling Street and around the corner on Sultan Street, watching them go into the Chinese drugstore. Disgusting, Butch thought: he takes her into a shop that specializes in such things as tiger penis, rhino horn, assorted plants and herbs, maybe Spanish fly, for all he knew. An aphrodisiac shop. Not a place to take a lady.

Stationing himself near the door, he watched what went on in the lewd shop as best he could, cursing the traffic noises that prevented him from hearing the skullduggery and drug dealing that had to be taking place.

The old Chinaman directed Libby into cooking up some sort of goop from his shelves. LSD maybe—Butch had heard that anyone could make acid in just about any cobbled-together chemistry lab. He was shocked to see Libby drawn into such shady activity. But perhaps it was possible she didn't know the real nature of the concoction the Chinaman had her make.

He took out his notebook and wrote:

SLICK WILLY: Joanie, this old man is the best chemist in Kuala Lumpur. Everyone calls him *Catmandu.*

JOANIE: Why do they call him cat-man-do?

SLICK WILLY: A number of reasons. Some say he experiments on cats with his drugs. Others say he runs a cat house over in the Chow Kit area, a place where he sells various of his chemicals, along with cocaine and other drugs he gets from American gangsters.

Not bad, Butch told himself. He glanced across the street and saw a man wearing a Stetson emerge from the Mandarin Hotel. Butch snapped his notebook shut, slipped it into a pocket in his robe, and watched the bogus cowboy walk to a waiting cab.

Of course the two drug dealers would stay in the same hotel, Butch realized. Why hadn't he thought of it earlier? That man had to be the one arrested in the airport. Butch stared, his anger growing. How did he get out of jail so fast? A payoff of some sort, how else? There was so much money to be had from drugs that police, jailers, anybody could be bought.

Butch knew his play would be even more crucial than ever, given this turn of events. He would have to have two villains in the drama. He took his notebook out and wrote, "Billy-Bob Johnson, called *the King of Cocaine* by the druggers in Chicago and *Cowboy Bob* by the members of his gang, swaggered out of the Chinese hotel."

The King stood by the cab, flashing a handful of bills and, as far as Butch could see, making a big deal out of giving money to the cab driver. The King waved at someone across the street. Butch walked toward the Mandarin, looking at the men Cowboy Bob waved to. Local thugs, Butch noted. Dangerous-looking men. Chicago dealers must have men such as those on the payroll all over the world, Butch thought, even right here in Kuala Lumpur. Men with names like—like what? He looked at them again, then wrote "Anwar the Knife and Killer Kaliayani, assigned as body guards to the King of Cocaine."

Butch felt creative excitement growing within him, and he knew that the gangsters gave him material of social significance to work into in his art. It was better material than he had when he wrote the play that slammed Rufus and Albert for ruining his favorite picnic spot.

Just what the turkeys deserved, Butch thought as he entered the Mandarin Hotel. And I'll nail these pushers, too—get the goods on them, then tell all of Kuala Lumpur about it in the best play I ever wrote.

Butch had already began thinking of which of his students at Ringling University might be cast in some of the parts in the play, and he was making a list of prominent Malaysians to invite to opening night.

In the lobby of the Mandarin, Butch pretended to examine a display of travel brochures while the cowboy talked to the man at the registration desk. It was an easy matter to get into the elevator with the King of Cocaine and ride to his floor. Butch felt the hair on his neck prickle when he stood next to the King, but he kept his face a blank mask of oriental inscrutability.

His creativity, as usual in times when he felt he was taking risks in his field research, ran at full tilt. That guitar case—what a great prop. He could stage some dramatic scenes where the King took bags of white powder and weapons out of it. But no Tommy guns. Too obvious, too much something an audience would expect to be in a guitar case. Grenades, maybe. Or a flame-thrower.

As soon as he saw the King go into room 402, Butch went to the men's room on the mezzanine, locked himself in a toilet booth, and removed his robe and pointed hat. From a pocket in the robe, he took his travel kit that had everything he needed for quick transformation of his face. With astringent and cotton pads, he removed Yap Ah Loy. Looking into the tiny mirror he propped on the commode tank, he took brushes and swabs and subtle make-up and put on the face of a European tourist, complete with mustache and a Lenin beard, then donned a batik shirt, a roll canvas hat and a small camera dangling around his neck.

Butch collapsed his pointed Yap-Ah-Loy hat, rolled up the robe, and put them, along with his travel kit, into a plastic shopping bag.

Then he went to the lobby and registered under the name Claude Boggle. "When I stayed here before," he told the clerk, "I stayed in room 409. A fine room it was, I'll tell you. Can you give me the same room?"

When he got to his room, Butch opened the door enough so that, were he inside, he could see if anyone came to or left room 402, just across the hall and down a few doors. Then he walked to the room of the King of Cocaine and looked back.

Damn. It was a bit too obvious that his door stood open. He went to the hall light close to his room, popped open the fixture covering, and took out the light bulb, using a handkerchief to keep from burning his hand. That would make his cracked door a little less noticeable, but not by much.

Minutes after he took up his post behind his door, Butch saw Cowboy Bob, the King of Chicago Cocaine, emerge. That just might serve as a title, Butch thought: *The King of Chicago Cocaine Comes to Kuala Lumpur*. Catchy.

He jotted the idea into his notebook while glancing at the lighted numbers over the elevator. Cowboy Bob went to the Mezzanine, probably to the coffee shop. Butch hoped so. A cup of decent coffee sounded great to him. The only cup he had that day was the horrible local stuff in the Sun Wah with the other American drug pusher pretending to draw him, then Libby. The Mandarin would have American coffee, something he could order in his present role as Claude Boggle. If he had remained Yap Ah Loy, he would be compelled to order the local coffee, which he knew to be a dark, evil-tasting brew powerful enough to leap out of the cup and wrestle him to the floor.

In the coffee shop, Butch sipped his coffee and watched the King of Chicago Cocaine play the part of Cowboy Bob the country bumpkin with admirable ease. Pouring milk over the steamed rice was perfect, a bit of stage foolery Butch himself might have made up. He wrote up stage directions for a possible coffee shop scene while the drug kingpin ate.

When Cowboy Bob left the Mandarin, Butch knew on instinct where he was heading. To the Sun Wah. And the two thugs, the local body guards, followed him. Butch followed Anwar the Knife and Killer Kaliayani, marveling at how easy criminal detective work could be and at how simple the police must be not to have someone watching these gangsters.

On the walk down Sultan Street to Petaling, Butch looked into the Chinese herb shop where the old man had cooked up the LSD for the other drug dealer. A young Chinese man stood behind the counter; the old man, the American drug dealer, and Libby were nowhere to be seen. I'll have to catch up with Kent and Libby later, Butch thought, hurrying after the two local hoods and the cowboy from Chicago.

Cowboy Bob talked to the same watch salesman the other dealer, Kent Day, had given so much attention to. Was that significant? Butch decided it was, especially when the cowboy bought a watch, handing the dealer something. Money? Maybe a bag of dope? Butch couldn't tell; he was too far down the street, behind the local boys assigned to guard the big cheese from Chicago.

Butch played the tourist by taking a few photographs, but not of any of the drug dealers. Then he walked past the two locals to a tailor across the street and down a way from the Sun Wah. Why wasn't Cowboy Bob going into the coffee shop, as Kent had done, Butch wondered.

He saw why when Bob bargained for and purchased an evil-looking lock-back knife. He's arming himself, Butch saw, for what? Does he expect trouble?

Cowboy Bob turned to Anwar the Knife and Killer Kaliayani, spun his knife high into the air and caught it by the handle with arrogant ease. Butch flinched. This was a dangerous man, a man to be wary of, not a person to cross. Maybe being a detective wasn't such an easy job, after all—at least not for the macho, muddle-minded folk Butch figured usually became cops.

Like Rufus Lombard and that fink whatzisname? Butch dredged up the name Albert and an image of a slope-shouldered round boy with arms like a gorilla, but couldn't remember his last name. When he was in high school in Peoria, Butch made the mistake of telling Rufus about a private lake just out of town, accessible via a maze of dirt roads. It had posted signs up all over the place, and barbed wire strung around it.

The gate stayed open. Beside the gate was a sign that said, "Private Property. For use of Employees of Nu-oil Only." But anyone could drive across the cattle guard and go right up to the lake. It was a favorite retreat for Butch—a great place for swimming and fishing.

Or it was a favorite retreat until Rufus and Albert and some of the other stupid football jocks went out there and chased the cows around. Rufus bragged about it at school: he and the others planned to catch one of the cows and do disgusting things to it. But all of the cattle were skittery, and after chasing them for an hour, Albert shot one of them in the eye with a pistol. "It fell over and shook like one of those cheap machines at the Laundromat," Rufus reported to the idiot gang standing around the flag pole after school. They all thought the tale wonderful and funny.

The next time Butch drove out to the lake, he found the gate padlocked and a new sign by it threatening to prosecute trespassers. Rufus and Albert, in a moment of casual brutality, had caused the owners of the lake to lock Butch out.

Butch didn't forget their offenses. When he wrote a play staged by students at Butler University, Butch included caricatures of Albert and Rufus, changing their names a bit and making them sleazy fools.

Right after high school, Rufus and Albert joined the Peoria police force. By now, they're probably detectives, Butch thought—unless they tried following someone like Cowboy Bob and got whittled down to size when he found them stumbling around behind.

Butch went into a tailor's shop and looked at sample fabric. That way, he could keep an eye on Cowboy Bob and his lock-back knife without being seen. The tailor hovered a little too close, pushing his services, until he noticed Anwar the Knife and Killer Kaliayani go up to Cowboy Bob in a threatening way. The tailor went to the door of his shop and watched. Butch saw the scene through the plate glass window.

He saw the little gangster threaten Cowboy Bob with a knife and watched the American criminal burst into a frenzy of violence. Butch expected at any moment to see Cowboy Bob whip out his knife and carve Anwar and Kaliayani into bloody chunks.

But he didn't. The man was so confident of his power that he dispatched his adversaries with his bare hands. Butch remembered riding in the elevator at the Mandarin with the Chicago killer, and he felt his chest tighten in fear. I was a little arrogant, myself, Butch thought, vowing not to get that close to Cowboy Bob again.

When the violent American broke Anwar's knife with his boot, Butch took out his notebook and wrote. It was such beautiful stage business, such a fine and convincing symbol of the villain's evil. In that simple, casual act, he said to the men he had just pummeled half to death—as well as to any other local gangsters who might be watching—that he could have used Anwar's knife to slit the rogue's throat, but chose not to. Tough and dangerous as Anwar and Kaliayani might be, the American hoodlum found them unworthy as adversaries, not worth the effort to kill, and he said as much by breaking the knife.

When Cowboy Bob walked away, Butch left the tailor's shop. He paused to look at Anwar the Knife and Killer Kaliayani, who were in no shape to notice him or much of anything. So they weren't body guards at all. Likely members of a rival drug ring. Butch whistled, again impressed with the man from Chicago. He knew who Anwar and Kaliayani were from the first, yet he had smiled and waved at them, even turned his back to them. That's a kind of confidence that betrays the sort of ruthless violence Butch knew he could present on stage, now that he had so much material to work with.

# 7

"We must all be actors," the gatekeeper told the serving girl, "for it is the only way to control our mistress."
—Virginia Li, "The Amah and the Tyrant"

Noland washed his hands, taking care not to rub soap into the places on his knuckles that Mehinder's bony face had nicked. He hated what he had just done, hated that gross sensation of feeling Mehinder's nose give way under his fist, hated the sight of Ibrahim and Mehinder writhing in pain.

"But," he said to his image in the mirror, "the alternative is something I would hate worse. Better them than me."

If he thought bluffing those men into leaving him alone might have worked, Noland certainly would have done it. It had worked with Mehinder in the jail. But that rabid little Ibrahim. He fancied himself a mean man with a knife—and probably was, too, given the chance. He didn't bluff so easily. Old Hank had taught Noland to bluff when you think you have a good chance to pull it off, but always be prepared to have the bluff called.

"And when bluffing is out of the question," Hank had said numerous times, "pound the dog pucky out of them." Noland noticed that Hank almost never bluffed, perhaps because he enjoyed pounding the dog pucky out of men who belittled him. But Noland found no pleasure in such violence, even if he did learn Hank's methods.

Noland sat on the bed in his hotel room and called the EXXON office, reporting to the secretary who answered that he was in town. Then he considered calling Suppriah.

He took out her number, picked up the phone, then set it down again. Surprising her might be more fun than talking on the phone. And Noland felt the need of some fun after all the unpleasantries. The bust at the airport. Hashim's jail. Having to kick the butts of those morons from the jail who followed him around. He felt the need of talking with a friend, but there were none around. Kent Day—that nice fellow from the flight over—would be a good person to see. He, at least, was a normal person, whereas everybody in Malaysia seemed to be weird. But there was no way to know where Kent was.

It had to be Suppriah, then. She wasn't weird. Her letters had been charming, full of wit and grace. It would be good to spend some time with a regular person. He told himself he could avoid disappointment by expecting only that: a regular person. Not a soulmate. He remembered the delicious high he always felt when he had been with his high school sweetheart back in Shamrock. "Virginia Holmes," he said her name aloud. Now there was a sweetie for you. Trouble was, she was a Texas woman, and so his dreams of her being his soulmate had to end in disaster.

Noland knew from hard experience that Texas women—though he always called them "girls"—were no damned good. Sure, they had plenty of potential, but like as not, they would turn out like Virginia Holmes.

On the airplane to Malaysia, he had told Kent about Virginia, about how the two of them seemed destined for one another, about her purity and grace and beauty.

When Virginia got elected cheerleader, she refused to go onto the football field in the skimpy uniform Shamrock High provided, choosing instead to make her own, which included a skirt that covered her knees. Noland told Kent about the skirt and about how delighted he was that she was so modest. But he did not tell how she worked out a number of routines for cheers in which she and the other cheerleaders whirled around, causing her modest skirt to fly out and reveal high-hip leotards and an abundance of Virginia that normally was kept out of sight.

Noland told Kent of loving Virginia "beyond sex, in the purist way, like Adam and Eve in Paradise." He didn't mention the dates that took them out on Pakan Road after dark, the titillating touching and kisses in which she thrust her tongue aggressively into his mouth. Nor did he tell about the time her parents went to Oklahoma City for the weekend.

For some weeks, Virginia suggested the drive to Pakan Road every night, and every night she let Noland know in every way she knew short of saying it in actual words that it was time he forgot his high-minded scruples and idealistic vision of their love and got on with what their passion dictated. But he seemed determined to save himself for his wedding night.

Not that he said it in so many words. But he thought he believed he ought to help Virginia remain pure until the night after they stood before the altar of the First Baptist Church, where he would promise to love and honor her and she would promise to love, honor, and obey him.

The reality, though, was that Noland was scared. Scared of the wrath of the community, should she get pregnant, scared of losing Virginia's love if he did not give in and do what she wanted. He sought information in the high school library about how to keep a girl from becoming pregnant, but found nothing because years before, the principal had removed all books even remotely dealing with sex from library shelves.

Noland knew about rubbers—everybody knew that much. He had gone to the restroom of the Shell service station over in Mobeetie, inserted a couple of quarters in a special machine bolted to the wall, and got a package of Golden Trojans that he kept in a secret place in his wallet. But rubbers seemed so crass, so deliberate, and he felt guilty for even having one on his person. It was evidence enough that he was planning to do something he knew to be dead wrong. The Golden Trojan had to stay in the secret place in his billfold not because he was afraid anyone would ever go through his things and find it; it was there so he would not have to see it on a daily basis, so he could try to forget its presence, forget that he was being so scheming and purposeful in planing an immoral act.

Noland also feared that, should he use the rubber there in the seat of his pickup out on Pakan Road in the dark, he might make some sort of mistake, perhaps a bad one. Virginia would think him less than a man. She might even laugh.

The thought of her laughing at him—even while she was probing his mouth with her determined, hot tongue—caused him to know that there was no way he could get the Trojan on. He told himself it would be like trying to put a glove on a piece of cooked spaghetti.

He had seen an ad in a magazine for a book called *Sane Sex Life and Sane Sex Living* that was supposed to tell everything a woman wanted from love making. Moreover, it would tell numerous ways to prevent pregnancy. It cost only twenty bucks and would arrive in the mail in a plain brown wrapper. So he ordered it, but not without feeling guilty. That was two weeks before the night out on Pakan Road when he told Virginia he loved her and would love her forever and she said, with impatience, "I love you, too, Noland, but dern it. People in love make love, don't they?" He admitted it was so, though he felt cornered, somehow. "Then show me how much you love me, Noland," she said, kissing him in a way that he regarded as an assault rather than a show of affection.

Show her? The notion was downright terrifying. Suppose he couldn't show her? What, after all, did he know about how to please a girl? He drew back from her with sudden inspiration and said, "People who really love each other take the love act seriously. Like it is something holy. They do it when they have plenty of time, and in the comfort of a home, and in bed. Not on a hot night on a country road on the nylon seat covers of a pickup, with the windows rolled up on account of mosquitoes and them all sweaty and uncomfortable. That would be . . . uh, be screwing. People who are in love make love with each other. They don't screw each other."

Noland thought that speech sounded pretty good. Idealistic. Pure of motive. Perhaps the best thing about it was it got him out of a tight corner. Virginia sat back and looked at him. She was impressed, he thought, maybe flattered to hear such evidence of how purely he loved her. "I want you, Noland," she said without passion. "I guess I want you worse than I have ever wanted anything." She pulled her blouse down over her exposed breasts. "Snap me, please." She turned so he could fasten her brassiere. "Take me to the Sonic."

At the Sonic Drive-In, she drank a Coke and sat on the pickup seat with her back against the door and her feet in his lap. "Friday night," she announced, "my parents will go visit relatives in Oklahoma City. I'm not going." She gave her attention to the Coke, leaving a silence he thought she wanted him to fill somehow. The thought of her at home, alone, on Friday night made him quite jumpy.

"You can come over," she said. Noland remained silent. "The house is fully screened against mosquitoes, and there are a number of beds to choose from." Noland tried to figure out if she were angry or sarcastic or what.

Then he realized that she was simply in love, and that girls probably showed their love in ways different from guys. She needed him to make love to her as proof that he cared, as a consummation of the coming together of their souls, as a declaration that they would always be together.

And maybe as a test of some kind. The idea of their bodies loving because of the matching of souls appealed to him. The notion of a test got him to shaking inside. When he took her home that night, she said, "They leave at six in the evening. You be here no later than eight." And she kissed him in her peculiar, exciting way, with her tongue darting around in his mouth.

The next several days were a misery. Noland vacillated among elation at the coming event, guilt for wanting Friday to come, and fear that it would arrive before he had figured out how to behave.

He monitored the arrival of the mail each day, and each day felt disappointment wash over him when the book didn't arrive.

Friday, at four in the afternoon, the mailman stopped at Noland's home. Noland watched from the porch while the mailman dug through the tray beside him, picked up a couple of envelopes, and put them into the box at the edge of the street. Then the mail jeep started moving off, and Noland knew he was doomed to face Virginia with no useful information at all. He was about to go into the house in despair, when the jeep stopped and backed up. The mailman reached behind the tray and pulled out a package.

The one in plain brown paper Noland had been praying for. He took the package to his room, locked his door, and ripped the paper off the book. He went straight for the section on birth control and read with increasing discomfort. The rhythm method seemed too cumbersome since it required so much careful planning. Oddly, the book didn't mention the pill, but that didn't matter since he knew it was something only a doctor could give out, and that a girl had to take one each day no matter if she did anything or not. So it would have to be a rubber, after all—unless Virginia was on the pill. Fat chance of that, he thought, in Shamrock Texas. Not that she would, anyway, even if they handed them out at school like candy. Taking the pill would mean she planned to do things. Virginia wasn't that kind of girl.

It's a good thing, he told himself, he had planned for such a turn of events by driving over to Mobeetie to get a fresh Trojan from the Shell station—in case the one he had carried around for several months was old and rotten and maybe leaky.

He spent the next hour reading the section on foreplay,

memorizing the recommended moves. After that, he read the main section on the big act itself, and was disappointed to find it uninformative and general. Then he looked at the title page and the notes on the book's publication history.

"First published in 1919?" he said aloud. Shit. What did they know about sex back then? He had seen photographs of people of that era, old yellowing ones in a trunk that once belonged to his great-grandmother. All the guys wore three-piece suits and had on funny round glasses and the women were all big as stock tanks and had their bodies encased in formidable black dresses with high white collars. None of them ever smiled—no doubt because they had to go through life ignorant about most things, like sex. Victorians, Noland thought. That's what they were—and they all thought sex caused baldness and warts and hair to grow on the palms of your hands. No wonder there was no mention of the pill. Victorians didn't know anything about sex. It was a wonder, in his view, that they managed to have kids at all.

He shut the book and stuck it under his mattress. So his manual on how to do it was about a hundred years old. He showered again—his third for the afternoon—and with resignation began dressing for the evening.

He half expected Virginia to meet him at the door in some skimpy gown and to jump his bones as soon as he walked in, giving him the old tongue and breathing hot in his ear. They would fall on the floor and roll around, clinching in passion, ripping at each other's clothes, and do it right there in the living room, on the carpet in front of that wall with all the photographs of Virginia and her family looking down at them while Virginia clawed red streaks on his back with her nails in the height of her passion, and afterward she would cry and cling to him, telling him how beautiful it was and that she would love him forever. He would stroke her hair, holding her cheek to his chest, and know that it was more than bodies that merged with such wild abandon. It was souls.

Such a vision of the night's event cheered him up and made him a little more eager for what he was beginning to think of as a major life event. At least it would be for her, since she was no doubt a virgin, and loss of that mystical quality called *virginity* was always something that girls were supposed to get all weepy about. He would be losing his virginity, too, and it seemed like an event of major proportions. Maybe not like it would be to a girl, he thought, but major enough.

Virginia met him at the door wearing the same outfit she had worn to Shamrock High School that day. It surprised him to see how casual she seemed about it all—no special dress, and not even a shower, he realized with a start. But then she probably showered that morning, and girls don't sweat like men do. He was a little disappointed that she didn't jump on him in the living room, as he had imagined it. But then he remembered that the whole point was to have a bed.

They sat in the living room, in separate easy chairs with most of the room separating them, and talked about small things. How she planned to try out for the lead role in the school play again this year. And of course she would get the part. How he had spent Saturday welding a new hitch on the back of his father's pickup, then took a couple of hours to learn the guitar backup to a new song. New to him. She scowled at the mention of the guitar. He had on more than one occasion insisted she listen to some dumb song he wrote for her, sung, she felt sure, to the tune of a song the cowboys on his dad's ranch liked to sing to the cows.

She switched to talking about how she was applying for a scholarship at Wayland Baptist University, which got him off of the business about the guitar and the cowboy songs and to telling how he thought he might go to Amarillo College. Auto mechanics, maybe.

She told how her parents had left for the whole weekend, then looked at him with amusement in her eyes. "I'll have to do it, won't I?" She stood. "I don't mind. Come on, Noland." She led him out of the living room, down a hall, and into her bedroom.

How do we get out of our clothes? he wondered. Does she expect me to take hers off? Do I wait for her to help me with mine? He tried to remember how they got naked in the vision he had earlier when he thought they would maybe make love on the floor. But the memory was of a blur of activity with them somehow dressed one minute and nude the next. Then he tried to recall anything in *Sane Sex Life* that would be of help, but couldn't remember any instructions for undressing.

While he stood frozen in uncertainty, Virginia closed the blinds, shut the door, and began undressing. Just like that? he thought, watching her in both relief and disappointment. In his view, the removing of the clothes ought to get more attention, more ritual. For sure more than just sitting on the edge of the bed and pulling off his socks, the same as he did every night before going to sleep.

What about the light? She had left it on, but maybe that was just an oversight. Love was something mysterious, magical, like the night, he thought, and it needed darkness to emphasize the mystery. He turned off the wall switch.

"Hey," Virginia said, "no light? Then at least open the closet door and turn the closet light on so we will have some notion of where each other is." He did as she said and found the effect was most pleasing. She looked so soft and beautiful, lying on the bed, nude before him in the soft light. When she reached for him, he realized with a start that he was standing there like a fool, admiring her face and hair.

He joined her and got the foreplay over with according to the handbook, as best as he could remember it. Now what, he wondered. The rubber. Damn. It was still in his wallet, and that was in his pants on the floor beside the bed. He reached with one hand so she wouldn't know and groped around while she clung to him, her mouth like a leech on his, her tongue busy. She didn't seem to notice the missing hand, and he managed to snag the pants by one leg, drag them around until he found the right pocket, and pull out the wallet. Getting the Trojan out was a little more difficult, but he did after a couple of tries, and he even uttered a few little moaning sounds, like hers, so she would know he was involved.

Then there was the problem of getting the rubber on, which struck him as a worse problem than getting out of his clothes had been. When she began to urge him over on top, he figured it was time, so he said, "This will just take a minute," sat on the edge of the bed and began struggling with opening the packet.

"What will just take a minute?" Virginia sounded cross.

"The uh . . . whatchama callit. The rubber." He pulled out the rubber and held it up to the light so he could figure out what to do with it.

"Rubber? Whatever for? Oh, silly, you don't need that."

"I don't?" Then he remembered what he had read about the rhythm method. Yeah, that was it. Virginia was a careful girl—he had always known that about her. At that moment it made sense to him that she would not have planned the events of the evening unless her period had coincided with her parent's trip to Oklahoma. He tossed the rubber aside and got back to Virginia.

Everything went well until he discovered that fitting together for the big event wasn't as easy as he had thought. After several failures, he again sat on the edge of the bed. "Vaseline," he said, frowning, trying to remem-ber what the handbook said. "Or jelly-lubricant, that's what we need."

"Over there," she said, pointing at her chest of drawers, "Top drawer, on the left." He opened the drawer and felt around inside. "Left side," she said. "The left."

He found a small jar, removed the lid, scooped out a large portion of goo, and, in the semi-darkness of the room, applied enough so there would be no possibility of failure to fit next time.

In an instant, though, he knew something was wrong, bad wrong. What he put on stung like a wasp, and, too late, he got a whiff of what he had opened. "Just a minute," he said, and hurried out the door and across the hall into the bathroom. When he hit the light switch and looked at the jar, his fears were confirmed. *Vicks,* the jar's label said.

He tried washing it off, but the menthol seemed to have worked into the pores of his skin. Water turned burning into freezing, and his member shrunk smaller than he ever remembered seeing it. He heard a twitter and looked up.

Virginia stood in the doorway to the bathroom, nude, looking at the jar of Vicks on the vanity and at him holding the tiny dead thing. And she laughed.

Noland pushed past her, gathered his clothes, and retreated to the living room, where he dressed in record speed. He could hear her laughter, and it seemed to go on and on.

It was a week before he got the nerve to speak to her again. Of course he was still in love with her, even if he had thought some rather mean thoughts about her and the stupid way she laughed. But they were, after all, soulmates, so he called her. She seemed polite enough, but told him no, she thought it best if they did not go out together again. Ever. He was about to protest when she started laughing again, and that made it easier to accept the end of the romance.

Still, Noland thought about her, and he grieved the loss for years. Virginia got her scholarship to Wayland, and she was kicked out after less than two semesters. Too much wild partying, Noland heard whispered about Shamrock. With boys. Maybe tobacco was involved, and even alcohol. The next thing he heard about her was that she had fallen in love with some trucker and had moved in with him, that the trucker got her to enroll in a course in diesel mechanics at Texas State Technical College out on the old air force base in Amarillo.

Noland had not told Kent about the Vicks or about Virginia's laughter. "I never knew what happened to her and me," he said. "She went crazy and threw away all we had going. Later, she got kicked out of college for screwing around, then run off with a trucker to Kansas City, became a diesel mechanic, I heard tell. And her so pretty and all, so tiny and feminine. It just don't make sense her working on trucks, much less on truck drivers. She might have turned into some kind of whore, but there is a part of me that still loves her, same as always."

"They say first love cuts the deepest," Kent said.

"And it's the truth. I try to think of her like she died, which I suppose is kind of what happened, at least to the innocent little girl I knew and loved."

Noland sat in his room in the Mandarin and told himself that from an older, wiser perspective, he knew the real problem with Virginia. She was a Texas girl. Now you take Suppriah—she never had a chance to even consider the bad choices Virginia made. Oriental girls grew up ignorant of all the bad things Texas girls had laid out before them, every day. Maybe, he thought, girls in Shamrock took a little longer than big-city girls to get around to doing super dumb things, but get around to it they did.

It would be refreshing to see Suppriah. But, he reminded himself, I got to expect just a nicer than usual girl, not a soulmate, or I'll end up disappointed, like as not.

He looked at the phone and again considered calling Suppriah. But just talking to her on the phone sounded so unappealing. Noland went to the main entrance of the hotel and asked the doorman to flag down a cab.

When the driver stopped in front of a gigantic house, Noland said, "This couldn't be the right place."

"Is. Look at number on gate," the driver said.

Noland got out, looking with skepticism at the wrought-iron gate, the yard lush with banana trees, bougainvillea, hibiscus, and other flowering plants. "Wait for me," he told the driver.

An old man met him at the gate. "Yes?" the man asked.

"I am here to see Miss Suppriah Krishna."

"You have appointment?"

Noland shook his head.

"Tell me name, then. I tell the madam." Noland gave his name. The old man shuffled up the driveway to the front door and pounded on it. A pretty oriental face appeared at the door, looked at Noland, who still waited outside the locked gate. The face disappeared and the door closed.

I believe that girl looked scared of me, Noland observed. The old man pounded on the door again. This whole damn country is weird, Noland thought. The old man banged on the door several more times. When it opened, and Suppriah stood there, more beautiful even than the photo-graph Noland had.

She listened to the gate keeper, then leaned out to look at Noland, showing no signs of recognition. And it's not like she don't have a whole bunch of pictures of me, Noland thought, irritated.

The gate keeper let Noland in, and he went up to Suppriah, taking off his Stetson. "Howdy, Miss Krishna," he said.

Suppriah looked confused, glanced at the gate keeper, back at Noland, then said with hesitation, "Would you like to come in, Mr. Fritch?"

In the living room Noland knew for sure something was amiss. The marble floors, the carved banisters on the staircase, the paintings on the walls, the spacious, high-ceiling room, and the elegant furniture confirmed his earlier estimation: a rich person lived here. Suppriah's letters had hinted at a more Spartan life style. As they sat down, Suppriah said, "Mr. Fritch, there seems to be some sort of misunderstanding here."

"I sure enough think so."

"I explained to your friend, Mr. Kent Day, I believe his name was, that I had never heard of you."

"Kent! He called you?"

"Yes. He needed the name of a lawyer to help you with your difficulties with the local police. I gave him a name of a famous lawyer. But that was just a bit ago." She looked puzzled. "Mr. Che Mothar must be quite good to have managed your release so soon."

"And you never wrote me letters? Never read mine?"

"Letters, Mr. Fritch?"

"Here," Noland took out his billfold, removed the photograph of Suppriah and handed it to her. "I sent the mail to your address. It was in that ad in *The Dallas Morning News.*"

Suppriah looked at the photograph then back at Noland. Her brows went up as in surprise, and she looked around the room, fixing her attention on a door beside the stairs. Raising a single finger to her lips, she stood and walked to the door, taking care to make no noise.

So Suppriah was as odd as everybody else, Noland thought. The whole dang country ought to be on a leash.

Suppriah pulled the door open. The pretty young lady Noland had seen earlier jerked up and stepped back.

"So you listen at the door," Suppriah said. "Do come in and clarify your part in this mystery." Suppriah's voice had a phony sweet edge to it that Noland thought sounded mean. The girl came into the living room, her head down. "Mr. Fritch, I want to introduce you to Jenny. Jenny, look up, please, so Mr. Fritch can see you."

Jenny turned so Suppriah could not see her face and glanced at Noland, offering a tiny, mischievous smile before looking at her feet again. Noland stood up. "No need to stand, Mr. Fritch. Jenny is a domestic servant in my household."

"Howdy, Miss Jenny," Noland said. "What is your last name?"

"Please, Mr. Fritch, do sit down. Jenny is the only person who could have taken my photograph from the drawer in my room. She is the perpetrator of an unkind hoax, and she does not deserve your courtesy."

Jenny mumbled something. "I beg your pardon?" Noland said.

"Speak up, girl," Suppriah said.

Jenny lifted her chin and looked at Noland. "I said, my name is Virginia. Virginia Li."

Noland found that information stunning. He sat down. "Virginia?" he whispered.

"I won't stand for any more nonsense. Your name is Jenny L.E.M. Mr. Fritch, her name is most assuredly not Virginia Li. Jenny, how could you ever have done something so vicious to me and to Mr. Fritch?"

Virginia looked again at her feet.

"Answer me, girl."

Noland took a deep breath, let it out with a slow hiss. "Looks like this girl made some funny mistakes, but what's the harm? I got some right charming letters out of the deal and got to meet you and see your beautiful home."

"I'll not have a servant pilfering from my private bureau drawers."

"She just took a picture. And I gave it back. You keep it, and all's well. Virginia, you wrote some of the nicest, most amusing letters I ever seen, and I want to thank you for that." He stood up.

"Jenny is barely literate. It is not possible that she wrote letters of any kind. She has an accomplice in this matter, Mr. Fritch, but I shall get to the bottom of it." Suppriah seemed even more outraged watching Noland walked to Virginia and offered a handshake. "She is an amah, Mr. Fritch, please. Do not treat her as if she were a lady. She is a servant—a thieving and deceitful servant, unworthy of your American charm."

Jenny took his hand, meeting his eyes with hers, even daring to smile.

Noland leaned close to Virginia and whispered, "Mandarin Hotel. Room 402. Call me."

"What was that? What are you two whispering about?" Suppriah stood, angry.

"Just thanking her for the letters. They were, as I said, right amusing."

"You are a fool to be taken in by her, Mr. Fritch. She and whoever wrote those letters have some scheme to get your money. Perhaps mine, as well. Jenny and I have much to discuss. Please." She gestured toward the front door, then walked to it.

As soon as Suppriah turned her back, Noland winked at Virginia. She nodded and smiled, then looked down when Suppriah opened the door and turned to Noland. "Good afternoon, Mr. Fritch," Suppriah said.

It wasn't until he got into the taxi that Noland thought of asking Suppriah if she knew where to find Kent. No percentage in going back and asking now, though, not with her madder than a wet hen. "Where to go?" the driver asked.

"I'm Noland Fritch from Texas. What's your name?"

Startled, the cab driver said, "Hock Chew. From Port Klang. Where you want to go?"

"Mr. Hock Chew from Port Klang, about taking the two of us to a fancy restaurant?" Noland felt the need to celebrate but wasn't sure why, "where I can treat the two of us to a couple of big old thick steaks."

As the gate keeper locked Noland out, Suppriah turned to Virginia in quiet fury. "Why did you send my photograph to that crass American, Jenny?"

Virginia looked at Suppriah, noting how she stood, feet apart and arms akimbo. Her servant-bashing stance. Virginia was all too acquainted with that hostile body language, and she knew what would follow: interrogation in a low, almost sweet voice, asking leading questions designed to make Virginia not only confess her sins against a trusting master but feel the depth of her own folly and unworthiness to serve in such a home as Suppriah's. When the mistress of the manor had humbled her wayward servant, she would shake her head and make clucking sounds with her tongue, saying "Jenny, Jenny, I don't know what to do with you."

Which was a lie. By that time in the scolding, she knew the punishment to impose, and she always pronounced her sentence with a sad, benign look on her face. That look was a lie, too, Virginia knew. Suppriah enjoyed wielding her power, enjoyed seeing the servant cringe before her.

Virginia wasn't all that good at cringing, a fact that seemed to annoy Suppriah. To keep her job, Virginia had learned to look at her feet and keep her face blank. The gate keeper did the act far better, rounding his shoulders and wincing at key moments of accusation. He demonstrated the stance once when Suppriah and her husband had gone to Cameron High-lands for vacation. "You do it like this," he explained, speaking Malay. He stood before the mirror in the hall, groveling and wincing until Virginia's peals of laughter broke his composure.

"You do that with such sincerity," Virginia said.

"Yes, yes." The gate keeper laughed. "I practice before a mirror. I have worked for Lady Spider for five years, longer than anyone else."

Lady Spider, Virginia remembered. She looked at Suppriah: how appropriate. This time, Virginia knew she would have to endure the sickly-sweet insults longer than ever, and the punishment would be to lose her job.

That realization caused Virginia to lift her chin and fix a cold, hard look on her face. She moved her feet apart and put her hands on her hips in deliberate mockery of Suppriah.

"Will you answer my question, or will you just stand there looking like an arrogant fool?"

"I will confess to making a mistake in sending your picture. Had I known it would go to a man of such quality, I surely would have sent my own."

"And just what do you mean by that?" Suppriah looked alarmed, as if she found the situation slipping from her control but wasn't sure how. As Jenny L.E.M., Virginia had never spoken with obvious intelligence to Suppriah.

"Extrapolate whatever meaning suits you best." Virginia turned to leave.

"And just where do you think you are going" Suppriah's voice became shrill.

Virginia turned to her with a genuine smile. That quavering voice was something new from the Spider Lady. "Why Suppriah Krishna," Virginia said, mocking Suppriah's phony sweet, servant-bashing voice and being familiar with her name, "Whatever makes you think I would remain in this household after your display of bad manners and poor breeding before that American gentleman? I resign my job here, effective immediately." She turned toward the servant's quarters at the back of the house.

"You cannot quit." Suppriah's voice became more shrill and loud. "Not until I fire you."

Even as Virginia responded with laughter, Suppriah appeared to realize how silly she sounded. She retreated to her bedroom upstairs.

Virginia had little to pack. Her few items of clothing and cosmetics fit into a plastic shopping bag with room to spare. She put on her only good dress: a tailored black and white outfit that showed her legs to good advantage without being lewd about it, fit tight around her tiny waist, and hinted at more of a bosom that she actually possessed. She lifted the mattress on the bed, took out Noland's letters, and put them into her purse.

At the gate, she handed her house keys to the old gate keeper. "Give these to the Spider Lady," she said. He whimpered and winced, then smiled at Virginia's appreciative laughter.

Virginia found it a bit upsetting to be without a job, but only a bit. She had other resources. Meager ones, to be sure, but resources, nevertheless. There was Uncle Feng out on Crab Island.

He would take her in, allow her to sleep on a mat among his hoard of children in his tiny fisherman's house. Or there was the money she saved during the year she worked for the Spider Lady, enough to provide food and shelter until she could find another job.

Virginia was no stranger to work, nor to poverty, though the poverty had not come until recent years. Until her father died, she lived in comparative ease with her parents in a flat in Petaling Jaya, just outside Kuala Lumpur. Her father, Li Soon Hock, had worked as an instructor of computer science at Taylor's College during the day. In the evenings he did odd jobs for a number of wealthy men—painting, repairing houses, fixing leaky roofs, unstopping drains. In the early mornings, he delivered *The New Straits Times* on his motor scooter to fifty houses in Petaling Jaya.

Virginia knew little of her father. She knew he snored at night, that he loved pork and ate it almost every meal, that he invested in gold and jade jewelry, that he valued education and saw to it that Virginia got to go to the University of Malaya. He seemed concerned that Virginia chose to study literature at the university, but he supported her choice, telling her that she would have to go on for a PH.D. and be a university teacher herself.

During Virginia's third year of college, Li Soon Hock died of a heart attack while dragging a dead tree he had just cut down in the yard of one of his evening customers.

Her mother, Chen Weng, got a job keeping books for a small company specializing in insecticides, but her income amounted to little. They moved several times to smaller and cheaper flats, selling furniture and the jewelry Soon had bought. By the time Virginia finished the third year at the University of Malaya, she and her mother were broke and had nothing more to sell except for an old IBM Model C electric typewriter.

The typewriter was something Virginia wouldn't even consider selling. Her father had spent the equivalent of a small gold and jade ring for it, then he gave a week of late-night work sessions cleaning, adjusting, and preparing it for his daughter's use. Virginia wrote term papers and short stories on it. The papers earned her high grades; the stories got her some attention from the Kuala Lumpur literary set. One story appeared in an anthology of Malaysian fiction, and another won second place in *The New Straits Times* short story contest.

Even before the Mercedes truck ran over Chen Weng on the Federal Highway, it had become clear that Virginia would not be able to register for another semester at the University of Malaya. Getting a PH.D. was out of the question, and many people with B.A. degrees even in practical subjects such as business management and computer science found it necessary to take menial jobs just to survive.

Virginia mourned her mother's death, then set it behind her. She had to, for there was no money to live on, and she had to find employment. She worked as a fish monger, selling the horse mackerel and red snapper her uncle Feng and his older sons caught in the Straits of Malacca. But she hated handling fish for 12 hours each day.

One Sunday, Virginia overheard two affluent women in Sungei Wang shopping center discussing the difficulties of getting and keeping good domestic help. A good amah, they agreed, needed to be honest, bright enough to follow simple orders, and uneducated enough to be happy with her status as a servant. She needed to come with references from other employers, but amahs were such an ignorant, transient lot that they seldom bothered to get and keep letters, so hiring anyone was risky. When the women mentioned how much an amah made, Virginia decided to give it a try. The pay was slight, but it amounted to far more than she made selling fish.

She used the IBM Model C to write her own letters of reference, creating in them the personality of Jenny L.E.M., a simple, uneducated, impeccably honest drudge of a worker who toiled long and hard for the mistress of the household.

The letters and a newspaper ad got her a job, but she lost it a week later because her cooking skills were so poor. So she bought cook books and learned to cook well enough to keep her next job, which was in the household of Suppriah Krishna, the Spider Lady.

The job paid better than had her previous one, and she had the luxuries of a fan and a black-and-white television in her room. At first, Virginia puzzled over these items being provided, but she found out that they were not for her enjoyment so much as to provide the Spider Lady with means of punishment. When Suppriah became angry with her amah, she threatened to remove either the fan or the TV.

Within a month of moving into the Spider Lady's home, Virginia began looking for ways to get back at Suppriah for the periodic sessions of servant-bashing, as Virginia thought of them. Suppriah seemed to regard her fussing as necessary for proper training and maintenance of servants. Between sessions, she was polite enough to the gate keeper, the gardener, and to the amah. But when Suppriah entered one of her foul moods, she

119

made life miserable. The gate keeper told Virginia that her lot in life was to bear such insults as the Spider Lady decided to mete out. All Virginia had to do was look guilty, shuffle around, and wince during the scoldings.

Virginia thought otherwise. On her weekends off, she went to Uncle Feng's home and pounded out short stories on her typewriter, stories of wealthy, shallow women who abused their servants. One of Virginia's stories appeared in *Modern Malaysian Women*, a slick magazine published in Kuala Lumpur, and another came out in a literary journal that circulated among the literary groups associated with area universities. Virginia was certain that Suppriah read neither of the stories.

One evening Virginia sat in her room sweating because the Spider Lady, in a moment of anger, had removed her fan. Virginia found it difficult to contain her anger. She turned on the TV in an attempt to focus her attention on something other than her fury and the heat. On the last part of the evening news was a spot about how unscrupulous men in places like the United States and Germany exploited lovelorn women in the Philip-pines, Thailand, and Malaysia by contacting them through newspaper ads suggesting marriage, luring them out of the country, and forcing them to work in bordellos.

Then, while Virginia watched a popular American television series about depraved and wealthy people in Dallas, a way occurred to her that might cause the Spider Lady a moment or two of discomfort.

The next day Virginia contacted an advertising agency and paid for an ad in an American newspaper. "I don't care which one," she told the clerk, "so long as it is a large paper that gets circulated in Dallas."

When Noland Fritch's response to the ad arrived at the Krishna household, Virginia intercepted the letter. She steamed it open, found Noland's photograph and read his request for a photograph of Suppriah. Virginia took a photograph from the Spider Lady's bureau and sent it to Noland, along with a letter that presented the writer as charming, innocent, and vulnerable. The best-case scenario, in her mind, was for this macho cowboy to come to Kuala Lumpur and somehow spirit Krishna away, perhaps lock her in a whorehouse in Dallas.

Virginia knew something so dramatic would not happen. But it seemed possible to her that something embarrassing to Suppriah could come of her exchange with the Texan.

The next few letters from Noland, however, caused Virginia to realize her original intent with the ad would never work. Noland turned out to be a charming, if somewhat male chauvinist, interesting man and not the Texas whoremaster she had envisioned answering the ad. She enjoyed writing to him, and she used her letters as a way to express some aspects of herself she could not share with anyone in Malaysia. Noland's letters became important to her, and she watched the mail with such persistence that the gate keeper teased her about it.

Virginia greeted the news of Noland's coming to Malaysia with both depression and hope. His arrival would spell the end of their correspondence. But it might mean getting him aside somehow, explaining the origins of their correspondence, and perhaps keeping his friendship in spite of the earlier lies.

Salvaging the relationship with Noland seemed unlikely, though—or it did until he had taken her hand, leaned close, and whispered his invite-tion to call him.

On the bus heading toward the Klang Bus Station in downtown K.L., Virginia worried that, now, with his knowledge of her being a mere domestic servant, Noland would regard her as an object to be used, a sexual plaything, and not a person at all. What if he did that? She reread some of his letters and affirmed that Noland would do no such thing. Still, it was possible.

At the Mandarin, she took the elevator to the fourth floor. When she stepped out of the elevator, she saw two men trying to break into a room. Noland's room. A Malay man bent over the lock, and a larger man watched. The large one held a black box.

They jerked up and looked at her. The larger man, a dark Indian fellow with one eye swollen nearly shut, appeared sinister enough to her —but the short Malay man scared her more with his feral little hostile eyes. It was too late to back away; they could catch her before the elevator doors closed.

Virginia approached the men. "I suppose you hotel employees have to change locks every time a customer checks out without returning the key." She tried to make herself sound as simple and sincere as she could. "I'm looking for room 509. I have sort of a date with a man who said his room was 509. Could you point me in the right direction?"

The smaller man grunted something and the larger one put a hand on his arm, holding him in place. "One floor up," the big man said. "If man

121

not there, maybe you and me have a sort of date?" He grinned at her.

"Maybe next time. Thanks." She got back on the elevator and went to the lobby. On a house phone, she called Noland's room but got no answer. Relieved, she sat in the lounge area by the door to wait for Noland. Should she tell the hotel authorities about the men, she wondered. Might that get Noland in some sort of trouble? It seemed safest to wait, to tell only Noland about the two men.

A few minutes later, the large Indian with the swollen eye and the mean-looking Malay man came down the stairs. The smaller one went out the front door; the larger one came up to her chair. "Man not want date?" he asked, grinning and looking at her legs.

"Yes, he did." Virginia looked at her watch. "He will be down in a minute or two."

"Later, you and me?"

"Maybe later."

The man grinned at her, took one last look at her legs, and left.

Hock Chew drove Noland to The Coliseum, explaining it to be an old hotel once frequented by Somerset Maugham. Noland looked around at the stained walls of the hotel's restaurant, the cheap Formica café tables and unswept floor and decided the place held more promise than the coffee shop at the Mandarin. "Hock," he said, "except for the funny painting on the wall, this place might be a steak house on the town square back in Clarendon, Texas."

"Steak good here. Sizzling steak." Hock apparently found it strange to be invited to eat in the middle of the afternoon.

They ate steaks served on cast iron platters heated so much that the meat hissed for several minutes after being set in front of them. Noland thought the meal so good that, to the evident amazement of Hock and the waiter, he ordered another steak for himself.

After the meal, Hock took Noland back to the Mandarin. "You give Hock good steak," the driver said, "I take you to hotel. Free."

As Noland got out of the cab, he noticed Mehinder and Ibrahim across the street. Annoyed, Noland crossed Sultan Street and walked toward the two. Mehinder stepped back, tripping on Ibrahim. "You two guys are dumber than dog shit," Noland said. "If I find you out here next time I come out, I'll stuff you both into that sewer," he pointed at a hole by the sidewalk that might once have had an iron grate over it. Mehinder looked at the hole and took another step back. He seemed to believe the threat. Ibrahim might have believed it, too, but he stood his ground, glowering at Noland.

Giving them one last slow and insolent look, Noland walked to the entrance of his hotel.

8

Through primitive art—mainly wood carvings of animist deities—
Malaysian jungle people seek to control the uncontrollable in
their universe.

—Dr. L. LeMaster, "The Psychology of Primitive Art"

Kent decided it was time to get out of the sun. When he left the
lawyer's office, he had a taxi take him to Central Market. There he saw
Libby watching someone from behind a display of tee shirts. Not wanting
more contact with her right then, he left the mall, heading toward the
building across the river that looked as if it were made from white lace. On
the foot bridge, he stopped to draw the blind beggars.

One, a rotund fellow with a paunch, played a portable synthesizer,
a loud instrument that produced organ music, complete with drums and
heavy base notes. The other two, dark women with fixed, unseeing eyes,
slapped tambourines. All three sat on the cement walkway at the edge of
the river bridge; passers-by dropped coins into a can sitting on top of one
of the synthesizer speakers. Kent put some coins into the can, then
stepped aside and drew the musicians. A small crowd gathered around
him, watching his hand move a pen around. After that, Kent wandered up
the river to a mosque set where two muddy streams converged. He stood
on the cement walk beside the rivers and drew the mosque and the men
sitting in the shade of palm trees beside it.

When he became aware that his face stung from the sun, Kent
started back to the hotel. Beside Central Market, he saw Libby and a
peculiar-looking fellow getting into a taxi. The man with Libby looked
nervous and uncomfortable from the heat.

As Kent watched the cab move into the traffic he considered
Libby's invitation. Dinner at her place. That sounded good. "But Petaling
Jaya is so far out, and cabs charge more late at night," Libby had said. "It
might be better if you planned to stay the night." That part worried him.

Kent had looked at her to determine her meaning. She seemed to see the question in his eyes and added, "Please don't get me wrong. I have a couple of guest rooms, and you would stay in one of them. Friends among the Americans here do that sort of thing all the time because of the distances and the problems with transportation. Few of us have the nerve to get cars because of the wild way Malaysians drive and because they drive on the left side here."

When Kent hesitated, Libby noticed and offered him an out. Since this was his first day in the country, and since he was still suffering from jet lag, maybe he would like to call her later and let her know if he would come. She had written her address and phone number down for him.

In some ways, Kent found Libby as interesting a woman as he had met. He took out the two business cards she had given him. One identified her as a gemologist; the other as a *bomoh*, which she had explained was a Malay spiritual healer. "I'm having some printed that say *Libby LeMaster, Senseh*," she told him, "which is something like a Chinese version of a Bomoh, only a tiny bit more scientific, since the senseh deals with herbs. Old Me Sing Ng who concocted the poultice for my knee is a senseh."

"And you trust those herbs to cure your knee?" Kent found it bizarre that she would use a witch doctor's brew instead of something from a real drug store.

"I'm willing to give it a try. If the scratch gets inflamed, I'll put some first-aid cream on it."

Libby had explained that she had other business cards, but that he would have to wait until an appropriate time before she would give him any of them. Kent found her making and remaking identities as represented by the odd business cards an interesting if outrageous aspect of Libby's personality. She was different from Rita, far different. Still, the relationship with Rita was too fresh, too painful for him to rush into anything with another woman.

Kent stood in the Central Market parking lot, replacing Libby's cards in his wallet and looking around to get his bearings. To his right was the lace building and beside it the post office. To his left he saw the blue-tinted ceramic tower that he had identified earlier as a Hindu temple, and beyond it the much higher dirty building with a sign saying "Mandarin Hotel" on the top. He walked across the parking lot toward the hotel, trying not to look at faces lest he feel compelled to stop in the sun and draw.

In the lobby of the Mandarin, Kent saw Noland engrossed in a conversation with a pretty Chinese woman. It was a scene he wanted to do in pastels: the meeting of east and west in a juxtaposition of cowboy—complete with checkered red-and-white shirt, Stetson hat, jeans and boots—and oriental woman dressed in stark black and white, like a yin-yang symbol. At first glance, the two would look like a most unlikely pairing of cultures. But Kent thought if he could just capture the intense interest on the Chinese woman's face, the way she gave all of her energy to the man sitting beside her; and if he could get Noland's body language down—the tension in his back and neck as he turned to the woman beside him—the resulting piece of art would say much about the illusion of opposites, about the potential for bridging vast but artificial differences human beings construct among themselves.

Kent opened his pad to a clean page and began blocking out the scene before him. Part of the reconciliation of opposites he wanted to put into the art had to do with the sexual energy he sensed snapping and popping in the air around Noland and the woman. But only part. He had to integrate somehow the clothing, the contrasting racial features, the interesting combination of personalities. It seemed impossible, but the challenge gripped him, and Kent drew with speed and intensity.

When the Chinese woman noticed him and tapped Noland's arm, Kent sighed. He wanted just a few more minutes, seconds, even, before setting the drawing aside for later work in color. But he had enough down, he thought, to guide him when he found time to give energy to the work again. He shut the pad.

"Kent Day, as I live and breathe." Noland stood.

"Hello, Noland. I'm glad to see the misunderstanding at the airport finally got cleared up."

"Got sprung this morning. Did you have anything to do with that?"

"This morning? Maybe. Probably not, though I did commission a lawyer to get you out, a Mr. Che Mothar bin somebody-or-other. His name was given to me by . . ." Kent glanced at the woman beside Noland. "By your friend—the one whose phone number you gave me."

"Suppriah Krishna. The Spider Lady. By golly, it might turn out that she's good for something, after all."

"The Spider Lady?"

"Yeah, she," Noland turned to the woman beside him. "But I'm ruder than a hog with his front feet in the trough. Kent, this here is Virginia. Virginia Li. Virginia, this is my good buddy, Kent Day." While Kent and Virginia shook hands, Noland continued: "Virginia, she's been telling me about Suppriah, who never wrote a single letter to me at all, it turns out. Virginia wrote all of them."

Libby had the taxi drop her off first. She had enjoyed about as much of Miles as she could stand for one day and felt the need to get away from the sweating, nervous and compulsive man. Besides, she needed to get her house in order for Kent.

She knew he would be coming, and she told herself how pleased she was that he would be there because he found her an interesting person, not because he was looking for sexual activity. Most men that she knew would be there, their tongues hanging out because of her inadvertent suggestion of sexual contact in inviting him to stay the night. But that in itself would have been enough to keep Kent away—she recognized the alarm in his non- verbal request for clarification. Of course, she had not intended to imply the night held more than dinner, visiting, and sleep in separate rooms. Libby walked through the house, picking up note cards, books, and scraps of paper: the debris of the research scholar.

Perhaps, she considered, she did on some level mean to invite Kent into intimacy with her. Perhaps. But there was no conscious intent there. Sure, she found him attractive. Part of the attraction had to do with the way he drew her with clothes on in spite of the fact that she posed nude.

As soon as she had recovered from the shock of seeing the drawing, she began to wonder about his motives in drawing her thus. He thought her too vulnerable, standing there nude, so he instinctively offered protection. Clothing protects. It offers identity, Libby thought, and shields from prying into what we really are. It protects our sexuality. Kent's desire to protect was to Libby at once touching and irritating. It was a male response, and implicit in it she found a sense of superiority. Annoying. Implicit also was a desire to give, perhaps to nurture. Libby liked that idea. Perhaps he wanted to deny her any sexuality, to drape her in clothes as Muslim men in Saudi Arabia cloak their women to deny them any identity as sexual beings. Libby had looked at the drawing and rejected such a notion. The clothing he put on her body both covered and teased with promise. He definitely drew her as a sexual being.

When she had shifted her attention from the clothing to the face in the drawing, Libby was stunned to see what Kent had done. It was as if he had seen into the center of her being, for he had somehow put aside the facade of toughness Libby thought she presented to the world. Kent's drawing showed her as a soft and loving person, a person vulnerable to pain. She liked to think of herself as prickly on the outside, like a cactus plant, but soft and flexible on the inside, and the soft, vulnerable part of her was something she kept secret. Yet Kent looked beyond the prickly exterior, something she had never known a man to do. And his ability to do so pleased her.

Libby ran a damp mop over the living room floor, picking up bits of dust and lint from the marble. With a start she realized that she had not yet questioned her own role in posing nude for Kent. Had he ever asked for her to remove her clothes? No. Reflecting on their exchanges made it clear that she had assumed he had asked. So she brought her own constructs to the situation, her own needs. What were they? Her need to have an interesting man approve of her body?

That idea angered her. Libby snatched up a book from beside the couch and jammed it into the bookcase. Why should she care if a man—any man—approved or disapproved of her appearance? She glanced around the living room and decided it looked too bare of statements about her personality.

The only thing in sight, other than normal furniture, was the ugly little Garuda from Thailand. It sat almost out of sight in one corner, a hawk- man with wings spread and face fierce enough to do what it was designed to do: frighten off evil spirits, deflect bad luck from the area. She needed other objects set here and there in the room, artwork of the spirit, of the strange and mystical, the unusual, the bizarre.

Libby considered other motives that might have led her to undress without being asked. A need to express her contempt for normal social restrictions. She liked that one better, much better. A desire to expose who she really was.

Yes, she thought. Clothing has a way of disguising our real selves, and removing it could well be a symbol of removing masks. To remove the masks, though, implied trust, and what basis did she have to trust Kent when he first approached her in the coffee shop with his shy request? None. So she was trusting to the point of making herself vulnerable.

She wanted to be vulnerable, then. Vulnerable to a man. Libby found that a repulsive idea. But her very repulsion, like her anger over the notion that she might need the approval of a man, gave some weight to the observation.

Libby went into her office, opened the glass doors to the display case, and removed her temple bells from Nepal, both the cymbal bells tied on each end of a leather string and the normal-looking bell with a clapper suspended inside and handle made to represent a highly-stylized thunder-bolt. She also picked up the carved figure of a meditating Buddha, something she had bought from a street hawker in Bali.

On the way into the living room, she demanded honesty of herself. You need approval of a male, approval of your sexuality. You really did intend Kent to hear a sexual innuendo in your invitation, then withdrew it when you saw he would reject such a proposal. You do want to make yourself vulnerable to a man, to subject yourself to his judgment, to reveal your inner self, even if it means there might not be reciprocation.

She put the bells on the coffee table and the Buddha on top of the book case, stood back and surveyed the room again. It was better, but still not quite right. She went to her bedroom upstairs to get Bumbun, the carved wooden snake deity she had bought from a Bumbun tribesman of Orang Asli on Carry Island. Bumbun, her favorite piece of primitive art, had the body of a snake, the head of either a dog or a dragon, and a single arm that ended in a three-clawed paw. She put Bumbun on an end table in the living room. There. She nodded her approval, feeling the room reflected some of the tastes of Libby LeMaster. If I could only put my self-concept in order as easily, all would be well, she thought with a sigh.

Should I be so hard on myself, she asked. After all, she had ascribed mainly good motives to Kent. Why assume that her own reasons for moving with such unusual directness into a relationship with him to be devoid of either caution or admirable motives? She had, after all, looked at his aura and at his signature, and both told her Kent was a man to be trusted. A *person* to be trusted, she corrected.

Be honest, Libby, she admonished. A *man*. Had a woman approached her with the same request, she would have responded in a different way. Perhaps it would not even have occurred to her that a request for posing from a woman artist was a request for posing nude.

Why does being honest for me always lead me into accusations and feelings of guilt, she wondered, annoyed with herself.

Kent listened to the account of Virginia's seeing the two men breaking into Noland's room. "We need to report this," he said.

"It would be better not to," Noland said. "Police would come, and I have had it with local police."

"Then let's at least go check out your room. If anything is missing, then we discuss reporting the matter?"

Noland grunted, noncommittal. He, Virginia, and Kent went to the room. "Those idiots still think I have drugs somewhere." Noland looked at the way the intruders had scattered his clothes about. His guitar case lay empty and partly crushed on the floor.

Kent looked in the bathroom. "I don't think you want to see this, Noland," he said. The guitar lay in the shower where someone had stepped on it, cracking the body, then ran water into it. Kent watched Noland's face as he came into the bathroom and saw the guitar. About all the face showed was surprise and regret.

"I do wish those boys hadn't done that," Noland said.

"Noland," Virginia said, her voice strained. "Oh, Noland, I forgot about the black box. The big one with the swollen eye had it in his hand. I had forgotten."

Kent and Noland stepped into the bedroom again. Virginia stood in the center of the room, pointing into the closet.

On the top shelf sat a small box wrapped in black paper and taped with black electrician's tape. Noland reached for it.

"No, Noland," Virginia said.

"Wait," Kent warned. "If the intruders left that, it likely has something dangerous in it."

"Yeah." Noland stepped back to Virginia and put an arm around her.

"The condition of the room, the guitar, the black box—don't they put this matter in a different light?" Kent asked. "Shouldn't we at least inform the house detective here at the hotel?"

"Yeah. I just plain don't like cops, though." Noland began gathering his clothes and stuffing them into the suitcase. "Let them poke around with the busted guitar and the box. I'm taking my clothes. They might decide to lock them up for evidence, for all I know, maybe keep them for a couple of years."

"You ought not stay in this room, you know."

"Yeah. I'll get another."

"That might not help. Those men knew you were in this one. How about staying in my room?"

Noland stood up, picking up the suitcase. "Your room?" He glanced at Virginia.

Kent noted the glance at Virginia. He came to a sudden decision about Libby's invitation. "I won't be needing the room tonight. I have an engagement for dinner that includes accommodations for the night."

"Kent, my boy," Noland put a hand on his shoulder and grinned. "You are one helluva fast worker."

I'm a fast worker? Kent thought as they left the room.

Butch Gaston watched them come out of the room and stand before the elevator. That girl again, he said to himself. Mata Hari, he had named her when she came before.

Butch squinted out the peep hole. He had gone to a plumbing supply shop on Petaling Street and bought the putty that held a tiny sliver of mirrored glass at just the proper angle on the outside of his door so he could see down the hall when he looked through the spy. It seemed safer to watch that way than to run the risk of the drug dealers noticing his door open.

Butch had seen Anwar the Knife fumble with the lock on Cowboy Bob's door, with Killer Kaliayani standing just behind him holding a lethal- looking box. A bomb, maybe. Then Mata Hari stepped off the elevator and watched them. Butch couldn't hear what they said to each other, but it looked to him as if Mata Hari knew those men. They chatted and did some pointing and waving. In a way, he was glad not to know the exact exchange, for it gave him the opportunity to come up with an explanation himself, a dramatic one he could work into his script. A beautiful, deadly woman would spice up the plot.

He knew that some people in the audience might groan at the cliché of having an oriental lady named "Mata Hari" as a character, but he just might go with it, anyway. Hardly anyone knew that *mata* was the

131

Malay word for *eye* and *hari* meant *day*. *Mata Hari*, then, was the Malay word for the sun. He would work that background into the script somehow, so his villainess would be thought of as "The Eye of the Day." Butch wrote in his notebook, "Mata Hari is as pitiless and cruel as the tropical sun," knowing it to be a great line but unsure about just who would utter it on stage.

Just as the American drug dealers and Mata Hari got on the elevator, Butch realized that the cowboy had his suitcase with him. They were abandoning the room, and he was about to lose them.

Butch opened his door, pulled the blob of putty and the mirror from beside the peep hole, and went to the elevator to watch the numbers over the door.


Libby hung up the phone, aware that she was grinning in a satisfied, almost childish way. *Confirmio,* she thought, I was right. Kent will be here for dinner and for the night.

She looked at her watch and decided there was plenty of time to walk to night market. Not all of the stalls would be set up yet, but the fruit and vegetable vendors would be there, most of them.

In the kitchen, she checked the steamed rice. Done to perfection, she told herself with both pride and annoyance. So was the chicken curry. "The way to a man's heart is through his stomach," her mother used to tell her. Even as a child, she thought such an attitude cheap, for it made women into culinary whores. Libby realized she stood in a kitchen, barefooted, holding the lid to a pot containing a gourmet meal, thinking about the man who would enjoy the food. And she felt a surge of anger at Kent as well as at herself.

She could take the chicken curry and the done-to-perfection rice out to the trash. When the man arrived, she could say she wasn't up to cooking, that she hated to cook, that she would take him to Syed's restaurant. And she would pick up the tab. She could do that, all of that, and it would be fine with Kent.

Libby replaced the lid and turned off the flame under the pot. Having such a choice and knowing Kent would feel fine about eating out made it okay not to choose to trash the food. The flash of anger at Kent, she told herself, was misdirected. And, so long as she remained in charge, so long as she did not relinquish control of her actions to her mother's stupid aphorisms, she could choose to be domestic when she wanted, even be barefoot in the kitchen, if she chose.

What she chose to do right then was go to market for the makings of an exotic fruit salad.

Going to night market took Libby out of her neighborhood of luxury bungalows, past a long series of shop houses, through an area of vacant lots grown over with secondary-growth jungle, and to an open area that, during working hours, served as a parking lot for a factory that made batteries. Libby wandered among the stalls, picking up items here and there: two starfruit, a small hand of finger-length bananas, an orange, an apple, two ripe mangos, a small guava, grapes, and a pineapple. The vendors all knew her by sight, and they haggled over prices in order to practice their English with such a beautiful *hantu putih*, or white ghost, as some of them referred to her.

The vendor she bought the pineapple from did a great deal of rolling of his eyes, spreading his palms, and speaking about starving children that Mem was denying proper nourishment by beating his prices down so much. He also grinned most of the time so she would understand it was all an act. As he handed her the plastic bag with the pineapple in it, he leaned toward her and said, "Mem, did you see the one in black who follows you? Watches you?" He raised his brows and nodded toward the crowd behind Libby.

She turned in time to get a glimpse of a dark figure vanish behind some stalls. "Who is it?" She asked the fruit vendor. He shrugged and turned to another customer.

The walk home seemed longer to Libby, especially the stretch from the jungly area past the shop houses. Twice she stopped and looked behind her, and both times the figure in black slipped out of sight before she could get a good look. The first time the one following her simply stepped behind some bushes beside the road. The second time was a bit more unnerving. The shadowy black figure seemed much closer, just a few doors back on the row of shop houses. When she turned, Libby saw only a snatch of black as someone stepped into the entrance of a shop.

By the time she got home, her heart pounded and the straps on the plastic bags she carried bit into her fingers. She locked the iron grate over the front door and looked out. The door afforded a clear view of the street, clear enough to establish that no one had followed her into her own neighborhood.

She walked around the house, making sure all the doors were secure. Glancing at her watch, she found herself wishing the time for Kent's arrival would hurry.

Kent had carried his case of art supplies out to the taxi. If Libby proved to be as comfortable a person to be with as he hoped, then he would do some work at her place, perhaps that night, perhaps in the morning. The images crowding in his head cried for further work in some medium. Pencil, if nothing else. He preferred ink to pencil, pastels to ink. Best of all would be oils, but that would require nailing together a frame and stretching canvas across it. He could do that, though, if there were time to work in oil.

Libby seemed relieved to see him, as if she had counted on his coming so much that she feared great disappointment if he did not come. Kent carried his over-night bag and art supplies through the door, casting a wary eye on her. Perhaps he should have found another hotel room. He hesitated in the threshold, worrying about feeling trapped.

"Your room," she said, "is right in there. I sleep in the master bedroom, upstairs."

Reassured, Kent deposited his load in the room she indicated, a large room with a double bed, a vanity, a table with a computer on it, and a door opening to a bathroom. Far more luxurious and larger than the hotel room, Kent observed, thinking he ought to be back in the hotel and the lovers he left there ought to have all this space.

"The computer," Libby said, speaking from the living room, "is mainly a word processor for my writing. Use it, if you wish."

It wasn't until they were almost through dinner that Libby told Kent about the black figure stalking her. When she began the account, Kent was only half listening. He found the chicken curry so peppery that his forehead became damp, and he heaped more rice on his plate to cut the fire. For every other bite, he ate something crunchy and cold from the fruit salad, which was made from items new to him. The meal amounted to sensory overload: Kent went from feeling spices fill his mouth with yellow-green fire, steaming and burning all the way to his stomach, to feeling the cold balm of tropical fruit restore him enough for another assault by the curry. But even the fruit had an explosive, acid feel to it buried just under the facade of sugar and exotic flavor.

Kent found eating Libby's cooking an experience more than merely a meal, and he gave himself to the experience in much the same way he gave himself to painting. Libby's voice was out there, but on the periphery of his awareness, while he concentrated on the oxymoronic cacophony of fiery curry and sweet fruit animating his body like surges of current through a light bulb. He listened mainly to his body, pausing from time to time to recall what Libby had just said so he could make an appropriate social noise.

When he became aware that she was telling about something distressing, he put down his fork and looked at her. "This man followed you all the way home?"

"No. Not all the way. But enough to have me scared, really scared. I practically ran the last block. I was so relieved when you arrived. Then I got angry at myself for thinking of a man in terms of being a protector."

"But, of course, you weren't thinking of me as a protector any more than," he almost said than does a child when it goes to a parent with fear of the darkness. But that simile made him the parent and Libby the child. She would not see that as a comforting comparison. He cast about for a substitute simile. "Any more than I thought of Rita as a protector when I sought her during thunderstorms. Her presence helped me feel less alone, less vulnerable somehow, when the lightening claps split the air. She gave comfort, not protection from danger. Perhaps comfort is more important."

He speared a piece of mango with his fork and looked at the odd shade of yellow with an artist's curiosity about color, then noted that Libby had a slight yellow smear on the corners of her mouth from the fruit. Kent, caught up in puzzling through the mystery of the dark figure following Libby, was unaware of how he looked at that yellow stain and of how he let his eyes rove over the lines and shadows of Libby's face, returning again and again to the mouth. It was the habit of the artist as well as his need to understand the emotions at play on her face.

Then he realized that Libby watched his eyes, perhaps regarding the frankness of his attention to her mouth as sexual.

"You are charming, Kent Day."

Her intonation seemed to say that she needed to beware of charm. But he knew she had no reason to be cautious.

"Do you suppose," Kent asked, "that this evening's incident is related in some way to that block of ice that nearly hit us?"

Libby stared, surprised. She had always prided herself with her ability to read people, to anticipate their actions, at least in some general sort of way. That ability was what led her into becoming a psychologist. Of course, she sometimes misread people, or failed to look closely enough at the signs. She remembered misreading Al Lutz back in that San Francisco clinic when he presented her with his prosthetic foreskin. But his behavior was based on pathology, often a difficult thing to fathom. She had made the mistake of not heeding the potential for violence she saw in that fellow, Che, at Cole's party. Worse, she surprised herself with that quick slap to his cheek, as if she were a wronged virgin at a high school sock hop in a movie set in 1958 and Che the horny, insensitive jock who expected the slap as just and proper punishment for his wandering hands.

Her surprise focused on catching herself at being distrustful, not being wrong about where Kent was heading with his observations. The distrust had come as an automatic response, based on such situational evidence. Had she bothered to remember Kent's relief when she showed him they were to stay in separate rooms, Libby told herself, she might not have been so quick to assume he was up to something.

"I've considered the dropping of the ice and the black figure to be connected, somehow," Libby said. "Likely there is a link." Che. He would hardly think the slap appropriate—in fact had said so with his threat. Libby told Kent about the incident, describing Che only as a local man she met in passing at a social gathering. "I thought his threat pure male bluster, born of testosterone poisoning. You know, the macho male's fragile sense of himself based on some distorted vision of his own sexual identity."

Kent seemed to look at her with greater interest, as if the turn in the conversation from the mundane to something dramatic somehow made her more appealing. She liked the way his eyes took in her face, her lips, perhaps imagining drawing them, perhaps kissing them. She wondered if he would be able to feel the sting of the curry peppers that animated her lips at the moment, perhaps making them look more rosy. She fell silent under the searching intensity of his eyes, her lips parting slightly and her head tilting a tiny bit in surprise.

Kent Day is a romantic, Libby observed. This time, his look has to be sexual. She admitted to herself that his frank display sexual interest pleased her, and she wondered if he was about to suggest they adjourn to a bedroom. That possibility pleased her, too, even if she would have to refuse. For now. This is all a bit rapid, she told herself, knowing from hard experience that emotional flames that burned with sudden heat and light burned out just as suddenly, leaving her damaged and empty.

"This might sound a bid strange to you," Kent said, "coming from me now, seemingly out of nowhere, but right now, more than anything else in the world I want . . ." he faltered. Libby, certain now of his intent, wanted him to go ahead and verbalize his passion, even if she would be compelled to find a way to rebuff it without hurting his feelings. She smiled and nodded.

"I want to try drawing you, just as you are, sitting there across the table from me." He blushed.

Libby tried to contain her astonishment. "Please," she said, gesturing in a vague way, "get your art pad. I'll sit right here."

## 9

I'm just a young cowboy picking these strings,
a-wishing for a woman to adore,
a-hoping this mournful song of mine brings
some girl to love me once more.
—Noland Fritch, "Guitar Picking Blues"


Noland sat on the bed, dressed in only a towel. When he had emerged from the shower, Virginia turned her back. "I will bathe now," she said. Noland told himself that the evening had been perfect, that the moment of waiting on the bed with the towel wrapped around him while he imagined water running over Virginia's wonderful body was a delicious moment, a final tease after several hours of putting off being alone together.

Such moments of waiting held promise of the kind of perfection he had sought for so long. And yet absolute perfection seemed elusive, even while he listened to the sounds of Virginia completing her bath. The cracks in the plaster up high, near the ceiling, annoyed him, as did the water stains over the bathroom door. He noticed dust mice in the corners and long strings surfacing in the carpet because of wear. Not the ideal room for a blending of bodies and souls.

Earlier, as Kent had gathered his art supplies and clothes for an over-night stay somewhere, Noland envisioned Kent rushing into sex with some girl, a beautiful Malaysian girl like Suppriah, for example. A quick kiss at the door, tossing his art stuff and clothes bag on the nearest chair to free up his hands for easy touching of breasts, then zip zip into a bedroom for peeling off clothes and grappling, sweaty and hot in the humid Kuala Lumpur evening. Go for it Kent, Noland thought. Nothing wrong with a little screw now and then—so long as you understood it for what it really was. The best damn exercise available.

There were several women back in Amarillo Noland went to see with a fair degree of regularity, women who understood about exercise, who would have Noland horizontal within minutes of his walking in the door. Hell, they didn't even do much talking, he thought: the girls along Amarillo Boulevard didn't expect conversation. Just exercise and money.

That evening Noland knew he could expect more than exercise, and the contrast of his expectations with what Kent seemed about to do lifted Noland's spirits. Virginia just might be the one, he thought, she just might well be. Might be, hell. She is the one.

Kent had left his room in a hurry, promising to take care of the unpleasant business with the house detective. Virginia and Noland watched Kent leave, then turned to each other in silence, each stepping back to look at the other. Virginia seemed to fear Noland would try to take her right then, proving to be little more than another insensitive man. He could tell she needed time to get used to him, to learn about him if sex were to have any meaning.

"You know this city a bunch better than I do," Noland said. "How about let's go look around the pretty spots of Kuala Lumpur, then go out to dinner someplace fancy?"

She looked relieved and named the Sakura, a restaurant she said she had never gone into. But she heard it was elegant. Until dinner time, she offered, they could walk around the downtown area and look at interesting buildings.

From the walk along the Klang river, Virginia pointed out the railway station, a series of minarets and spires as beautiful as anything in the entire city, she said. "But don't ever go inside."

"Why not?" Noland leaned against the cement railing separating the sidewalk from the drop into the river. He stayed close enough to Virginia to feel the heat from her body, but didn't touch. Not yet. He knew it to be enough to feel her presence, to get whiffs of her delicate perfume, to look at her perfect complexion, her tight figure, her nice ankles.

"Inside is not so elegant. Trains park there, and travelers wait on benches."

"That beautiful building is ugly on the inside?"

Virginia hesitated. "Not so ugly. Functional. Perhaps noisy from the trains, and smelly from diesel exhaust, and hot. No one goes inside the station to admire the building. But everyone loves to look at it from the outside. It is the most famous building in all of Kuala Lumpur."

Beyond the railway station stood the National Mosque, also a beautiful building, but not so dramatic as the railway station. "And that is the post office," Virginia pointed with her thumb held straight on top of her fist, "and beside it the Bumi building."

Noland watched her hand. "Why do you point like that, with your thumb?"

"I don't, always. Many Malaysians think pointing thus," she extended her index finger, "means the same as this," she drew in her index finger and extended her middle finger. "What do you call doing this?"

Noland flushed. It didn't seem right for Virginia to be flipping the bone around like that.

"The British," she continued, not seeming to notice Noland's discomfort, "do it like this," she held up both her index and her middle fingers, stuck out her chin, slit her eyes, and gave her hand two quick jerks.

Her holding up those two fingers didn't strike Noland as particularly nasty until she shook them in front of that mean facial expression. He flinched.

"What do you call doing this in Texas?"

"Uh, the bird. Flipping the bird. Or shooting the finger."

"Malays," she said, shaking her index finger toward the National Mosque, "flip the bird like this. But Chinese are trilingual and can switch about as the occasion demands." She held up two fingers, then stood, her arm extended over the river railing, holding up her middle finger, aiming the gesture at the railway station.

Noland stared. Jesus Christ on a crutch, he said to himself, I wish Virginia wouldn't stand there and do that.

As they walked around the city, Noland enjoyed the long shadows and the relative coolness of evening air. She showed him the Federal Court building, and across from it the Tudor structure of the old Selangor Club set on a broad expanse of green lawn used for cricket. The club once was for exclusive use of the snooty British rulers, Virginia explained, but in recent years had become a playground for the snooty Malays who controlled the government.

It was clear that Virginia loved Kuala Lumpur. After her gaffe with shooting the finger in such a gross and public way, Virginia seemed to revert to the innocent, beautiful girl Noland found so achingly attractive.

Her Chinese features and British-flavored accent made her appear to Noland as exotic as the minarets on the railway building. Everything he looked at seemed fresh and bright.

"Never have I seen Kuala Lumpur so lovely," Virginia said.

Noland understood. He felt it too: the transforming of reality that comes from shared vision, from seeing while in a state of grace. Grace, for Noland, came not from any sort of religious system. It came, he told himself, from blending two people into one. Before sharing vision with Virginia, Kuala Lumpur for Noland amounted to little more than an odd-looking city full of weird people. But it had become a beautiful place. He had dreamed of escaping his utter aloneness in the world through merging with another for so many years that he kept marveling that the experience finally seemed upon him.

Noland tried to express some of what he felt, but words became blocky things, stubborn in their refusal to be shaped into coherent meaning. He stammered what he felt were some inadequate phrases about the way everything seemed so clear and clean, realizing even as he used those words that he sounded absurd. Hydrocarbons in the downtown air bit into his lungs and stung his eyes, and a distant cloud haze obscured the mountains northeast of the city, making them into gray lines.

Virginia looked at him, her face solemn, and pressed her hand on his arm. "I understand, Noland," she said as his voice trailed off, defeated by the impossibility of communicating something so complex. "I understand."

What she felt most was a vast relief that Noland in person seemed to be as charming as the persona she got glimpses of in his letters, that he appeared to be a man with whom she could talk about herself in ways that were important.

She was unwilling, though, to tell herself that she was in love with him, as he seemed to want. Charmed, maybe. She found him attractive in a number of ways, not the least being his little-boy manner of stumbling around when he tried to talk of his feelings. But not in love. It seemed to her that Noland wanted her to feel love or something like it, even if he had not said so.

"You do feel it, I can tell you do," Noland said with an intensity that Virginia found both charming and a little scary.

At the Sakura, Noland looked at the menu, recognizing many items, finding most quite beyond his experience. What the heck was *nasi goring*? Or, for that matter, what would a fried noodle look like? He felt so good about the evening with Virginia that he almost told her to order for them both, figuring that whatever she ordered would be something wonderful. He was about to make that suggestion when he saw an item in the seafood section: "fresh sole baked under fresh salamander." Then he saw something even more disquieting. "Hairy Fungus," the menu said, "with Spice Bones." Suppose Virginia ordered by naming one of those funny words like *nasi goring*, and it turned out to be salamander or gizzards or fungus or something even more disgusting? He had heard the Chinese were fond of eating seventeen-year-old duck eggs that looked like lumps of tar. Suppose she ordered something like that?

To play it safe, to keep from risking a jarring of the evening, he ordered a hamburger for himself. Virginia ordered some sort of noodle soup, but neither one of them ate much. For Noland, part of his lack of appetite came from having had such a late lunch with Hock Chew from Port Klang. Also, his stomach seemed to quiver inside him when he looked at Virginia.

She felt nervousness, but her unsettled feeling came more from conflicting emotions dominated by fear. This handsome foreigner clearly wanted much more than friendship. Virginia would have gladly settled for having him for a companion, even a lover, at least for a while. But she knew he wanted much more, and wanted it immediately. He would adore her, his gestures and intonation and facial expressions said. She admitted to herself that she had encouraged him in subtle ways the entire evening.

Virginia found the unspoken offer of being adored a heady prospect, but she feared the price Noland might extract from her. A man like that might be smothering.

The Spider Lady was smothering in a much less pleasant way. A relationship with Noland held promise of freedom from the likes of the Spider Lady, and from poverty. Virginia imagined a future with him that included travel and luxuries. And she feared for herself, feared that for such luxuries she might bind herself to a man who demanded she adore him in return. That could be a problem if he turned out to be insufferable in some way.

Virginia reviewed the complicated situation as she showered. He sat in there on the bed, waiting for much more than sexual activity. Could she perform up to his expectations? She wasn't worried about the sex. It was a phrase he had used during dinner that bothered her. Soulmates.

"All my life," Noland had said, "I've been lonely. For years I've looked for the person I could connect with. I had about given up on the idea of becoming soulmates with anyone."

There it was, then. He had not spoken of his offer to her, but she understood. He would adore her, take care of her, make her into a rich Texas lady, give her a world she never dreamed of possessing, and all she had to do was share the very essence of her being, allow another to enter with an intimacy that . . . . That what? she pushed herself not to back away from the scary place her thoughts seemed to lead. What was it? Fear of intimacy? Fear of being vulnerable? Fear of loss? Noland seemed to like the term *soulmates* a bit too much to suit her. She wished she had never used it in that ad for the Dallas paper.

With a heavy sigh, she turned the water off, her heart rate increasing as time ran out. An odd thought, she told herself. He's just a man in there, waiting for pleasure.

But as she dried, she admitted that what awaited in the other room was nothing so simple as that.

Kent drew with increasing speed and increasing frustration.
Libby watched. "Kent?"
He set the drawing on the table and threw the pencil down. "Sometimes, sometimes . . ." Kent let his voice trail off.
"Sometimes?"
"The moment leaves. A slight shift either in me, in the way I see my subject—or else a shift in the light, maybe. Emotions change, and what I wanted to find with my hand evaporates. I don't know. Sometimes I hate being an artist. Better to be a fisherman or a carpenter. Years ago, I would tear up the failed art, smear it, or feed it to the Dumpster or the fire place. Then I taught myself patience. Wait, wait and hope that somehow the magic vision would return. Sometimes it does, though always in a different form, and my eyes see the magic and my hand strives."
Kent held up his hand and turned it, looking at it. "This hand is smart and can do some astounding things with a pencil or ink or oil. But

143

it isn't smart enough, and what it does isn't enough, even when the magic is upon me and I feel excitement coursing through my entire body, and light and shade yield their secrets. Even when I sense success in seeing and understanding, the shadow of failure descends, and what I know is out there doesn't make it through this hand."

"You demand perfection of yourself?"

"Not perfection, exactly. At least I don't think of it as perfection. Completion. Years ago I thought the problem was lack of competent skill. That excuse is gone, now." Kent felt tear roll down his cheek.

"Your art often gives you pain?"

Kent wiped his cheek with a quick, impatient movement, looked at Libby and smiled. "You get me to talking about myself so cleverly that we do little talking about you. Who are you, Libby LeMaster, gemologist, bomoh and soon-to-be-senseh?"

"Would you like my card?" She stood up. "Join me in the living room and I'll get my business card for you. It tells my true identity. But you must agree to let me see some of who you are, too, Mr. Kent Day. You must let me see more of that art pad."

They sat on a rattan couch. Libby handed Kent a card that said "Libby LeMaster, Palmist and Spiritual Advisor."

"My spirit for sure needs advising. Here," he offered her his palm.

"At a quick glance, I would say that your life line has few breaks in it, your head line runs directly into the mound of Apollo, your heart line is a mess of zig-zaggedy crosses, your line of finance almost invisible, your mound of Venus," she took his hand and rubbed a finger over the area below his thumb, "healthy. Quite healthy."

"Yeah?" Kent looked at his palm. "That bad, is it?"

"A wonderful palm. Wonderful. Soft. Elongated. Plenty of interesting lines. Yours is an ancient soul, an artist's soul. Only two bracelets of life. But no matter. Do you have trouble making up your mind about matters of the heart?"

"Do you read my palm by asking questions?"

Libby laughed. "Partly. The lines give me a starting point." She turned his hand to examine the base of his little finger. "Two—perhaps three affairs of the heart. This one," she pointed to a crease beneath the finger, "has a break in it. A love affair that didn't work out. But it was important—look how deep and long the line is before it splits. Have you been married?"

"A long involvement, yes. Marriage? No." Kent thought about Rita. Beautiful, loving, supportive Rita. Cold, damaging Rita.

"Would you like to tell me about her?"

"She helped me with my art." Kent withdrew his hand and rubbed his palm on his pants.

Rita liked red. She wore a red beach robe when she first walked into the Hotel Galvez where Kent worked as artist-in-residence as the Singing Artist who wooed tourists with wit, charm, and an occasional song while drawing them in caricature. Kent watched her go to the bar with several hefty-looking women and order a drink. It seemed to Kent that she cultivated a kind of mean, hard look that some young Texas women affected— but on the lady in red, the facade wasn't quite convincing. Not to Kent.

He sat a short distance away by his easel and studied Rita by drawing her face in exaggerated form. But instead of exaggerating the false overlay of toughness, he emphasized the softness around her eyes, the warmth her occasional smile revealed. When one of the women she was with pointed out to the group that the Singing Artist appeared to be drawing one of them, they trooped over to Kent and looked at his work.

"Honey, I don't believe he quite has your number," one of the women said. They laughed a mean, critical laugh. Rita glanced around at her companions, and for a second, Kent saw her anger at the women.

"He might be dangerously close to the truth," Rita said, looking at Kent, releasing the mean, hard expression she seemed to hold in place for her friends. But only for a moment.

"Bullshit," one of the women said, and the others laughed again.

"Okay, buster," Rita said, clearly playing to her companions, "you got the face a little too goody two-shoes. Can you make up for the blunder by putting a real body under it?" She opened the red robe and dropped it to the floor, revealing a perfectly-sculptured body clad only in a red bikini. That act got her hoots, whistles and laughter from the women.

Kent drew with speed, putting a voluptuous body under the caricature of Rita's face. Working with pastels, he drew her with a red bikini that slipped here and there, revealing over-sized nipples and a patch of pubic hair. "Compliments of the house," he said when he handed her the drawing.

Kent could see his jab at her had hit home when she first looked at the completed drawing. She shot him a quick, wounded look that had nothing of anger in it. Then she forced a laugh, one that, Kent noted, did not involve her eyes. "Faces you can't do worth a shit," she pronounced. "But bodies you seem to know."

Kent told Libby about the laughter Rita got with that line, about how she contrived to usher the group out of the bar after he gave her the drawing, about how she paused in the doorway, looking back at him with that same wounded expression on her face. He told about the guilt he felt for misusing his talent in hurting the woman in red.

That night Rita knocked on the door to his room. She came in, still wearing the robe but not wearing the artificial hard look. Kent began with an apology, but she stopped him. "I'm the one who needs to apologize."

"What happened that evening," Kent told Libby, "exists as a kind of blur in my memory. Rita spoke with great intensity and feeling about everything. She loved so much of the world, and she seemed to see with the eyes of an artist. She wasn't an artist of any kind—but her attitudes seemed so similar to mine. Somehow we found ourselves lying on the floor, the lights turned their dimmest, and Vivaldi's *Four Seasons* playing on my stereo. I have little memory of how it happened, but we became lovers, Rita and I, there on the carpet in the dim light with the notes of 'Spring' flowing around us. I think she had nothing on under her red robe—but the next day, I couldn't remember for sure. She stayed the night, then the next and the next. Her personal items appeared in greater number in my suite until one day I realized that something significant had happened in my life. I had become half of a couple. It wasn't something I had planned on."

Rita began throwing her energy into making Kent's drawings known beyond the tourist set in Galveston. She had him draw political cartoons for her amusement, then, later, showed Kent copies of *The Texas Observer* and other such journals featuring the cartoons.

In just a few weeks, Kent began to notice that all was not right with their sexual relating. Rita had plenty of passion, and she loved what went on in their bedroom, or at least she did most of the time. The exceptions resulted in her pulling away in fright, then demanding the light be turned on before she could continue. Even then, there were times Kent felt she regarded their coupling as some sort of imposition.

Kent's response was to become impotent. He didn't tell Libby about that part, though. He acknowledged there were problems with their sexual relating, then went on to talk about Rita's influence on him as an artist.

More and more he turned to serious art, doing commercial items and political cartoons only upon demand. Rita tried to check this trend, subtly at first, then with open hostility. "Why paint like that?" she asked one evening as he worked in oils. "No one will buy it."

Astounded and more than a little hurt by her tone, Kent said, "Commercial art earns me a living. Real art allows me to be alive." But Rita did not understand.

She began to be absent from their suite, sometimes for several nights running. She would return without explanation, engage him in love making, draw away, and cry. One evening, after such a frustrating attempt to be close, Kent pushed for an explanation.

And he got more than he could have guessed. Rita covered herself with her red robe and sat on the bed beside Kent, her knees drawn up under her chin. "There is an old joke in the Big Thicket over in east Texas where I grew up, to the effect that a virgin in the Big Thicket is a girl who can out-run her brothers." Her eyes filled with tears. "You could add the word *uncles* to that joke, I guess. The truth is, Kent, I never was a very fast runner." She tried to say a few more words, but couldn't get them out. For the next few moments, she cried with an intensity that frightened Kent. When he put his hand on her shoulder, she twisted away, rolled off the bed, and sat on the floor, holding her hands up in front of her, looking at him with eyes full of fear.

Kent took a pillow and went to the living room for the night. He slept little. In the early morning hours, Rita came to him, embarrassed. He sat on the couch, holding her, stroking her hair. She told him how touched she was with his tenderness, that she knew his impotence had been a result of his body understanding that she hated to have a penis in her, even while she enjoyed the loving closeness.

"At first, Kent," Rita said, putting her cheek against his, "it was so good with you that I thought my problems with men were over. But they came back in the darkness, and I got scared again, and I went back to . . . to . . . ." She sobbed, and he could feel her fear.

"I won't hurt you, Rita."

"No. I understand that." She forced herself to quit crying, drew back and looked at him. "It's just that I have to tell you, and I'm afraid of what you will do." Kent looked puzzled but said nothing. He waited.

"Women don't frighten me."

Kent remembered the scene in painful detail, remembered telling Rita that he would try to be understanding of her need to get away from him from time to time, that he would try not to question where she had gone, that he would try to accept her back as if she had gone to visit relatives. But he could promise nothing beyond trying. He remembered wondering if he would find it more difficult or less so if Rita had insisted on going away to lie with another man instead of with a woman. Or maybe it was *women*, several women that she needed to share her body with—he wondered about that, but he wasn't about to ask for details. Would it be more difficult to feel in competition with a man rather than with a woman?

Kent had no answer. He remembered how her absences threw him into depression and pain. He remembered, but he did not tell Libby. To her he said:

"Rita would have damaged me as an artist. She began to disparage anything I painted or drew that couldn't be readily turned into cash. I had to get away from her, but when I brought up the subject of our parting, she would cry and cling to me, and always my nerve failed."

Kent did not tell Rita that he had a chance to become one of the cultural exchange artists in the Selangor-Texas twining of Malaysian and US states. He took care of all plans for departing the country without her knowing, and when the time came to leave, he took only a few possessions —his clothing and art supplies—and left one evening when she was gone to visit her "relatives." He wrote her a note saying he would be in some tropical country for a year, that he would not return to Galveston, ever, and that he valued the memories of their better times together. Then he caught a bus to Houston, where he stayed in a motel until time for his flight to leave for Malaysia a few days later.

"All that pain," Libby said, "and it's all so recent. You're still in a state of mourning the lost relationship."

"Maybe. More than anything, though, I feel numb when I think about Rita."

"Numb and cautious. Understandably so."

Kent looked at her. Was it that obvious? He shrugged. "You're an excellent palmist. You make a few impressive remarks about the lines on my hand, ask a couple of leading questions, and I lay open part of my soul for you." He looked at his palm. "I see what you mean by the lines just being a starting point. Impressive. Especially when we came in here for you to tell me something about you, for a change."

"I'm better at listening than at talking about myself."

"So I've noticed. Perhaps you can tell me about you, now?"

"Another business card?" she offered.

"One with the truth on it?"

"All of them are truthful. What would you like to ask me about gems? Or about Malay spiritual healing? Or about palmistry?"

Kent laughed. "Okay, okay. Slip me another bit of the truth with another card. Getting to know you, Libby, is like studying stray bits of tile that ultimately make a mosaic."

"When you get me assembled, let me know. I would much like to take a look at the entirety, myself. Here," she picked up her purse from beside the couch, dug out two more cards, and handed one to Kent."

"*Libby LeMaster*," Kent read, "*purchasing agent for Master and Master Antiques, Oklahoma City.* Your company?"

"The first Master on the card refers to my father, the second to my older brother. And, yes, I added *Le* to my name myself. I got the idea from Daniel Defoe, who was born just plain old Daniel Foe. Any questions?"

Amused, Kent said, "Just one. May I look at the other card in your hand?"

"The ceramic chips—do they make a pattern yet?" She handed him the card.

"Vaguely. *Dr. Libby LeMaster, Lecturer in Psychology, Ringling University at Malaysia.* Is this one on the level?"

"Kent Day."

"Okay, okay." He whistled. "No wonder you know how to get me to talking about myself. A psychologist."

"B.A. in English literature, University of Oklahoma, MA in psychology, North Texas State, PH.D. in psychology, The University of California at Santa Cruz. Internship in counseling, Rozendall Clinic, San Francisco. Research specialty: the paranormal. First job after completing training: teaching in Malaysia for a university whose home campus in

Oklahoma I have never seen. Two books, six articles."

"An impressive resume, Dr. LeMaster."

"There. That's part of the reason I carry around business cards. People adjust how they relate with me according to what symbols they see on the cards, and that one," she thrust her finger at the card Kent held, "gets people to call me *doctor*. The title sets up barriers."

"Libby, then."

"Yes. Libby. And you, Kent, promised me a peek into your art pad in exchange for information about me."

"But a résumé tells so little," Kent protested.

"Then dig it out. Fairly. I'm not totally adverse to talking about myself. May I?" She reached for the art pad on the coffee table.

"You also carry around the cards as a way to experiment with identity. Much like your addition to the name you were given at birth."

"An astute observation. And true. Oh, Kent, this drawing of the food hawker is superb." She flipped forward and back through the pages, studying some pieces with great attention, glancing at others. On one page she stopped, startled. "Butch," she said. "Butch Gaston. Where did you meet him?"

Kent looked at the drawing. "He sat right across from me in the Sun Wah. He was there when you walked in."

"Really? His back to me, maybe? Kent, it would be most unlike for this man to see me and not speak."

"Remember the Chinaman with the robe and pointy hat?"

Libby frowned in thought. "Yeah—I think I remember him. But that wasn't Butch."

"Maybe not. But under the false shadows from makeup, that," Kent tapped the drawing, "is what I saw. Mainly. And you say he is a friend of yours?"

"I most definitely did not say that."

"His disguise was excellent. I knew something had to be wrong somewhere, but it took me a while to see what it was and to find the real face under that makeup. Libby, do you suppose this Butch fellow had anything to do with the ice falling? Or with the man in black following you tonight?"

"Hardly. Well—he could be the man in black, I guess. But Butch isn't capable of anything violent."

150

Libby sketched in some background on Butch: his questionable academic credentials from some seeming mail-order graduate school, his teaching drama for Ringling in Oklahoma, then coming to Malaysia to teach speech; his love of theater; his bragging about having written several plays that were staged in some drip-water college in Illinois or Iowa or one of those other square-looking states in the center of the US map. "He's almost the classical nerd," she said. "Butch loves to tell you trivial things, such as the fact that he finds the pepper steak at Jothy's better than anywhere else—which is okay, I suppose. But he tells about it at such great length, then the next time he sees you, he will repeat the observations. Butch is a bore, more than anything else."

And a bit on the dense side, Libby said. "At a recent faculty dinner party, I had the misfortune of being seated across the table from him. He made one inane observation after another."

She had let most of them pass. But when he commented that he thought women in southeast Asia were better off and happier than women in the United States, she felt compelled to comment. "Women in Malaysia," she said, "are routinely denied positions of importance in both business and industry. The Muslim men dress their women in sacks, and many have to wear that odd head gear that covers everything but their face."

"Those women get up in the morning and put on the sacks, as you call them," Butch pointed out. "Nobody forces them to dress like that. And those same women are the very ones who seem so happy, so free of problems that torment American women."

"The pressure is indirect, Butch, even if the women submit. In a place where circumcision of female infants is still practiced openly by a few people and no one in the society makes a public issue of the mutilation, I would say women have severe problems."

"As I understand it," Butch said, "circumcision for women doesn't hurt any more than it does for men. Besides, it's a non- issue, as far as I can see. In the first place, the idea of female orgasm is an invention of women's liberation advocates. At least in my experience the idea is a myth."

At that point, Libby had given up the discussion. "How could you hold an intelligent conversation with a person like that?" she asked Kent.

"Astounding," Kent said. "Simply astounding. Not only that, but I don't believe if I were Butch, that I would have told something like that on myself."

"I thought of that. And, you know, he had the temerity to ask me for a date? No kidding. That same evening."

"Maybe he was angered by your refusal? I mean enough to . . ."

"To arrange for fifty pounds of ice to fall on my head, you mean. Hardly. He's such a wimp."

"How about to scare the daylights out of you by following you in a spooky black costume?"

Libby considered the suggestion. "Maybe. I'll confront him with it and watch his responses. If he pulled such a trick on me, he'll be sorry."

## 10

Passion fruit, mango, and durian beg
that art and nature be matches;
the artist must create a cloisonne egg
and brood with bright wings till it hatches.
— Coleman Farquart, *An Asian Mystery*


Coleman examined his collection of medals, pleased because each amounted to a declaration of his eccentricity, of his genius. From time to time, Cole worried that he might not be a creative genius at all but a genuine eccentric striving to be an artist. But most of the time he knew better: it took the creative imagination of a true artist to present such a bizarre facade to the world. The facade, then was a work of art, a creation, an edifice. The reality—the ultimate reality—had to be the creative spirit behind the medals and other outrageous behavior.

He selected two medals that Miles seemed to hate above all others and penned them to his shirt. Miles proved useful as a gauge of how effective the medals were. If Miles hated them, Cole could be assured that the medals would draw plenty of attention—and never mind that the attention might be critical. Many people had examined Salvador Dali's paintings just to see what kind of art such a nut would produce, and some gave it serious critical attention as a way to criticize the man. Thus, Cole figured, Dali became famous enough to change the world of art. I'll do the same as a poet, Cole affirmed, but more. Much more.

In the living room, Cole found Miles scowling at the bound volume of poetry on the coffee table. Poor Miles is so transparent, Cole thought. "From the look on your face," he said, "I can see that you have been enjoying my latest poems." Miles looked pained, but he grunted an amiable sound and nodded. Cole said, "We must discuss them, sometime. But for now, have you given any more thought to going to Genting Highlands with the Batu Blue retreat?"

"It would be a good trip."

"Am I to take it, then," Cole asked, surprised with his easy victory, "that you will go?"

"Yes."

"Excellent. Excellent. Miles, you have the spirit of the true artist. I know that you hold yourself out to the world as a teacher and a technical writer, perhaps, but under that facade, you are as true an artist as anyone I know."

Miles jerked and stared. By golly, Cole thought, I hit on something. Cole had always figured that Miles thought his graffiti was good only for useful harassment of enemies. Of course, Cole knew better: Miles was a true artist, functional and dedicated. No one that Cole knew understood graffiti as art, especially the graffiti writers themselves. Can it be that he sees himself as artist? Cole wondered. "I must urge others to go. Libby. She is an artist of reading people. Butch needs to be there, too, since he's a playwright, and a good one, from what I have heard. And Roseta, that lovely Malay woman—she is an artist if I ever saw one. She certainly needs to be there." Cole watched Miles, enjoying his consternation over being told that he was an artist. He positively fidgeted like a boy caught with his hand in a cookie jar, Cole thought, amused. Maybe I ought to tell him right now about Batu Blue. And about my knowing he likes to write graffiti.

But that would ruin the timing of the retreat, maybe cause Miles to withdraw and refuse to join the group effort. Cole enjoyed making Miles squirm a bit, but it wasn't such a good idea to hit him with too much at once, given the timing. Cole understood that Miles valued his anonymous status—as a good graffiti artist should.

When Coleman had gone back to the Ringling main campus to report to the president on the status of the cooperative project in Malaysia, he had found the opportunity to see Miles in action as a socially-dedicated artist. The tidy little bits of verse and prose that appeared here and there on campus, usually typed and always laminated in plastic, amounted to the most effective satirical attacks that Cole had ever witnessed.

President Vernon Hackler, new to Oklahoma and new to being a university president, seemed determined to make his mark on Ringling. He wanted new buildings sporting bronze plates that said, "Built During the Administration of President Vernon Hackler." The bad news for him was the university needed no new buildings. Hackler suggested tearing down several of the older ones but perceived that the Board of Directors would balk at the idea.

Then he found the Building Renovation Fund, a little-used pool of money that had grown to a staggering amount over the decades from private donations being put there by a provost who often did not know what to do with gifts from wealthy alumni. None of the buildings needed much renovation, but that did not stop Hackler. He decided to shift the focus of the university to make it, as he stated publicly, a more "student-oriented campus." He hired a consulting firm from Muleshoe, Texas, to do an in-depth study of the university's long-term needs, paid the firm too much, and it concluded what President Hackler directed it to find. The library needed to be closer to the center of the campus, the gym needed to be farther away to encourage students to get exercise by walking to it, and the ROTC building needed to have closer academic ties to the university so its image would improve.

Hackler appointed a committee of professors who made recommendations based on the findings of the consulting firm, recommendations Cole was certain Hackler directed and rewrote. To the astonishment of the academic community, the university president published his Grand Plan calling for moving the gym into the building that had for sixty years housed the library, moving the library into the basement of the ROTC building, and converting the current gym into the Vernon Hackler Museum of Oklahoma Sports.

The faculty had stood by in stunned silence while Hackler stirred the campus around. Even the students said little when they found it necessary to stoop in the narrow corridors of the new library stacks in the basement of the ROTC building, and those who did object were directed to the new library director, Colonel Stringlie, the campus ROTC commander, a one-time public relations officer who got his training in the American press conference rooms in Viet Nam. Cole knew that Hackler made the Colonel head librarian because he was so good at using charts, graphs, and statistical data to illustrate the superiority of the new library.

Some few faculty objected to rearranging the campus and making a man with a degree in military science the library director, but they were younger, inexperienced people without tenure, and Hackler fired them out-of-hand. No effective voice of protest arose until an anonymous graffiti artist became angry about the university president's usurping what Miles regarded as the best swimming hole on Lake Texhoma.

When Vernon Hackler built himself a cozy new office off campus, the graffiti artist pointed out the absurdity of spending university money for such frivolities by mounting a campaign that sent the president on a witch hunt, an angry purge of faculty and staff he thought might be responsible for the graffiti.

The new presidential office was located on university property at the edge of Lake Texhoma, a spot that for years had been reserved for student and faculty use. "Highhanded Hackler hoards the swimming hole," read one piece of graffiti that appeared in most of the restrooms on campus. A week later, another appeared. Cole tried to remember the wording: "Putting President Hackler's office on the university swimming hole is tantamount to dumping shit into Lake Texhoma." Or something like that. Cole remembered the effects: the thin-skinned Hackler became livid with anger over the criticism of his choice of office space.

He assigned an army of maintenance men to clean up the offending notes—something that proved difficult since the artist had put them on the walls of the restrooms with some sort of super glue that required the maintenance men to chip the notices off with chisels, often damaging the walls. And President Hackler recruited an assortment of toadies to watch the restrooms day and night.

Not that such vigilance did much good. The artist simply put his notices up elsewhere. His next choice was the glass doors of most of the buildings on campus.

Cole found him sticking up some graffiti late one night. Catching sight of Miles in the act of publishing his art was a serendipitous bit of good luck, as Cole saw it. He happened to be working late on composing a poem set in the campus chapel when the artist came sneaking out of the bushes.

Cole's idea for the poem was to draw upon religious imagery and imagery of darkness at the same time, so he had gone to the Chapel late at night, let himself in through the side door, and sat on one of the pews in the darkened building to let the atmosphere of the place soak in.

A fine bit of motion in the moonlit bushes just beyond the window caught Cole's attention, and he moved to the window to see what it was. A shadowy figure crouched under an arborvitae bush, stirring something in a jar on the ground. Cole watched until he had the good fortune of seeing the artist move for a moment into a shaft of moonlight.

Miles Osborn.

What an unlikely person to become dedicated to a social cause, Cole thought; what an unlikely person to be an artist of any kind.

Miles smeared something on a card in his hand, then slunk around to the front of the Chapel to scratch and tap on the door. As soon as Miles had gone, Cole opened the door to see what art Miles had left there. It was a wonderful piece of graffiti glued to the small glass pane in the center of the door, attached with something that smelled like plastic:

Hackler's Grand Plan is truly absurd;
Flush away, flush away Hackler the turd.

The local paper ran an article on the graffiti, but would not print it "because," said the article "of its obscene turn of phrase." Obscene or not, students and faculty alike enjoyed repeating it and laughing.

Miles' graffiti so angered Hackler that he committed what the academic community thought of as the ultimate absurdity of bringing legal action against "the John Doe or John Does" responsible for the graffiti.

The lawsuit had to be left pending because no one knew the identity of the accused—no one but Cole, and he wasn't about to tell. Hackler claimed publicly that his purpose in initiating the law suit was to vindicate himself in an open court, but most saw his real purpose as being to intimidate the graffiti artist—and hence all opposition—into silence.

It disturbed Cole some that Miles did not address the real issues on campus: the gutting of the library building to make it into a gym and cramming the library's holdings into the basement of the ROTC building. But then, Cole concluded, many artists don't realize their own power, and often they are myopic about social issues. They needed training to focus their energies.

Miles' next bit of graffiti appeared on the hall walls of several buildings, including the hall just outside Hackler's office. "This is clearly an inside job," Hackler declared at a press conference. "The slanderer has to be someone who has free access to university buildings, someone who would not be suspected of committing such criminal acts. He or she is a coward and a vandal who walks along, maybe in a crowd, seeming only to brush against the walls, but leaving vile items stuck here and there, items that cause permanent damage to the wall surface. The university has commissioned a private investigating firm to locate the vandal or vandals, and hundreds of volunteers from the faculty, staff, and student body have agreed to keep an around-the-clock vigil on campus. When we catch the guilty parties, they will face criminal as well as civil court action. And I can guarantee that, if the vandals continue, we will catch them."

President Hackler fired two young English professors because they had published poetry in various literary magazines and hence were potentially the graffiti artist. Others he suspected, the tenured professors whom he could not fire without facing court action from them, Hackler reassigned to the new Ringling campus in Malaysia. But the notices kept appearing.

The kind of passive-aggressive bravery Miles illustrated through his actions had astounded and pleased Coleman. He began working to get Miles involved in the Malaysian branch of the university—just as he had recruited several other artists.

Even as he prepared to leave for Malaysia, Miles continued to affirm himself as a dedicated artist: he wrote a bumper sticker and attached it to President Hackler's Mercedes. "Follow me to Ringling's sewer hole at Lake Texhoma," the bumper sticker said. It remained on the car for two days, much to the amusement of the academic community. The presidential toadies were too fearful of pointing it out to Hackler because he had on several occasions punished bearers of bad news. Hackler found out about it when a photograph of the back of his car appeared in the town's weekly newspaper. That week, three university employees whom Hackler suspected of being capable of perpetrating such atrocities were fired: a non-tenured professor of government, the secretary of one of the deans, and a janitor.

Hackler did not bother explaining the firings, but the faculty senate, made braver by the successes of the graffiti artist, demanded an explanation of the termination of the professor. Hackler declared he and the professor had developed certain "philosophical differences," then refused to discuss the matter further because "such exchanges are not productive." Angered, the faculty senate prepared a university-wide vote of no confidence to show the governing board of the university the general displeasure with Hackler.

Cole knew that by the time he engineered Miles' transfer to Petaling Jaya to teach on the Malaysian campus, the presence of Miles as artist was no longer needed on the main campus, for the graffiti had set in motion events that would result in the firing of an academic dictator. Cole had been so impressed with the power of Miles' art that he saw to it he and Miles were designated to be roommates. That way, Cole could better train Miles to use his art for serious purposes.

"How many members of the Batu Blue group will be going to Genting Highlands?" Miles asked.

"All of them, I hope. Of course," Cole lowered his voice, frowned, and leaned toward Miles, "many will forget, and we have to call them to make sure they'll go." He hoped Miles would catch the hint. Miles remained silent. Cole tried being direct: "Will you help me with the phoning?"

"How long will the group be there, anyway?" The annoyance in Miles' voice was clear.

Cole sat back and sighed. Better not push, not yet, he thought. "I have reserved hotel rooms for the entire weekend." He pulled a list of members out of his pocket. "I probably ought to be the one who makes the calls, though."

Kent directed the taxi to the Mandarin, dreading having to deal with the house detectives and perhaps the police, but certain it would be better for him to do it than leave the task to Noland. Noland seemed so unpredictable—one minute he would be the essence of Texas gentility, the next he might talk about how he trained to do effective barroom brawling. He's just a big, over-grown kid, Kent thought, a romantic who might even read Danielle Steele novels in secret and goes more than once to every Rambo movie that comes out.

Kent had started to tell Libby about Noland and Virginia, but decided not to since her life seemed complicated enough as it was. Kent sat in the taxi, watching the slow crawl of morning traffic on the Federal Highway between Petaling Jaya and Kuala Lumpur, and wondered about the real reasons for not telling Libby about Noland. Perhaps he was fearful that Libby would not like the big cowboy. But why should that matter? Kent liked him, even if there were sides to Noland that could be unsavory. Maybe, Kent thought, I'm afraid she will condemn me because she disliked the company I keep. Kent shrugged, deciding the impulse not to mention Noland was silly. He opened his sketch pad and drew Libby's face from memory.

When he arrived at the hotel, Kent looked at his watch, deciding it was a little early to wake up the love birds. Libby would not be meeting him for another hour, so there was no rush about gathering clothing to take to the mountain resort for the weekend. I'll let them sleep, Kent decided, while I take care of the business with the intruders in Noland's room.

Noland lay in bed, reviewing the events of the previous evening and night. Virginia slept beside him, her head on his arm. She snored, and her face sagged in a strange way that make her look moronic. Still, Noland concluded, she had real beauty, even if her mouth was open and a line of saliva strung from her lips onto his arm. The moisture hanging from Virginia's mouth reminded Noland of calf slobbers, and her sleeping face even seemed to have the same bovine, vacant quality a calf had when it looked up from its business of nosing around in the grass. Anyway, Noland affirmed, she would have real beauty when she awoke and arranged her face in a normal way.

He remembered other, similar mornings, ones that seemed grotesque parodies of the current one. It wasn't the first time he had awakened in a hotel with a woman's sleeping head on his arm. Some of those women he had trouble identifying in the early morning hours. Once, in Abilene, he had awakened thus and looked with horror at the creature beside him. She had no eyebrows, only lines drawn above her eyes with some sort of ink-looking stuff. No eye lashes, either, Noland remembered, shuttering. Her sleeping eyes had reminded him of the turtles he used to see asleep on logs in the creek near Shamrock: rubbery flaps of skin covered beady little reptilian dots that had an empty way of looking at him when the skin rolled back. The rest of his bed mate looked little better than those lashes eyes. She appeared hard, tough, and Noland thought if he looked, he might find knife scars on her from fights in bars. Probably she carried a switch-blade in her purse.

This is not good, he told himself, trying to make his mind work in spite of a hangover. Where had this dog of a woman come from? He dragged out a few images of buying drinks for a beautiful lady in some truck-stop bar out on Interstate 20. Beautiful? Noland glanced again at the rubbery eyelids and drew in a breath between his teeth. God, was I that drunk, or did I dump the beautiful lady and get picked up by the turtle woman? He thought of Willy Nelson singing, "I never went to bed with an ugly woman, but I woke up with a few."

A vague memory came to him. Had he smashed a truck driver in the face for trying to spirit off his woman? It had to be the same woman, he realized. Ugly. Coyote ugly, he thought, remembering an old joke and understanding the truth of it for the first time. "Coyote ugly," the joke went, "describes a strange woman that you find sleeping on your arm when you wake up in a hotel you don't remember checking into, and she is so ugly that, rather than waking her up, you chew your arm off to get away."

Then, Noland thought, there's double coyote ugly—when you gnaw off your other arm so she won't recognize you later.

Instead of being amused, Noland felt a flash of anger at himself for ever finding the jokes funny. Hell, he had told himself through the alcoholic haze of a hangover, they weren't a bit funny. Those jokes had to be the unvarnished truth.

He looked again at Virginia. She might be a bit odd-looking in her sleep, but she certainly wasn't coyote ugly. Noland moved his arm and Virginia came awake, her mouth closing with a plopping sound and a hand reaching up to wipe away the slobber.

She looked at him and smiled. "Good morning, Mr. Noland, the dragon-man. You were a dragon of virility last night. How is it with you this morning? She giggled, snuggled closer to him, and rubbed her tongue over his nipple. "Oho. The dragon lives," she said in mock astonishment. Within seconds, she was straddling him, moving with rhythmic determination.

Noland noticed her morning breath and almost joked about her being the dragon lady, but decided the timing wasn't exactly right for that. He liked what she was doing, though he felt a twinge of disappointment to realize that she seemed to be rushing the act, as if to get it over with, and that, while the love making amounted to playful intimacy, it hardly approached an act that bonded souls.

Afterward, Noland sat on the bed, savoring a profound sense of melancholy, and wishing he had his guitar. He would sing to Virginia, if old Mehinder Dave and Abraham hadn't gone and busted the guitar. He would sing of lovelorn, dying cowboys and pretty little women. Of truck drivers and long, empty Texas highways and yearning for love that lasted forever. "You like American music?" he asked, raising his voice so Virginia could hear him over the drone of the shower.

"Yes. I seldom listen to anything else. Most Malaysians love music from America." Virginia hummed a rock tune to herself. Noland glanced at his imitation Rolex.

"You just sit tight, darling," he said, pulling on his pants. "I'll be gone an hour or so. Maybe less."

"Will you come back?"

"With bells on. Nothing could keep me away, Virginia."

In the lobby, Noland asked the desk clerk where he could find a music store that sold guitars.

Libby had packed as soon as Kent left. She chose a belt purse and put her clothes for the weekend into a nylon hand bag. The Batu Blue retreat had slipped her mind until Cole called the previous night. Probably her memory lapse, she decided, came because of all the exciting and scary events of the past couple of days. Kent entering her life. The ice nearly killing her on Petaling Street. The figure in black. Kent coming to her home for the night.

She piddled around the kitchen, glancing at the clock. It had been Kent's idea that he go back to the hotel alone, that she meet him later. She didn't like that plan but did not object when he proposed it. The water on the stove began to boil, and Libby poured some into a cup with a seabag. So here stands Libby LeMaster, she thought sourly, killing time—and for what? So you can be with a man, Libby. Now you think life has no meaning without being in the presence of a man? I have only a limited amount of time to get on with the business of living, and every moment is precious, a bright, hard little jewel glimmering between the darkness of the womb and the nothingness of death—and I kill time. Squander it, toss it to the wind like so much sand, watch it drain grain by grain from the hourglass of my life while I do nothing but wait. Most people wait their lives away, Libby knew, and she had scorn for them. They killed the very thing that they could least afford to slay when they killed time. And here I am, doing the same, she accused. For a man.

And such an odd one. Shifting her attention to Kent soothed her anger somewhat. Not so odd, she affirmed; in fact he is much like me, in many ways. She stirred her seabag around, lifted it out with a spoon, wrapped the string around it and squeezed the water into the cup. Like wanting to protect himself from intimacy while he's so vulnerable from just moving out of a relationship. I've done that. Like the way he sees sexual contact as an extension of a loving relationship, not just a physical act. Rare for a man. Doesn't that make him worth waiting for?

But to *kill* time. Libby couldn't stand the thought. She turned to the sink, poured out the cup of tea, buckled on her waist purse, and went to the phone to call a cab.

On the way to the Mandarin, Libby wondered how Kent would take her coming early. And coming up to his room. He had told her to wait in the lobby, like he was afraid she would come up and rape him or something. A silly notion, she concluded, given her having stood before him, nude, in the same room, and given his coming to her house to spend the night and their retiring like Victorian lovers, chaste and pure, going to separate rooms without so much as a brushing of lips or even clasping of hands.

So who was he to distrust her, much less tell her what to do? She would do as she pleased, come early, since that pleased her, go to his room. Such actions would speak with eloquence of her determination in refusing to have someone else dictate how she structured her day, not to mention showing him that she could be trusted to respect his desire to remain sexually aloof. For the time being, anyway.

When she entered the hotel, Libby remembered that she was to call an out-station cab before ringing Kent's room. That way, the cab would be there soon and they could be on their way. Kent said he liked the idea of spending the weekend at a mountain resort with a group of artists.

When she told Cole she would invite a first-rate artist, he expressed his approval by lowering his voice and telling her in sincere tones how he appreciated her sensitivity to the needs of the Batu Blue group. Libby knew if she had been talking to Cole in person instead of on the phone, he would have leaned close and frowned in a profound way while delivering his positive reinforcement for her bringing another artist to his group.

She glanced at the hotel's house phone, rejecting calling the Genting cab yet and rejecting calling Kent's room. She would just go up there and announce her presence, perhaps sit in his room while he dressed. He would have to learn to trust her. She left her bag with the bell captain, then turned to the elevator.

Libby felt a moment of doubt as she reached to knock on the door. Aren't I being a bit pushy? Shouldn't I respect his desire to protect himself in his own way? A wave of tenderness washed over her, of affection for Kent's artistic nature, his genius with capturing beauty on paper with his drawings, his unmade characteristic of wishing to relate with her without allowing the prospect of going to bed together to get in the way. She hesitated only a moment, then knocked.

The door opened about four inches, stopping at the end of the safety chain, and Libby found herself looking at the face of a beautiful Chinese woman. Flustered and embarrassed, Libby stepped back and looked at the room number above the door. "Yes?" the woman said.

"I, uh, was looking for Mr. Kent Day. But I guess I got the wrong room."

"Oh, this is the right one. Kent isn't in right now. Could I take a message for him?"

"No. No. Forget it." Libby turned away and ran to the elevator. So much for his being an unusual male, Libby told herself. And I was so taken in. She let the anger move through her while riding down in the elevator. What now? Go home, refuse to answer the phone for the day?

Libby snorted at the idea. That was too juvenile a response for her to consider. She walked with measured, deliberate steps to the lounge where Kent had directed her to wait for him.

Mata Hari and the American kingpins had to be somewhere in the hotel. Butch felt certain of that. Likely they had another room on the sixth floor, but through carelessness, Butch had let them get to it without discovering the room number.

They were cool ones, those Americans—cool enough to draw the police into their games with the local hoodlums. After they left the room to take the elevator to the sixth floor, Butch had gone back to his peep-hole, reattached the mirror, and stood squinting through the spy. A plain-clothes cop came to the druggers' room, let himself in with a pass key, and left in haste. An hour later, he returned, escorting another plainclothes cop and four uniformed police into the room. They all left with equal haste, and an hour after that, the bomb squad showed up dressed like goalies in a hockey match. When they left, one carried a black box.

Butch took notes on the activities, unsure how he could work the turn of events into his play, but convinced that such dramatic stage business would rivet an audience's attention. While he wrote, he marveled at the way the gangsters had brought the police into the affair, having them remove the bomb, dealing with the law as if they were just ordinary citizens. It wasn't until the next morning that it occurred to Butch that perhaps the police were on the Americans' payroll. A chilling thought, he realized, and told himself that he would have to be careful not to turn to any police for aid. Doing so could be like the fellow Butch read about in an American newspaper who encountered a rattlesnake, so he picked up a stick to defend himself—and the stick bit him. He hadn't looked at the stick-like object he grabbed, and it turned out to be another rattlesnake.

Butch stayed at the door, peeking out each time he heard a sound, for another hour before he concluded that the gangsters would not return to the room, not that night, anyway. So he tried to get some sleep.

The next morning, he awoke early, put on his tourist disguise, and went to the coffee shop for a quick breakfast before stationing himself in the lounge on the ground floor to watch for Mata Hari and the others.

Kent came in carrying what looked like an over-night bag and his props to make people think he was a genuine artist. So I was wrong, Butch thought. One of them did go out again, and I missed following him.

Butch stood, stretched, and pretended to continue reading the newspaper. Perhaps it would be possible to follow the gangster to the other room. But Kent vanished into the office of the hotel management, so Butch returned to the easy chair. What was he doing in there, Butch wondered. Maybe the hotel people were—By god, that had to be it. When the realize-tion hit him, Butch felt it like a physical blow. Those druggers owned the hotel managers, maybe even the hotel itself.

Of course. Why else would men with so much money to throw around on such matters as buying off the entire Kuala Lumpur police force choose to stay in a cheap hotel like the Mandarin? Proximity to the drug market on nearby streets wasn't a good enough explanation—as Butch had thought before. The entire hotel had to be a part of the scheme to introduce big-time drug trafficking into Malaysia.

Butch glanced around, no longer feeling safe. He would have to be careful in that den of vice and corruption or he could simply vanish from the face of the earth. They might tie an anchor to him and dump him into the South China Sea. Or carve him into chunks and run him through an industrial gauged garbage disposal, then drain the red soup that had been his body into the Klang river. It seemed certain they would do some such thing to him if a low-ranking pusher, posing as a porter or a desk clerk, took notice of his interest in the big bosses or their Chinese mistress.

Butch felt his heart racing and the panic in him rise. Was writing a play, however successful it might become, worth such risks?

Just as he leaned toward deciding an artist ought to observe life from afar instead of plunging into the heat and dust of humanity's battles, Libby walked in.

Butch watched her pause, look at the red house phone on the wall, glance into the lounge—looking directly at him but without recognition—then check a bag with the bell captain and get on the elevator. The lights above the elevator door told Butch Libby went to the sixth floor. So she knew about the other room. She was in deeper than he had figured, and without a doubt she had placed herself in extreme danger.

He envisioned a Malaysian hatchet man assigned to eliminate Libby. Hatchet man. The term caused him to break out in a sweat as he imagined Libby being chopped into small enough pieces to fit into a plastic bag, then carried dripping to a leafmold grave on some rubber tree plantation and buried for the ants and grubs to finish destroying.

Sometimes the artist must venture into the dust and heat, Butch affirmed, proud of himself, but still aware of his heart racing. He would save Libby, if nothing else, then perhaps withdraw into the artist's ivory tower to watch the world's reflection indirectly in the magic mirror, weaving his dramatic tapestry so others could better understand and hence cure the ills of the world.

Then another thought occurred to him. Libby seemed the perfect model for a character who would be the logical dramatic counterpoint to Mata Hari. He would call her Joanie. She would be light-skinned and fair headed, somewhat tall—all the things that Mata Hari was not. Kind, loving, naive, delicate, fragile. He pulled out his notebook and took notes. That string of adjectives did not fit his understanding of Libby, of whom he was a bit afraid. But no matter. She would merely serve as the base for the character he would create. He would have to get Mata Hari and Joanie on stage together to show the contrast between them. But how? That part stumped him, and as he worked on the problem, Libby came out of the elevator.

She walked straight toward him, her fingers alternately clinching into fists and shooting out straight. Butch adjusted the newspaper so he could watch her while pretending to read. She sat on the couch across from him and crossed her arms on her chest, a gesture Butch had learned to write into stage directions to suggest his character was closing herself off from emotional contact with others. Something about the determined way Libby walked in and seemed to take over the couch rather than just sitting on it frightened Butch. He looked at her face, her set jaw and the knit brows, and he concluded that she was unhappy about something. She seemed to be feeling some strong, negative emotion.

Disappointment, maybe? Butch wondered. He felt he ought to go over to her, tell her of the danger she was in, get her out of that sinister hotel. But she looked scary. Maybe, just maybe she was angry about something. If that was it, he thought he better not speak to her right then. He knew that some people focus their anger on those who would help them, and he had no desire to be the object of Libby's wrath. Better to wait a bit, let her cool down, if it is indeed anger that has her all stirred up, then talk to her.

He remembered and elaborated upon his fantasy of Libby's dismembered body being dragged in a plastic bag across the shaded soil of the rubber tree plantation, leaving little trails of blood from twig-punctures in the bag. And he tried to work up his nerve to do what he knew he had to do. As Shakespeare said, he admonished himself, "Screw with courage on the sticky place," and get out there into the ongoing human tragedy, strike a blow for humanity and justice, forsake the artist's lofty tower long enough to get Libby out of this hotel and save her from those ruthless gangsters.

Not a bad speech, that, Butch thought, wondering if he shouldn't write it down before he forgot the wording.

He had begun folding his paper, girding himself for facing a still-distraught Libby, when the phony artist emerged from the manager's office behind her. Too late, Butch realized, as Kent spotted Libby. For now, anyway.

Kent looked at Butch, and he lifted the paper, dropping the folds from it, to block the gangster's scrutiny. He shifted around so he could see Libby just beyond the edge of the paper. She sat there, soothing some wrinkles out of her slacks, unaware of Kent behind her.

"Hello, again, and so soon," Kent said. He walked around the couch and sat beside her.

"Hello," she said in an aloof way, crossing her legs. Kent glanced at Butch, who had to shift the paper again, cutting off the couch from his line of vision. He decided he would have to settle for listening lest Kent think him interested in what was going on.

"It didn't take long to pack for the weekend at Genting," Libby said.

"Have you called an out-station cab?"

"Not yet."

Kent fell silent, and Butch sneaked a quick a peek at him. Kent sat fidgeting, rubbing his hands on his knees. "Libby, there are some things I need to tell you. I should have done it earlier, but for some reason did not. It's about this friend. A person I just met, actually." Kent laughed a dry, nervous laugh.

"You don't have to tell me, Kent."

"But I do. I've been thinking about the Genting trip, about getting away for the weekend, and I think it might be good for my friend to go along, if that's all right with you. But first, I want you to know about a series of rather bizarre incidents."

Butch, captivated by Kent's tone and certain he was about to learn something of genuine significance, lowered the newspaper to look Kent and Libby. After all, Butch thought, I am disguised. Libby had not recognized me, and she looked right at me. Twice.

But when the paper dropped to his lap, Butch found Kent looking at him. He faltered, started to pick up the paper again, realized that such a gesture would be a bit transparent, and looked beyond Kent and Libby, pretending to be interested in what the desk clerk was doing.

Kent looked at Butch, then said, "Libby, what did you say that man's name was—the one under the pointy Chinese hat and the make-up? Butch Gaston, wasn't it?"

He knows, Butch thought. My god, he found out. Butch looked at Kent, expecting him to reach into his pocket for a pistol. His stooges would be nearby with their guns and ropes and knives, waiting for the word from the boss, and in no time at all, butch thought in a panic, I'll be red soup running down the drain toward the Klang river.

He jumped to his feet, the newspaper scattering on the floor, and sprinted to the front door, jerked on the handle and banged his head from trying to get out before he had the door open wide enough. Butch envisioned the desk clerk taking a pistol from a drawer and firing. He jinked through the door, hunkering down and jumping to one side, feeling his back tingle in anticipation of the bullets.

Looking back at the entrance to the hotel to see if one of the hired guns might be there to take a few shots at him, Butch ran into Noland.

Noland grunted in surprise but stood firm, swinging his guitar case out of harm's way. Butch bounced to one side, flailing his arms, and fell stunned to the sidewalk. He gasped for breath and felt his vision constricting to a tiny spot of cement. He was also aware that he had scraped his cheek and that something warm ran down his face. As the air began to come easier into his lungs, he found himself staring without comprehension at a pair of lizard hide cowboy boots.

"That there looks like a nasty gash, little fellow," Noland said. "Here, we'll get you inside and fix you up real good."

Butch felt a hand under one arm, a hand backed by enormous strength that lifted him to his feet. He found himself staring nearly nose to nose at the face of the King of Chicago Cocaine. *Take me inside and fix me up good*, Butch thought in wild panic, envisioning the red soup that had been his body pouring into a sewer. He twisted away from the gangster's grip and ran.

"Jesus H. Cristo," Noland muttered in astonishment, "this is for sure a country full of screwballs." People along the sidewalk stopped to stare as Butch scrambled across the street, lurching this way and that, running toward the Klang Bus Station.

## 11

Tin mines transubstantiate jungle manna to gall;
Now only the artist can save Eden from a fall.
—Coleman Farquart, *Asean Doublets*


Che Mothar Bin Dr. Hazri dropped six coins into the slot machine and pulled the handle. The painted wheels blurred then snapped into place: watermelons, oranges, grapes, and one double bar. Nothing. Exactly what he hoped the day would come to—nothing. But he knew better, for people were scheduled to suffer, maybe even to die, people like that supposed amah, Jenny L.E.M. or whatever her real name was. She wasn't one of his Thai or Filipino girls, so far as he could determine. Whoever she turned out to be, Che knew that Bayang would have some nasty work for Che. How nasty this time? Che wondered. And will I do it? The question amused him, and he allowed himself a thin-lipped smile.

He dropped six more coins into the machine, telling himself even as he did so what a foolish business this was, feeding the magic machine. Magic because of its ability to make your money into its money, always dribbling a few coins back and flashing its lying signs proclaiming how easy it was to win, always taking more than it gave and yet casting some sort of spell over you, compelling you to feed it more coins, for the next play just might ring the bells and flash the lights on the top of the machine to announce you had won really big.

He pulled the handle. Two stars appeared and a return of five coins registered on the win meter. Down only one coin that time, a victory of sorts. As he dropped six more coins into the slot, someone touched his shoulder. He ignored the touch, knowing what he would see if he looked back. Bayang's toady. The wheels spun then chinked into place with a satisfying similarity of colors: three grapes. The win meter added thirty coins, bringing Che's winnings up to nearly half the number of coins he had lost. The toady cleared his throat.

Che turned from the machine, slit his eyes, and looked at the man beside him.

"Boss say they come. Say you need to know." The message delivered, the man turned and walked away.

Che watched him. A shabby little devil of a Thai, Che thought. Or maybe Filipino. Some Chinese, some Malay, some Indian, and a European or two went into the making of most of Bayang's toadies. Bayang himself revealed mixed racial stock with his Chinese eyes, dark skin, Malay nose, and hair that might be worn by an African. A tangled noodle dish of ancestors. Arab traders who would sell you their brothers' teeth for the right price. Thai head hunters. Maybe some of those fierce fellows from the cannibal islands down south.

But of course, he wasn't the real boss, nor was his name *Bayang*. He registered at the hotel as Abu Segrin Wong, his idea of a joke, Che supposed, that stringing of Malay, Indian and Chinese names into one, combining the three dominate racial groups of Malaysia. No one seemed to know his real name. The toadies who traveled with him called him *boss;* members of the first line on the streets of K.L., people like Mehinder who had never seen him, referred to him as *orang bayang*, the shadow man. Che didn't call him anything to his face, for he seemed to lack identity in the way he represented the unnamed men with big money, men from Bangkok or maybe Manila, men who would sell you more than their brothers' teeth, more than you needed, more than you asked for.

Six more coins, a pull on the handle, the whirl of colors, a scattering of fruit, and coins gone. Six more. Che fed the machine with a compulsion he hated, and soon he watched only the stubborn win meter, ignoring the spinning disks, for they mattered not at all. Only the red digital readout of the win meter was of importance.

Che had once scorned those who sat at slot machines, back when he studied at the University of Malaya and then at the University of London, where he read law. He courted Lisa then, blond, fair-skinned Lisa who covered her breasts with elegant sweaters, breasts three times larger than any Malay woman's, breasts he once wanted to see and touch with a passion that robbed him of all reason. Later, he came to believe that he married Lisa because it was the only way he could get her to take off her sweater.

Lisa came to Kuala Lumpur with him, and almost without his noticing it, children dropped from her while he made himself known first as a lawyer then as an official in the ruling Malay political party. Money came with the government post, and a house just off Ampang street, near the International School of Kuala Lumpur where Lisa sent their children, a house as elegant as the homes of the ambassadors from other countries, ambassadors who were his neighbors and party guests and fellow members of the Selangor Club.

Then he stumbled. A minor thing, he thought: a mistake in backing the wrong idea about allocation of Borneo resources, but not so minor from the point of view of some ministers, who netted him with the ISA, the Internal Security Act that allowed the government to imprison without a hearing anyone deemed a threat to the security of the country. The official stand of the government was that he worked with those who would stir racial strife between the ruling Malays and the economically powerful Chinese community.

Che went to jail, knowing the charges to be a sham, knowing he would be out in mere weeks, knowing he had too many friends in high places to stay locked up for long. Most government officials of any importance had at one time or another done time under the ISA. It was part of political life for successful Malays.

But the weeks dragged into months, his friends dropped away, and he even heard the rumors that many had noticed how remarkably Chinese he looked. And there was that English wife, they whispered—not a person for a Malay of real importance to be married to, especially when the party leader disliked anything British.

Che put himself on hold, refusing to think much about the world beyond the walls of his cell. Lisa came as often as the government allowed, which wasn't often, and she assured him that his children were fine, that they excelled in school, that there was plenty of money to run the house. She brought him books of handicrafts and curious things to do with his hands in the long hours of ISA confinement. He became quite good at clipping butterfly wings and arranging them into mosaics depicting Malaysian rural life. Doing the butterfly art proved satisfying, something he would continue later as a hobby, though he came to fancy himself a real artist, enough so that he sought association with other artists in the Batu Blue group.

After nearly two years of prison, someone in the government deemed him harmless, and Che got out. But his life seemed to be in shambles. The Malays in power made it clear that if he tried to regain political position, the ISA would be invoked again; his family, he found, lived with no domestic servants because money ran short, and in a matter of months he would lose his house. Lisa had grown larger, her breasts becoming parodies of themselves, and she seemed to sweat most of the time.

Law firms in Kuala Lumpur had no openings for him, so he opened his own practice. Few clients came. He put his house up for sale. Then Bayang came with a distasteful but legitimate offer of business. Bayang represented an organization that supplied cheap domestic help in the form of Filipino women willing to work as amahs in the households of the wealthy in Kuala Lumpur. Che's job would be to secure the proper papers for them to come into the country legally. He didn't like the work, and he knew doing it would mean further alienation from the elite Malay political structure, for there was much official sentiment against bringing foreigners into the Malaysian labor force. But Bayang offered so much money— enough that Che could take his house off the market and, within just a few months, hire several of Bayang's amahs himself.

Then Bayang came with a special case. One Malaysian client wanted an amah who was only 14 years old. He would accept none of the other women Bayang offered, and he was willing to pay a high premium to get the girl.

"He wants her as his personal plaything," Che objected, repulsed by the idea.

"I don't ask customers to write a job description," Bayang said. "They pay, I supply, you make it legal."

"This is different," Che said. Yes, Bayang agreed. Different because the customer offered so much money, most of which would go to Che. Bayang named the amount, and Che sat back in his chair in astonishment.

It seemed like such a small matter, the looping around the law and beyond the law, the tiny lies necessary to get the right papers. Che worked with a name, Maria Alonzo, an abstraction, and not a little girl at all. Besides, she would be a woman soon enough. Better, he told himself, to be a woman in Kuala Lumpur than a lost and hungry little girl in Manila.

Bayang's next deal offered more of a problem: eight domestic servants, ages 16 to 19, for a single household in Jahor Baru, just north of Singapore. "Change their ages," Bayang directed. "And use these addresses as places of employment." He gave Che a list of eight different homes in Jahor. "The addresses are real ones, but you must make up names for the families that live there." Then he handed Che an envelope stuffed with cash, and he left.

Che told himself he shouldn't take the case, that he would be aiding in setting up a house of prostitution. But he counted the money and knew he would do as Bayang directed. Che helped bring more women into the country who would be prostitutes, and there were more cases of lying about the ages of little girls, one as young as nine, a child from Bangkok. Che objected to that case, but not with any real conviction.

Bayang announced that he would no longer come to Che's office, that Che would come to see Bayang at an office near the Genting Hotel whenever summoned for more work.

Che bought a Mercedes and brought more servants to his home (a gate keeper, two yard men, a driver to take his children to school, a night watchman). Lisa seemed unimpressed, but then she wasn't so impressive herself with her spreading figure and tendency to be morose when she wasn't surly. He gave her a tiny budget each month, not near the amount she had before he stumbled on the ISA, for he feared she might grow independent with money available. She often showed him pieces of art and fine furniture for their home, and he always paid for the items. He liked living with luxury, and buying such things kept Lisa quiet.

Then he met Ani in the gambling casino at Genting. A month later, he found himself telling Lisa about her. "She is Malay," he said. "My own culture calls to me."

"You want a divorce?" Lisa asked. "If so, I am certainly willing to discuss terms."

"No."

"I do."

"I don't."

"Then why tell me about your whore?"

The words enraged him. Ani a whore? After an ugly scene in which Che reminded Lisa that she depended on him for money, that she could not leave no matter what, he stormed off to the Selangor Club for a few drinks. Alone in the bar he asked himself why he had told Lisa about Ani. But he had no answer.

Che left all walk-in cases that came to his law office in Kuala Lumpur to his assistant, Ros, a bright doormat of a Malay woman just out of law school at the University of Malaya. Che busied himself with one client, Bayang. Paperwork he required amounted to little, so Che had increasing amounts of time for Ani, whom he kept in luxury at Genting Highlands Hotel. Clients began to come into his office in greater numbers. He got some cases he deemed insignificant, ones Ros handled with intelligence, calling upon him to do the courtroom part if the case promised publicity. Some of them got his name in the paper with a frequency that alarmed Bayang but pleased Che.

He found out about the heroin and cocaine on the same weekend Lisa disappeared.

Bayang, who always dealt in cash, handed Che a stack of five hundred ringgit bills. "Count them," Bayang directed. Che counted the bills, staggered by the amount.

"You want me to do something that I cannot do," Che said, fearing that he would not find a way to refuse whatever Bayang wanted.

"Not at all. This is payment for something you have already done." Some of the prostitutes Che had secured papers for, Bayang explained, worked as mules, a few of them even made several trips between Bangkok and Kuala Lumpur to carry China White, high-grade cocaine that got top money from wealthy customers. Some carried heroin for the street users in Kuala Lumpur.

"This is too dangerous," Che objected. "The government kills dealers in dadah. The death penalty is automatic."

Bayang scowled. "Do not lecture me. If anyone is caught, it will be one of the mules or one of our street clerks like those vile men that call themselves 'the Burning Tigers.' None of them knows you or me."

"Still," Che said, "it is beyond me to deal in such matters." He put the stack of bills on Bayang's desk.

"Do you remember Maria Alonzo?" Bayang asked. He opened a drawer in his desk.

Che knit his brows. Maria Alonzo—that name seemed familiar, but he couldn't pin it down.

"This is only one of several photographs." Bayang handed him a large color photo showing a little girl touching the stiff member of a man. The girl had only buds for breasts and no pubic hair at all.

Che had always disliked Bayang, but at that moment he hated the man. "You said we deal only in amahs," Che said with fury.

"To you, Che, I have never made such a claim, for you are intelligent enough to know it to be a lie. Would you like to see other photographs of Maria? I have better ones. And of course there are similar pictures of other young girls you have brought into the country. But I see you take no joy in such matters." He took the photograph from Che's hands. "You are a good lawyer, Che. The best in our organization. You earn your money."

Che understood the implied threat: take the money and accept the fact that he dealt in drugs or face charges of trafficking in children as prostitutes. He had no doubts that Bayang would come up with a way to publicize Che's crimes with no risk to himself at all.

Bayang pushed the stack of ringgit notes back in front of Che then stood and looked out the window so Che would not have to pick up the money while being watched.

Back in his room, he made furious love to Ani, bruising her so she cried out. Then they argued, though later Che could not remember what the disagreement was about. He went to the casino, handed a floor clerk one of Bayang's five hundred ringgit notes and ordered the man to bring him change as he needed it. For the next several hours he sat at a slot machine jerking the lever with such violence that a small crowd gathered. When he decided to leave for Kuala Lumpur and had the clerk gather and cash his coins, he found himself staring at over one thousand ringgit.

At his home in Kuala Lumpur, the gate keeper did not come out. Annoyed, Che leaned on his horn, then got out and opened the gate himself. Just as he was about to get into the car to drive it to the carport, he glanced at the house and sensed something wrong. He walked to the front door, peering in windows on the way. The house looked empty.

Inside he found his home stripped of everything, furniture, artwork, Persian carpets. Everything. He walked through each room, numb, looking at kitchen cabinets standing open and empty, at closets with only a few stray metal hangers in them, at drawers sitting on the floor, and at walls with nails on them where paintings had hung.

Lisa took everything, he told himself, and he sat on the floor of his bedroom and cried. Loss of Lisa and his children and the house full of expensive art and furniture seemed too great to bear, or it seemed so for the time he covered his face with his hands, feeling hot tears run between his fingers.

But when he drove away from the house, he felt more anger than anything else. How could Lisa do such a thing to him, when he was still reeling from the discovery that he had been involved in drug deals, when his financial world seemed to be turning into a nightmare? He needed the comfort and stability of his home and family at such a time, and it felt so unfair of Lisa to deny him what he needed. He drove his Mercedes through the streets of Kuala Lumpur, his fury growing. In his imagination he saw Lisa standing before him, fat and insolent, and he imagined striking her with his fists. Hard.

At the Selangor Club, he calmed himself over a gin and tonic. There would be more time, he had told himself, for Ani, for playing in the casino, for lounging around the Club.

Che dropped in six more coins and pulled the lever. Lisa had seemed to drift into his life and then out, as had the children, as had Ani and Celia Hong and Nor Habib and Waneta Krishnan. The win meter jumped by thirty coins and Che glanced down to see what did it. Watermelons. He made a quick calculation, estimating he had lost only sixty ringgit since sitting down. Not bad. A glance at his watch told him he still had time to gamble and even eat a meal before going to his room to wait for the call from Bayang. It might take quite some time for the first line street people to catch that Chinese woman, Jenny, who seemed to be the Americans' contact for pushing drugs in Kuala Lumpur, and even longer to get her ready to tell what she knew. The Burning Tigers would do it and with great efficiency, then call Bayang through his chief toady. Bayang and Che would question her.

Che didn't look forward to that since what the Burning Tigers would do to Jenny might not be pretty. After she talked, Bayang would decide what to do with the woman and perhaps the two Americans. If Bayang asks me to commit even greater crimes, Che told himself, this time I will say *no*.

He looked at his hands, noting that the copper-nickel coin had blackened them. If only the American cowboy and the artist had never come, or at least that strange man, Coleman, had arranged his odd retreat elsewhere. Genting had been the logical spot for such a gathering, of course; the other resorts—Frasier's Hill and Cameron Highlands—were too far from Kuala Lumpur. Genting was not a long drive, the roads went through lovely mountain jungles, and the hotel had all necessary facilities. Still, Che hated the thought of all the artists being in the hotel at the time Bayang dug to the bottom of the mystery of the woman in black who, he claimed, had been following Che around Kuala Lumpur.

That tall, blond American woman would be somewhere in the hotel, too. Che didn't know what he would do about her, but he was sure Bayang would suggest something disgusting.

Miles stood by the Genting Hotel elevators, as Roseta had directed him. She would take care of the rooms, she had said, and that was just fine with him. Clerks always annoyed him, especially Malaysian clerks who never seemed to speak loud enough—and those who did have the volume spoke such poor English that Miles couldn't understand them, so they might as well be whispering like the others. But take the Chinese. They were by god the only ones who knew the value of speaking out, though they sing everything, Miles thought, in a cadence that makes them sound like comic imitations of characters in an Italian opera, so that their English comes out sounding like Cantonese or Mandarin or whatever the hell their own language is called. Indians spoke in low tones, though audibly enough. It's the dang Malays, Miles affirmed, who drove a body to distraction. He watched Roseta dealing with a Malay man at the check-in counter, a man who muttered as bad as the rest of them.

She looks plenty good, Miles thought, wearing that Mexican-style dress. He had never seen her in anything but a *baju karum*, the shimmery, ankle-length dress worn by those Malay women who choose not to drape themselves in black tents. But today she wore a white cotton dress with flowers embroidered all over it. "From Mexico," she had explained earlier that day. "I bought it in Singapore."

Miles put Roseta's bag on the floor and wiped his hand on his pants. Hey-Soos, he grumbled, why would she carry so much stuff for just a weekend? His own clothes fit into a small plastic shopping bag. But Roseta had to have a leather grip stuffed to bulging with a mere weekend's worth of clothes. And so heavy. He flexed his fingers and looked at Roseta coming toward him. For her, he acknowledged, he would be willing to carry twice so much. He liked her for a number of reasons, he told himself —one being that she always projected enough so he could hear her speak. Rare for a Malay.

"We are in room six eighty," she announced as she punched an elevator button.

"What?"

"Six eight zero." They got aboard an elevator with several other people. Roseta stood close and took his arm. He tried not to show his surprise.

On the bus from Kuala Lumpur, Roseta had explained how it would be better if they passed themselves off as a married couple—better for her in case there was any suspicion of khalwat on the part of any officials who noticed them.

"Khalwat?" Miles had asked.

"Close proximity. In Malaysia it is a crime for an Islamic woman to

178

be in close contact with a male unless he is her father or husband."

"And you are Islamic?" The question of her religion had never occurred to him.

"Not any more. Maybe not ever, though I grew up with Islam. But that isn't the point. The problem is that I look Malay, and most Malay women are Islamic. This," she took a simple gold band from her purse, "is a fake gold ring I bought in Central Market." She slipped it on and held out her hand. "I am now married, for a weekend, anyway."

"Might any officials ask about us?"

"It is not likely. But the guards at the hotel, they tend to be nosy. I will show my ring, and that should do. If they ask more questions, I was born Roseta Gonzales in a city in your country. Name a city for me."

"A city?"

"Yes. A city where someone like me could be born. Are not the Americans born of Mexicans darker? Don't they have black eyes?"

"Brown, yes. Uh, San Antonio."

"Is that a good city for Mexican people, San Antonio?"

"It's a city in Texas, about the size of Kuala Lumpur. Many Mexican people live there."

"Then," she had looked at her ring again, "I was born of the Gonzales family in San Antonio. I am a Texan by birth and a Mexican by heritage. You like my Mexican dress? Ecclesiastic police will not even look at me twice."

The elevator stopped on the sixth floor. Roseta nudged Miles. "Our floor," she said with a slight giggle. He allowed her to lead the way. On the bus, he had assumed that the marriage guise ended with her fake gold ring. He hadn't thought about the matter, but if he had, he would have assumed that they would take separate rooms. But she said "our room." Singular. And she named only one number.

By the time they got to room 680, Miles felt excited by the strange turn of events, even if he also felt just a bit cornered.

"I have to go," Butch said. "I have to. But I don't like it."

"Relax. Not even your own mother would recognize you." Cole reached across the front seat of the van and patted his shoulder. "You look sort of like Hal Holbrook in his Mark Twain makeup, only maybe a little older. When you came up to my place with those glasses on and tapping around with that stick, I was certain you were just an old blind guy about to try to sell me some brooms."

Butch turned off of Kuching Street toward Batu Caves. "This route will take us longer than the new highway, but it's the only way I know. If you're in some kind of a hurry, I'll stop and try to get directions for going the faster way. But this one takes you through some magnificent jungle. The drive up to Genting Highlands is better than getting there, in my opinion—if you take this old narrow road."

"Take the jungle road. I'm in no hurry. There are some things I want to talk with you about, anyway."

"About those gangsters?"

"Butch, maybe, just maybe those men are what they appear to be. Libby called me today to say Noland and his Malaysian girlfriend will be joining the Batu Blue group. It seems he is a geologist, here as an employee of EXXON. She also said the one named Kent Day is an artist. A fine one, she said."

"Saying it doesn't make it true."

"Maybe it does, if you say it in the right way. You're an artist, a playwright, Butch. You know a play doesn't present the factual truth of what's out there in the world. Artists don't work that way. They take the truth only as a starting point, as the raw material for art, and the art they make becomes more true than facts."

Butch looked at Cole, noting the way he strained toward him against the confines of the seat belt and shoulder strap, the way his face looked squashed down into a fanatical frown, the way his medals and ribbons pulled the front of his shirt out of shape. Maybe Miles is right, Butch thought. Cole might not have all his marbles in one bag.

"The truth," Butch said, "is that Libby has become trapped somehow with some dangerous men, and she needs someone to show her the danger she faces."

"Your truth."

"The truth, dammit."

"Maybe."

They let a few kilometers slip by in silence. Butch drove past a row of hawker stands with bananas and mangosteens hanging from them, and piles of spiky durian on the ground beside them; past houses on stilts almost hidden by rambutan trees, tapioca bushes, and banana leaves; past a hillside covered with rubber trees. Ahead, they could see the mountains lifting the jungle into the sun.

"Butch," Cole said, "you never have asked me the purpose of the Batu Blue."

"To encourage creative writers and the like, right? You're all the time encouraging me to do more writing, especially about things in Malaysia. I never joined your group, Cole, because I don't want other writers to influence me. I am my own man."

"Would you be surprised if I told you that in the most crucial way, you already are a member of the group, even as you work to stay apart from it?"

Butch glanced at him. "Yes," he said with uncertainty.

"The purpose of the retreat is to reveal to Batu Blue its real purpose, though most of them know at a gut level. You know, and you're already working hard to achieve its goals. You've read Eliot, right?"

"T. S. Eliot?" Butch remembered struggling with some impossible poetry back in a lit class at Butler University. "You mean stuff such as 'The Waste Land' and the like?" He couldn't remember any other titles. All he could dredge up was his wrestling with poems that made no sense at all, crap poems, he had called them. And he remembered how, late one night before a literature exam, he had sat in a stupor, staring at a page in his lit book with Eliot's name on it. Idly he anagrammed Eliot's name, and the result caused him to bolt upright in his chair. *Toilet*. That was what T. Eliot spelled backward. No wonder he wrote crap poems. Butch hooted with laughter. He couldn't wait to tell his literature teacher what he had discovered. The next day, when he shared what he termed "Butch Gaston's Contribution to Literary Criticism" with the teacher, the man was not amused. Butch failed the exam, and he later told some people in the student union that the teacher had failed him because of that little joke.

"Yes," Coleman said. "He had this idea, see, that the poet served to civilize society. The poet *refined their sensibilities*, he said. I think the man had something there, only it isn't just the poet. It's artists of all kind. They don't just create beauty or entertain. Some of them don't even do that, really. Many works of literature and other forms of art like painting are far from beautiful, and often they are so painful that only someone weird would enjoy them. Artists," Coleman lowered his voice and leaned toward Butch, pulling against the shoulder strap, "serve a vital social function. Absolutely vital."

Butch thought of how his play had blasted some of his old enemies in high school. "That's right," Butch said. Then he remembered "The

Waste Land," that crap poem by old man Toilet. "Some artists do, anyway," Butch added.

"Precisely. Precisely. Some do, others struggle to, even if they don't know what they're about." Coleman waved his hand at the jungle they were driving through—trees nearly a hundred feet high, bamboo thickets, vines, lianas. "Butch, how long ago do you suppose all of Malaysia was like this? A couple of generations? Three? The people here were barely out of the stone age when Europeans came with their technology and jerked them out of the trees and into the twentieth century. Look at the Kuala Lumpur valley. Just a couple of decades ago, as I understand it, there were hardly any automobiles at all. Now the traffic congestion and air pollution are enough to stagger a citizen of Los Angeles. Malaysia might be the most beautiful country in the world right now, but how long will that last? They are chopping down the rain forests for hardwood, turning the land inside out for tin, and killing their citizens on the highways and in factories. They know no restraint and plunge into folly with their headlong fall into technology that far outstrips their older, simpler jungle mentality. Malaysia might well be doomed, Butch."

Butch felt as he often had in classes at Butler where abstract ideas were discussed. Like he was missing something, like the others in the class saw things he could not. And, as always, he suspected that there was nothing to see. They made the simple into something complex because of some perverse desire to sound profound. He looked at Coleman's flushed face and found it easy to conclude that the man didn't understand Eliot any more than Butch or anyone else did. "What is the point?" Butch demanded.

"The point, ah yes the point," Coleman held out his palm and punched it with an index finger. "The point is that perhaps more than any place on earth, Malaysia needs her artists, and those artists cannot afford to muddle along, blind to their real purpose. No. There isn't time. They must see the need to redouble the efforts to refine sensibilities, to civilize the people of the jungles, to keep them from destroying themselves with tools of technology that seem to promise so much but deliver only death blows to the earth and water and bend the human spirit to the path of materialism."

"Batu Blue will save Malaysia?" Butch was amazed.

"It would be a start, a gleam of hope, a bright little spot of optimism in a country already plunging into the gloom of technology and despair. And if the artists knew of their mission, they could go about it more systematically. In the Batu Blue retreat, I shall tell them. You said you won't come to any of our meetings, so I'm telling you now. Not that you need much of a nudge, Butch. You are already dedicated to writing a play of social satire. You're going there to gather more material for your drama, isn't that right?"

"No. Yes. I'm going to try to find a way to save Libby. Maybe I'll get some material for a play while I'm at it—if I can figure out a way to watch that Kent fellow without him knowing who I am. He has some sort of uncanny ability to see through my disguises."

"Not the one you have on now, he won't. Butch, if you get a chance, take a close look at the artist's pad you say he carries as a prop, see if he isn't a real artist, after all. Artists who paint people have a way of seeing beyond superficial makeup in ways the rest of us cannot—Kent's trained eye could be how he saw through your tourist guise in that hotel. Try checking out Kent first, before following the cowboy. And if you find out anything, let me know. Be warned, though, that I shall leave a message for all members of the Batu Blue group with the main desk, telling them where my room will be so they will have a central place for messages. Kent and the cowboy will know where I am through Libby."

"Don't do that, Cole. You don't realize the danger you put yourself in."

"I doubt it will be dangerous for anyone in such a public place as Genting Hotel, no matter what those Americans turn out to be. But do keep an open mind about them, Butch. Often people are exactly what they seem to be."

Butch considered the possibility that Cole could be right, but he didn't believe it. Still, it was worth checking out, so long as he took the proper precautions.

Miles unbuttoned his shirt. Joining Roseta sounded like a wonderful idea. She had unpacked her clothes as soon as they walked into the room, "so they won't wrinkle," she explained as she hung items in the closet. Miles sat on the bed and watched her every move, as if she were performing some feat of extraordinary interest. Yet when she turned from the closet, he couldn't remember the color or shape of a single garment she had put into it. "I need to freshen up a bit," she said, taking some small items from the bottom of her bag. "A shower would feel good." That was when she had turned to him with a shy smile and said in little more than a whisper, "you can join me, if you want."

It took him long minutes to recover from the shock of it. Of course he wanted to shower with her. He pulled his shirt half off, hesitated, then put it back on and began fastening the buttons again. It seemed all a bit too quick and too frightening to suit him.

"Miles," Roseta called from the bathroom, "will you hand me my shampoo? It's in the small zipper part of my bag."

He turned the bag over a couple of times before locating the part she referred to, found the shampoo, and walked into the bathroom.

She had pulled the shower curtain back and stood exposed in the tub, water running over her body. Miles drew in a quick breath between his teeth. Their eyes met, and though Miles felt an almost overpowering urge to look at her body, he knew he couldn't, not with her looking him in the eye. She held out her hand and he placed the shampoo bottle into it; neither broke eye contact. "Thank you, Miles," she said. Then she looked down at herself and added in a low voice, "It is all right to look."

He looked down, then glanced at his shirt, realizing that he had buttoned the bottom button in the third hole so the shirt hung at a crazy angle. His hand shot up, lifting the shirt front into a little wad to keep her from seeing how absurd he looked.

"Oh, Miles," she said watching him fumble with his shirt, "I'm so relieved you decided to join me. I was beginning to be afraid that I had offended you."

Miles unbuttoned his shirt without letting go of the spot he held bunched up. He dropped the shirt on the floor, then took off the rest of his clothes and stepped into the shower with her.

They bathed in a silent, business-like way, slipping past each other to share the stream of water, handing the soap back and forth. She did not shampoo her hair, but Miles gave the matter no thought. After they toweled dry, Miles followed her into the bedroom. She reached into her bag for panties, then turned to look openly at Miles for the first time. "You are a beautiful man, Miles Osborn."

"So are you. Uh, a woman. A beautiful woman, I mean."

"I have never showered with a man before." She put on the panties and picked up a bra. Miles searched through his plastic bag for clean underwear but somehow couldn't locate them. He didn't believe her disclaimer about showering, but right then, her lie didn't seem to matter so much.

She stepped over to him and turned her back. "Fasten me, please." She held the ends of the bra so he could reach them. He fumbled with the bra until he managed to fit the hook into the eye. She turned to him, standing close. "It would be all right with me, if you kissed me now." She turned her face up to him and closed her eyes.

He bent toward her and set his lips against her cheek. She shifted, her lips seeking his, finding them, then pressed her body against his. Miles felt dizzy. Somehow they were on the bed together, touching and nuzzling each other with a passion Miles had never felt before. As he lifted himself to enter her, a number of unrelated, crazy thoughts ran through his mind: how did her panties come off, and her bra? He had seen her put them on, hadn't he, and even helped? And what was he doing with this forward woman, one who was so experienced with men that she could come out of her clothes, such as they were, with seeming magic? But the thoughts were like a distant movement on the horizon, and Roseta's body was right there, against his, her breath coming in quick gasps, even as his did, and nothing seemed to matter except their coming together as he pushed into her.

She cried out in pain and he pulled back, rising on his arms and knees. "I've hurt you," he said, alarmed.

"Only a little. It's nothing." She pulled him toward her again.

"No. Look, I've made you bleed." He stood beside the bed, and looked at her.

"It's okay, it's okay," she whispered.

"Oh, my god," Miles rushed into the bathroom, wet a wash cloth and brought it to her. He sat beside her as she dabbed herself with the cloth.

"It won't happen again," she said.

"No. Just that once."

He looked at her with such awe and tenderness that Roseta felt tears come to her eyes. I've got him now, she told herself. But rather than feeling victorious, all she felt was an overpowering tenderness for him.

"Would you like to finish making love now?" she asked, knowing how he would answer, feeling sure she had a man beside her who was not the typical male.

"No. Not now. We need to think about all this."

She smiled, pleased with him and with herself for guessing his response. Then he startled her by leaping to his feet and declaring, "I've always lived alone." He grabbed his bag of clothes and fled into the bathroom. "Not by myself," he raised his voice so she could hear over the sound of the tap, "since roommates like Cole don't count. But alone, nevertheless."

Roseta put on clothes. Miles continued talking: "Never even a live-in lover and certainly no one who would think of marrying me. People back in Oklahoma think I'm odd, and they are probably right. Just a nerd, a woman said once, a woman in the administration building who didn't think I could hear, an older woman who worked as a clerk there. The younger ones laughed, the pretty ones who glanced at me from the corners of their eyes and smirked and formulated phrases to explain me away, phrases like *just a nerd.* So I pretend I don't hear such remarks or see the way they fix me with judging or indifferent eyes, the way you would look at a bug in a collection, one stuck on a pin and varnished, suspended over a slip of paper with a Latin name typed across it. I walk off, maybe pretending to whistle to myself, and take out my note pad and write . . ." His voice trailed off.

Roseta pulled her Mexican style dress over her head and glanced in the mirror. It's better than a Malay dress, she thought. Still, she wished she had some jeans and a tee shirt like she had seen American women wear. Miles entered wearing boxer shorts and an undershirt. "So I don't know. I just don't know." He sat on a chair and dropped his chin to his chest.

"I know. I know you are more of a man than anyone I've ever met." She sat on the arm of the chair and put her hand on his shoulder. "Maybe even more than Jamal would have become."

"Jamal?" Miles looked at her with some alarm.

She smiled again, glad to see he would not like to have a rival. "My brother. Remember what I told you when we met in Central Market?"

Miles sighed with obvious relief. "I'm not sure. Do you mean that business about how you needed some help in finding out something about the lawyer who grabbed Libby and got slapped for his effort? Che?"

"Yes, Che. He killed Jamal. He was only sixteen, my brother, not much more than a child."

## 12

The art of mosaic reached its greatest heights in Malaysia among those who clip jungle butterfly wings to create beauty beyond the art of nature.
—Che Mothar Bin Dr. Hazri, "Malayan Folk Art"

Noland took his guitar out of its case, sat on the bed and grinned at Virginia. "Used to," he said, "I sat up late, out on the porch back in Shamrock, and practiced picking. Chet Atkins was my hero, then. I learned this piece from one of his records."

Virginia sat on a stuffed chair listening to the music. Noland played much better than she expected, even if the piece had a bit too much of the twanging, sliding notes she associated with American country-and-western music. "Very nice," she said when he finished. "Will you play another for me?"

"That one is called 'The Wildwood Flower,' a favorite in Texas. This next one is a mite different, and you have to forgive the mistakes. I can't play 'La Malagueña' like Chet does."

Virginia watched his hands, feeling that there was no way he could be striking so many notes with only ten fingers. From time to time, Noland shut his eyes tight and shook his head, indicating he had made a mistake. But Virginia heard no mistakes, only fluid, beautiful music that moved through her, filling her with excitement. She looked at Noland with new respect. His next piece was New Orleans blues with a beat he achieved through striking bass notes with his thumb while playing high notes with his fingers, producing a melody that seemed filled with pain and crying. Virginia felt great tenderness for him.

When the last notes of the blues number died away, Noland strummed some chords, holding his fingers on the neck of the guitar like a contortionist. And he began singing in a resonate, deep voice a song of wandering long, empty Texas roads, of drifting like the wind, of isolation and loneliness. When he stopped singing, Virginia saw his eyes were moist. "I wrote that song," he said, his voice husky, "at a time I thought I was doomed to be alone forever."

The tone of his voice and the way he looked at her worried Virginia. She stood up. "Noland, you have such talent. You are a real artist, and you didn't tell me."

"I don't know about being an artist. But I wanted to show you, not just tell you I could do some things with a guitar. Talking about it always sounds like empty bragging."

"Will you play some more for me? Later? Right now I would like to go down to the casino. I've heard about it for years, but never seen the gambling machines and the gamblers."

Noland looked pleased. "I knew a girl named Virginia once, back in Texas, who hated my guitar. Course, I wasn't so practiced up back then, but my picking wasn't all that bad, either."

In the casino, Virginia walked around, looking with awe at the people marking keno, at the way the croupier raked away all the chips at the roulette tables, at the way people fed coins to the slot machines. She knew that Noland watched her with amusement. "This here," he said, "is nothing but a den of iniquity. But the slots can be fun. You want to try?"

"I don't know how."

"I'll show you." He got some change from a clerk sitting by the bank of slot machines and instructed Virginia in what to watch for when the wheels spun and stopped in patterns of color and numbers. On her third coin, five grapes lined up, the win meter jumped, and bells rang. "That's how it gets you hooked," he said. "A small win that looks and sounds big. Then you put all the coins you won back into the machine, and more." She played in silence, Noland standing close. "Have you ever been in love?"

The main reason she suggested leaving their the room was to put off dealing with such a question. But there it was. She dropped several more coins into the machine, pulled the lever, and shook her head. "Loving is dangerous. People change or die or go away. My father died. My mother. And I knew a man once, one I might have learned to love, given time. He taught me much in his bed about . . ." she bit her lip and turned to him. "I hope what I say doesn't hurt. Or disappoint. I don't know. Maybe I talk too much. I hope you know that my name is a lie. I was no virgin when we met."

"Neither was I, Virginia. The past doesn't matter."

Relieved, she turned again to the slot machine. "But it does matter, Noland. The man I mentioned. Married. With children. He lied to me, and he said he loved me. I believed, and even if I feared loving, I wanted to learn. Some part of me did. Then he left, and the emptiness of his going hurt. Not as much as it would have had I allowed myself to love him. But it hurt."

"I was in love, once," Noland volunteered. "Ever since, I've been looking for it again. I had come to believe I might not ever find it."

"I've never found it." She turned to him again. "Noland, do not rely on me. Do not. I defend against love, and even if we pleasure each other in bed, it is my belief that I will never find it. Please do not be hurt."

She looked at the slot machine with distaste. "This grows wearsome, this machine with its lights and wheels. Can we go elsewhere? Perhaps to dinner?"

After dinner, they returned to their room where Noland played his guitar for her again, and again she felt moved by the music, by the feeling way he made the blues vibrate from the strings. Then he set aside the guitar and they made love.

She stretched and sighed her contentment in the afterglow of loving.

"I think I've found it," Noland said. She stiffened a bit, and he added with haste: "I didn't mean to offend you."

"Oh, Noland, I'm not offended." She sat up. "I'm a bit frightened, perhaps."

"Of me?"

"Of what you need—maybe of what I need. *Finding it*, as you spoke of love, could be the beginning of pain." She stood and began dressing. "I'll be going for a walk now. Just around the hotel." He sat up. "No. You stay here. I need to be alone." She laughed at the seriousness of his face. "I'll be back. You know I'll be back. And quite soon."

When he saw the policeman and the other man coming up the stair well, Miles went into the ninth floor hall. As the exit door open behind him, he ducked into the custodian's closet. Pushing the closet door nearly shut, Miles peeked out. But the two men didn't come into the hall, not until the Chinese woman left her room.

Miles watched the policeman and his companion nearly sprint to catch up with the woman and grab her from behind. The bigger man put his hand over her mouth and the smaller one, the policeman, pulled his revolver and thrust it into her face. She didn't struggle much. The big dark- skinned fellow seemed to be enjoying himself as he dragged the woman back down the hall to the stairs. The policeman kept glancing toward the elevator.

As soon as the exit door closed, Miles went to it. He listened until he felt it safe to open the door a tiny bit and take a look. One floor down, the two men dragged the woman out of the stair well. Miles counted to five then went down the flight of steps and cracked the door. He watched the two men and the woman disappear into the second room on the left side of the hall. The scene, he told himself in deliberate understatement, seemed a bit more spectacular than anything he had expected when Roseta instructed him to follow the one she called Virginia.

Now what? Miles asked himself. Report to Roseta? He didn't know where to find her. Tell the policeman he had seen standing by the exit to the casino? That might do no good at all; a man in an identical uniform had just helped grab the woman who, no doubt, was Virginia. She came from Virginia's room, anyway.

He stood frozen in indecision, feeling he had to tell someone what he had witnessed, growing fearful the men would come out of the room, see him peeking through the exit door, and come after him. He glanced at the room number on the second door, then he went one more floor down, entered the hall and headed for the elevator.

Miles had thought finding the room of the Chinese woman and the cowboy rather easy, except for having to talk with Cole. He made such a big deal out of it, inviting him in, adjusting some of the medals on his shirt just to call attention to them, big-shotting around on the phone to the main desk. Then he tried to pump Miles for why he needed the information. Miles answered in a vague way and got out of there, located Virginia and Noland's room, then stationed himself in the stairwell to watch the door. After about twenty minutes the cop and the big dark fellow came up the stairwell.

When Miles had slipped into the custodian's closet, he told himself hiding was a by god strange business for him. But after showering with Roseta and making love with her—and discovering she had yielded her virginity to him, he had found himself willing to do whatever she asked. Her amazing account of her brother and of her recent attempts to learn more about Che confirmed for Miles that Roseta had to be the most interesting person he had ever met.

They had gone to one of the hotel restaurants for dinner and talked of food and weather and other trivial things that somehow seemed not so trivial to Miles. Then they walked about the hotel, looked around in the casino, walked among the crowd on the ground floor, window shopped in the gallery of stores beyond the registration desk. Roseta stood beside a window displaying jewelry and sighed. "Time with you, Miles, runs so quickly. But now I must get to work. You will help me?"

"Yes. What should I do?"

She had given him instructions in their room while she put a weird black dress over her regular clothes, then put on black head gear and a veil. She looked to Miles like an Islamic from Saudi Arabia. When she left, she said she was going to spy on Che. Miles objected to that, but she laughed. "I'll be perfectly safe," she said. "He won't even see me. And if he does look my way, all he will see is a black lump of a person. There is no way he will know who I am."

Many things about the story Roseta had told astounded Miles. She was a lawyer. Amazing. He and Cole always assumed her to be an artist who worked with water colors. Hadn't Cole told him that? Even more mind- boggling was that she worked for Che—and the turkey hardly knew her. He saw her at the Batu Blue meetings dressed as Roseta, and yet he never recognized her as Ros, his legal assistant.

When Miles expressed his astonishment about the matter, Roseta waved her hand in annoyance. "Che," she said, "never takes women seriously enough to pay any attention to details that don't concern him. All he sees of me as Ros is a shapeless woman in black with only her face showing, a face that never wears make-up and never looks directly at him, one he has no reason to examine closely. And as Roseta, I have long black hair to change the way I look, and make-up and a dress that suggests a woman instead of the black sack that could be hiding anything from an old stick of a woman to one thick as a cow. As Roseta, I am simply another woman, one he apparently doesn't find appealing as a sex object. He sees Ros only as a machine to do his law work."

As a Dakwah fundamentalist Islamic woman who cloaks everything but her eyes with black cloth, she explained, she could follow Che various places and discover a great deal about the men he dealt with and the women he seduced, adding to what she learned from watching him as Ros and Roseta. Over a period of time, she compiled a great deal of information about Che, some of it quite damning. But she needed more, she told Miles. For her brother's sake.

"Che murdered your brother?" Miles had demanded.

"Not outright. He did it through the legal machinery of Malaysian law." Roseta's voice had trembled when she told about Jamal.

Miles got on the elevator and punched G. As the machine dropped him to the ground floor, he took out his note pad and wrote, "Two men kidnaped Virginia and forced her into room 836." He scowled at the note, then added "Fear for her."

On the ground floor, Miles walked to the center of the gigantic lobby. There were people everywhere, mostly Chinese, all busy rushing here and there. Miles hesitated and looked around, hoping to catch sight of Roseta in her black sack, feeling sure it was useless. He went toward the sign that said "Tandas" and entered the door with the logo of a male on it.

At least a dozen men were in there, some standing by the latrine, some washing at the lavatories and drying their hands. Miles considered taping the note inside one of the booths. He reread his graffiti and decided this was not the place for it.

He would by god leave it on Cole's door, that's what he would do. Then he would wander around looking for Roseta.

In front of Coleman's room, Miles pulled some tape from his pocket. Just as he stuck his note to the door, it opened. "Hello, Miles," Coleman said. "Are you involved in another graffiti campaign?"

The two men in police uniforms bound her hands while a third man held her tight against his body, one hand over her mouth. He laughed without humor. "You and me have sort of date now," he kept repeating, "sort of date." He stank of tobacco and rancid sweat.

"Now her legs," one of the phony policemen said. He stepped back while the smaller man wrapped something around her ankles. Virginia thought the man standing in front of her looked Malay, though he was clearly a mixture of a number of races.

"Are you afraid, Jenny L.E.M.?" he asked. She stiffened upon hearing that name. "Good, good. I see you are, a little. Ibrahim, show her your knife."

Ibrahim finished tying her legs, stood and grinned at her. He produced a knife with a heavy blade for her to inspect. The man holding his hand over her mouth laughed again. He ran his other hand up to her

192

breasts.

"Sort of date," he said.

"When Mehinder takes his hand away from your mouth, you must remain quiet until I tell you to speak," the Malay-looking man said. "If you make any noise at all, Ibrahim will use his knife. He is quite skillful with it. Put her there," he motioned to a stuffed chair. "Prop her feet." Mehinder set her in the chair, knelt beside her and cupped her breasts with his hands. He laughed. "Save that for later, Mehinder. Right now we have some business to conduct." Ibrahim put the ottoman under her legs. Virginia saw that her hands and feet were bound with strips of leather. "I have only a few questions. You will answer them truthfully. What is your real name, Jenny L.E.M.?"

"Virginia Li."

"I doubt that. Where are you from?"

"Petaling Jaya." Ibrahim grabbed her hair and pinned her head against the back of the chair. His knife flashed toward her and she felt a sharp slap on her cheek.

"Ibrahim, don't do anything like that again unless I tell you." The man interrogating her sat down on the ottoman beside Virginia's legs. "He hit you with the flat part of the knife. You are lucky. And smart. If you had cried out, he might have cut your throat. Ibrahim, you stand over there. My ways, Virginia or Jenny or whatever your name is, are more refined and more effective. Ibrahim, take off your shoe."

Ibrahim looked dumfounded. Mehinder laughed and shoved the small man toward the bed where he sat and removed his shoe.

"For now," the man on the ottoman said, "I'll pretend that I believe you are from Petaling Jaya. But be careful with how you answer the other questions. Who do you work for?"

"You will not believe anything I say, I can see that."

"I might. Try me. Who do you work for?"

"Nobody. I just lost my job as amah for Suppriah Krishna."

"But you work for someone else. What kind of dadah did your American friends bring into Malaysia?"

"Noland and Kent? Noland came to work for EXXON. Kent is an artist, invited here by the Sultan of Selangor. They are not dealers in drugs."

"You disappoint me. Ibrahim, give me your sock. Mehinder, get a towel." Mehinder chuckled and went into the bathroom. Ibrahim, a puzzled frown on his face, pulled off his sock. The man on the ottoman leaned toward her and grasped her nose. "Open your mouth," he commanded. Virginia kept her mouth clamped shut. "Ibrahim, bring your knife. We will pry it open."

Virginia opened her mouth. The man stuffed Ibrahim's sock into it and tied a leather strip around her head so she could not spit out the sock. "Think about what is in your mouth," he said. "Think about Ibrahim's feet, about where he walks barefoot, about how he dislikes bathing. I suspect he has fungus growing between his toes. It is so common in the tropics. Can you taste the sock? Mehinder, put the towel there." Mehinder dropped a bath towel on the arm of the chair.

"I will tell you an amusing story. Perhaps you know it already. Have you been to Nepal? You won't nod or shake your head? No matter. Just outside of Kathmandu, on the rocky ground between the forks of a river, a strange man lives in a hut he built from river sticks. The locals call him *Bahadura*, which means the Brave One. He calls himself *Nalayaka*, or the Unfit. Everyone in the valley knows of him, and tourists go stand on the banks of the river, hoping to see him. Bahadura has lived there for many years. Some think he is a holy man and bring him food. That is because of what he does, once each year. He cuts away a small part of his body. Many years ago he began with parts of his fingers, then worked his way up his arm. Now he has only a stump left of that arm. No one knows how he does it, for he performs his ritual privately, inside the hut of sticks. He somehow cuts through the flesh and saws through the bone. Mehinder, put her hand on the towel."

Virginia struggled, but it was no use. Mehinder pressed her hand on the arm of the chair, against the towel, and spread her fingers. "Ibrahim, take the end of that one," the man pointed to the little finger on her left hand. Virginia squirmed about and made muffled sounds, watching in horror as Ibrahim sliced away the first joint of her finger.

Libby ordered two glasses of starfruit juice. Kent opened his art pad to a clean page and made a quick sketch of the waitress leaning over Libby, peering into the drinks menu, her pencil poised over the order form. "Are you an artist, sir?" the waitress asked.

"Yes, he is," Libby said.

"May I see what you just drew?" The waitress came to his side of the table. Kent sighed and looked around the room. The table he sat beside seemed to be in the middle of the crowded lobby, but in fact was off to one side somewhat just behind the roped off area that served as a cocktail lounge. Nearly everyone he saw was Chinese. The only exceptions were Libby and a man in a preposterous white suit and sunglasses who strolled toward the lounge, searching the floor before him with a walking cane.

"Is this me?" The waitress put her finger on Kent's drawing.

"Not yet. It's just blocking. The lines tell me how you stood just a minute ago. Later perhaps I will fill in the details." Kent watched the blind Caucasian stop when he touched the rope close to Libby. He paused, felt along the rope with the cane, then walked behind Kent.

"Are there others in your book that you have finished?" the waitress asked. Kent nodded. "May I look?" She held out her hand. Kent handed her the pad.

"Does this happen often?" Libby asked as the waitress looked through the drawings.

"Not so often back in the States. Here, I don't know yet."

Butch stopped and watched the waitress flip through Kent's pad. So the man is an artist, after all, Butch thought, and a damn good one.

"Some of these are very beautiful. Others—not so nice. If you finish drawing me while you are at Genting, you will let me see it, yes?" The waitress closed the art pad and set it in Kent's hands as if she were handing him a menu.

As the waitress walked away, Libby leaned forward and whispered, "Kent, the people here are often so frank about their observations." She sat back and laughed. "More than once, I have had people, perfect strangers, ask me why my nose is so tall."

Kent laughed. "That seems cheeky, coming right out with what's on their minds like that. And yet I could take a lesson from them." He became serious. "That uncomfortable confusion this morning at the Mandarin could have been avoided if I had told you about Noland and Virginia from the start." He opened the pad and began work on the sketch of the waitress.

Butch stood so he didn't exactly face Kent and watched him draw. Astonishing, Butch thought. The man is a genuine artist. And a good one. He tried to hide his surprise. Probably, he thought, Libby wouldn't look at him—but if she did, the dark glasses would keep her from seeing that he watched Kent.

"Set that business behind you, Kent. It doesn't matter. What concerns me most is the bomb those two fellows planted in Noland's room. The only bothersome thing about what happened this morning is that funny man, Butch. Odd as it might sound, he appears to be involved some-how with the planting of the bomb. As soon as we get back to PJ, I'll find him and get some answers out of him. That or wring his neck."

Butch's hand went automatically to his neck. He decided it was time to get away from the lounge area, away from Libby and her wrath. Though he took care to play the role of the blind man, he wasn't so sure the disguise was necessary anymore, except, of course, to avoid having to answer to Libby.

Disappointment washed over him as he considered the prospect of losing the basis in reality for his great dramatic work, disappointment that was far greater than his relief to find Libby not in danger, after all.

"Are we avoiding what we came to the lounge to discuss?" Kent asked.

"Yes."

"What about it, then?"

Earlier, as Kent and Libby stood behind Noland at the hotel's reception desk and heard him request just one room for him and Virginia, Libby asked under her breath, "How are we going to do this, Kent?" He had hesitated, searched for the proper answer, then pointed toward the lounge and suggested the two of them get a refreshment.

The waitress set glasses of yellowish juice in front of them. "Sharing a room would save money, and I would be comfortable with that," Libby said. "What about you?"

Kent thought about Rita and Hotel Galvez, about how she posed for him in her red bikini, about the explosive, wild passion his touch had awakened in her. All of that, he told himself, was so long ago and half a world away. "Sharing a room," he said, feeling the hair on the back of his neck prickle, "makes sense to me, too."

"Do you want to get the room, or shall I?"

"Would you mind? I would meet you by the elevator with our bags."

It helps, Kent thought, looking at Libby on the elevator, that she is tall—a reminder that she is far, far different from Rita.

Inside the room, they set their bags down and Libby turned to him. Kent knew he must look frightened when she suggested they go for a walk around the artificial lake outside, then go for dinner. She's showing me she will give me space, he thought. When they returned to the room, Kent felt more relaxed about the matter.

"So many things about you are attractive, Kent Day. Your immense talent with art—the way you can capture so much of what is inside a person in lines that have such elegant simplicity. The way you treat me as a friend, and work to understand who I am. The way you worried about my feelings when you realized I had found Virginia in your room." She touched her fingertips to his cheek then dropped her hand.

"You got a room with only one bed."

Libby nodded. "You did tell me to get the room. Also, we were in here before. Did you not notice then?" She unbuckled her waist purse, dropped it on the bed and looked at him, brows raised.

"Would you be amused if I told you I have performance anxiety?" He kissed her neck. Both kept their hands by their sides. "And that I'm almost terrified."

"I fear beginnings," she said. "They have a way of circling about and becoming endings. The only thing that keeps me from running out the door is that I have no expectations."

"Then we start on even ground." He put his hand on her cheek, brushed his fingers down her neck and unbuttoned the top button of her blouse. She began unbuttoning his shirt while they stood, inches apart, each watching the other's hands. As Kent worked with the second button, images of Rita flashed through his mind. He remembered her twisting away from him in the dark, turning on the light, unable to continue their touching. Remembered the discovery that she both liked and hated the thought of him entering her, remembered his impotence and how Rita sometimes overcame that with her hands and lips and tongue, remembered her cowering on the floor, terrified of him as she blended him with the ghosts of her past. The images that came to him had a vividness and immediacy that denied time, and Hotel Galvez seemed not so far away. His hands began trembling, and the button slipped this way and that, remaining caught in the buttonhole. "Likely I will be impotent," he whispered.

"That doesn't matter. Not at all." She took his hands, placed them on her hips, and unfastened the button he had been worrying with. As she took the next one, someone knocked on their door.

They jumped apart, and both laughed. "I feel like I did when I was sixteen and my father turned on the porch light in the middle of my first kiss," Libby said. The knock came again, harder and insistent.

Kent felt somehow it was exactly the right thing for her to say. "There will be more time," he said, "later." He felt both relief and disappointment.

Libby went to the door and looked out the spy. "It's Noland, and he looks quite agitated." She opened the door.

"Sorry to bust in on you like this." Noland looked at Libby's partially-buttoned blouse. "I have lousy timing. It's Virginia. She left to go for a short walk—just for a few minutes, she said. It's been some time, now, and she hasn't showed up. I thought maybe she came by your room or called or something."

"Come in, Noland." Libby stepped back.

"We haven't seen her," Kent said. "But we'll help you look."

"Probably it's nothing." Noland looked up and down the hall, then entered the room. "But after that thing in my room back at the other hotel turned out to be a bomb, I'm just jumpy as hell. I should never have let her go off by herself, not for a minute."

"Noland," Libby said, "people do not chain each other up. Virginia had a perfect right to go for a walk."

Noland looked pained. "You know what I mean," he said. "That business about the bomb has me scared for her."

"Did you get Coleman's message when you checked in?" Libby asked. "I got the one for me and Kent at the main desk."

"That funny thing about batso blue meeting in his room? Virginia said it came from the man you told us about on the way up here who likes to gather artists and writers around him."

"Virginia said that? Then there is a remote possibility that she called him or went to his room."

"Maybe." Noland looked doubtful.

"It's worth calling and checking, anyway." Libby went to the phone and called the operator. "Ring Coleman Farquart, please."

"Sorry about all the trouble, Kent," Noland said.

"No problem."

"I've been so long in finding this lady. An entire lifetime. Then I get careless, for just a minute—"

"Noland, she's somewhere in this hotel, probably doing something perfectly reasonable. I doubt that we need to worry at all."

Libby put the phone down and reached for the purse she had dropped on the bed. "Come on," she said, sweeping past them to the door. "Cole said his roommate from PJ is in his room, and he knows something about Virginia. Something about her being in trouble."

"Cover her eyes," the man on the ottoman said. Mehinder tied a strip of cloth around Virginia's eyes. "Now get out of here." Ibrahim and Mehinder left the room. The man picked up the phone, dialed four numbers, and said a single word: "Ready."

Within minutes Bayang and Che came in. "Anything yet?" Bayang asked.

"No. But she is the right girl, and I have her ready to tell you whatever you want to know."

"Take off her gag."

"Where did all the blood come from?" Che asked.

"It's nothing. Just part of the persuasion from the Burning Tiger boys."

"I don't like it."

"You don't get paid to like it," Bayang snapped. "Just shut up and listen. We're likely saving your neck."

While the man in the policeman's uniform took off her gag, he spoke to Virginia in low tones: "You will speak only when asked and you will make no other sounds. Remember my story about Bahadura. If you do not do as we ask, I will cut away another piece of you, then another, until you have only a stump hanging from your shoulder, like Bahadura."

"I am Bayang, the Shadow Man. You will answer my questions." Bayang took out some papers and read from one: "'To whom it may concern: Miss Jenny L.E.M. has been employed in my household for the period of two years as a domestic servant. I found her to be a hard worker, impeccably honest, and a creative cook.' Jenny, what did I just read from?"

The focus of Virginia's attention had been on the pain in her finger. While she had been aware of the events in the room since Ibrahim used his knife on her hand, they seemed almost unreal, like they were happening to someone else. Even the threat to chop more pieces from her arm had come to her as a voice from a distant room. But something about the way Bayang spoke caught her full attention. For all their threats, she had not believed the other men would do more than cause her to feel pain. But the coldness in this man's voice said he could take her life.

"I wrote that," she said.

"It goes on to say you are illiterate. I suppose you wrote that, too?"

"Yes."

"Then, my dear Jenny, we have something of a problem. If you wrote the letter, you are obviously not illiterate. You are obviously a liar. Is that correct?"

"I needed a job."

"You will not sidestep my question."

"Yes. I lied in that letter."

"You understand what I will do to you if you lie to me? I refer, of course, to what I will do after all the unnecessary pain and suffering."

"Yes. You will take my life."

"Then we understand each other perfectly. How often do you masquerade as a Dakwah?"

"I never have."

"Are you telling me that you have never cloaked yourself in black Islamic robes and a veil in order to follow a certain lawyer, to spy on him?"

Virginia felt a knot of fear growing in her stomach. "I worked as an amah. I wrote stories about the experience, publishing them under my real name, Virginia Li. I have never spied on anyone."

"Be careful. I am a patient man, but not a stupid man. I can check on your claim to have published stories. How did you first meet the tall man called Noland?"

Virginia had hoped for such a question, something that would allow her to talk at some length, to cause as much time to go by as possible without these men hurting her again, or doing worse. She began her account with the cruelties of the Spider Lady that drove her into taking out an ad in *The Dallas Morning News*. Sensing that the truth, bizarre though it was, would not be enough to keep the men in the room quiet, she elaborated on the truth. The Spider Lady became a woman who seduced all her male servants, forcing them to do disgusting things with her until they quit. The only man who could stand her sexual games over any period of time was the old gate keeper. Virginia told of how she had hidden so she could watch what the Spider Lady made the gate keeper do.

The men in the room listened without interruption.

On the elevator Noland demanded, "Any of you chewing gum?"

"I am," Coleman said. "And I think Miles is, right Miles?"

"Give it to me," Noland said.

"I think I have a pack in my pocket." Coleman put a hand into his pants pocket.

"No. I want the piece you're chewing." The elevator stopped on the eighth floor. As they got off, Noland added, "Hurry." He snatched the gum as soon as Coleman had it out of his mouth. "Which way?" Noland turned to Miles. Miles pointed and Noland took off in a run. The others followed.

Noland stopped in front of a door and stuck Cole's gum over the spy. He stepped back, gesturing with impatience at the group coming up the hall, then pointed to the number over the door and raised his brows in question.

"Yes," Miles said. Noland's index finger shot up to his lips. He stepped up to the door and knocked three times.

Roseta, who had followed Che to the room, then waited behind the door to the stairs, pulled off the black gown and hood and rolled them up to carry under one arm. Miles was out there, along with Coleman and Libby and her new friend, Kent—all watching whatever the big cowboy was doing. Roseta decided she could join the group safely enough. And she wanted to see what happened when Che and the other man came to the door.

Miles looked at Roseta in astonishment and started to speak. She shook her head and nodded toward Noland.

"Who is it?" a voice asked. Noland knocked again. He put his hand on the door knob and turned his shoulder to the door. When the door opened to the length of the safety chain, Noland hit the door with his shoulder with such force that the wood screws on the chain gave and the door smashed into the face of the man in the police uniform. Noland slammed the door into him again, then rushed into the room.

He caught Che hard in the stomach with his right fist. Bayang moved back and stumbled against the bed just as Noland hit him in the face. Noland looked at Virginia. "My god," he said at the sight of the blood. Che tried to stand. Noland grabbed his coat and jerked his head against the wall. The impact made a dull cracking sound.

Libby knelt beside the man by the door. The others crowded into the room. "Noland?" Virginia said while he worked to untie her blindfold. Kent unbound her feet. "Noland," she said, breaking into tears.

"Your hand," he said.

"It hurts." She held up her hands while Noland cut the straps with his pocket knife. "But I will be all right." She fought back tears.

Roseta took Virginia's hand and looked at her little finger. "Che did this," she said. "The animal."

"Who are all these people, Noland?" Virginia asked. He looked around.

"Friends," he said. "Right, Libby?"

"That's right. Her name is Roseta." Libby turned Che over and felt in his coat pocket. Miles nudged him contemptuously with his shoe. "Dead?" he asked.

"No." Libby stood up. Noland had Virginia on her feet, holding her and stroking her hair.

"There are others," Virginia said. "One has a pistol."

"Close that door," Noland said to Coleman, who stood beside the door looking with astonishment at the scene in the room. As he turned to the door, Coleman saw Butch coming down the hall, feeling in front of him with his cane.

"Good grief, Butch," Coleman said. "Stop the blind man act and get into this room. There's people out there with guns."

"Guns?" Butch hurried into the room, and Coleman shut the door. "Oh, sheeeit," Butch said backing into Coleman when he saw Noland.

"Stop that, Butch. Noland just saved this lady's life. You were absolutely wrong about him."

"I was?" Butch took off the dark glasses and looked around in bewilderment.

Libby examined the man on the bed. "Broken nose, I think," she said. "Likely he will be out for some time." She looked up and saw Butch. "The blind European?" she said.

"It's Butch, dressed as a character actor," Coleman said. "He followed us here."

"Two others," Virginia said. "There were two others. One a big Indian fellow, one a little man they called Ibrahim, the one who cut my hand."

"Mehinder and Abraham," Noland said. "The ones who planted the

202

bomb."

"Bomb?" Roseta asked.

"Jesus Holy Christ," Butch said. "Another bomb." He pulled out a pad and wrote something on it.

"Stop that," Coleman said, slapping at Butch's pad.

"They left just a few minutes ago," Virginia said. "Ibrahim has a pistol. He's dressed like a policeman."

"They could come back any time," Kent said. "I don't like this."

"Let's all get to my room," Coleman said.

"No," Libby said. "Not safe. Maybe we should call hotel security."

"No cops," Noland said.

"He's right." Kent pointed at the man on the floor by the door. "They might turn out to be like that one. We'd better leave here fast."

"Butch has a van," Coleman said. "It would hold us all. We could drive to my place in Petaling Jaya."

"My van?" Butch asked, confused.

"Trust me," Coleman said.

"My place would be better," Libby said. "Virginia, can you make it with your hurt hand?"

"Yes."

"Who all will go?" Butch asked.

"All of us," Libby said. "Right now, without going to any of our rooms."

"That's right," Noland said.

"We ought to split into two groups to be less conspicuous when we go to the van," Coleman said.

"No splitting up," Noland said. "Kent, look out in the hall and see if anyone is there. We gotta get to the elevator."

"I don't know about all this," Butch said.

"Dammit, Butch," Libby said, "Haven't you made enough trouble?"

"Butch," Coleman said, "we have to get out of here, and your van is the only logical way. Stop being the playwright and help us."

"Okay," Butch said. "Let's go to the van."

"Get a wash cloth for Virginia's hand," Noland said. Coleman stepped into the bathroom.

As the others filed out of the room, Roseta caught Miles' arm. "Lift him up," she gestured at Che. Without questioning her, Miles took Che's shoulders and heaved him to a sitting position.

"We need to go," Libby said, looking back. When she saw Roseta struggling to put the black gown over Che's head, Libby went back into the room. "Help me lift him a little higher, Miles," she said. "Roseta, hurry."

"Come on," Kent said. "We need to shut this door."

"Twenty more seconds," Libby said. "There. Set him in the chair." Roseta straightened the cloth on Che's head and fastened the veil over his face.

## 13

Into the jungle, into the jungle
of monkeys that hoot and sing,
Noble Noland led his people
where leeches suck and scorpions sting.
—Coleman Farquart, *An Asian Mystery*

Bayang felt as if he were drowning. He tried sitting up, but the effort brought a surge of pain to his head, and even then the feeling of drowning persisted. He rolled to his side and drew a hand up to his face. Blood, he noted, still running from his nose. He pushed himself up on one elbow and looked around the room, squinting against the ache in his head.

A woman in Dakwah black, her face covered, slumped on one of the chairs. She seemed to be asleep. Raul sat on the floor by the door, holding his head. "Raul," Bayang said. The man on the floor grunted. "Raul, get up."

"Yes, Boss."

"Where is Che?" Bayang stood, winced, and sat back on the bed. "And who is that woman?"

"Who broke the door?" Raul stood and leaned against the wall.

"This Dakwah devil woman has the shoes of a man." Bayang jerked the veil off of the figure on the chair. "Che."

"Che?" Raul went to the chair, leaned over and peered into Che's face. "Che don't look so good." He put his fingers to the side of Che's throat.

"Alive?"

"Yes." Raul lifted Che's eyelid. "But no one is home. Che will be useless for some time."

"Get the keys to his Mercedes. Take them to those animals, Mehinder and Ibrahim. Tell them to find the cowboy American and cut his throat."

Raul lifted the black robe and felt in Che's pockets. "What will I do with Che?"

Bayang scowled. "Put his veil back over his face and let him sleep. Send the boys after the American, then get me a taxi for the airport."

Butch drove down the mountain road from Genting, taking the bumps and curves as fast as he dared. Once he understood that the men with the guns in the hotel were the same ones he had seen plant the bomb in Noland's room, no one had to urge him to hurry. Cole had told him about Noland breaking into the room to rescue Virginia. "He hit them hard and sudden," Cole said, a note of awe in his voice. "That man is tough and powerful and quite far from being a criminal. You saw the way he treats the woman he took away from those thugs."

So I lost a villain, Butch thought. But I gain a protagonist who appears to be a genuine hero. And that scene in the room back there— dynamite for theatrics. The girl with her finger cut off by the genuine villains, the coming of Noland like the cavalry thundering in, just in the nick of time. Butch envisioned one of the men in the room chopping off the girl's finger, then pressing the knife to her throat, about to dispatch her when the door flew open and Noland leaped into the room like an occidental Bruce Lee, spinning in a blur of action, but using his fists, American-style, instead of kicking and delivering oriental karate chops. Butch glanced in the rear-view mirror, hoping to catch a glimpse of Noland, but knowing it was already too dark.

Kent sat in the far back with Libby. Noland fussed over Virginia's hand. Libby tore a washcloth into strips for a bandage. Miles sat by Roseta just behind the driver's seat. In the rear-view mirror, Butch had seen Miles put his arm around Roseta before darkness made seeing in the van impossible.

As the van approached the speed bump just before the Genting road teed into the old Kuala Lumpur highway, Cole said, "There's a car behind us."

"I've seen the headlights," Butch said. "It could be anyone." He turned right at the intersection.

"Wrong way," Roseta said. "Kuala Lumpur is the other direction."

"I came from this direction," Butch said.

"This is the old road. The intersection to the new one is the other direction." Her voice had a certainty to it that caused Butch to slow.

"What about it?" he directed the question to others in the van.

"Should I turn back?"

"It would get us home faster," Libby said. "I understand this old road winds around a great deal."

"I have no opinion on the matter," Miles said.

"Turn back," Roseta urged him.

"It might be better," Cole said, then added "Here comes the car I thought might be following us." Butch slowed, looking for a place to turn around. A black Mercedes pulled up beside his van, and Butch saw Killer Kaliayani lean out the window with something in his hand.

"You stop," he yelled. Butch shifted into a lower gear and speeded up. The Mercedes kept up easily, and the man shouted something Butch couldn't hear, then fired a pistol at the van. Butch pulled hard on his steering wheel, ramming his front fender into the side of the Mercedes.

Startled, Mehinder braked the Mercedes and pulled away. When he did so, he ran off the road into a small ditch. Ibrahim leaned out of the window as the Mercedes came to a halt. He fired several more times at the van.

The glass of the rear windshield shattered and Kent felt a tearing in the fleshy part of his shoulder, just above the armpit. He ran his hand over the spot and felt something wet.

"Kent," Libby said, "he hit you."

"Not bad." Kent's shoulder felt heavy as if, he thought, a doctor had just injected him with an antibiotic in thick oil.

"Butch," Libby said, "can you turn on the dome light?"

Butch glanced at the stalled Mercedes in his side mirror. "In just a minute or so," he said. "I think their car got stuck. Let me round this bend first. There." He switched on the light.

"How bad is it?" Cole asked.

"Bad," Libby said.

"Not so bad," Kent corrected. "It doesn't hurt much."

"There's no turning back now," Butch said. He took the curves so fast the tires squealed and he had to drift into the other lane for stability.

"Back there," Roseta said, "several curves back—look. Headlights coming, fast." Butch turned off the dome light.

"There's a dirt road ahead," he said. "If I remember right, it's just beyond a bridge. If the curves on the mountain block us from the car behind, I'm going to take that road and cut off my lights. Maybe we can go back up the mountain if the car passes us."

"Try it," Noland said.

The van rounded a curve and crossed a narrow bridge. "Hang on." Butch hit the brakes and turned hard to the left. The road ran straight into dense jungle. "This will be a bit scary, but the lights have to go, and I don't dare hit the brake for a while on account of the braking lights." He squinted ahead, measuring the distance to a bend in the road, switched off the headlights, and began down-shifting.

"It worked," Libby said. "The car just went past this road." Branches brushed the van on both sides; some scraped the top. The darkness ahead was complete. Just as Butch forced the gear shift into first, the van hit a bump then pitched forward down a steep incline.

Butch turned on the lights and pushed at the brakes. He feared braking hard lest the van flip forward. Those in the back of the van slammed forward against the seats in front of them. Kent grunted when his shoulder hit the seat back, and Noland muttered, "Crappo." He began reaching for Virginia even as he fell forward.

When the ground leveled some, Butch had to contend with the trees. He managed to avoid them by jerking the wheel with such violence that his passengers were tossed about. The van had come nearly to a halt when he hit the outcropping of rock.

At first he didn't see it. Then it was too late. The front wheels bounced once and the frame of the van hit the rock. Butch turned off the engine. "That's all she wrote," he said. "We are high-centered." He turned off the headlights.

"Virginia?" Noland said.

"I'm all right."

"Kent, your shoulder," Libby said.

"Back up the hill, look." Roseta clutched Miles' arm.

"They won't drive down here. Even Abraham isn't that dumb," Noland said.

"Kent?" Libby said.

"Not bad," Kent said. "Not good, but not so bad."

Noland opened the side door. "Damn. Somebody cut the dome light." Butch reached toward the light, found the switch. "That must have given them a fix on us. Let's get out of this tank," Noland said.

"I can't see a damn thing," Miles said.

"This way, everybody," Noland said. "Everyone join hands right over here." Outside the van, Noland listened with astonishment to the night sounds of the jungle. The chirps, buzzes and croaks came from insects, he decided.

"I have a flashlight," Butch offered.

"Don't turn it on. Can you rustle up that stick you used when you pretended to be a blind man?"

"I'll get it."

"Virginia, you hold the back of my shirt with your good hand. Libby, take ahold of Virginia and Kent, and stay in a line. And you with the walking stick, get it to me, then get back in the back of the line with that other guy."

"Their names are Cole and Butch," Libby said.

"Look up the hill," Virginia said. "Torches."

"That's what the people here call flashlights," Libby said. Two tiny spots of light flickered on the hill behind them, appearing and disappearing behind the trees.

"They will be maybe thirty minutes or more picking their way down here," Noland said. "I'll poke around with this cane in front of me and head down hill. It looked like a clear shot for good way down, or did to me before Cole turned off the lights to his van."

"Butch," Libby corrected, "Butch's van."

"Butch, then. Everybody lined up? Virginia? Your hand all right?"

"Yes."

"Kent? You doing any good?"

"Fine. Lead on."

"Stay lined up, and everybody hang on to the person in front. Who's last back there? Butch?"

"Yes."

"You'll be rear guard. Keep an eye over your shoulder. If you see those flashlights get much closer, let me know. But don't talk loud."

"Got it." *Rear guard*, Butch thought, pleased.

"What's making all that noise?" Miles asked.

"Bugs," Virginia said. "Some are night birds."

"Big ones?" Miles' voice quavered a bit.

"Small. All small."

"I don't like this," Miles said.

"Not worth a shit," Butch agreed, grinning into the dark. "But Cowboy Bob seems to know what he's doing."

"Noland," Libby said. "Butch, his name is Noland Fritch."

209

"Can the chatter," Noland said, though he doubted their voices carried far because of all the competition from the insects. He swung the cane in front of him, at first walking blind. But as his eyes adjusted, he began to see some shapes in front of him illuminated by faint moonlight that filtered through the cloud cover. After about five minutes of walking, they entered the trees. Butch said:

"Noland? Killer Kaliayani and Anwar the Knife are heading back up the hill."

"Who?" Libby asked.

"The guys from the black Mercedes. They gave up. I can just catch glimpses of their lights going back up the hill."

"Mehinder and Abraham," Libby said. "Noland says their names are Mehinder and Abraham."

"Ibrahim," Virginia said. "He is the mean little one who cut my finger."

"They'll wait for morning," Miles said, "then come shoot us."

"Those two guys," Noland said, "are idiots studying to become morons. In the dark like this, neither one of them could find his belly button with a both hands and a compass. But they don't give up, I've learned that much about them. Come daylight, they could be dangerous."

"So what do we do?" Butch asked.

"Put some distance between us, then get some rest. Soon as it's light, we move on again. There's a branch up ahead. We'll head for it and follow it down a ways."

"A branch?" Virginia asked.

"Creek. I can hear the water now and again. Back in the Pecos Wilderness, the rule is if you want to find civilization, go downhill till you find a creek, then follow it. People all the time build settlements along flowing water. Same must be true here."

Coleman found that his literary medals pulled the front of his shirt and banged his chest as he walked over the uneven ground. He began removing them and throwing them into the darkness.

Noland led the group stumbling through the night until they neared a stream. "Ground's too rough to move much more," he announced. "We bed down here."

"Bed down," Miles said in amazement.

"Everybody but one person. Probably it isn't necessary, but it wouldn't hurt for us to post a watch. I'll take the first one."

"Stand watch?" Butch said. The words sent a shiver of pleasure through him. "I sure would like to take the first shift, Noland. You get some rest. We need our leader to be fresh and alert."

"You sound like a man with some outdoors experience," Noland said, grinning into the darkness. Libby coughed. "You have a wrist watch?"

"Yessir."

"Two hours. You wake me in two hours."

"Three," Butch said.

"What's that rotten smell?" Kent asked.

"Smells like dead fruit that turned jelly in the sun," Noland said.

"Durian," Virginia said. "We are somewhere near a durian tree, and the fruit is ripe."

"Butch, you still got that flashlight?" Noland asked. "Shine it around a bit."

Butch turned on the light. It flickered and went out. He bumped it on his leg and it came back on, producing a feeble light. "Batteries are nearly gone."

"This looks fine," Noland said. "No underbrush right around here. If anybody has to take a whiz, go behind that tree over there. But nobody wander off. We'll make camp by this big tree."

"Butch, hold the light over here," Libby said. "Kent, sit there," She pulled him close to the trunk of the tree, sat him down, and began unbuttoning his shirt. The flashlight flickered and Butch bumped it again.

"So much blood, Libby said. But the bleeding has stopped. Right there, Butch, hold the light right there. Kent, the bullet went on through, but it cut you up doing it. Cut you up bad. The bullet must have flattened when it hit the glass. Anyone have a knife?"

"Here," Noland dug into his pocket for the lock-back knife he had bought on Petaling street. Virginia cut some strips from the bottom of her blouse and wrapped them around Kent's shoulder. "How's that?"

"Better. But it hurts like fire when I move it."

"I'll make you a sling." She cut more of her blouse.

"After a while," Cole said, "you sort of get used to the rotten fruit smell. But it's still there, like the night sounds."

"In the morning, we'll need all the strength we have," Noland said. "Everybody try to get some sleep, even if you think it isn't possible."

"I hear a mosquito," Miles said.

"Nobody could hear a mosquito in all this noise," Cole said.

211

"I do. We'll all get malaria."

Noland popped his contacts out into his palm, put them into his mouth for cleaning, then shoved them into the watch pocket of his jeans. He stretched out on the ground, pulling Virginia down beside him.

"Can you sleep like this?" she asked. "I mean, the ground is all rocky and covered with roots."

"You lie here, sort of on my shoulder and side. Prop your hurt hand on my chest. I'll sleep, all right. This isn't exactly the Hilton, but it isn't as lumpy as a bed of west Texas hard scrabble."

Virginia snuggled against him. *Hard scrabble*? she wondered. Noland smelled vaguely of sweat, but not in an unpleasant way. It seemed impossible for anyone to perspire in the cool mountain air, but Noland had done so. She put her hand on his chest as he instructed. It felt better there, elevated a bit. And his body heat warmed her in a pleasant way.

"I just killed a mosquito," Miles announced.

"Like as not you just got the only one around," Noland said. "Mosquitoes don't like thin mountain air. You hardly ever find them in the high country of New Mexico or Colorado. Down on the Texas plains, it's a different story. Come a little rain, and mosquitoes come boiling out of the buffalo wallers and chew you to death at night. This is pure heaven here. Dang few mosquitoes and no rattle snakes. In west Texas, the rattle snakes would climb right in your sleeping bag, looking for a little warmth."

"Don't talk that way, Noland," Virginia said.

"Snakes." Miles jumped to his feet.

"Miles," Roseta said, "Lie down."

"Snakes?" Cole said.

"Cobras," Miles said. "Jungles are full of cobras, right? And we're lying on the floor of the jungle, right where they crawl around."

"This is a rain forest," Libby said, "not a jungle."

"Cobras are the same as any other snake," Noland said. "Cold blooded. Get them a little cool, and they go right to sleep. They don't like a mountain top any more than a rattler would. Now if we was down in the jungle around the Kuala Lumpur valley, like as not they would be all around us. But not up here. Cobras don't live in the high jungle, so don't get your panties all in a wad."

Kent laughed, but doing so sent a stab of pain through his shoulder. Libby patted him and made shush sounds. She sat leaning against the trunk of a tree, cradling Kent's head in her lap. "You lie down, too," Kent told her.

"Nothing doing. I never sleep more than four hours per night, and there's no way I could sleep right now. You rest."

Miles settled back down beside Roseta. Just as she pulled him close to her, something crashed through leaves and hit the ground with a loud thump. "What the hell was that?" Miles bolted upright.

"Please," Roseta said. "A branch fell, or a tree. Parts of the jungle are always dying and falling."

"Rain forest," Libby said.

"But that was right over there, not more than ten feet away," Miles said.

Roseta patted his arm. "Noise carries well in the jungle. It was close to us, Miles, but it was nothing to be frightened about. I once passed a night in the government bunk house in Taman Nagara, the national park where there is nothing but jungle and river and the Orang Asli. The bunk house had many windows, and we heard the night sounds. Jungles are always noisy."

"Was he right?" Miles asked. "I mean about there being no cobras in a mountain jungle?"

"You will not be bothered by cobras," Roseta said. She knew Noland to be wrong, but she thought he knew that. There was no point in Miles worrying, so why tell him cobras lived all over Malaysia? She pulled him against her, took his hand and put it on her leg.

"Roseta," he whispered, "did you take your dress off?"

She giggled and pulled his hand higher so he could feel the cloth. "No. I had to tear it up the seam so I could walk. Your hand feels good. Warm. Keep it right there while you go to sleep."

Miles thought of their touching back at the Genting Hotel and felt himself stir. I must be perverted, he told himself, to think of that sort of thing out here. Then he remembered the Orang Asli. They procreated in the jungle, didn't they? It could be done, then. The thought warmed him, and he began to relax, all thought of cobras forgotten.

Everyone drifted off to sleep except for Butch, who knew he had to keep alert to guard the group. Even Libby put her head against the tree and fell asleep. They came awake to the sound of Coleman screaming.

"What is it? What happened?" Butch knelt beside Coleman. When Butch touched him, Coleman stopped screaming.

"Something attacked me." His voice was high and thin.

Butch bumped the flashlight. "I don't see anything. Nothing came into camp, or I would have heard it."

"It bit my leg," Coleman said. Noland and Roseta went to Coleman. Butch shined the light on his leg. "It hurts like fire. And look," his voice went up a pitch, "I'm bleeding."

"Right there," Roseta said, guiding Butch's arm, "put the light there. It's just a durian, Cole. A durian fell on your leg."

"That's a fruit?" Noland touched the durian. "It feels like a petrified porcupine."

Coleman laughed with relief. "Attacked by a wild fruit," he said.

"Durian fall when they're ripe," Roseta said. "They fall from high in the tree and can be dangerous because they're so heavy and have so many spikes."

"Can you stand on that leg?" Noland asked.

"I think so. But it hurts like crazy."

"Butch, bring the light over here. Roseta, come help me take a look at the trunk of this tree." The light flickered and went out.

"I think it's a goner this time." Butch bumped it several more times. "I might as well throw it away."

"No. Give it to me. I want to throw it the opposite direction from where we will go." Noland took the flashlight and heaved it into the darkness. They listened as it clattered and bounced, quieting some of the jungle sounds. "That might give Mehinder and Abraham cause to think we walked that direction. Roseta, can you recognize the trunk of a durian tree from feeling it?"

"No."

"Then we need to move camp to someplace that smells different. Everybody up. Kent? You okay?"

"He's not so good," Libby said. "He has a fever."

"I can walk." Kent's voice was weak.

"Virginia?"

"Over here."

"Cole? Your leg?"

"It hurts, Noland, but Virginia and Kent must hurt worse. Let's move on."

"I'll stay on this side to keep anyone from falling into the creek," Butch said.

"Good idea. Everybody grab ahold of somebody else. We go

downhill, the same direction as the creek. Ready? Small steps, everybody. The ground is mighty rough."

Noland led them into the dark. He could make out a few shapes from the moonlight filtering through the trees, but the shapes blurred and seemed to drift around out of focus because his contacts were still in his watch pocket. Mostly he moved by feel, using Butch's cane to test each step.

Kent leaned on Libby. He could feel the fever in his body, and his head throbbed. Coleman limped, clinching his teeth each time he had to put any weight on his sore leg. Virginia held Noland's shirt with her good hand. Roseta stayed right behind, touching her and guiding Miles.

After counting one hundred and fifty steps, Noland said, "Roseta, are we under any durian trees?"

"I think not. The smell becomes faint."

"Then we stop here," Noland said. "Funny thing about how there seems to be so little brush. Just trees and rocks and roots popping out of the ground. Not what I thought a jungle would be like."

"This is a rain forest, as I observed earlier," Libby said.

"In the jungle movies, the guys in the pith helmets are all the time hacking with big knives just to get through," Noland said. "How come there's no brush? Is that the difference between a jungle and a forest? No brush?"

"A jungle is a confusion and a chaos of growing things," Coleman said. "A place of wild and intense vitality. A place of danger and beauty. What we have ventured into is most assuredly a jungle."

"Some call this jungle," Roseta said, "some call it forest. It's all the same. Small plants don't grow so well under the shade of the tall trees."

"A mosquito just bit me," Miles said.

"Everybody try to get back to sleep," Noland said. "Butch, I think it's about time for me to take the watch."

"Not yet. I have another hour and a half to go."

"You call me, okay?"

It took some time for them to find ways to feel even remotely comfortable on the ground. Miles kept muttering about the roots and rocks. Libby wouldn't let Kent lie down until she felt satisfied the spot she chose was smooth enough for him to rest. When he did stretch out, she lay beside him and took his head on her shoulder.

"Another mosquito," Miles announced. "Probably one of those

striped ones that carry dengue fever. Don't they call it 'break-bone fever?' Or is it 'black water fever?' Not that it matters, since we'll all die of malaria, anyway."

"Go to sleep, Miles," Roseta said, placing his hand on her leg again.

When she thought the others had gone to sleep, Virginia pulled closer to Noland and pressed her lips against his cheek. She could tell he was awake, even if he seemed not to respond. Putting her mouth close to his ear, she whispered, "Who would have ever thought I would find it in the middle of a mountain jungle?"

Noland opened his eyes, seeing only faint shapes of the trees above them. A root protruding from the ground lifted his shoulder in an annoying way. He disliked the damp feeling of the ground, and the night creatures shrieked in pitches that hurt his ears. Yet he felt he had never had a more delicious moment in his life. "Virginia, I, I . . ." he grasped at words, but they slipped away somehow.

"You don't have to say it," she whispered. "It's enough just to know. You sleep now." She kissed his cheek again and settled her head on his shoulder.

Just as the pre-dawn sun gave enough light to see by, Noland awoke with a start. He lifted Virginia's hand with great care and set it on her own breast, then sat up. Butch stood a few feet away, holding a tree branch like a shepherd's staff. Libby sat with Kent's head in her lap. Coleman lay sleeping in a fetal position. Miles and Roseta slept tangled in each others' arms. "Be full light soon," Noland said. "Butch, you should have woke me up."

"We need you fresh and rested." Butch looked pleased with himself.

"He's right," Libby said. "You are the only one of us with any experience in a wilderness."

Noland stood, picked up Butch's cane and put it under his belt, like a sword. He dug in his watch pocket. "Seems like knowing how to get around the Pecos Wilderness don't count for much out here. Where's my other contact?" He moistened the one lens and put it into an eye, winced, and took it out. He put it back into his mouth, then tried it on the other eye.

"What is it, Noland?" Virginia sat up.

"My contacts. Can't find but one. The other hurt my eye. Must have had something on it." He blinked furiously. "Got it in the wrong eye, but that can't be helped. Must have nicked the other eyeball something fierce." He bent and squinted at the ground. Butch and Virginia helped him look. "No use spending much more time. We got to move on. How's Kent?" Noland looked at Libby.

"Bad. I think the fever went down some, but he's still hot." She had sat up earlier in the morning and took Kent's his head in her lap.

"Can he walk?"

"I can walk," Kent said. "Sort of." He looked up at Libby's face and thought she must look like the Madonna from the view of the child, and more than anything else right then he wanted to draw Libby from that perspective. The thought of it stirred him with excitement—the Madonna from the perspective of the Christ child. He remembered that other artists had thought of doing that—but it would not matter. His would be better, for she would have Libby's face and have a canopy of leaves over her head with streaks of yellow and reddish clouds showing beyond the green. Dawn and beatitude and Libby's slight smile. Heaven on earth.

"Mosquitoes must have drained two pints of my blood in the night," Miles said.

"Can I help you, Kent?" Noland extended a hand. Kent took it and stood in an unsteady way. Libby took his arm and checked the other to make sure it was in the sling.

"Your blouse will never be the same," Kent said. She had torn it from the bottom hem all around, making bandages, until she made her midriff bare.

As they walked downhill, Noland became convinced that they followed a path. The rocky jungle floor and the profusion of roots snaking out of the ground made it difficult to know for sure, but it looked as if people used the area beside the creek as a trail of sorts.

The creek dived into a deep ravine, vanishing into rocks and brush. They had to walk away from the water. "We'll get back to it before long," Noland said. As they moved away from the sound of water falling over rocks, the sky darkened and a wind came up, stirring the tops of the trees.

Then the rain began. At first, they heard it hitting the leaves high overhead, but none reached the ground. Then large, fat drops fell from the leaves. "In west Texas, a rain would mean nobody could follow our trail," Noland said. "It could also mean flash floods building up in the arroyos to drown anything unlucky enough to get caught in a wash. Here, we don't leave tracks to speak of, and a flash flood doesn't seem likely, except in the area around the creek."

"Roseta is freezing to death," Miles said. "I'm cool, myself, maybe for the first time since coming to Malaysia. Never mind about the malaria we all got in the night from mosquitoes. We're all going to die of pneumonia." At first, Miles walked with his hand cupped over his shirt pocket, protecting his graffiti pad. But it got soaked, in spite of his care. He glanced at Coleman, remembering that Cole somehow knew of his graffiti—and had known for some time. Miles didn't like anyone knowing about his art, but if someone had to be in on it, it might as well be Cole, who could keep a secret.

"Do you realize," Coleman said, "that around the base of some of those trees are patches of wrinkled-leafed pepperonium? The floor of the jungle is crawling alive with house plants."

"When we get back," Butch said, "I'm going to write a trilogy about our adventures. Three three-act plays, all of them set in the jungle."

Virginia eyed the men in the group. No wonder so many Malays felt contempt for Americans, she thought. With the exception of Noland—and maybe Kent—these men are crazy.

They crossed a flat area where the trees thinned and ankle-deep grass grew. The ground felt soft. "A boggy spot," Noland said. "Won't take long in the rain for this place to turn into swamp. Hurry out of it."

They reached hard ground again and walked for a while in silence. "Kent needs a rest," Libby said.

"Kent?" Noland said.

"Maybe two minutes. Then I can move on."

"Five minutes everybody," Noland said. "We're taking the line of least resistance through the jungle. Likely it's a trail that doesn't see much use. What it means is that Mehinder and Abraham will come the same way, and they move a bunch faster than we do. Cole, how's your leg?"

"At first it felt so stiff I thought I would have to hop back to civilization. Now it's limbered up. It's just bruised and uncomfortable."

Libby helped Kent sit down. "I'll be right back," she said. She walked several paces beyond the trail to a thorny shrub with yellow flowers, picked some leaves and put them into the purse she wore strapped around her waist.

Noland sat on a root close to a tree that looked as if it had vines wrapping its trunk. He took out his one contact, wet it in his mouth, and tried it on the other eye. "Damn," he said and popped it into his palm again, then put it back in the wrong eye. He guided Virginia into sitting on his lap. She held her hand out away from contact. "How is it?" he asked, nodding toward the hand.

"Numb, mostly. My feet hurt worse." She began taking off her shoes.

"That tree," Coleman said, "the one behind Noland. Look at it. A Malaysian rosewood, maybe a hundred feet high. It's probably nearly three hundred years old—and look at it. Doomed. That thing wrapping around it is a strangler fig."

"My god, you have a black worm stuck to your foot," Noland said.

Virginia laughed. "Listen everyone. When we walked in the grass, I got a leech on my foot. They like to crawl into your shoe for a drink of blood. You should all open up your shoes to see if anybody is in there." She pulled the leech off and tossed it away from her.

"Leeches?" Miles said, alarmed. He went into a frenzy of pulling at his shoes.

"It's all right." Roseta patted his arm. "They do not hurt, and they do not carry disease."

"It's the rain," Libby said. "I read that when it rains in the jungle, leeches become a real problem."

"Two of them," Coleman said. "I have two of them on one ankle. They're stuck on like hooks."

"Pull them off," Virginia said.

"Leeches," Miles said with a frantic note in his voice. "Look at them. My feet are crawling alive with them."

"There are only," Roseta counted, "five. Five, Miles."

"You call that *only*? Look at them, fat as balloons. And after last night, I don't have any blood to spare."

"It's like a giant, wormy tick, all pumped up and ripe." Noland looked at a leech on his foot. He pulled it off. "Don't hurt or itch, though."

"Gross, Noland," Miles said. "You just grabbed it and yanked it off. Gross. Look at the way you're bleeding."

"They inject something in the skin to keep the blood from clotting," Libby said. "That means you will bleed for a good while, but it won't hurt you."

Noland pulled his boots back on. "Everybody tug the little bastards off and let's move on."

Butch found no leeches on his feet, nor did Libby. She pulled three from Kent's ankles and found another crawling on his sock. Roseta took the leeches from her own feet, then turned to help Miles. He sat on a root, clamped his eyes shut, and let her take care of the problem. "I wouldn't walk through that grass again for a hundred million dollars," he said.

Virginia watched Miles with contempt. If Noland acted like that for even a minute, she thought, I would never let him touch me.

When they were all on their feet again, Noland said, "I don't like to be the voice of gloom and doom, but those guys that are following us likely are only about thirty minutes back there. An hour at most. If we don't find people soon, we'll need to think of finding ways to hide or trap them."

When the rain stopped, monkeys began singing to them in choruses of hoots. Butch, who had seen such monkeys in the Singapore zoo, explained that they were large, black creatures who blew up balloons of air in their throats and squeezed it out, cupping their hands over their lips to help with the hooting sounds. "I think they're telling us that this is their part of the jungle."

"They're warning each other about us," Roseta said. "We will hear them but not see them because they think we are hunters. The Orang Asli hunt them with poisoned darts. They eat them."

"Eat monkeys?" Miles said. "That's by god downright gross. Worse than getting leeches."

"I saw a tiny hand once," Virginia said, "not much bigger than your thumb, floating in a pot of stew in a hawker's stand in Kuala Lumpur."

"Gross," Miles said.

"Looks like we do some climbing down," Noland said. He had come to a place where the terrain slanted an a difficult angle in one place and dropped off as a sheer cliff in another. A third alternative was to angle off on a fairly easy and obvious trail that sloped gradually down the mountain.

"We have four choices: take the easy trail, jump off the cliff, turn back, or go down that," he pointed. "Mehinder and Abraham will expect us to go for the trail. I say we work our way down the harder one."

The others gathered and looked at the decent. "Not so bad," Kent said. "It could be worse. There seems to be plenty of things to take hold of, and the climb down looks almost like stairs."

"This is definitely a trail," Noland said. "Crude and rough, but a trail. Soon as we get to the foot of this climb, we head off through the jungle just in case those boys with the guns figure out they missed us and come back this way."

The climb down took nearly an hour, much longer than Noland wanted it to. Often they had to turn around facing the mountain and climb down from root to root, from foothold to foothold as if climbing a ladder. For the most part it was possible to hold on to a tree or branch and step down. Progress for Coleman and Kent went especially slow. Sometime on the way down, the rain stopped.

As they reached near-level ground again, they heard voices above them, but there was no way to see where they came from because the trail down had twisted through trees and brush. Everyone turned to Noland. He raised his fingers to his lips, then pointed the direction for them to take.

He led them away from the trail, across a small rise winding around trees that rose high into the air. They descended the rise to the edge of a pool of clear water fed by a waterfall, a small stream of water coming from a cliff about three meters above the pool. "We go up there," Noland pointed, "and rest behind those bushes until we feel safe about going down stream again. Don't anybody make any noise, no matter what."

"I would drink that water," Butch said.

"Better not," Virginia warned.

"We might all have to later," Noland said. "But right now, we should tough it, just to play it safe."

"I vote for that," Miles said.

"It isn't a voting matter," Noland said. "Them that wants to, drinks. But do it fast cause we need to get to the bushes."

"Lead on," Butch said.

They pushed their way into the bushes near the place where the water fell from the cliff. "Get comfortable as possible," Noland said. "Sit down or lie down, but for chrissake don't move around much or make any noise."

Miles had the hardest time making himself sit on the leaves and twigs. He knew there had to be things among them that slithered and bit or stung, or worse. Butch dropped his staff-like branch and sprawled, oblivious to the discomforts of the rocks and twigs. He felt dead tired after staying awake all night, and he welcomed the rest, no matter how rough the ground. Miles watched him fall to sleep. "Like a goddam baby," he muttered, feeling irritated with Butch.

Libby set to work tearing more bandages from her blouse. "Better stop that soon," Noland said, meaning the ripping sounds. Kent watched her through fevered eyes, wishing he felt well, wishing he had his art supplies. She seemed not even to notice that she exposed the lower half of her breasts with the last round of cloth ripped from her blouse. Kent thought she looked even more like the Madonna for being partly exposed like that. He allowed her to unwrap his shoulder. She made clucking noises with her tongue when she saw the red streaks on his arm and breast and the yellow oozing from his wound.

Unzipping the pouch on her waist, she took out some leaves, crushed them, then put them on his wound. He winced but did not draw away. "*Bulang*," she said. "It will help with the pain and might help some with the infection." She wrapped the wound with the strips she had just torn from her blouse, then put his arm back into the sling.

Noland watched Libby work, mainly looking at her nipples flashing pink as she lifted her arms, exposing her breasts beneath what remained of her blouse. Virginia, amused, whispered to Noland, "You sleep on the ground, climb around in a mountain jungle until you're half dead, make yourself blind in one eye and see poorly out of the other, and yet you still look."

"Some few sights are positively amazing," he said. Virginia agreed. Libby seemed unaware that she was no longer fully dressed or that anyone watched her.

She had Miles' undivided attention. Roseta stared in astonishment, never having conceived that anyone could have breasts that large or that white.

Butch screamed and jerked to a sitting position, clutching his wrist. Miles saw a movement on the ground beside him where Butch had been sleeping.

Roseta saw the scorpion, a big one. It was over three inches long and stood on a twig, its tail poised above its head. Miles, seeing only a vague movement on the ground, bunched his fist and smashed the scorpion, then almost screamed himself as pain shot through his hand.

"What's going on?" Noland asked.

"Scorpion," Roseta said. "Miles killed it."

"Everybody get still. That scream will bring Mehinder and Abraham here for sure."

"That was brave," Roseta said. "But perhaps not such good judgment." She took Miles' hand and looked at the red spot at the base of his little finger.

"Crush this and put it on the sting," Libby said, handing Roseta a leaf from her purse. "It should help with the pain and draw some of the poison out."

"No," Miles said. "Don't touch it."

"I would take one of those," Butch said. Roseta passed him the leaf.

"Quiet," Noland said. "Someone is coming." He took Butch's cane from his belt.

Ibrahim walked to the edge of the pool, his pistol in hand. He paused to look around, saw the bushes near the top of the waterfall, and headed toward them. He and Mehinder must have split up on the top of the hill, Noland thought, and that is a real piece of luck. He felt he could handle one of them, given the element of surprise. Tightening his grip on the cane, he drew his legs beneath him, ready to jump.

Ibrahim paused beside a bush less than a meter from Noland and tried to look into it. Noland waited until Ibrahim reached with the pistol to part some leaves in the brush, then sprung forward and swung the cane, hitting both the pistol and Ibrahim's thumb.

The weapon fell from Ibrahim's hand. Noland stood, the cane poised for another blow. Ibrahim looked with surprise at the American seeming to materialize out of the brush, then dived for the pistol at the same time Noland moved for it. Noland kicked it into the pool below, then brought the cane down hard on Ibrahim's back.

Libby picked up the branch Butch had carried all morning and stepped out of the bush, circling it to come up behind Ibrahim. As she approached, she saw him come suddenly to his feet, saw the knife flash toward Noland and plunge deep beneath his rib cage, angling upward.

Noland looked surprised, dropped the cane and put his hands on Ibrahim's, and for a moment the two men stood together, in the parody of a greeting, the tall American looking perplexed at the small, dark Asian who grinned and twisted the handle of his knife.

Noland fell back off the cliff, into the pool. "What I told you," Ibrahim shouted after him: "What I told you!"

Libby swung the branch in a wide ark and hit Ibrahim's face as if she were batting a ball. Without stumbling, Ibrahim fell straight back on the ground.

"Noland," Butch shouted, "My god, Noland." He ran to the edge of the cliff, paused for a second, and jumped into the water.

Virginia, who had seen the knife go into Noland's heart, felt as if the pain from her severed finger surged through her whole body. It took great effort for her to stand and move toward Ibraham. She glanced into the pool below, seeing only Butch splashing around on the surface. "Noland, Noland," she whispered. "I should not have let you in." Tears ran on her cheeks. "But I did. I did."

She squatted on the ground beside Ibrahim and picked up a rock the size of the man's head. The effort shot a needle of pain through her injured hand.

Libby watched but said nothing. Virginia lifted the rock above the skull she intended to crush and held it for a long moment. The pain in her finger increased, and she looked at the bloody bandage. Shifting her position, she brought the rock down hard on Ibrahim's hand. "For Noland," she said. Picking up the rock, she moved to the other side of the body and smashed the other hand. "For me," she said.

"Virginia."

She looked up at Libby, Roseta and Kent, unsure which one had spoken her name. Coleman was farther back, stooping and holding his leg. All watched her in silence. Virginia stood up. This isn't happening to me, she told herself—not to me. To someone else, but not to me. She looked around, feeling a heavy kind of numbness grip her much as she did when Suppriah stood, arms akimbo, and spoke cruelty in a sweet voice. I will not hang my head and be a victim, she told herself. Never again.

Virginia gave her head a sharp jerk to banish the image of Suppriah, then looked at the people around her. They stared at her with a kind of awe, she could see that. But she did not understand it.

"Mehinder will be somewhere near," she said. "Come." She walked down the incline. Libby stayed back for a moment, stooped beside Ibrahim and took a plastic card from his pocket. Virginia led them down the incline to the edge of the pool where Butch and Miles pulled Noland's body from the water. "Leave it," she said. "It has no life."

Butch dragged the body onto a flat, bare rock by the pool and knelt beside it. "Noland, Noland," he said and began to cry in low, whimpering sobs. The body lay on its back, its eyes open, staring, its mouth agape and filled with water. Blood streamed from the wound, running watery across the rock and into the pool.

Kent watched Virginia stand beside Noland, watched the water flowing from her eyes. But she made no sound at all. He forced himself to look at the body of his friend. Roseta went to Butch and put her hand on his shoulder.

"It has no life," Virginia repeated, then turned to Libby. "Can you dive?"

"Dive?"

"There," Virginia pointed. "You can see the weapon on the bottom. Can you get it? Perhaps we will need to use it if the other man comes."

Butch stood up. "Yes," he said. "Yes. We'll kill him." His voice had a wild, almost insane quality to it. He waded into the edge of the pool and stood for a moment where Noland's blood made the water pink. Raising his arms, fists clinched, he shouted, "We'll kill them all," then dived toward the pistol.

# 14

Monkeys see the jungle as a place to hoot and play;
city folk see cobra fangs and tigers with their prey
and call the jungles evil things that must be kept at bay;
loggers see the jungle as a way to get their pay,
while poets weep to see the ancient jungle hauled away;
painters save the jungle with an image that can stay,
painting vivid jungle scenes in shades of green and gray.
　　　　　　　—Coleman Farquart, *An Asian Mystery*

Virginia didn't know how to use the pistol Butch gave her, but she carried it anyway. No one else in the group had ever handled a pistol, either. "If we must use it," Butch had declared, "I could figure out how to make it fire. But we shouldn't experiment on account of the sound."

"We follow the running water," Virginia said, turning.

"We should bury—"

"Hush, Butch," Libby said. She took Kent's arm and followed Virginia.

Kent glanced uneasily back at Noland's body. Leaving it that way didn't seem proper, and yet Virginia was right. It had no life. Taking time for some sort of burial would be an act for the benefit of the living, and they couldn't risk taking the time. I'll complete the painting of him and Virginia sitting in the lobby of the Mandarin, Kent vowed, telling himself that doing so would be a more fitting expression of his feelings about the man than would a feeble attempt at burial. Kent knew Noland would live on in the painting, after a fashion, and Noland's search for completion would be what Kent would strive to celebrate in the piece of art.

Kent watched Virginia move downhill, then double back to report the way clear for at least a hundred meters. "She knew Noland such a short time," he said after Virginia walked ahead again. Libby said nothing; they walked on. "She would have learned to love him," he added.

"All of us already had, some," Libby said. "Virginia more than the rest."

"And yet look at her."

"She's doing what Noland would have done. For him. And for her.

Kent, right now, she's avoiding her grief, denying it. She needs us to need her help. Which, of course, we do."

They walked over an hour before Kent began to falter and stumble. Libby helped him sit down so he could rest against a tree. Virginia, who had walked ahead to find the best way down a steep incline, was nowhere in sight. "He's burning with fever," Libby said. "Miles, help me." She took off what was left of her blouse. "Take this to the creek, rinse it, and bring it to me with plenty of water in it. We have to get his fever down."

Miles had a difficult time getting to the water, though the climb into the ravine would, under normal circumstances, have been easy. His hand throbbed, and he felt dizzy. When he got back with the wet cloth, he didn't notice Libby's bare breasts.

Kent saw that something appeared to be wrong with Miles but decided the problem might be with his own fevered perception. He sat leaning his head against a tree and watched Libby rub the wet cloth on his face and arm. The water seemed freezing cold. It felt good to close his eyes, to relax and let Libby wash the heat from him. When he heard Butch say, "Berak?" he opened his eyes.

A small, dark man who wore what appeared to be blue bathing trunks and held a tube of some sort, stood looking at him. Virginia was beside him. Kent blinked hard and looked at the man. The tube, Kent realized, had to be a blow pipe the forest people used to hunt monkeys. The man had a bamboo case suspended on a rope that wrapped his waist. From the case protruded the pith ends of darts for his blow pipe. "That isn't Berak," Libby said. "But I'll bet this man came from the same tribe. Bumbun?" she asked the man. He grinned, nodded, and stared at her breasts.

"This is Sabak," Virginia said. "He speaks some English. He says he has a house just over there," she pointed. "There are nine families in his kampung."

"We made it, then. We are very glad to meet you, Sabak." Libby turned back to Kent. "His fever runs high. Soon he will feel cold, and we will need to wrap him."

"Where's the pistol?" Butch asked.

"I threw it into the water when I saw Sabak coming with his blow pipe and darts. I thought it best not to seem unfriendly in any way."

"Man sick," the Bumbun tribesman said. "We take it for home, get well him. Man walks?"

"I can walk," Kent said. He tried to get up but found the effort beyond him.

"How far?" Libby asked.

"I would guess about ten minutes," Virginia said. "Let's help him to his feet. Miles?"

Miles, who sat on the ground with Roseta squatting beside him, looked up but said nothing. "Now what?" Libby turned to him. "Miles?"

"The scorpion," Roseta said.

"Can he walk?"

"I can walk just fine," Miles said. "But I doubt I can jump very high." His statement made perfect sense to him. The others looked at him and then at each other.

"Guide him, Roseta," Virginia said. "Butch, come help Kent."

"Not that side." Libby's voice went up an octave. "Not his wounded side." Butch shrank from her. He took Kent's other arm, pulled him to his feet, then nearly fell. Sabak handed Libby his blow pipe, pushed Butch aside and pulled Kent's arm over his shoulder.

"Fall to me," he said.

"He means lean on him," Libby said. The man's shoulder was the same height as Kent's armpit, and Kent leaned on him like a crutch. Sabak grinned again and began walking.

When they reached the Bumbun village, a boy about fifteen years old and a young woman came to help with Kent. The boy wore cut-off jeans and a tee shirt with the letters TCU across the front. The woman wore a sarong tied above her breasts. She wanted to have Kent taken into one of the houses, but Sabak shook his head. The steps up to the doors of the houses consisted of logs with notches cut into them; the houses stood on stilts nearly two meters off the ground.

Libby led Kent and Sabak into the shade under one of the houses. A woman brought a straw mat, shooed away a dog and several chickens, and put the mat on the ground for Kent. About a dozen women and children gathered to stare at Libby's white breasts and to look in round-eyed wonder at the rest of the group. Two little girls and a boy, all under five years old, squatted beside the grass mat and looked at Kent. The little girls wore only woven grass bracelets and anklets; the boy wore nothing at all.

Coleman, Roseta and Miles sat on another grass mat brought by one of the women. Libby sat beside Kent, cooling his forehead with the rag that had been her blouse. Virginia stood under a nearby house, clutching her hurt hand and talking with the man who had helped Kent. Butch walked around the other houses, looking at them and trying to talk with the people.

"*Tolong, saya nak air*," Libby said to one of the women. She smiled and shook her head. "I need some water." She sighed. "You don't speak Malay, then." The woman smiled again, continuing to shake her head. Through sign language, Libby communicated that she needed water. The woman brought an aluminum pan, darkened from the cookfire. She also held out a sarong, gesturing that she would show Libby how to tie it so it covered her breasts.

Libby looked down at herself as if she were just discovering her state of undress. She stood up and allowed the woman to tie the sarong under her arms, just over her breasts. "That looks good on you," Kent said. "But I think I liked the natural look better."

Libby knelt beside him again. "I thought you were too feverish to notice."

"I'm cold."

"You're too hot, Kent, even if you feel cold. It's the fever that has your thermostat all out of order."

The women, seeing Kent begin to shiver, brought blankets. Libby looked at them and grimaced. Likely they were crawling alive with vermin. "A trade-off," she said, spreading the blankets on Kent.

"I could have used one of those last night," Coleman said.

"It's even cooler at night during the rainy season," Libby said. "Roseta, how is Miles?"

"Better, I think. Sometimes a scorpion sting will make a person odd, for a while."

"I'm not odd," Miles said in a querulous tone.

"He is even better than I thought," Roseta said.

"What about that other man?" Coleman asked. "The other one with a gun?"

"I doubt he would come here," Libby said. "Too many people."

"These people wouldn't stop someone like that," Cole said.

"They would. They have blow pipes with darts that would kill a person in minutes. You saw the one I carried for the Bumbun."

"That is correct," Roseta said. "Malaysians—even city Malaysians—know a pistol is of little use against a tribe with blow pipes and poison darts."

Butch returned and sat on the mat beside Coleman. "Cole, these people live in houses made of bamboo and palm fronds. There isn't the sign of a wheel anywhere around. And yet they have electricity."

"Electricity?" Coleman found the idea absurd. "In the middle of the jungle?"

"See for yourself." He waved his hand at the houses. "Each of these places has a television antenna."

Virginia and Sabak came from under the other house. "We are close to a chemist," she said. "Just over that hill, in a row of shop houses."

"Chemist?" Kent said.

"A Drug store. Oh, Kent, that means medicine for your fever and your wound." Libby stood in excitement. "I'll go right away."

"No," Virginia said. "You stay with Kent. I'll go—you tell me what to get."

"Aspirin. But Malaysians don't use that much, do they? If there isn't any aspirin, bring whatever the chemist recommends for fever. And ask for something to disinfect a wound—something not damaging to tissue. First aid cream, maybe. We need to put some on your finger, too."

As Virginia left, Miles asked Sabak about electricity in the village. "No lectric," he said.

"I saw television antennas. How do you run the televisions?"

"Battery. From car. Kampung man buy cheap TV. *Putih dan hitam.* Black and light only. Buy battery. When battery finished, take to mans there," he pointed the direction Virginia went, "get battery filled for TV."

"But," Miles said, "Nobody here speaks English—except for you, of course. And yet you still watch television?"

"Miles, you feel better." Roseta leaned her head on his shoulder. Sabak looked blank.

"*Cik bercakap Bahasa Malaysia?*" Do you speak Malay? Libby asked.

"*Sedikit, sedikit,*" Sabak said.

"So you speak only a little Malay? And does anyone else in the kampung speak Malay or English?"

"No."

"Wait a minute," Butch said, a flash of understanding coming to him. "If nobody here speaks English or Malay, except for this guy, and all Malaysian television is broadcast in one of those languages, how do the people here understand what they watch?"

Miles muttered, "Jesus, Butch," and Roseta patted his arm.

"Exactly," Libby said, hiding a smile. "Do the people of the kampung watch television every day?"

"Night only. Yes."

"That's it," Butch said. "A powerful symbol—just the thing I need for my tragedy."

"Tragedy?" Coleman asked. Butch turned to him, his brows lifted high so his eyes showed white all around.

"Tragedy, yes. What else could it be? I have enough material just since walking into the hotel at Genting for a trilogy. Villains who capture and mutilate beautiful and defenseless women. A cast of innocents who suffer," he swept his hand around, indicating the group beneath the house, "and a larger-than-life hero who meets a tragic fate because of hubris."

"All of that is material for an epic poem," Coleman said. "But Noland hardly suffered from hubris. A kind of biological fate did him in. He had on only one contact lens, and that on the wrong eye because the other eye was scratched. So he saw the world dimly, and with no depth of vision. That little man wouldn't have touched him had it not been for Noland's problems with the contact lens."

"Hubris," Butch insisted.

"I saw little exaggerated pride in Noland," Kent said.

"Cole is right, Butch," Libby said, "Noland simply couldn't see. Physically, he couldn't. And he was blind in other ways. Noland was essentially a good, trusting man, so it did not occur to him that someone would come at him with a knife like that—so sudden and with such vicious intent. In a way, he died because of his own good qualities."

"He was a great man," Butch declared. "A great man. A kind of modern-day prince. He took care of us, helped us escape, fought for us, and he died for us."

"The right material for an epic poem."

Miles looked from Coleman to Butch, shaking his head. Those two were by god loony and deserved to be exposed in some choice graffiti. Noland was an ordinary man, not unlike Miles himself, a man who had just fallen in love, perhaps for the first time—just as Miles had—and he wanted to protect his woman from men who would harm her. His death was a kind of absurd accident, something that would not have happened had it not been for the chain of events that led him to the confrontation in

231

the jungle with the rabid little man and his knife. Miles felt certain Noland would have hated to hear these jerks sitting around talking about him like he was a character in a poem or a play, a thing to be analyzed into oblivion. More than anything else right then, Miles wanted a dry piece of paper and a pen so he could lash out at Butch and Cole. It would be so easy, he thought, to stick it to them:

> Coleman and Butch, Butch and Cole
> desecrated Noland's soul
> talking twiddle and garbagey words,
> stacking intellectual turds.

Miles smiled a toothy, mean smile, pleased with himself.

Virginia returned with medication. While Libby tended to Kent, Virginia reported that she had called the taxi center at Genting and ordered two out-station cabs to take them to Kuala Lumpur.

"Telephoned?" Butch asked in astonishment.

"Yes. Just over that hill is a surprisingly large community. The highway between Kuala Lumpur and the east coast is just a little way from here."

"We're not in the middle of a jungle, after all?" Butch sounded more disappointed than surprised.

"Jungle finished," Sabak said. "Log trucks come. Malay government with saw. Cut down jungle. Rain make rivers to mud, fish die, many fish. Wild pig go, monkey soon finished. Bumbun learn to eat rice, live in house. House good. Rice—bah. Very worse than sago. Not good like pig. Young Bumbun wear city shirt, want city, run from Bumbun, tap tree and dig mine, ruin more, more jungle. Jungle Malaysian no more, finished. Only jungle edge here, part of jungle there. Bumbun say, 'why you cut jungle, turn over earth for mine, plant tree that bleed white? Jungle home for Bumbun.' Malay government say jungle not belong to Bumbun. Belong to government. Who government to take jungle, make Bumbun eat rice, drive away pig? Who government?"

The group sat in awkward silence, none of them looking at Sabak except for Kent. Virginia cleared her throat. "We should go to the shop house. The taxis will be here soon."

Kent stood before a window, watching it rain. Behind him stood two make-shift easels holding a piece of canvas nearly three meters long and over a meter high. "An absolute masterpiece," Libby had declared, though Kent felt it far from adequate. Behind it, leaning against the wall, stood another canvas, blank and waiting.

Kent watched the rain lash the frangipani and mango trees in Libby's yard and thought of the boy in Sabak's village, the one who had worn the TCU tee shirt. That boy saw such rain so often that he would take no notice of it. His world seemed so small to Kent, so circumscribed by the remaining jungle, the tiny kampung, the small community just over the hill from his village. And yet he looked each night into the window of a black-and-white television at a world of Hollywood movies, of American situation comedies, of Malaysian news broadcasts and talk shows. A mute window, for the boy understood none of the languages on the television, Kent thought with wonder. What would such a boy—one who hunted monkeys with poisoned darts—make of the world he saw through the magic window, the world of people who spoke in strange languages and did such incomprehensible things to each other?

What, for that matter, Kent wondered, what do I understand of the jungle with its dealing out death in sudden violence, as when Noland stood on the edge of that cliff with a knife thrust hot under his ribs?

Kent watched an oleander bush in the yard, a plant trimmed into a tree, lean from the wind and rain and fall to the ground. "That happens frequently," Libby said from the doorway behind Kent. "The gardener will prop it up with some sticks, trim it, and it will bloom and look fine until another hard wind."

"It rains nearly every day," Kent said. "Water falls as if the entire South China Sea were being poured upon us. And yet Malaysians call this the dry season." He adjusted the strap on his shoulder. Another few days, and he could do without the sling. Then his painting would go faster, though everyone who looked at the gigantic jungle scene supported by two easels expressed amazement at how fast he painted. Kent turned back to his work.

"Kent, the painting is as perfect as anything I could ever imagine," Libby said.

Kent envied her ability to be satisfied; his own eyes told him of the inadequacies in the work. Especially in the face of Virginia. She stood in a Malaysian jungle by a pool of water, pointing toward the waterfall in the background, seeming to request something of the person looking at the painting. On the flat rock, just behind her, lay a body of a man wearing a plaid shirt, jeans, and cowboy boots. From his side came a trickle of blood, spilling on the rock and running into the water. Noland's face lay hidden behind Virginia. Virginia's eyes brimmed with tears, and yet there was a tough kind of determination there, something that defied death and defeat, a kind of stubborn affirmation of life and hope.

Libby said that face made you feel like either crying or saluting, depending on how you looked at it. Kent liked the assessment, and yet he felt if he made just a few alterations he might better capture what he had seen in Virginia that day in the jungle. And he wanted desperately to make the proper changes, to complete the painting so he could feel free to paint another scene that he held inside him, a scene that seemed to swell and grow so that he imagined it bursting out of him in an explosion of light and color.

Butch came to talk to Kent every day. He proclaimed he labored long and hard on the first part of the tragedy of Noland Fritch, that the writing went well, and he was confident of producing a masterpiece. Coleman came to Libby's house almost as often, each time bringing a few lines of his epic to share. He read with great intensity, frowning and backing Kent around the room with the way he thrust his face into Kent's.

Kent understood little about poetry, and what Cole wrote sounded okay to him. Libby seemed to like it. Kent did wonder about the heavy rhythm of the lines. They sometimes sounded jerky and too self-conscious, like Cole was a bit too taken with the idea of producing art.

Roseta had come only twice—accompanied each time by Miles—once to take a deposition from Kent, Libby, and Virginia, and once to announce she had settled the matter about the bomb that had been found in the Mandarin. Mehinder, she said, sat in jail since his finger prints were all over the bomb. Likely Ibrahim's were, too, but his fingers were in no shape to take prints for comparison. The bandages would come off in a few days, though.

At Kent's request, Roseta had taken care of informing EXXON about Noland's death and telling them where to find the body. She also contacted the office of the Sultan of Selangor to explain why Kent had not shown up at the meeting of artists that had been scheduled in Shah Alam.

"Che is still walking around, free," Roseta had said. "But that won't last long. My guess is that he will be arrested next week. I already have his Filipino boss in jail—thanks to Libby's having taken his passport from him before we left the hotel. That act, and the taking of the identification cards from Che and, later, Ibrahim, were strokes of genius. Having those items has enabled me to bring the full force of Malaysian law to bear on those people."

Roseta looked at Libby. "I have more freedom now. Perhaps not so much as you, but I will never again wear the black robes and terrible head covering that I had to wear when I worked for Che. And the Dakwah cloak we draped over Che in that hotel room is gone from my wardrobe forever. I wore it, once, to spy upon you when I felt unsure of your relationship with those surrounding Che. You walked to the market to buy fruit."

"Roseta. That was you? And I assumed the shadowy person in black to be a man."

"Please accept my apologies for making you upset."

"It's all right. At least the mystery is solved. Have you learned from Che or any of the others who tried to kill me with that block of ice?"

"No. Likely I will not ever find out."

Miles hung back, listening but saying nothing. Roseta went on to say her career as a lawyer finally felt underway, that many clients sought her since the press gave her so much publicity for being the key to breaking up a major human trafficking gang that also dealt in illegal drugs. Miles scowled at the mention of her career. Kent noticed that, from time to time, he took out a small pad and scribbled in it.

Libby had told Kent that Miles was in love in a desperate, even comic way. But he didn't quite know how to cope with Roseta's insistence that, if he married her, he had to reside in Kuala Lumpur so she could pursue her career.

Kent stepped back and looked at his rendering of Virginia's face in the painting. Still not quite right, he told himself. Virginia stayed in Libby's house, but she seldom came into the room where Kent painted the jungle scene. The day before, he had found Virginia looking at the work, weeping in silence. "When I complete it, Virginia," he told her, I want you to have it."

Her hand went to her mouth. "Oh, Kent," she said. "I want to learn to look at it without crying, but there is too much pain. I can't seem to let go. Why can't I let go?" Kent reached toward her to brush away a tear; she took his hand and pressed his palm against her cheek. He had looked up at that moment and seen Libby watching from the doorway.

That night, Libby had told him how his gift of the painting was the right thing to do for Virginia. "Learning to see herself as you saw her that day will help her, Kent, more than I can with all my counseling skills."

After making love with Libby that night, Kent lay beside her, listening to the sounds of night birds, crickets, and frogs, sounds that had a comforting, steady quality. The image of his jungle Madonna floated before him: her face concerned, tilted downward, her breasts partly exposed beneath a blouse torn mostly away and fringed with threads. The image became almost tangible there in the darkness, like something apart from him, something already painted, completed to perfection, saying all he knew to be possible and in no need of further work. "Remember that the human body is holy," Sister Corazon told him so many years before. He could sense her behind him, looking at the painting he envisioned hanging in the Malaysian night, saying "Yes. Yes." In the background, behind the Madonna, stood the primordial jungle, intensely green, the leaves overhead alive to the drops of rain gathering upon them.

Kent added another dab of paint to Virginia's face on the canvas, leaned back to examine what he had done, then removed the dab with a finger.

"Kent," Libby said, "Remember what Virginia said to you yesterday when you gave her the painting?"

"Yes."

"Can you do what she thinks she cannot?"

He looked at Libby and felt the image he had to try to capture seem to grow and move inside him. "Perhaps I can." He put the brush down. With her encouragement, he thought, it'll be easier attempting the Madonna. And maybe this time I'll get it right. "Help me set this jungle scene over there," he said, "against the wall. Then we'll put the blank canvas on the easel."

www.ingramcontent.com/pod-product-compliance
Lightning Source LLC
Chambersburg PA
CBHW020359030726
47496CB00007B/2219